D1485753

EVERYMAN,

I WILL GO WITH THEE,

AND BE THY GUIDE,

IN THY MOST NEED

TO GO BY THY SIDE

C015115390

EVERYMAN'S POCKET CLASSICS

BEDTIME
STORIES

EDITED BY DIANA SECKER TESDELL

EVERYMAN'S POCKET CLASSICS

Alfred A. Knopf New York London Toronto

THIS IS A BORZOI BOOK
PUBLISHED BY ALFRED A. KNOPF

This selection by Diana Secker Tesdell first published in
Everyman's Library, 2011

Copyright © 2011 by Everyman's Library
A list of acknowledgments to copyright owners appears at the back
of this volume.

All rights reserved. Published in the United States by Alfred A. Knopf,
a division of Random House, Inc., New York, and in Canada by
Random House of Canada Limited, Toronto. Distributed by
Random House, Inc., New York. Published in the United Kingdom
by Everyman's Library, Northburgh House, 10 Northburgh Street,
London EC1V 0AT, and distributed by Random House (UK) Ltd.

US website: www.randomhouse.com/everymans

ISBN: 978-0-307-59494-5 (US)
978-1-84159-608-2 (UK)

A CIP catalogue reference for this book is available from the
British Library

Typography by Peter B. Willberg
Typeset in the UK by AccComputing, North Barrow, Somerset
Printed and bound in Germany by GGP Media GmbH, Pössneck

BEDTIME
STORIES

Contents

A. S. BYATT

THE THING IN THE FOREST

THERE WERE ONCE two little girls who saw, or believed they saw, a thing in a forest. The two little girls were evacuees, who had been sent away from the city by train, with a large number of other children. They all had their names attached to their coats with safety-pins, and they carried little bags or satchels, and the regulation gas-mask. They wore knitted scarves and bonnets or caps, and many had knitted gloves attached to long tapes which ran along their sleeves, inside their coats, and over their shoulders and out, so that they could leave their ten woollen fingers dangling, like a spare pair of hands, like a scarecrow. They all had bare legs and scuffed shoes and wrinkled socks. Most had wounds on their knees in varying stages of freshness and scabbiness. They were at the age when children fall often and their knees were unprotected. With their suitcases, some of which were almost too big to carry, and their other impedimenta, a doll, a toy car, a comic, they were like a disorderly dwarf regiment, stomping along the platform.

The two little girls had not met before, and made friends on the train. They shared a square of chocolate, and took alternate bites at an apple. One gave the other the inside page of her *Beano*. Their names were Penny and Primrose. Penny was thin and dark and taller, possibly older, than Primrose, who was plump and blonde and curly. Primrose had bitten nails, and a velvet collar to her dressy green coat. Penny had a bloodless transparent paleness, a touch of blue in her fine lips. Neither of them knew where they were going, nor how long the journey might take. They did not even know why they were going, since neither of their mothers had quite known how to explain the danger to them. How do you say to your child, I am sending you away, because enemy bombs may fall out of the sky, because the streets of the city may burn like forest fires of brick and timber, but I myself am staying here, in what I believe may be daily danger of burning, burying alive, gas, and ultimately perhaps a grey army rolling in on tanks over the suburbs, or sailing its submarines up our river, all guns blazing? So the mothers (who did not resemble each other at all) behaved alike, and explained nothing, it was easier. Their daughters they knew were little girls, who would not be able to understand or imagine.

The girls discussed on the train whether it was a sort of holiday or a sort of punishment, or a bit of both. Penny had read a book about Boy Scouts, but the children on the train did not appear to be Brownies or Wolf Cubs, only a mongrel battalion of the lost. Both little girls had the idea that these were all perhaps *not very good* children, possibly being sent away for that reason. They were pleased to be able to define each other as 'nice'. They would stick together, they agreed. Try to sit together, and things.

The train crawled sluggishly further and further away from the city and their homes. It was not a clean train – the upholstery of their carriage had the dank smell of unwashed trousers, and the gusts of hot steam rolling backwards past their windows were full of specks of flimsy ash, and sharp grit, and occasional fiery sparks that pricked face and fingers like hot needles if you opened the window. It was very noisy too, whenever it picked up a little speed. The engine gave great bellowing sighs, and the invisible wheels underneath clicked rhythmically and monotonously, tap-tap-tap-CRASH, tap-tap-tap-CRASH. The window-panes were both grimy and misted up. The train stopped frequently, and when it stopped, they used their gloves to wipe rounds, through which they peered out at flooded fields, furrowed hillsides and tiny stations whose names were carefully blacked out, whose platforms were empty of life.

The children did not know that the namelessness was meant to baffle or delude an invading army. They felt – they did not think it out, but somewhere inside them the idea sprouted – that the erasure was because of them, because they were not meant to know where they were going or, like Hansel and Gretel, to find the way back. They did not speak to each other of this anxiety, but began the kind of conversation children have about things they really disliked, things that upset, or disgusted, or frightened them. Semolina pudding with its grainy texture, mushy peas, fat on roast meat. Listening to the stairs and the window-sashes creaking in the dark or the wind. Having your head held roughly back over the basin to have your hair washed, with cold water running down inside your liberty bodice. Gangs in playgrounds. They felt the pressure of all the other alien children in all the other carriages as a potential gang. They shared another square of chocolate, and licked their fingers, and looked out at a great white goose flapping its wings beside an inky pond.

The sky grew dark grey and in the end the train halted. The children got out, and lined up in a crocodile, and were led to a mud-coloured bus. Penny and Primrose managed to get a seat together, although it was over the wheel, and both of them began to feel sick as the bus bumped along snaking country lanes, under whipping branches, dark leaves on dark wooden arms on a dark sky, with torn strips of thin cloud streaming across a full moon, visible occasionally between them.

* * *

They were billeted temporarily in a mansion commandeered from its owner, which was to be arranged to hold a hospital for the long-term disabled, and a secret store of artworks and other valuables. The children were told they were there temporarily, until families were found to take them all into their homes. Penny and Primrose held hands, and said to each other that it would be wizard if they could go to the same family, because at least they would have each other. They didn't say anything to the rather tired-looking ladies who were ordering them about, because with the cunning of little children, they knew that requests were most often counter-productive, adults liked saying no. They imagined possible families into which they might be thrust. They did not discuss what they imagined, as these pictures, like the black station signs, were too frightening, and words might make some horror solid, in some magical way. Penny, who was a reading child, imagined Victorian dark pillars of severity, like Jane Eyre's Mr Brocklehurst, or David Copperfield's Mr Murdstone. Primrose imagined – she didn't know why – a fat woman with a white cap and round red arms who smiled nicely but made the children wear sacking aprons and scrub the steps and the stove. 'It's like we were orphans,' she said to Penny. 'But we're not,' Penny said. 'If we manage to stick together . . .'

The great house had a double flight of imposing stairs to its front door, and carved griffins and unicorns on its balustrade. There was no lighting, because of the black-out. All the windows were shuttered. No welcoming brightness leaked across door or window-sill. The children trudged up the staircase in their crocodile, hung their coats on numbered makeshift hooks, and were given supper (Irish stew and rice

14

pudding with a dollop of blood-red jam) before going to bed in long makeshift dormitories, where once servants had slept. They had camp-beds (military issue) and grey shoddy blankets. Penny and Primrose got beds together but couldn't get a corner. They queued to brush their teeth in a tiny wash-room, and both suffered (again without speaking) suffocating anxiety about what would happen if they wanted to pee in the middle of the night, because the lavatory was one floor down, the lights were all extinguished, and they were a long way from the door. They also suffered from a fear that in the dark the other children would start laughing and rushing and teasing, and turn themselves into a gang. But that did not happen. Everyone was tired and anxious and orphaned. An uneasy silence, a drift of perturbed sleep, came over them all. The only sounds – from all parts of the great dormitory it seemed – were suppressed snuffles and sobs, from faces pressed into thin pillows.

When daylight came, things seemed, as they mostly do, brighter and better. The children were given breakfast in a large vaulted room. They sat at trestle tables, eating porridge made with water and a dab of the red jam, heavy cups of strong tea. Then they were told they could go out and play until lunch-time. Children in those days – wherever they came from – were not closely watched, were allowed to come and go freely, and those evacuated children were not herded into any kind of holding-pen, or transit camp. They were told they should be back for lunch at 12:30, by which time those in charge hoped to have sorted out their provisional future lives. It was not known how they would know when it was 12:30, but it was expected that – despite the fact that few of them had wrist-watches – they would know how to keep an eye on the time. It was what they were used to.

Penny and Primrose went out together, in their respectable coats and laced shoes, on to the terrace. The terrace appeared to them to be vast, and was indeed extensive. It was covered with a fine layer of damp gravel, stained here and there bright green, or invaded by mosses. Beyond it was a stone balustrade, with a staircase leading down to a lawn, which that morning had a quicksilver sheen on the lengthening grass. It was flanked by long flower-beds, full of overblown annuals and damp clumps of stalks. A gardener would have noticed the beginnings of neglect, but these were urban little girls, and they noticed the jungly mass of wet stems, and the wet, vegetable smell. Across the lawn, which seemed considerably vaster than the vast terrace, was a sculpted yew hedge, with many twigs and shoots out of place and ruffled. In the middle of the hedge was a wicket-gate, and beyond the gate were trees, woodland, a forest, the little girls said to themselves.

'Let's go into the forest,' said Penny, as though the sentence was required of her.

Primrose hesitated. Most of the other children were running up and down the terrace, scuffing their shoes in the gravel. Some boys were kicking a ball on the grass. The sun came right out, full from behind a hazy cloud, and the trees suddenly looked both gleaming and secret.

'OK,' said Primrose. 'We needn't go far.'

'No. I've never been in a forest.'

'Nor me.'

'We ought to look at it, while we've got the opportunity,' said Penny.

There was a very small child – one of the smallest – whose name, she told everyone, was Alys. With a *y*, she told those who could spell, and those who couldn't, which surely included herself. She was barely out of nappies. She was quite extraordinarily pretty, pink and white, with large pale blue

16

eyes, and sparse little golden curls all over her head and neck, through which her pink skin could be seen. Nobody seemed to be in charge of her, no elder brother or sister. She had not quite managed to wash the tearstains from her dimpled cheeks.

She had made several attempts to attach herself to Penny and Primrose. They did not want her. They were excited about meeting and liking each other. She said now:

'I'm coming too, into the forest.'

'No, you aren't,' said Primrose.

'You're too little, you must stay here,' said Penny.

'You'll get lost,' said Primrose.

'You won't get lost. I'll come with you,' said the little creature, with an engaging smile, made for loving parents and grandparents.

'We don't want you, you see,' said Primrose.

'It's for your own good,' said Penny.

Alys went on smiling hopefully, the smile becoming more of a mask.

'It will be all right,' said Alys.

'Run,' said Primrose.

They ran; they ran down the steps and across the lawn, and through the gate, into the forest. They didn't look back. They were long-legged little girls, not toddlers. The trees were silent round them, holding out their branches to the sun, breathing noiselessly.

Primrose touched the warm skin of the nearest saplings, taking off her gloves to feel their cracks and knots. She exclaimed over the flaking whiteness and dusty brown of the silver birches, the white leaves of the aspens. Penny looked into the thick of the forest. There was undergrowth – a mat of brambles and bracken. There were no obvious paths.

Dark and light came and went, inviting and mysterious, as the wind pushed clouds across the face of the sun.

'We have to be careful not to get lost,' she said. 'In stories, people make marks on tree-trunks, or unroll a thread, or leave a trail of white pebbles – to find their way back.'

'We needn't go out of sight of the gate,' said Primrose. 'We could just explore a little bit.'

They set off, very slowly. They went on tiptoe, making their own narrow passages through the undergrowth, which sometimes came as high as their thin shoulders. They were urban, and unaccustomed to silence. At first the absence of human noise filled them with a kind of awe, as though, while they would not have put it to themselves in this way, they had got to some original place, from which they, or those before them, had come, and which they therefore recognized. Then they began to hear the small sounds that were there. The chatter and repeated lilt and alarm of invisible birds, high up, further in. The hum and buzz of insects. Rustling in dry leaves, rushes of movement in thickets. Slitherings, dry coughs, sharp cracks. They went on, pointing out to each other creepers draped with glistening berries, crimson, black and emerald, little crops of toadstools, some scarlet, some ghostly-pale, some a dead-flesh purple, some like tiny parasols – and some like pieces of meat protruding from tree-trunks. They met blackberries, but didn't pick them, in case in this place they were dangerous or deceptive. They admired from a safe distance the stiff upright fruiting rods of the Lords and Ladies, packed with fat red berries. They stopped to watch spiders spin, swinging from twig to twig, hauling in their silky cables, reinforcing knots and joinings. They sniffed the air, which was full of a warm mushroom smell, and a damp moss smell, and a sap smell, and a distant hint of dead ashes.

Did they hear it first or smell it first? Both sound and scent were at first infinitesimal and dispersed. Both gave the strange impression of moving in – in waves – from the whole perimeter of the forest. Both increased very slowly in volume, and both were mixed, a sound and a smell fabricated of many disparate sounds and smells. A crunching, a crackling, a crushing, a heavy thumping, combined with threshing and thrashing, and added to that a gulping, heaving, boiling, bursting steaming sound, full of bubbles and farts, piffs and explosions, swallowings and wallowings. The smell was worse, and more aggressive, than the sound. It was a liquid smell of putrefaction, the smell of maggoty things at the bottom of untended dustbins, the smell of blocked drains, and unwashed trousers, mixed with the smell of bad eggs, and of rotten carpets and ancient polluted bedding. The new, ordinary forest smells and sounds, of leaves and humus, fur and feathers, so to speak, went out like lights as the atmosphere of the thing preceded it. The two little girls looked at each other, and took each other's hand. Speechlessly and instinctively they crouched down behind a fallen tree-trunk, and trembled, as the thing came into view.

Its head appeared to form, or become first visible in the distance, between the trees. Its face – which was triangular – appeared like a rubbery or fleshy mask over a shapeless sprouting bulb of a head, like a monstrous turnip. Its colour was the colour of flayed flesh, pitted with wormholes, and its expression was neither wrath nor greed, but pure misery. Its most defined feature was a vast mouth, pulled down and down at the corners, tight with a kind of pain. Its lips were thin, and raised, like welts from whipstrokes. It had blind, opaque white eyes, fringed with fleshy lashes and brows like the feelers of sea-anemones. Its face was close to the ground, and moved towards the children between its forearms which were squat, thick, powerful and akimbo, like a cross between a monstrous washerwoman and a primeval dragon. The flesh on these forearms was glistening and mottled, every colour, from the green of mould to the red-brown of raw liver, to the dirty white of dry rot.

The rest of its very large body appeared to be glued together, like still-wet papier-mâché, or the carapace of stones and straws and twigs worn by caddis-flies underwater. It had a tubular shape, as a turd has a tubular shape, a provisional amalgam. It was made of rank meat, and decaying vegetation, but it also trailed veils and prostheses of man-made materials, bits of wire-netting, foul dishcloths, wire-wool full of pan-scrubbings, rusty nuts and bolts. It had feeble stubs and stumps of very slender legs, growing out of it at all angles, wavering and rippling like the suckered feet of a caterpillar or the squirming fringe of a centipede. On and on it came, bending and crushing whatever lay in its path, including bushes, though not substantial trees, which it wound between, awkwardly. The little girls observed, with horrified fascination, that when it met a sharp stone, or a narrow tree-trunk, it allowed itself to be sliced through, flowed sluggishly round in two or three smaller worms, convulsed and reunited. Its progress was achingly slow, very smelly, and apparently very painful, for it moaned and whined amongst its other burblings and belchings. They thought it could not see, or certainly could not see clearly. It and its stench passed within a few feet of their tree-trunk, humping along, leaving behind it a trail of bloody slime and dead foliage, sucked to dry skeletons.

Its end was flat and blunt, almost transparent, like some earthworms.

When it had gone, Penny and Primrose, kneeling on the

moss and dead leaves, put their arms about each other, and hugged each other, shaking with dry sobs. Then they stood up, still silent, and stared together, hand in hand, at the trail of obliteration and destruction, which wound out of the forest and into it again. They went back, hand in hand, without looking behind them, afraid that the wicket-gate, the lawn, the stone steps, the balustrade, the terrace and the great house would be transmogrified, or simply not there. But the boys were still playing football on the lawn, a group of girls were skipping and singing shrilly on the gravel. They let go each other's hand, and went back in.

They did not speak to each other again.

The next day they were separated and placed with strange families. Their time in these families – Primrose was in a dairy farm, Penny was in a parsonage – did not in fact last very long, though then the time seemed slow-motion and endless. These alien families seemed like dream worlds into which they had strayed, not knowing the physical or social rules which constructed those worlds. Afterwards, if they remembered the evacuation it was as dreams are remembered, with mnemonics designed to claw back what fleets on waking. So Primrose remembered the sound of milk spurting in the pail, and Penny remembered the empty corsets of the vicar's wife, hanging bony on the line. They remembered dandelion clocks, but you can remember those from anywhere, any time. They remembered the thing they had seen in the forest, on the contrary, in the way you remember those very few dreams – almost all nightmares – which have the quality of life itself, not of fantasm, or shifting provisional scene-set. (Though what are dreams if not life itself?) They remembered too solid flesh, too precise a stink, a rattle and a soughing which thrilled the nerves and the cartilage of their growing ears. In the memory, as in such a dream, they felt, I cannot get out, this is a real thing in a real place.

They returned from evacuation, like many evacuees, so early that they then lived through wartime in the city, bombardment, blitz, unearthly light and roaring, changed landscapes, holes in their world where the newly dead had been. Both lost their fathers. Primrose's father was in the Army, and was killed, very late in the war, on a crowded troop-carrier sunk in the Far East. Penny's father, a much older man, was in the Auxiliary Fire Service, and died in a sheet of flame in the East India Docks on the Thames, pumping evaporating water from a puny coil of hose. They found it hard, after the war, to remember these different men. The claspers of memory could not grip the drowned and the burned. Primrose saw an inane grin under a khaki cap, because her mother had a snapshot. Penny thought she remembered her father, already grey-headed, brushing ash off his boots and trouser-cuffs as he put on his tin hat to go out. She thought she remembered a quaver of fear in his tired face, and the muscles composing themselves into resolution. It was not much, what either of them remembered.

After the war, their fates were still similar and dissimilar. Penny's widowed mother embraced grief, closed her face and her curtains, moved stiffly, like an automat, and read poetry. Primrose's mother married one of the many admirers, visitors, dancing partners she had had before the ship went down, gave birth to another five children, and developed varicose veins and a smoker's cough. She dyed her blonde hair with peroxide when it faded. Both Primrose and Penny were only children who now, because of the war, lived in amputated or unreal families. Penny developed crushes on poetical teachers and in due course – she was clever – went to university, where she chose to study developmental psychology. Primrose had little education. She was always being kept off school to look after the others. She too dyed her blonde curls with peroxide when they turned mousy and faded. She got fat as Penny got thin. Neither of them married. Penny became a child psychologist, working with the abused, the displaced, the disturbed. Primrose did this and that. She was a barmaid. She worked in a shop. She went to help at various church crèches and Salvation Army reunions, and discovered she had a talent for story-telling. She became Aunty Primrose, with her own repertoire. She was employed to tell tales to kindergartens and entertain at children's parties. She was much in demand at Hallowe'en, and had her own circle of bright yellow plastic chairs in a local shopping mall, where she kept an eye on the children of burdened women, keeping them safe, offering them just a *frisson* of fear and terror that made them wriggle with pleasure.

The house aged differently. During this period of time – whilst the little girls became women – it was handed over to the Nation, which turned it into a living museum, still inhabited by the flesh and blood descendants of those who had built it, demolished it, flung out a wing, closed off a corridor. Guided tours took place in it, at regulated times. During these tours, the ballroom and intimate drawing-rooms were fenced off with crimson twisted ropes on little brass one-eyed pedestals. The bored and the curious peered in at four-poster beds and pink silk *fauteuils*, at silver-framed photographs of wartime Royalty, and crackling crazing Renaissance and Enlightenment portraits of long-dead queens and solemn or sweetly musing ancestors. In the room where the evacuees had eaten their rationed meals, the history of the house was displayed, on posters, in glass cases, with helpful notices, and opened copies of old diaries and records. There were reproductions of the famous paintings which had lain here in hiding during the war. There was a plaque to the dead of the house: a gardener, an under-gardener, a chauffeur and a second son. There were photographs of military hospital beds, and of nurses pushing wheelchairs in the grounds. There was no mention of the evacuees whose presence appeared to have been too brief to have left any trace.

The two women met in this room on an autumn day in 1984. They had come with a group, walking in a chattering crocodile behind a guide, and had lingered amongst the imagery and records, rather than going on to eavesdrop on the absent ladies and gentlemen whose tidy clutter lay on coffee tables and escritoires. They prowled around the room, each alone with herself, in opposite directions, without acknowledging each other's presence. Both their mothers had died that spring, within a week of each other, though this coincidence was unknown to them. It had made both of them think of taking a holiday, and both had chosen that part of the world. Penny was wearing a charcoal trouser suit and a black velvet hat. Primrose wore a floral knit long jacket over a shell-pink cashmere sweater, over a rustling long skirt with an elastic waist, in a mustard-coloured tapestry print. Her hips and bosom were bulky. They coincided because both of them, at the same moment, half saw an image in a medieval-looking illustrated book. Primrose thought it was a very old book. Penny assumed it was nineteenth-century mock-medieval. It showed a knight, on foot, in a forest, lifting his sword to slay something. The knight shone on the rounded slope of the page, in the light, which caught the gilding on his helmet and sword-belt. It was not possible to see what was being slain. This was because, both in the tangled vegetation of the image, and in the way the book was displayed in the case, the enemy, or victim, was in shadows.

Neither of them could read the ancient (or pseudo-ancient) black letter of the text beside the illustration. There was a typed explanation, or description, under the book, done with a faded ribbon and uneven pressure of the keys. They had to lean forward to read it, and to see what was worming its way into, or out of, the deep spine of the book, and that was how they came to see each other's face, close up, in the glass which was both transparent and reflective. Their transparent reflected faces lost detail – cracked lipstick, pouches, fine lines of wrinkles – and looked both younger and greyer, less substantial. And that is how they came to recognize each other, as they might not have done, plump face to bony face. They breathed each other's names, Penny, Primrose, and their breath misted the glass, obscuring the knight and his opponent. I could have died, I could have wet my knickers, said Penny and Primrose afterwards to each other, and both experienced this still moment as pure, dangerous shock. But they stayed there, bent heads together, legs trembling, knees knocking, and read the caption, which was about the Loathly Worm, which, tradition held, had infested the countryside and had been killed more than once by scions of that house, Sir Lionel, Sir Boris, Sir Guillem. The Worm, the typewriter had tapped out, was an English Worm, not a European dragon, and like most such worms, was wingless. In some sightings it was reported as having vestigial legs, hands or feet. In others it was limbless. It had, in monstrous form, the capacity of common or garden worms to sprout new heads or trunks if it was divided, so that

25

two worms, or more, replaced one. This was why it had been killed so often, yet reappeared. It had been reported travelling with a slithering pack of young ones, but these may have been only revitalized segments. The typed paper was held down with drawing-pins and appeared to continue somewhere else, on some not visible page, not presented for viewing.

Being English, the recourse they thought of was tea. There was a tea-room near the great house, in a converted stable at the back. There they stood silently side by side, clutching floral plastic trays spread with briar roses, and purchased scones, superior raspberry jam in tiny jam jars, little plastic tubs of clotted cream. 'You couldn't get cream or real jam in the war,' said Primrose in an undertone as they found a corner table. She said wartime rationing had made her permanently greedy, and thin Penny agreed, it had, clotted cream was still a treat.

They watched each other warily, offering bland snippets of autobiography in politely hushed voices. Primrose thought Penny looked gaunt, and Penny thought Primrose looked raddled. They established the skein of coincidences – dead fathers, unmarried status, child-caring professions, recently dead mothers. Circling like beaters, they approached the covert thing in the forest. They discussed the great house, politely. Primrose admired the quality of the carpets. Penny said it was nice to see the old pictures back on the wall. Primrose said, funny really, that there was all that history, but no sign that they, the children, that was, had ever been there. Penny said no, the story of the family was there, and the wounded soldiers, but not them, they were perhaps too insignificant. Too little, said Primrose, nodding agreement, not quite sure what she meant by too little. Funny, said Penny, that they should meet each other next to that book, with that picture. Creepy, said Primrose in a light, light cob-web voice, not looking at Penny. We saw that thing. When we went in the forest.

Yes we did, said Penny. We saw it.

Did you ever wonder, asked Primrose, if we *really* saw it?

Never for a moment, said Penny. That is, I don't know what it was, but I've always been quite sure we saw it.

Does it change – do you remember all of it?

It was a horrible thing, and yes, I remember all of it, there isn't a bit of it I can manage to forget. Though I forget all sorts of things, said Penny, in a thin voice, a vanishing voice.

And have you ever told anyone of it, spoken of it, asked Primrose more urgently, leaning forward, holding on to the table edge.

No, said Penny. She had not. She said, who would believe it, believe them?

That's what I thought, said Primrose. I didn't speak. But it stuck in my mind like a tapeworm in your gut. I think it did me no good.

It did me no good either, said Penny. No good at all. I've thought about it, she said to the ageing woman opposite, whose face quivered under her dyed goldilocks. I think, I think there are things that are real – more real than we are – but mostly we don't cross their paths, or they don't cross ours. Maybe at very bad times we get into their world, or notice what they are doing in ours.

Primrose nodded energetically. She looked as though sharing was solace, and Penny, to whom it was not solace, grimaced with pain.

'Sometimes I think that thing finished me off,' said Penny to Primrose, a child's voice rising in a woman's gullet, arousing a little girl's scared smile which wasn't a smile on Primrose's face. Primrose said:

'It did finish *her* off, that little one, didn't it? She got into its path, didn't she? And when it had gone by – she wasn't anywhere,' said Primrose. 'That was how it was?'

'Nobody ever asked where she was, or looked for her,' said Penny.

'I wondered if we'd made her up,' said Primrose. 'But I didn't, we didn't.'

'Her name was Alys.'

'With a *y*.'

There had been a mess, a disgusting mess, they remembered, but no particular sign of anything that might have been, or been part of, or belonged to, a persistent little girl called Alys.

Primrose shrugged voluptuously, let out a gale of a sigh, and rearranged her flesh in her clothes.

'Well, we know we're not mad, anyway,' she said. 'We've got into a mystery, but we didn't make it up. It wasn't a delusion. So it was good we met, because now we needn't be afraid we're mad, need we, we can get on with things, so to speak?'

They arranged to have dinner together the following evening. They were staying in different bed-and-breakfasts and neither of them thought of exchanging addresses. They agreed on a restaurant in the market square of the local town – *Seraphina's Hot Pot* – and a time, seven-thirty. They did not even discuss spending the next day together. Primrose went on a local bus tour. Penny asked for sandwiches, and took a long solitary walk. The weather was grey, spitting fine rain. Both arrived at their lodgings with headaches, and both made tea with the teabags and kettle provided in their rooms. They sat on their beds. Penny's bed had a quilt with blowsy cabbage roses. Primrose's had a black-and-white

28

checked gingham duvet. They turned on their televisions, watched the same game show, listened to the inordinate jolly laughter. Penny washed herself rather fiercely in her tiny bathroom: Primrose slowly changed her underwear, and put on fresh tights. Between bathroom and wardrobe Penny saw the air in the room fill with a kind of grey smoke. Rummaging in a suitcase for a clean blouse, Primrose felt giddy, as though the carpet was swirling. What would they say to each other, they asked themselves, and sat down, heavy and winded, on the edges of their single beds. Why? Primrose's mind said, scurrying, and Why? Penny asked herself starkly. Primrose put down her blouse and turned up the television. Penny managed to walk as far as the window. She had a view with a romantic bit of moorland, rising to a height that cut off the sky. Evening had caught her: the earth was black: the house-lights trickled feebly into gloom.

Seven-thirty came and went, and neither woman moved. Both, indistinctly, imagined the other waiting at a table, watching a door open and shut. Neither moved. What could they have said, they asked themselves, but only perfunctorily. They were used to not asking too much, they had had practice.

The next day they both thought very hard, but indirectly, about the wood. It was a spring day, a good day for woods, and yesterday's rain-clouds had been succeeded by clear sunlight, with a light movement of air and a very faint warmth. Penny thought about the wood, put on her walking-shoes, and set off obliquely in the opposite direction. Primrose was not given to ratiocination. She sat over her breakfast, which was English and ample, bacon and mushrooms, toast and honey, and let her feelings about the wood run over her skin, pricking and twitching. The wood, the real and imagined wood – both before and after she had entered it with Penny – had always been simultaneously a source of attraction and a source of discomfort, shading into terror. The light in woods was more golden and more darkly shadowed than any light on city terraces, including the glare of bombardment. The gold and the shadows were intertwined, a promise of liveliness. What they had seen had been shapeless and stinking, but the wood persisted.

So without speaking to herself a sentence in her head – 'I shall go there' – Primrose decided by settling her stomach, setting her knees, and slightly clenching her fists, that she would go there. And she went straight there, full of warm food, arriving as the morning brightened with the first busload of tourists, and giving them the slip, to take the path they had once taken, across the lawn and through the wicket-gate.

The wood was much the same, but denser and more inviting in its new greenness. Primrose's body decided to set off in a rather different direction from the one the little girls had taken. New bracken was uncoiling with snaky force. Yesterday's rain still glittered on limp new hazel leaves and threads of gossamer. Small feathered throats above her, and in the depths beyond, whistled and trilled with enchanting territorial aggression and male self-assertion, which were to Primrose simply the chorus. She heard a cackle and saw a flash of the loveliest flesh-pink, in feathers, and a blue gleam. She was not good at identifying birds. She could do 'a robin' – one hopped from branch to branch – 'a black bird' which shone like jet, and 'a tit' which did acrobatics, soft, blue and yellow, a tiny scrap of fierce life. She went steadily on, always distracted by shines and gleams in her eye-corner. She found a mossy bank, on which she found posies of primroses, which she recognized and took vaguely, in the warmth of her heart labouring in her chest, as a good sign, a personal sign. She picked a few, stroked their pale petals, buried her nose in them, smelled the thin, clear honey-smell of them, spring honey without the buzz of summer. She was better at flowers than birds, because there had been *Flower Fairies* in the school bookshelves when she was little, with the flowers painted accurately, wood-sorrel and stitchwort, pimpernel and honeysuckle, flowers she had never seen, accompanied by truly pretty human creatures, all children, from babies to girls and boys, clothed in the blues and golds, russets and purples of the flowers and fruits, walking, dancing, delicate material imaginings of the essential lives of plants. And now as she wandered on, she saw and recognized them, windflower and bryony, self-heal and dead-nettle, and had – despite where she was – a lovely lapping sense of in-visible – *just* invisible life swarming in the leaves and along the twigs, despite where she was, despite what she had not forgotten having seen there. She closed her eyes a fraction. The sunlight flickered and flickered. She saw glitter and spangling everywhere. She saw drifts of intense blue, further in, and between the tree-trunks, with the light running over them.

She stopped. She did not like the sound of her own toiling breath. She was not very fit. She saw, then, a whisking in the bracken, a twirl of fur, thin and flaming, quivering on a tree-trunk. She saw a squirrel, a red squirrel, watching her from a bough. She had to sit down, as she remembered her mother. She sat on a hummock of grass, rather heavily. She remembered them all, Nutkin and Moldywarp, Brock and Sleepy Dormouse, Natty Newt and Ferdy Frog. Her mother didn't tell stories and didn't open gates into imaginary worlds. But she had been good with her fingers. Every Christmas during the war, when toys, and indeed materials, were not to be had, Primrose had woken to find in her stocking a new stuffed creature, made from fur fabric with button eyes and horny claws, or, in the case of the amphibians, made from scraps of satin and taffeta. There had been an artistry to them. The stuffed squirrel was the essence of squirrel, the fox was watchful, the newt was slithery. They did not wear anthropomorphic jackets or caps, which made it easier to invest them with imaginary natures. She believed in Father Christmas, and the discovery that her mother had made the toys, the vanishing of magic, had been a breathtaking blow. She could not be grateful for the skill and the imagination, so uncharacteristic of her flirtatious mother. The creatures continued to accumulate. A spider, a Bambi. She told herself stories at night about a girl-woman, an enchantress in a fairy wood, loved and protected by an army of wise and gentle animals. She slept banked in by stuffed creatures, as the house in the blitz was banked in by inadequate sandbags.

Primrose registered the red squirrel as disappointing – stringier and more rat-like than its plump grey city cousins. But she knew it was rare and special, and when it took off from branch to branch, flicking its extended tail like a sail, gripping with its tiny hands, she set out to follow it as though it was a messenger. It would take her to the centre, she thought, she ought to get to the centre. It could easily have leaped out of sight, she thought, but it didn't. It lingered and sniffed and stared nervily, waiting for her. She pushed through brambles into denser greener shadows. Juices stained her skirts and skin. She began to tell herself a story about staunch Primrose, not giving up, making her way to 'the centre'. She had to have a reason for coming there, it was to do with getting to the centre. Her childhood stories had all been in the third person. 'She was not afraid.' 'She faced up to the wild beasts. They cowered.' She laddered her tights and muddied her shoes and breathed heavier. The squirrel stopped to clean its face. She crushed bluebells and saw the sinister hoods of arum lilies.

She had no idea where she was, or how far she had come, but she decided that the clearing where she found herself was the centre. The squirrel had stopped, and was running up and down a single tree. There was a sort of mossy mound which could almost have had a throne-like aspect, if you were being imaginative. So she sat on it. 'She came to the centre and sat on the mossy chair.'

Now what?

She had not forgotten what they had seen, the blank miserable face, the powerful claws, the raggle-taggle train of accumulated decay. She had come neither to look for it nor to confront it, but she had come because it was there. She had known all her life that she, Primrose, had *really* been in a magic forest. She knew that the forest was the source of terror. She had never frightened the littl'uns she entertained at parties, in schools, in crèches, with tales of lost children in forests. She frightened them with slimy things that came up the plughole, or swarmed out of the U-bend in the lavatory, or tapped on windows at night, and were despatched by bravery and magic. There were waiting hobgoblins in urban dumps beyond the street-lights. But the woods in her tales were sources of glamour, of rich colours and unseen hidden life, flower fairies and more magical beings. They were places where you used words like spangles and sequins for real dew-drops on real dock leaves. Primrose knew that glamour and the thing they had seen came from the same place, that brilliance and the ashen stink had the same source. She made them safe for the littl'uns by restricting them to panto-mime flats and sweet illustrations. She didn't look at what she knew, better not, but *she did know she knew*, she recognized confusedly.

Now what?

She sat on the moss, and a voice in her head said, 'I want to go home.' And she heard herself give a bitter, entirely grown-up little laugh, for what was home? What did she know about home?

Where she lived was above a Chinese takeaway. She had a dangerous cupboard-corner she cooked in, a bed, a clothes-rail, an armchair deformed by generations of bottoms. She thought of this place in faded browns and beiges, seen through drifting coils of Chinese cooking-steam, scented with stewing pork and a bubbling chicken broth. Home was not real, as all the sturdy twigs and roots in the wood were real, it had neither primrose-honey nor spangles and sequins. The stuffed animals, or some of them, were piled on the bed and the carpet, their fur rubbed, their pristine stare gone from their scratched eyes. She thought about what one thought was *real*, sitting there on the moss-throne at the centre. When Mum had come in, snivelling, to say Dad was dead, she herself had been preoccupied with whether pudding would be tapioca or semolina, whether there would be jam, and subsequently, how ugly Mum's dripping nose looked, how she looked as though she was *putting it on*. She remembered the semolina and the rather nasty blackberry jam, the taste and the texture, to this day, so was that real, was that home? She had later invented a picture of a cloudy aquamarine sea under a gold sun in which a huge fountain of white curling water rose from a foundering ship. It was very beautiful but not real. She could not remember Dad. She could remember the Thing in the Forest, and she could remember Alys. The fact that the mossy tump had lovely colours – crimson and emerald, she said, maidenhairs, she named something at random – didn't mean she didn't remember the Thing. She remembered what Penny had said about 'things that are more real than we are'. She had met one. Here at the centre, the spout of water was more real than the semolina, because she was where such things reign. The word she found was 'reign'. She had understood something, and did not know what she had understood. She wanted badly to go home, and she wanted never to move. The light was lovely in the leaves. The squirrel flirted its tail and suddenly set off again, springing into the branches. The woman lumbered to her feet and licked the bramble-scratches on the back of her hands.

Penny had set off in what she supposed to be the opposite direction. She walked very steadily, keeping to hedgerows and field-edge paths, climbing the occasional stile. For the first part of the walk she kept her eyes on the ground, and her ears on her own trudging, as it disturbed stubble and pebbles. She slurred her feet over vetch and stitchwort, looking back over the crushed trail. She remembered the Thing. She remembered it clearly and daily. Why was she in this part of the world at all, if not to settle with it? But she walked away, noticing and not noticing that her path was deflected by fieldforms and the lie of the land into a snaking sickle-shape. As the day wore on, she settled into her stride and lifted her eyes, admiring the new corn in the furrows, a distant skylark. When she saw the wood on the horizon she knew it was the wood, although she was seeing it from an unfamiliar aspect, from where it appeared to be perched on a conical hillock, ridged as though it had been grasped and squeezed by coils of strength. The trees were tufted and tempting. It was almost dusk when she came there. The shadows were thickening, the dark places in the tumbled undergrowth were darkening. She mounted the slope, and went in over a suddenly discovered stile.

Once inside, she moved cautiously, as though she was hunted or hunting. She stood stock-still, and snuffed the air for the remembered rottenness: she listened to the sounds of the trees and the creatures, trying to sift out a distant threshing and sliding. She smelled rottenness, but it was normal rottenness, leaves and stems mulching back into earth. She heard sounds. Not birdsong, for it was too late in the day, but the odd raucous warning croak, a crackle of something, a tremulous shiver of something else. She heard her own heartbeat in the thickening brown air.

She had wagered on freedom and walked away, and walking away had brought her here, as she had known it would. It was no use looking for familiar tree-trunks or tussocks. They had had a lifetime, her lifetime, to alter out of recognition.

She began to think she discerned dark tunnels in the undergrowth, where something might have rolled and slid. Mashed seedlings, broken twigs and fronds, none of it very recent. There were things caught in the thorns, flimsy colourless shreds of damp wool or fur. She peered down the tunnels and noted where the scrapings hung thickest. She forced herself to go into the dark, stooping, occasionally crawling on hands and knees. The silence was heavy. She found things she remembered, threadworms of knitting wool, unravelled dishcloth cotton, clinging newsprint. She found odd sausage-shaped tubes of membrane, containing fragments of hair and bone and other inanimate stuffs. They were like monstrous owl-pellets, or the gut-shaped hair-balls vomited by cats. Penny went forwards, putting aside lashing briars and tough stems with careful fingers. It had been here, but how long ago? When she stopped, and sniffed the air, and listened, there was nothing but the drowsy wood.

Quite suddenly she came out at a place she remembered. The clearing was larger, the tree-trunks were thicker, but the fallen one behind which they had hidden still lay there. The place was almost the ghost of a camp. The trees round about were hung with threadbare pennants and streamers, like the scorched, hacked, threadbare banners in the chapel of the great house, with their brown stains of earth or blood. It had been here, it had never gone away.

Penny moved slowly and dreamily round, watching herself as you watch yourself in a dream, looking for things. She found a mock tortoiseshell hairslide, and a shoe-button with a metal shank. She found a bird-skeleton, quite fresh, bashed flat, with a few feathers glued to it. She found ambivalent shards and several teeth, of varying sizes and shapes. She found – spread around, half-hidden by roots, stained green but glinting white – a collection of small bones, finger-bones, tiny toes, a rib, and finally what might be a brain-pan and brow. She thought of putting them in her knapsack, and then thought she could not, and heaped them at the foot of a holly. She was not an anatomist. Some at least of the tiny bones might have been badger or fox.

She sat down on the earth, with her back against the fallen trunk. She thought that she should perhaps find something to dig a hole, to bury the little bones, but she didn't move. She thought, now I am watching myself as you do in a safe dream, but then, when I saw it, it was one of those appalling dreams, where you are inside, where you cannot get out. Except that it wasn't a dream.

It was the encounter with the Thing that had led her to deal professionally in dreams. Something which resembled

37

unreality had walked – had rolled, had wound itself, had *lumbered* into reality, and she had seen it. She had been the reading child, but after the sight of the Thing, she had not been able to inhabit the customary and charming unreality of books. She had become good at studying what could not be seen. She took an interest in the dead, who inhabited real history. She was drawn to the invisible forces which moved in molecules and caused them to coagulate or dissipate. She had become a psychotherapist 'to be useful'. That was not quite accurate or sufficient as an explanation. The corner of the blanket that covered the unthinkable had been turned back enough for her to catch sight of it. She was in its world. It was not by accident that she had come to specialize in severely autistic children, children who twittered, or banged, or stared, who sat damp and absent on Penny's official lap and told her no dreams, discussed no projects. The world they knew was a real world. Often Penny thought it was *the* real world, from which even their desperate parents were at least partly shielded. Somebody had to occupy themselves with the hopeless. Penny felt she could. Most people couldn't. She could.

All the leaves of the forest began slowly to quaver and then to clatter. Far away there was the sound of something heavy, and sluggish, stirring. Penny sat very still and expectant. She heard the old blind rumble, she sniffed the old stink. It came from no direction; it was on both sides; it was all around; as though the Thing encompassed the wood, or as though it travelled in multiple fragments, as it was described in the old text. It was dark now. What was visible had no distinct colour, only shades of ink and elephant.

Now, thought Penny, and just as suddenly as it had begun, the turmoil ceased. It was as though the Thing had turned away; she could feel the tremble of the wood recede and become still. Quite suddenly, over the tree-tops, a huge disc of white-gold mounted and hung, deepening shadows, silvering edges. Penny remembered her father, standing in the cold light of the full moon, and saying wryly that the bombers would likely come tonight, there was a brilliant, cloudless full moon. He had vanished in an oven of red-yellow roaring, Penny had guessed, or been told, or imagined. Her mother had sent her away before allowing the fireman to speak, who had come with the news. She had been a creep-mouse on stairs and in cubby-holes, trying to overhear what was being imparted, to be given a fragment of reality with which to attach herself to the truth of her mother's pain. Her mother didn't, or couldn't, want her company. She caught odd phrases of talk – 'nothing really to identify', 'absolutely no doubt'. He had been a tired gentle man with ash in his trouser turn-ups. There had been a funeral. Penny remembered thinking there was nothing, or next to nothing, in the coffin his fellow-firemen shouldered, it went up so lightly, it was so easy to set down on the crematorium slab.

They had been living behind the black-out anyway, but her mother went on living behind drawn curtains long after the war was over.

She remembered someone inviting her to tea, to cheer her up. There had been indoor fireworks, saved from before the war, Chinese, set off in saucers. There had been a small conical Vesuvius, with a blue touch-paper and a pink and grey dragon painted on. It had done nothing but sputter until they had almost stopped looking, and then it spewed a coil of fantastically light ash, that rose and rose, becoming five or six times as large as the original, and then abruptly was still. Like a grey bun, or a very old turd. She began to cry. It was ungrateful of her. An effort had been made, to which she had not responded.

The moon had released the wood, it seemed. Penny stood up and brushed leaf mould off her clothes. She had been ready for it and it had not come. She did not know if she had wanted to defy it, or to see that it was as she had darkly remembered it; she felt obscurely disappointed to be released from the wood. But she accepted her release and found her way back to the fields and her village along liquid trails of moonlight.

The two women took the same train back to the city, but did not encounter each other until they got out. The passengers scurried and shuffled towards the exit, mostly heads down. Both women remembered how they had set out in the war-time dark, with their twig-legs and gas-masks. Both raised their heads as they neared the barrier, not in hope of being met, for they would not be, but automatically, to calculate where to go, and what to do. They saw each other's face in the cavernous gloom, two pale, recognizable rounds, far enough apart for speech, and even greetings, to be awkward. In the dimness they were reduced to similarity – dark eyeholes, set mouth. For a moment or two, they stood and simply stared. On that first occasion the station vault had been full of curling steam, and the air gritty with ash. Now, the blunt-nosed sleek diesel they had left was blue and gold under a layer of grime. They saw each other through that black imagined veil which grief, or pain, or despair hang over the visible world. They saw each other's face and thought of the unforgettable misery of the face they had seen in the forest. Each thought that the other was the witness, who made the thing certainly real, who prevented her from slipping into the comfort of believing she had imagined it, or made it up. So they stared at each other, blankly and desperately, without acknowledgement, then picked up their baggage, and turned away into the crowd.

*   *   *

Penny found that the black veil had somehow become part of her vision. She thought constantly about faces, her father's, her mother's – neither of which would hold their form in her mind's eye. Primrose's face, the hopeful little girl, the woman staring up at her from the glass case, staring at her conspiratorially over the clotted cream. The blonde infant Alys, an ingratiating sweet smile. The half-human face of the Thing. She tried, as though everything depended on it, to remember that face completely, and suffered over the detail of the dreadful droop of its mouth, the exact inanity of its blind squinneying. Present faces were blank discs, shadowed moons. Her patients came and went, children lost, or busy, or trapped behind their masks of vagueness or anxiety or overexcitement. She was increasingly unable to distinguish one from another. The face of the Thing hung in her brain, jealously soliciting her attention, distracting her from dailiness. She had gone back to its place, and had not seen it. She needed to see it. Why she needed it, was because it was more real than she was. It would have been better not even to have glimpsed it, but their paths had crossed. It had trampled on her life, had sucked out her marrow, without noticing who or what she was. She would go and face it. What else was there, she asked herself, and answered herself, nothing.

So she made her way back, sitting alone in the train as the fields streaked past, drowsing through a century-long night under the cabbage-rose quilt in the B&B. This time she went in the old way, from the house, through the garden-gate; she found the old trail quickly, her sharp eye picked up the trace of its detritus, and soon enough she was back in the clearing, where her cairn of tiny bones by the tree-trunk was undisturbed. She gave a little sigh, dropped to her knees, and then sat with her back to the rotting wood and silently called the Thing. Almost immediately she sensed its perturbation, saw the trouble in the branches, heard the lumbering, smelled its ancient smell. It was a greyish, unremarkable day. She closed her eyes briefly as the noise and movement grew stronger. When it came, she would look it in the face, she would see what it was. She clasped her hands loosely in her lap. Her nerves relaxed. Her blood slowed. She was ready.

Primrose was in the shopping mall, putting out her circle of rainbow-coloured plastic chairs. She creaked as she bent over them. It was pouring with rain outside, but the mall was enclosed like a crystal palace in a casing of glass. The floor under the rainbow chairs was gleaming dappled marble. They were in front of a dimpling fountain, with lights shining up through the greenish water, making golden rings round the polished pebbles and wishing-coins that lay there. The little children collected round her: their mothers kissed them good-bye, told them to be good and quiet and listen to the nice lady. They had little transparent plastic cups of shining orange juice, and each had a biscuit in silver foil. They were all colours – black skin, brown skin, pink skin, freckled skin, pink jacket, yellow jacket, purple hood, scarlet hood. Some grinned and some whimpered, some wriggled, some were still. Primrose sat on the edge of the fountain. She had decided what to do. She smiled her best, most comfortable smile, and adjusted her golden locks. Listen to me, she told them, and I'll tell you something amazing, a story that's never been told before.

There were once two little girls who saw, or believed they saw, a thing in a forest . . .

NATHANIEL HAWTHORNE

YOUNG GOODMAN BROWN

YOUNG GOODMAN BROWN came forth at sunset into the street at Salem village; but put his head back, after crossing the threshold, to exchange a parting kiss with his young wife. And Faith, as the wife was aptly named, thrust her own pretty head into the street, letting the wind play with the pink ribbons of her cap while she called to Goodman Brown.

'Dearest heart,' whispered she, softly and rather sadly, when her lips were close to his ear, 'prithee put off your journey until sunrise and sleep in your own bed tonight. A lone woman is troubled with such dreams and such thoughts that she's afeard of herself sometimes. Pray tarry with me this night, dear husband, of all nights in the year.'

'My love and my Faith,' replied young Goodman Brown, 'of all nights in the year, this one night must I tarry away from thee. My journey, as thou callest it, forth and back again, must needs be done 'twixt now and sunrise. What, my sweet, pretty wife, dost thou doubt me already, and we but three months married?'

'Then God bless you!' said Faith, with the pink ribbons; 'and may you find all well when you come back.'

'Amen!' cried Goodman Brown. 'Say thy prayers, dear Faith, and go to bed at dusk, and no harm will come to thee.'

So they parted; and the young man pursued his way until, being about to turn the corner by the meeting-house, he looked back and saw the head of Faith still peeping after him with a melancholy air, in spite of her pink ribbons.

'Poor little Faith!' thought he, for his heart smote him. 'What a wretch am I to leave her on such an errand! She talks of dreams, too. Methought as she spoke there was trouble in her face, as if a dream had warned her what work is to be done tonight. But no, no; 't would kill her to think it. Well, she's a blessed angel on earth; and after this one night I'll cling to her skirts and follow her to heaven.'

With this excellent resolve for the future, Goodman Brown felt himself justified in making more haste on his present evil purpose. He had taken a dreary road, darkened by all the gloomiest trees of the forest, which barely stood aside to let the narrow path creep through, and closed immediately behind. It was all as lonely as could be; and there is this peculiarity in such a solitude, that the traveler knows not who may be concealed by the innumerable trunks and the thick boughs overhead; so that with lonely footsteps he may yet be passing through an unseen multitude.

'There may be a devilish Indian behind every tree,' said Goodman Brown to himself; and he glanced fearfully behind him as he added, 'What if the devil himself should be at my very elbow!'

His head being turned back, he passed a crook of the road, and, looking forward again, beheld the figure of a man, in grave and decent attire, seated at the foot of an old tree. He arose at Goodman Brown's approach and walked onward side by side with him.

'You are late, Goodman Brown,' said he. 'The clock of the Old South was striking as I came through Boston, and that is full fifteen minutes agone.'

'Faith kept me back a while,' replied the young man, with a tremor in his voice, caused by the sudden appearance of his companion, though not wholly unexpected.

It was now deep dusk in the forest, and deepest in that

part of it where these two were journeying. As nearly as could be discerned, the second traveler was about fifty years old, apparently in the same rank of life as Goodman Brown, and bearing a considerable resemblance to him, though perhaps more in expression than features. Still they might have been taken for father and son. And yet, though the elder person was as simply clad as the younger, and as simple in manner too, he had an indescribable air of one who knew the world, and who would not have felt abashed at the governor's dinner table or in King William's court, were it possible that his affairs should call him thither. But the only thing about him that could be fixed upon as remarkable was his staff, which bore the likeness of a great black snake, so curiously wrought that it might almost be seen to twist and wriggle itself like a living serpent. This, of course, must have been an ocular deception, assisted by the uncertain light.

'Come, Goodman Brown,' cried his fellow-traveler, 'this is a dull pace for the beginning of a journey. Take my staff, if you are so soon weary.'

'Friend,' said the other, exchanging his slow pace for a full stop, 'having kept covenant by meeting thee here, it is my purpose now to return whence I came. I have scruples touching the matter thou wot'st of.'

'Sayest thou so?' replied he of the serpent, smiling apart. 'Let us walk on, nevertheless, reasoning as we go; and if I convince thee not thou shalt turn back. We are but a little way in the forest yet.'

'Too far! too far!' exclaimed the goodman, unconsciously resuming his walk. 'My father never went into the woods on such an errand, nor his father before him. We have been a race of honest men and good Christians since the days of the martyrs; and shall I be the first of the name of Brown that ever took this path and kept'—

'Such company, thou wouldst say,' observed the elder person, interpreting his pause. 'Well said, Goodman Brown! I have been as well acquainted with your family as with ever a one among the Puritans; and that's no trifle to say. I helped your grandfather, the constable, when he lashed the Quaker woman so smartly through the streets of Salem; and it was I that brought your father a pitch-pine knot, kindled at my own hearth, to set fire to an Indian village, in King Philip's war. They were my good friends, both; and many a pleasant walk have we had along this path, and returned merrily after midnight. I would fain be friends with you for their sake.'

'If it be as thou sayest,' replied Goodman Brown, 'I marvel they never spoke of these matters; or, verily, I marvel not, seeing that the least rumor of the sort would have driven them from New England. We are a people of prayer, and good works to boot, and abide no such wickedness.'

'Wickedness or not,' said the traveler with the twisted staff, 'I have a very general acquaintance here in New England. The deacons of many a church have drunk the communion wine with me; the selectmen of divers towns make me their chairman; and a majority of the Great and General Court are firm supporters of my interest. The governor and I, too— But these are state secrets.'

'Can this be so?' cried Goodman Brown, with a stare of amazement at his undisturbed companion. 'Howbeit, I have nothing to do with the governor and council; they have their own ways, and are no rule for a simple husbandman like me. But, were I to go on with thee, how should I meet the eye of that good old man, our minister, at Salem village? Oh, his voice would make me tremble both Sabbath day and lecture day.'

Thus far the elder traveler had listened with due gravity;

but now burst into a fit of irrepressible mirth, shaking himself so violently that his snake-like staff actually seemed to wriggle in sympathy.

'Ha! ha! ha!' shouted he again and again; then composing himself, 'Well, go on, Goodman Brown, go on; but, prithee, don't kill me with laughing.'

'Well, then, to end the matter at once,' said Goodman Brown, considerably nettled, 'there is my wife, Faith. It would break her dear little heart; and I'd rather break my own.'

'Nay, if that be the case,' answered the other, 'e'en go thy ways, Goodman Brown. I would not for twenty old women like the one hobbling before us that Faith should come to any harm.'

As he spoke he pointed his staff at a female figure on the path, in whom Goodman Brown recognized a very pious and exemplary dame, who had taught him his catechism in youth, and was still his moral and spiritual adviser, jointly with the minister and Deacon Gookin.

'A marvel, truly, that Goody Cloyse should be so far in the wilderness at nightfall,' said he. 'But with your leave, friend, I shall take a cut through the woods until we have left this Christian woman behind. Being a stranger to you, she might ask whom I was consorting with and whither I was going.'

'Be it so,' said his fellow-traveler. 'Betake you the woods, and let me keep the path.'

Accordingly the young man turned aside, but took care to watch his companion, who advanced softly along the road until he had come within a staff's length of the old dame. She, meanwhile, was making the best of her way, with singular speed for so aged a woman, and mumbling some indistinct words – a prayer, doubtless – as she went. The traveler put forth his staff and touched her withered neck with what seemed the serpent's tail.

'The devil!' screamed the pious old lady.

'Then Goody Cloyse knows her old friend?' observed the traveler, confronting her and leaning on his writhing stick.

'Ah, forsooth, and is it your worship indeed?' cried the good dame. 'Yea, truly is it, and in the very image of my old gossip, Goodman Brown, the grandfather of the silly fellow that now is. But – would your worship believe it? – my broomstick hath strangely disappeared, stolen, as I suspect, by that unhanged witch, Goody Cory, and that, too, when I was all anointed with the juice of smallage, and cinquefoil, and wolf's bane'—

'Mingled with fine wheat and the fat of a new-born babe,' said the shape of old Goodman Brown.

'Ah, your worship knows the recipe,' cried the old lady, cackling aloud. 'So, as I was saying, being all ready for the meeting, and no horse to ride on, I made up my mind to foot it; for they tell me there is a nice young man to be taken into communion tonight. But now your good worship will lend me your arm, and we shall be there in a twinkling.'

'That can hardly be,' answered her friend. 'I may not spare you my arm, Goody Cloyse; but here is my staff, if you will.'

So saying, he threw it down at her feet, where, perhaps, it assumed life, being one of the rods which its owner had formerly lent to the Egyptian magi. Of this fact, however, Goodman Brown could not take cognizance. He had cast up his eyes in astonishment, and, looking down again, beheld neither Goody Cloyse nor the serpentine staff, but this fellow-traveler alone, who waited for him as calmly as if nothing had happened.

'That old woman taught me my catechism,' said the young man; and there was a world of meaning in this simple comment.

They continued to walk onward, while the elder traveler

exhorted his companion to make good speed and persevere in the path, discoursing so aptly that his arguments seemed rather to spring up in the bosom of his auditor than to be suggested by himself. As they went, he plucked a branch of maple to serve for a walking stick, and began to strip it of the twigs and little boughs, which were wet with evening dew. The moment his fingers touched them they became strangely withered and dried up as with a week's sunshine. Thus the pair proceeded, at a good free pace, until suddenly, in a gloomy hollow of the road, Goodman Brown sat himself down on the stump of a tree and refused to go any farther.

'Friend,' said he, stubbornly, 'my mind is made up. Not another step will I budge on this errand. What if a wretched old woman do choose to go to the devil when I thought she was going to heaven: is that any reason why I should quit my dear Faith and go after her?'

'You will think better of this by and by,' said his acquaintance, composedly. 'Sit here and rest yourself a while; and when you feel like moving again, there is my staff to help you along.'

Without more words, he threw his companion the maple stick, and was as speedily out of sight as if he had vanished into the deepening gloom. The young man sat a few moments by the roadside, applauding himself greatly, and thinking with how clear a conscience he should meet the minister in his morning walk, nor shrink from the eye of good old Deacon Gookin. And what calm sleep would be his that very night, which was to have been spent so wickedly, but so purely and sweetly now, in the arms of Faith! Amidst these pleasant and praiseworthy meditations, Goodman Brown heard the tramp of horses along the road, and deemed it advisable to conceal himself within the verge of the forest, conscious of the guilty purpose that had brought him thither, though now so happily turned from it.

On came the hoof tramps and the voices of the riders, two grave old voices, conversing soberly as they drew near. These mingled sounds appeared to pass along the road, within a few yards of the young man's hiding-place; but, owing doubtless to the depth of the gloom at that particular spot, neither the travelers nor their steeds were visible. Though their figures brushed the small boughs by the wayside, it could not be seen that they intercepted, even for a moment, the faint gleam from the strip of bright sky athwart which they must have passed. Goodman Brown alternately crouched and stood on tiptoe, pulling aside the branches and thrusting forth his head as far as he durst without discerning so much as a shadow. It vexed him the more, because he could have sworn, were such a thing possible, that he recognized the voices of the minister and Deacon Gookin, jogging along quietly, as they were wont to do, when bound to some ordination or ecclesiastical council. While yet within hearing, one of the riders stopped to pluck a switch.

'Of the two, reverend sir,' said the voice like the deacon's, 'I had rather miss an ordination dinner than tonight's meeting. They tell me that some of our community are to be here from Falmouth and beyond, and others from Connecticut and Rhode Island, besides several of the Indian pow-wows, who, after their fashion, know almost as much deviltry as the best of us. Moreover, there is a goodly young woman to be taken into communion.'

'Mighty well, Deacon Gookin!' replied the solemn old tones of the minister. 'Spur up, or we shall be late. Nothing can be done, you know, until I get on the ground.'

The hoofs clattered again; and the voices, talking so strangely in the empty air, passed on through the forest, where no church had ever been gathered or solitary Christian prayed. Whither, then, could these holy men be journeying so deep into the heathen wilderness? Young Goodman Brown caught hold of a tree for support, being ready to sink down on the ground, faint and overburdened with the heavy sickness of his heart. He looked up to the sky, doubting whether there really was a heaven above him. Yet there was the blue arch, and the stars brightening in it.

'With heaven above and Faith below, I will yet stand firm against the devil!' cried Goodman Brown.

While he still gazed upward into the deep arch of the firmament and had lifted his hands to pray, a cloud, though no wind was stirring, hurried across the zenith and hid the brightening stars. The blue sky was still visible, except directly overhead, where this black mass of cloud was sweeping swiftly northward. Aloft in the air, as if from the depths of the cloud, came a confused and doubtful sound of voices. Once the listener fancied that he could distinguish the accents of towns-people of his own, men and women, both pious and ungodly, many of whom he had met at the communion table, and had seen others rioting at the tavern. The next moment, so indistinct were the sounds, he doubted whether he had heard aught but the murmur of the old forest, whispering without a wind. Then came a stronger swell of those familiar tones, heard daily in the sunshine at Salem village, but never until now from a cloud of night. There was one voice, of a young woman, uttering lamentations, yet with an uncertain sorrow, and entreating for some favor, which, perhaps, it would grieve her to obtain; and all the unseen multitude, both saints and sinners, seemed to encourage her onward.

'Faith!' shouted Goodman Brown, in a voice of agony and desperation; and the echoes of the forest mocked him, crying, 'Faith! Faith!' as if bewildered wretches were seeking her all through the wilderness.

The cry of grief, rage, and terror was yet piercing the night, when the unhappy husband held his breath for a response. There was a scream, drowned immediately in a louder murmur of voices, fading into far-off laughter, as the dark cloud swept away, leaving the clear and silent sky above Goodman Brown. But something fluttered lightly down through the air and caught on the branch of a tree. The young man seized it, and beheld a pink ribbon.

'My Faith is gone!' cried he, after one stupefied moment. 'There is no good on earth; and sin is but a name. Come, devil; for to thee is this world given.'

And, maddened with despair, so that he laughed loud and long, did Goodman Brown grasp his staff and set forth again, at such a rate that he seemed to fly along the forest path rather than to walk or run. The road grew wilder and drearier and more faintly traced, and vanished at length, leaving him in the heart of the dark wilderness, still rushing onward with the instinct that guides mortal man to evil. The whole forest was peopled with frightful sounds – the creaking of the trees, the howling of wild beasts, and the yell of Indians; while sometimes the wind tolled like a distant church bell, and sometimes gave a broad roar around the traveler, as if all Nature were laughing him to scorn. But he was himself the chief horror of the scene, and shrank not from its other horrors.

'Ha! ha! ha!' roared Goodman Brown when the wind laughed at him. 'Let us hear which will laugh loudest. Think not to frighten me with your deviltry. Come witch, come wizard, come Indian pow-wow, come devil himself, and here comes Goodman Brown. You may as well fear him as he fear you.'

In truth, all through the haunted forest there could be nothing more frightful than the figure of Goodman Brown. On he flew among the black pines, brandishing his staff with frenzied gestures, now giving vent to an inspiration of horrid blasphemy, and now shouting forth such laughter as set all the echoes of the forest laughing like demons around him. The fiend in his own shape is less hideous than when he rages in the breast of man. Thus sped the demoniac on his course, until, quivering among the trees, he saw a red light before him, as when the felled trunks and branches of a clearing have been set on fire, and throw up their lurid blaze against the sky, at the hour of midnight. He paused, in a lull of the tempest that had driven him onward, and heard the swell of what seemed a hymn, rolling solemnly from a distance with the weight of many voices. He knew the tune; it was a familiar one in the choir of the village meeting-house. The verse died heavily away, and was lengthened by a chorus, not of human voices, but of all the sounds of the benighted wilderness pealing in awful harmony together. Goodman Brown cried out, and his cry was lost to his own ear by its unison with the cry of the desert.

In the interval of silence he stole forward until the light glared full upon his eyes. At one extremity of an open space, hemmed in by the dark wall of the forest, arose a rock, bearing some rude, natural resemblance either to an altar or a pulpit, and surrounded by four blazing pines, their tops aflame, their stems untouched, like candles at an evening meeting. The mass of foliage that had overgrown the summit of the rock was all on fire, blazing high into the night and fitfully illuminating the whole field. Each pendent twig and leafy festoon was in a blaze. As the red light arose and fell, a numerous congregation alternately shone forth, then disappeared in shadow, and again grew, as it were, out of the darkness, peopling the heart of the solitary woods at once.

'A grave and dark-clad company,' quoth Goodman Brown.

In truth they were such. Among them, quivering to and fro between gloom and splendor, appeared faces that would be seen next day at the council board of the province, and others which, Sabbath after Sabbath, looked devoutly heavenward, and benignantly over the crowded pews, from the holiest pulpits in the land. Some affirm that the lady of the governor was there. At least there were high dames well known to her, and wives of honored husbands, and widows, a great multitude, and ancient maidens, all of excellent repute, and fair young girls, who trembled lest their mothers should espy them. Either the sudden gleams of light flashing over the obscure field bedazzled Goodman Brown, or he recognized a score of the church members of Salem village famous for their especial sanctity. Good old Deacon Gookin had arrived, and waited at the skirts of that venerable saint, his revered pastor. But, irreverently consorting with these grave, reputable, and pious people, these elders of the church, these chaste dames and dewy virgins, there were men of dissolute lives and women of spotted fame, wretches given over to all mean and filthy vice, and suspected even of horrid crimes. It was strange to see that the good shrank not from the wicked, nor were the sinners abashed by the saints. Scattered also among their pale-faced enemies were the Indian priests, or pow-wows, who had often scared their native forest with more hideous incantations than any known to English witchcraft.

'But where is Faith?' thought Goodman Brown; and as hope came into his heart, he trembled.

Another verse of the hymn arose, a slow and mournful

strain, such as the pious love, but joined to words which expressed all that our nature can conceive of sin, and darkly hinted at far more. Unfathomable to mere mortals is the lore of fiends. Verse after verse was sung; and still the chorus of the desert swelled between like the deepest tone of a mighty organ; and with the final peal of that dreadful anthem there came a sound, as if the roaring wind, the rushing streams, the howling beasts, and every other voice of the unconcerted wilderness were mingling and according with the voice of guilty man in homage to the prince of all. The four blazing pines threw up a loftier flame, and obscurely discovered shapes and visages of horror on the smoke wreaths above the impious assembly. At the same moment the fire on the rock shot redly forth and formed a glowing arch above its base, where now appeared a figure. With reverence be it spoken, the figure bore no slight similitude, both in garb and manner, to some grave divine of the New England churches.

'Bring forth the converts!' cried a voice that echoed through the field and rolled into the forest.

At the word, Goodman Brown stepped forth from the shadow of the trees and approached the congregation, with whom he felt a loathful brotherhood by the sympathy of all that was wicked in his heart. He could have well-nigh sworn that the shape of his own dead father beckoned him to advance, looking downward from a smoke wreath, while a woman, with dim features of despair, threw out her hand to warn him back. Was it his mother? But he had no power to retreat one step, nor to resist, even in thought, when the minister and good old Deacon Gookin seized his arms and led him to the blazing rock. Thither came also the slender form of a veiled female, led between Goody Cloyse, that pious teacher of the catechism, and Martha Carrier, who had received the devil's promise to be queen of hell. A rampant hag was she. And there stood the proselytes beneath the canopy of fire.

'Welcome, my children,' said the dark figure, 'to the communion of your race. Ye have found thus young your nature and your destiny. My children, look behind you!'

They turned; and flashing forth, as it were, in a sheet of flame, the fiend worshippers were seen; the smile of welcome gleamed darkly on every visage.

'There,' resumed the sable form, 'are all whom ye have reverenced from youth. Ye deemed them holier than yourselves, and shrank from your own sin, contrasting it with their lives of righteousness and prayerful aspirations heavenward. Yet here are they all in my worshipping assembly. This night it shall be granted you to know their secret deeds: how hoary-bearded elders of the church have whispered wanton words to the young maids of their households; how many a woman, eager for widows' weeds, has given her husband a drink at bedtime and let him sleep his last sleep in her bosom; how beardless youths have made haste to inherit their fathers' wealth; and how fair damsels – blush not, sweet ones – have dug little graves in the garden, and bidden me, the sole guest, to an infant's funeral. By the sympathy of your human hearts for sin ye shall scent out all the places – whether in church, bed-chamber, street, field, or forest – where crime has been committed, and shall exult to behold the whole earth one stain of guilt, one mighty blood spot. Far more than this. It shall be yours to penetrate, in every bosom, the deep mystery of sin, the fountain of all wicked arts, and which inexhaustibly supplies more evil impulses than human power – than my power at its utmost – can make manifest in deeds. And now, my children, look upon each other.'

They did so; and, by the blaze of the hell-kindled torches,

the wretched man beheld his Faith, and the wife her husband, trembling before that unhallowed altar.

'Lo, there ye stand, my children,' said the figure, in a deep and solemn tone, almost sad with its despairing awfulness, as if his once angelic nature could yet mourn for our miserable race. 'Depending upon one another's hearts, ye had still hoped that virtue were not all a dream. Now are ye undeceived. Evil is the nature of mankind. Evil must be your only happiness. Welcome again, my children, to the communion of your race.'

'Welcome,' repeated the fiend worshippers, in one cry of despair and triumph.

And there they stood, the only pair, as it seemed, who were yet hesitating on the verge of wickedness in this dark world. A basin was hollowed, naturally, in the rock. Did it contain water, reddened by the lurid light? or was it blood? or, perchance, a liquid flame? Herein did the shape of evil dip his hand and prepare to lay the mark of baptism upon their foreheads, that they might be partakers of the mystery of sin, more conscious of the secret guilt of others, both in deed and thought, than they could now be of their own. The husband cast one look at his pale wife, and Faith at him. What polluted wretches would the next glance show them to each other, shuddering alike at what they disclosed and what they saw.

'Faith! Faith!' cried the husband, 'look up to heaven, and resist the wicked one.'

Whether Faith obeyed he knew not. Hardly had he spoken when he found himself amid calm night and solitude, listening to a roar of the wind which died heavily away through the forest. He staggered against the rock, and felt it chill and damp; while a hanging twig, that had been all on fire, besprinkled his cheek with the coldest dew.

The next morning young Goodman Brown came slowly into the street of Salem village, staring around him like a bewildered man. The good old minister was taking a walk along the graveyard to get an appetite for breakfast and meditate his sermon, and bestowed a blessing, as he passed, on Goodman Brown. He shrank from the venerable saint as if to avoid an anathema. Old Deacon Gookin was at domestic worship, and the holy words of his prayer were heard through the open window, 'What God doth the wizard pray to?' quoth Goodman Brown. Goody Cloyse, that excellent old Christian, stood in the early sunshine at her own lattice, catechizing a little girl who had brought her a pint of morning's milk. Goodman Brown snatched away the child as from the grasp of the fiend himself. Turning the corner by the meeting-house, he spied the head of Faith, with the pink ribbons, gazing anxiously forth, and bursting into such joy at sight of him that she skipped along the street and almost kissed her husband before the whole village. But Goodman Brown looked sternly and sadly into her face, and passed on without a greeting.

Had Goodman Brown fallen asleep in the forest and only dreamed a wild dream of a witch-meeting?

Be it so if you will; but, alas! it was a dream of evil omen for young Goodman Brown. A stern, a sad, a darkly meditative, a distrustful, if not a desperate man did he become from the night of that fearful dream. On the Sabbath day, when the congregation were singing a holy psalm, he could not listen because an anthem of sin rushed loudly upon his ear and drowned all the blessed strain. When the minister spoke from the pulpit with power and fervid eloquence, and, with his hand on the open Bible, of the sacred truths of our religion, and of saint-like lives and triumphant deaths, and of future bliss or misery unutterable, then did Goodman

Brown turn pale, dreading lest the roof should thunder down upon the gray blasphemer and his hearers. Often, awaking suddenly at midnight, he shrank from the bosom of Faith; and at morning or eventide, when the family knelt down at prayer, he scowled and muttered to himself, and gazed sternly at his wife, and turned away. And when he had lived long, and was borne to his grave a hoary corpse, followed by Faith, an aged woman, and children and grandchildren, a goodly procession, besides neighbors not a few, they carved no hopeful verse upon his tombstone, for his dying hour was gloom.

NEIL GAIMAN

TROLL BRIDGE

THEY PULLED UP most of the railway tracks in the early sixties, when I was three or four. They slashed the train services to ribbons. This meant that there was nowhere to go but London, and the little town where I lived became the end of the line.

My earliest reliable memory: eighteen months old, my mother away in hospital having my sister, and my grandmother walking with me down to a bridge, and lifting me up to watch the train below, panting and steaming like a black iron dragon.

Over the next few years they lost the last of the steam trains, and with them went the network of railways that joined village to village, town to town.

I didn't know that the trains were going. By the time I was seven they were a thing of the past.

We lived in an old house on the outskirts of the town. The fields opposite were empty and fallow. I used to climb the fence and lie in the shade of a small bulrush patch, and read; or if I were feeling more adventurous I'd explore the grounds of the empty manor beyond the fields. It had a weed-clogged ornamental pond, with a low wooden bridge over it. I never saw any groundsmen or caretakers in my forays through the gardens and woods, and I never attempted to enter the manor. That would have been courting disaster, and besides, it was a matter of faith for me that all empty old houses were haunted.

It is not that I was credulous, simply that I believed in all things dark and dangerous. It was part of my young creed that the night was full of ghosts and witches, hungry and flapping and dressed completely in black.

The converse held reassuringly true: daylight was safe. Daylight was always safe.

A ritual: on the last day of the summer school term, walking home from school, I would remove my shoes and socks and, carrying them in my hands, walk down the stony flinty lane on pink and tender feet. During the summer holiday I would put shoes on only under duress. I would revel in my freedom from footwear until the school term began once more in September.

When I was seven I discovered the path through the wood. It was summer, hot and bright, and I wandered a long way from home that day.

I was exploring. I went past the manor, its windows boarded up and blind, across the grounds, and through some unfamiliar woods. I scrambled down a steep bank, and I found myself on a shady path that was new to me and overgrown with trees; the light that penetrated the leaves was stained green and gold, and I thought I was in fairyland.

A little stream trickled down the side of the path, teeming with tiny, transparent shrimps. I picked them up and watched them jerk and spin on my fingertips. Then I put them back.

I wandered down the path. It was perfectly straight, and overgrown with short grass. From time to time I would find these really terrific rocks: bubbly, melted things, brown and purple and black. If you held them up to the light you could see every colour of the rainbow. I was convinced that they had to be extremely valuable, and stuffed my pockets with them.

I walked and walked down the quiet golden-green corridor, and saw nobody.

I wasn't hungry or thirsty. I just wondered where the path was going. It travelled in a straight line, and was perfectly flat. The path never changed, but the countryside around it did. At first I was walking along the bottom of a ravine, grassy banks climbing steeply on each side of me. Later, the path was above everything, and as I walked I could look down at the treetops below me, and the roofs of occasional distant houses. My path was always flat and straight, and I walked along it through valleys and plateaus, valleys and plateaus. And eventually, in one of the valleys, I came to the bridge.

It was built of clean red brick, a huge curving arch over the path. At the side of the bridge were stone steps cut into the embankment, and, at the top of the steps, a little wooden gate.

I was surprised to see any token of the existence of humanity on my path, which I was by now convinced was a natural formation, like a volcano. And, with a sense more of curiosity than anything else (I had, after all, walked hundreds of miles, or so I was convinced, and might be *anywhere*), I climbed the stone steps, and went through the gate.

I was nowhere.

The top of the bridge was paved with mud. On each side of it was a meadow. The meadow on my side was a wheat-field; the other field was just grass. There were the caked imprints of huge tractor wheels in the dried mud. I walked across the bridge to be sure: no trip-trap, my bare feet were soundless.

Nothing for miles; just fields and wheat and trees.

I picked an ear of wheat, and pulled out the sweet grains, peeling them between my fingers, chewing them meditatively.

I realized then that I was getting hungry, and went back down the stairs to the abandoned railway track. It was time to go home. I was not lost; all I needed to do was follow my path home once more.

There was a troll waiting for me, under the bridge.

'I'm a troll,' he said. Then he paused, and added, more or less as an afterthought, 'Fol rol de ol rol.'

He was huge: his head brushed the top of the brick arch. He was more or less translucent: I could see the bricks and trees behind him, dimmed but not lost. He was all my nightmares given flesh. He had huge strong teeth, and rending claws, and strong, hairy hands. His hair was long, like one of my sister's little plastic gonks, and his eyes bulged. He was naked, and his penis hung from the bush of gonk hair between his legs.

'I heard you, Jack,' he whispered in a voice like the wind. 'I heard you trip-trapping over my bridge. And now I'm going to eat your life.'

I was only seven, but it was daylight, and I do not remember being scared. It is good for children to find themselves facing the elements of a fairy tale – they are well equipped to deal with these.

'Don't eat me,' I said to the troll. I was wearing a stripy brown T-shirt, and brown corduroy trousers. My hair also was brown, and I was missing a front tooth. I was learning to whistle between my teeth, but wasn't there yet.

'I'm going to eat your life, Jack,' said the troll.

I stared the troll in the face. 'My big sister is going to be coming down the path soon,' I lied, 'and she's far tastier than me. Eat her instead.'

The troll sniffed the air, and smiled. 'You're all alone,' he said. 'There's nothing else on the path. Nothing at all.' Then he leaned down, and ran his fingers over me: it felt like butterflies were brushing my face – like the touch of a blind person. Then he snuffled his fingers, and shook his huge head. 'You don't have a big sister. You've only a younger sister, and she's at her friend's today.'

'Can you tell all that from smell?' I asked, amazed.

'Trolls can smell the rainbows, trolls can smell the stars,' it whispered sadly. 'Trolls can smell the dreams you dreamed before you were ever born. Come close to me and I'll eat your life.'

'I've got precious stones in my pocket,' I told the troll. 'Take them, not me. Look.' I showed him the lava jewel rocks I had found earlier.

'Clinker,' said the troll. 'The discarded refuse of steam trains. Of no value to me.'

He opened his mouth wide. Sharp teeth. Breath that smelled of leaf mould and the underneaths of things. 'Eat. Now.'

He became more and more solid to me, more and more real; and the world outside became flatter, began to fade.

'Wait.' I dug my feet into the damp earth beneath the bridge, wiggled my toes, held on tightly to the real world. I stared into his big eyes. 'You don't want to eat my life. Not yet. I – I'm only seven. I haven't *lived* at all yet. There are books I haven't read yet. I've never been on an aeroplane. I can't whistle yet – not really. Why don't you let me go? When I'm older and bigger and more of a meal I'll come back to you.'

The troll stared at me with eyes like headlamps.

Then it nodded.

'When you come back, then,' it said. And it smiled.

I turned around and walked back down the silent straight path where the railway lines had once been.

After a while I began to run.

69

I pounded down the track in the green light, puffing and blowing, until I felt a stabbing ache beneath my ribcage, the pain of stitch; and, clutching my side, I stumbled home.

The fields started to go, as I grew older. One by one, row by row, houses sprang up with roads named after wild-flowers and respectable authors. Our home – an ageing, tattered Victorian house – was sold, and torn down; new houses covered the garden.

They built houses everywhere.

I once got lost in the new housing estate that covered two meadows I had once known every inch of. I didn't mind too much that the fields were going, though. The old manor house was bought by a multinational, and the grounds became more houses.

It was eight years before I returned to the old railway line, and when I did, I was not alone.

I was fifteen; I'd changed schools twice in that time. Her name was Louise, and she was my first love.

I loved her grey eyes, and her fine light brown hair, and her gawky way of walking (like a fawn just learning to walk which sounds really dumb, for which I apologize): I saw her chewing gum, when I was thirteen, and I fell for her like a suicide from a bridge.

The main trouble with being in love with Louise was that we were best friends, and we were both going out with other people.

I'd never told her I loved her, or even that I fancied her. We were buddies.

I'd been at her house that evening: we sat in her room and played *Rattus Norvegicus*, the first Stranglers LP. It was the beginning of punk, and everything seemed so exciting: the possibilities, in music as in everything else, were endless.

Eventually it was time for me to go home, and she decided to accompany me. We held hands, innocently, just pals, and we strolled the ten-minute walk to my house.

The moon was bright, and the world was visible and colourless, and the night was warm.

We got to my house. Saw the lights inside, and stood in the driveway, and talked about the band I was starting. We didn't go in.

Then it was decided that I'd walk *her* home. So we walked back to her house.

She told me about the battles she was having with her younger sister, who was stealing her makeup and perfume. Louise suspected that her sister was having sex with boys. Louise was a virgin. We both were.

We stood in the road outside her house, under the sodium yellow streetlight, and we stared at each other's black lips and pale yellow faces.

We grinned at each other.

Then we just walked, picking quiet roads and empty paths. In one of the new housing estates, a path led us into the woodland, and we followed it.

The path was straight and dark, but the lights of distant houses shone like stars on the ground, and the moon gave us enough light to see. Once we were scared, when something snuffled and snorted in front of us. We pressed close, saw it was a badger, laughed and hugged and kept on walking.

We talked quiet nonsense about what we dreamed and wanted and thought.

And all the time I wanted to kiss her and feel her breasts, and maybe put my hand between her legs.

Finally I saw my chance. There was an old brick bridge over the path, and we stopped beneath it. I pressed up against her. Her mouth opened against mine.

Then she went cold and stiff, and stopped moving.

'Hello,' said the troll.

I let go of Louise. It was dark beneath the bridge, but the shape of the troll filled the darkness.

'I froze her,' said the troll, 'so we can talk. Now: I'm going to eat your life.'

My heart pounded, and I could feel myself trembling.

'No.'

'You said you'd come back to me. And you have. Did you learn to whistle?'

'Yes.'

'That's good. I never could whistle.' It sniffed, and nodded. 'I am pleased. You have grown in life and experience. More to eat. More for me.'

I grabbed Louise, a taut zombie, and pushed her forward. 'Don't take me. I don't want to die. Take *her*. I bet she's much tastier than me. And she's two months older than I am. Why don't you take her?'

The troll was silent.

It sniffed Louise from toe to head, snuffling at her feet and crotch and breasts and hair.

Then it looked at me.

'She's an innocent,' it said. 'You're not. I don't want her. I want you.'

I walked to the opening of the bridge and stared up at the stars in the night.

'But there's so much I've never done,' I said, partly to myself. 'I mean, I've never. Well, I've never had sex. And I've never been to America. I haven't . . .' I paused. 'I haven't *done* anything. Not yet.'

The troll said nothing.

'I could come back to you. When I'm older.'

The troll said nothing.

72

'I *will* come back. Honest I will.'

'Come back to me?' said Louise. 'Why? Where are you going?'

I turned around. The troll had gone, and the girl I had thought I loved was standing in the shadows beneath the bridge.

'We're going home,' I told her. 'Come on.'

We walked back and never said anything.

She went out with the drummer in the punk band I started, and, much later, married someone else. We met once, on a train, after she was married, and she asked me if I remembered that night.

I said I did.

'I really liked you, that night, Jack,' she told me. 'I thought you were going to kiss me. I thought you were going to ask me out. I would have said yes. If you had.'

'But I didn't.'

'No,' she said. 'You didn't.' Her hair was cut very short. It didn't suit her.

I never saw her again. The trim woman with the taut smile was not the girl I had loved, and talking to her made me feel uncomfortable.

I moved to London, and then, some years later, I moved back again, but the town I returned to was not the town I remembered: there were no fields, no farms, no little flint lanes; and I moved away as soon as I could, to a tiny village ten miles down the road.

I moved with my family – I was married by now, with a toddler – into an old house that had once, many years before, been a railway station. The track had been dug up, and the old couple who lived opposite us used it to grow vegetables.

I was getting older. One day I found a grey hair; on

another, I heard a recording of myself talking, and I realized I sounded just like my father.

I was working in London, doing A&R for one of the major record companies. I was commuting into London by train most days, coming back some evenings.

I had to keep a small flat in London; it's hard to commute when the bands you're checking out don't even stagger onto the stage until midnight. It also meant that it was fairly easy to get laid, if I wanted to, which I did.

I thought that Eleanora – that was my wife's name; I should have mentioned that before, I suppose – didn't know about the other women; but I got back from a two-week jaunt to New York one winter's day, and when I arrived at the house it was empty and cold.

She had left a letter, not a note. Fifteen pages, neatly typed, and every word of it was true. Including the PS, which read: *You really don't love me. And you never did.*

I put on a heavy coat, and I left the house and just walked, stunned and slightly numb.

There was no snow on the ground, but there was a hard frost, and the leaves crunched under my feet as I walked. The trees were skeletal black against the harsh grey winter sky.

I walked down the side of the road. Cars passed me, travelling to and from London. Once I tripped on a branch, half-hidden in a heap of brown leaves, ripping my trousers, cutting my leg.

I reached the next village. There was a river at right angles to the road, and a path I'd never seen before beside it, and I walked down the path, and stared at the partly frozen river. It gurgled and plashed and sang.

The path led off through fields; it was straight and grassy.

I found a rock, half-buried, on one side of the path. I picked it up, brushed off the mud. It was a melted lump of purplish stuff, with a strange rainbow sheen to it. I put it into the pocket of my coat and held it in my hand as I walked, its presence warm and reassuring.

The river meandered away across the fields, and I walked on in silence.

I had walked for an hour before I saw houses – new and small and square – on the embankment above me.

And then I saw the bridge, and I knew where I was: I was on the old railway path, and I'd been coming down it from the other direction.

There were graffiti painted on the side of the bridge: FUCK and BARRY LOVES SUSAN and the omnipresent NF of the National Front.

I stood beneath the bridge in the red brick arch, stood among the ice cream wrappers, and the crisp packets and the single, sad, used condom, and watched my breath steam in the cold afternoon air.

The blood had dried into my trousers.

Cars passed over the bridge above me; I could hear a radio playing loudly in one of them.

'Hello?' I said, quietly, feeling embarrassed, feeling foolish. 'Hello?'

There was no answer. The wind rustled the crisp packets and the leaves.

'I came back. I said I would. And I did. Hello?'

Silence.

I began to cry then, stupidly, silently, sobbing under the bridge.

A hand touched my face, and I looked up.

'I didn't think you'd come back,' said the troll.

He was my height now, but otherwise unchanged. His long gonk hair was unkempt and had leaves in it, and his eyes were wide and lonely.

75

I shrugged, then wiped my face with the sleeve of my coat. 'I came back.'

Three kids passed above us on the bridge, shouting and running.

'I'm a troll,' whispered the troll, in a small, scared voice. 'Fol rol de ol rol.'

He was trembling.

I held out my hand and took his huge clawed paw in mine. I smiled at him. 'It's okay,' I told him. 'Honestly. It's okay.'

The troll nodded.

He pushed me to the ground, onto the leaves and the wrappers and the condom, and lowered himself on top of me. Then he raised his head, and opened his mouth, and ate my life with his strong sharp teeth.

When he was finished, the troll stood up and brushed himself down. He put his hand into the pocket of his coat and pulled out a bubbly, burnt lump of clinker rock.

He held it out to me.

'This is yours,' said the troll.

I looked at him: wearing my life comfortably, easily, as if he'd been wearing it for years. I took the clinker from his hand, and sniffed it. I could smell the train from which it had fallen, so long ago. I gripped it tightly in my hairy hand.

'Thank you,' I said.

'Good luck,' said the troll.

'Yeah. Well. You too.'

The troll grinned with my face.

It turned its back on me and began to walk back the way I had come, towards the village, back to the empty house I had left that morning; and it whistled as it walked.

I've been here ever since. Hiding. Waiting. Part of the bridge.

I watch from the shadows as the people pass: walking their dogs, or talking, or doing the things that people do. Sometimes people pause beneath my bridge, to stand, or piss, or make love. And I watch them, but say nothing; and they never see me.

Fol rol de ol rol.

I'm just going to stay here, in the darkness under the arch. I can hear you all out there, trip-trapping, trip-trapping over my bridge.

Oh yes, I can hear you.

But I'm not coming out.

URSULA K. LeGUIN

THE POACHER

> ...And must one kiss
> Revoke the silent house, the birdsong wilderness?
> *Sylvia Townsend Warner*

I WAS A CHILD when I came to the great hedge for the first time. I was hunting mushrooms, not for sport, as I have read ladies and gentlemen do, but in earnest. To hunt without need is the privilege, they say, of noblemen. I should say that it is one of the acts that makes a man a nobleman, that constitutes privilege itself. To hunt because one is hungry is the lot of the commoner. All it generally makes of him is a poacher. I was poaching mushrooms, then, in the King's Forest.

My father had sent me out that morning with a basket and the command, 'Don't come sneaking back here till it's full!' I knew he would beat me if I didn't come back with the basket full of something to eat – mushrooms at best, at this time of year, or the fiddleheads of ferns that were just beginning to poke through the cold ground in a few places. He would hit me across the shoulders with the hoe handle or a switch, and send me to bed supperless, because he was hungry and disappointed. He could feel that he was at least better off than somebody, if he made me hungrier than himself, and sore and ashamed as well. After a while my stepmother would pass silently by my corner of the hut and leave on my pallet or in my hand some scrap she had contrived or saved from her own scant supper – half a crust, a lump of

81

pease pudding. Her eyes told me eloquently, Don't say anything! I said nothing. I never thanked her. I ate the food in darkness.

Often my father would beat her. It was my fate, fortunate or misfortunate, not to feel better off than her when I saw her beaten. Instead I felt more ashamed than ever, worse off even than the weeping, wretched woman. She could do nothing, and I could do nothing for her. Once I tried to sweep out the hut when she was working in our field, so that things would be in order when she came back, but my sweeping only stirred the dirt around. When she came in from hoeing, filthy and weary, she noticed nothing, but set straight to building up the fire, fetching water, and so on, while my father, as filthy and weary as she, sat down in the one chair we had with a great sigh. And I was angry because I had, after all, done nothing at all.

I remembered that when my father first married her, when I was quite small, she had played with me like another child. She knew knife-toss games, and taught me them. She taught me the ABC from a book she had. The nuns had brought her up, and she knew her letters, poor thing. My father had a notion that I might be let into the friary if I learned to read, and make the family rich. That came to nothing, of course. She was little and weak and not the help to him at work my mother had been, and things did not prosper for us. My lessons in reading ended soon.

It was she who found I was a clever hunter and taught me what to look for – the golden and brown mushrooms, woodmasters and morels and other fungi, the wild shoots, roots, berries, and hips in their seasons, the cresses in the streams; she taught me to make fishtraps; my father showed me how to set snares for rabbits. They soon came to count on me for a good portion of our food, for everything we grew on our field went to the Baron, who owned it, and we were allowed to cultivate only a mere patch of kitchen garden, lest our labors there detract from our work for the Baron. I took pride in my foraging, and went willingly into the forest, and fearlessly. Did we not live on the very edge of the forest, almost in it? Did I not know every path and glade and grove within a mile of our hut? I thought of it as my own domain. But my father still ordered me to go, every morning, as if I needed his command, and he laced it with distrust – 'Don't come sneaking back until the basket's full!'

That was no easy matter sometimes – in early spring, when nothing was up yet – like the day I first saw the great hedge. Old snow still lay grayish in the shadows of the oaks. I went on, finding not a mushroom nor a fiddlehead. Mummied berries hung on the brambles, tasting of decay. There had been no fish in the trap, no rabbit in the snares, and the crayfish were still hiding in the mud. I went on farther than I had yet gone, hoping to discover a new fernbrake, or trace a squirrel's nut-hoard by her tracks on the glazed and porous snow. I was trudging along easily enough, having found a path almost as good as a road, like the avenue that led to the Baron's hall. Cold sunlight lay between the tall beechtrees that stood along it. At the end of it was something like a hedgerow, but high, so high I had taken it at first for clouds. Was it the end of the forest? the end of the world?

I stared as I walked, but never stopped walking. The nearer I came the more amazing it was – a hedge taller than the ancient beeches, and stretching as far as I could see to left and right. Like any hedgerow, it was made of shrubs and trees that laced and wove themselves together as they grew, but they were immensely tall, and thick, and thorny. At this time of the year the branches were black and bare, but nowhere could I find the least gap or hole to let me peer through to the other side. From the huge roots up, the thorns were impenetrably tangled. I pressed my face up close, and got well scratched for my pains, but saw nothing but an endless dark tangle of gnarled stems and fierce branches.

Well, I thought, if they're brambles, at least I've found a lot of berries, come summer! – for I didn't think about much but food, when I was a child. It was my whole business and chief interest.

All the same, a child's mind will wander. Sometimes when I'd had enough to eat for supper, I'd lie watching our tiny hearthfire dying down, and wonder what was on the other side of the great hedge of thorns.

The hedge was indeed a treasury of berries and haws, so that I was often there all summer and autumn. It took me half the morning to get there, but when the great hedge was bearing, I could fill my basket and sack with berries or haws in no time at all, and then I had all the middle of the day to spend as I pleased, alone. Oftenest what pleased me was to wander along beside the hedge, eating a particularly fine blackberry here and there, dreaming formless dreams. I knew no tales then, except the terribly simple one of my father, my stepmother, and myself, and so my daydreams had no shape or story to them. But all the time I walked, I had half an eye for any kind of gap or opening that might be a way through the hedge. If I had a story to tell myself, that was it: There is a way through the great hedge, and I discover it.

Climbing it was out of the question. It was the tallest thing I had ever seen, and all up that great height the thorns of the branches were as long as my fingers and sharp as sewing needles. If I was careless picking berries from it, my clothes got caught and ripped, and my arms were a net of red and black scratches every summer.

Yet I liked to go there, and to walk beside it. One day of

early summer, some years after I first found the hedge, I went there. It was too soon for berries, but when the thorns blossomed the flowered sprays rose up and up one above the other like clouds into the sky, and I liked to see that, and to smell their scent, as heavy as the smell of meat or bread, but sweet. I set off to the right. The walking was easy, all along the hedge, as if there might have been a road there once. The sun-dappling arms of the old beeches of the forest did not quite reach to the thorny wall that bore its highest sprays of blossom high above their crowns. It was shady under the wall, smelling heavily of blackberry flowers, and windlessly hot. It was always very silent there, a silence that came through the hedge.

I had noticed long ago that I never heard a bird sing on the other side, though their spring songs might be ringing down every aisle of the forest. Sometimes I saw birds fly over the hedge, but I never was sure I saw the same one fly back.

So I wandered on in the silence, on the springy grass, keeping an eye out for the little russet-brown mushrooms that were my favorites, when I began to feel something queer about the grass and the woods and the flowering hedge. I thought I had never walked this far before, and yet it all looked as if I had seen it many times. Surely I knew that clump of young birches, one bent down by last winter's long snow? Then I saw, not far from the birches, under a currant bush beside the grassy way, a basket and a knotted sack. Someone else was here, where I had never met another soul. Someone was poaching in my domain.

People in the village feared the forest. Because our hut was almost under the trees of the forest, people feared us. I never understood what they were afraid of. They talked about wolves. I had seen a wolf's track once, and sometimes heard the lonely voices, winter nights, but no wolf came near the houses or fields. People talked about bears. Nobody in our village had ever seen a bear or a bear's track. People talked about dangers in the forest, perils and enchantments, and rolled their eyes and whispered, and I thought them all great fools. I knew nothing of enchantments. I went to and fro in the forest and up and down in it as if it were my kitchen garden, and never yet had I found anything to fear.

So whenever I had to go the half-mile from our hut and enter the village, people looked askance at me, and called me the wild boy. And I took pride in being called wild. I might have been happier if they had smiled at me and called me by my name, but as it was, I had my pride, my domain, my wilderness, where no one but I dared go.

So it was with fear and pain that I gazed at the signs of an intruder, an interloper, a rival – until I recognized the bag and basket as my own. I had walked right round the great hedge. It was a circle. My forest was all outside it. The other side of it was – whatever it was – inside.

From that afternoon, my lazy curiosity about the great hedge grew to a desire and resolve to penetrate it and see for myself that hidden place within, that secret. Lying watching the dying embers at night, I thought now about the tools I would need to cut through the hedge, and how I could get such tools. The poor little hoes and mattocks we worked our field with would scarcely scratch those great stems and branches. I needed a real blade, and a good stone to whet it on.

So began my career as a thief.

An old woodcutter down in the village died; I heard of his death at market that day. I knew he had lived alone, and was called a miser. He might have what I needed. That night when my father and stepmother slept, I crept out of the hut and went back by moonlight to the village. The door of the cottage was open. A fire smoldered in the hearth under the smokehole. In the sleeping end of the house, to the left of the fire, a couple of women had laid out the corpse. They were sitting up by it, chatting, now and then putting up a howl or two of keening when they thought about it. I went softly in to the stall end of the cottage; the fire was between us, and they did not see or hear me. The cow chewed her cud, the cat watched me, the women across the fire mumbled and laughed, and the old man lay stark on his pallet in his windingsheet. I looked through his tools, quietly, but without hurrying. He had a fine hatchet, a crude saw, and a mounted, circular grindstone – a treasure to me. I could not take the mounting, but stuck the handle in my shirt, took the tools under my arm and the stone in both hands, and walked out again. 'Who's there?' said one of the women, without interest, and sent up a perfunctory wail.

The stone all but pulled my arms out before I got it up the road to our hut, where I hid it and the tools and the handle a little way inside the forest under a bit of brushwood. I crept back into the windowless blackness of the hut and felt my way over to my pallet, for the fire was dead. I lay a long time, my heart beating hard, telling my story: I had stolen my weapons, now I would lay my siege on the great thorn hedge. But I did not use those words. I knew nothing of sieges, wars, victories, all such matters of great history. I knew no story but my own.

It would be a very dull one to read in a book. I cannot tell much of it. All that summer and autumn, winter and spring, and the next summer, and the next autumn, and the next winter, I fought my war, I laid my siege: I chopped and hewed and hacked at the thicket of bramble and thorn. I cut through a thick, tough trunk, but could not pull it free till I had cut through fifty branches tangled in its branches.

87

When it was free I dragged it out and then I began to cut at the next thick trunk. My hatchet grew dull a thousand times. I had made a mount for the grindstone, and on it I sharpened the hatchet a thousand times, till the blade was worn down into the thickness of the metal and would not hold an edge. In the first winter, the saw shivered against a rootstock hard as flint. In the second summer, I stole an ax and a handsaw from a party of traveling woodcutters camped a little way inside the forest near the road to the Baron's hall. They were poaching wood from my domain, the forest. In return, I poached tools from them. I felt it was a fair trade.

My father grumbled at my long absences, but I kept up my foraging, and had so many snares out that we had rabbit as often as we wanted it. In any case, he no longer dared strike me. I was sixteen or seventeen years old, I suppose, and though I was by no means well grown, or tall, or very strong, I was stronger than he, a worn-out old man, forty years old or more. He struck my stepmother as often as he liked. She was a little, toothless, red-eyed, old woman now. She spoke very seldom. When she spoke my father would cuff her, railing at women's chatter, women's nagging. 'Will you never be quiet?' he would shout, and she would shrink away, drawing her head down in her hunched shoulders like a turtle. And yet sometimes when she washed herself at night with a rag and a basin of water warmed in the ashes, her blanket would slip down, and I saw her body was fine-skinned, with soft breasts and rounded hips shadowy in the firelight. I would turn away, for she was frightened and ashamed when she saw me looking at her. She called me 'son', though I was not her son. Long ago she had called me by my name.

Once I saw her watching me as I ate. It had been a good harvest, that first autumn, and we had turnips right through the winter. She watched me with a look on her face, and

I knew she wanted to ask me then, while my father was out of the house, what it was I did all day in the forest, why my shirt and vest and trousers were forever ripped and shredded, why my hands were callused on the palms and crosshatched with a thousand scratches on the backs. If she had asked I would have told her. But she did not ask. She turned her face down into the shadows, silent.

Shadows and silence filled the passage I had hacked into the great hedge. The thorn trees stood so tall and thickly branched above it that no light at all made its way down through them.

As the first year came round, I had hacked and sawn and chopped a passage of about my height and twice my length into the hedge. It was as impenetrable as ever before me, not allowing a glimpse of what might be on the other side nor a hint that the tangle of branches might be any thinner. Many a time at night I lay hearing my father snore and said to myself that when I was an old man like him, I would cut through the last branch and come out into the forest – having spent my life tunneling through nothing but a great, round bramble patch, with nothing inside it but itself. I told that end to my story, but did not believe it. I tried to tell other ends. I said, I will find a green lawn inside the hedge ... A village ... A friary ... A hall ... A stony field ... I knew nothing else that one might find. But these endings did not hold my mind for long; soon I was thinking again of how I should cut the next thick trunk that stood in my way. My story was the story of cutting a way through an endless thicket of thorny branches, and nothing more. And to tell it would take as long as it took to do it.

On a day near the end of winter, such a day as makes it seem there will never be an end to winter, a chill, damp, dark, dreary, hungry day, I was sawing away with the woodcutters' saw at a gnarled, knotted whitethorn as thick as my thigh and hard as iron. I crouched in the small space I had and sawed away with nothing in my mind but sawing.

The hedge grew unnaturally fast, in season and out; even in midwinter thick, pale shoots would grow across my passageway, and in summer I had to spend some time every day clearing out new growth, thorny green sprays full of stinging sap. My passage or tunnel was now more than five yards long, but only a foot and a half high except at the very end; I had learned to wriggle in, and keep the passage man-high only at the end, where I must have room enough to get a purchase on my ax or saw. I crouched at my work, glad to give up the comfort of standing for a gain in going forward.

The whitethorn trunk split suddenly, in the contrary, evil way the trees of that thicket had. It sent the sawblade almost across my thigh, and as the tree fell against others interlaced with it, a long branch whipped across my face. Thorns raked my eyelids and forehead. Blinded with blood, I thought it had struck my eyes. I knelt, wiping away the blood with hands that trembled from strain and the suddenness of the accident. I got one eye clear at last, and then the other, and, blinking and peering, saw light before me.

The whitethorn in falling had left a gap, and in the maze and crisscross of dark branches beyond it was a small clear space, through which one could see, as through a chink in a wall: and in that small bright space I saw the castle.

I know now what to call it. What I saw then I had no name for. I saw sunlight on a yellow stone wall. Looking closer, I saw a door in the wall. Beside the door stood figures, men perhaps, in shadow, unmoving; after a time I thought they were figures carved in stone, such as I had seen at the doors of the friary church. I could see nothing else: sunlight, bright stone, the door, the shadowy figures. Everywhere else the branches and trunks and dead leaves of the hedge massed before me as they had for two years, impenetrably dark.

I thought, if I was a snake I could crawl through that hole! But being no snake, I set to work to enlarge it. My hands still shook, but I took the ax and struck and struck at the massed and crossing branches. Now I knew which branch to cut, which stem to chop: whichever lay between my eyes and that golden wall, that door. I cared nothing for the height or width of my passage, so long as I could force and tear my way forward, indifferent to the laceration of my arms and face and clothing. I swung my dull ax with such violence that the branches flew before me; and as I pushed forward the branches and stems of the hedge grew thinner, weaker. Light shone through them. From winter-black and hard they became green and soft, as I hacked and forced on forward, until I could put them aside with my hand. I parted the last screen and crawled on hands and knees out onto a lawn of bright grass.

Overhead the sky was the soft blue of early summer. Before me, a little downhill from the hedge, stood the house of yellow stone, the castle, in its moat. Flags hung motionless from its pointed towers. The air was still and warm. Nothing moved.

I crouched there, as motionless as everything else, except for my breath, which came loud and hard for a long time. Beside my sweaty, blood-streaked hand a little bee sat on a clover blossom, not stirring, honey-drunk.

I raised myself to my knees and looked all round me, cautious. I knew that this must be a hall, like the Baron's hall above the village, and therefore dangerous to anyone who did not live there or have work there. It was much larger and finer than the Baron's hall, and infinitely fairer; larger and fairer even than the friary church. With its yellow walls and red roofs it looked, I thought, like a flower. I had not seen much else I could compare it to. The Baron's hall was a squat keep with a scumble of huts and barns about it; the church was gray and grim, the carved figures by its door faceless with age. This house, whatever it was, was delicate and fine and fresh. The sunlight on it made me think of the firelight on my stepmother's breasts.

Halfway down the wide, grassy slope to the moat, a few cows lay in midday torpor, heads up, eyes closed; they were not even chewing the cud. On the farther slope, a flock of sheep lay scattered out, and an apple orchard was just losing its last blossoms.

The air was very warm. In my torn, ragged shirt and coat, I would have been shivering as the sweat cooled on me, on the other side of the hedge, where winter was. Here I shrugged off the coat. The blood from all my scratches, drying, made my skin draw and itch, so that I began to look with longing at the water in the moat. Blue and glassy it lay, very tempting. I was thirsty, too. My waterbottle lay back in the passage, nearly empty. I thought of it, but never turned my head to look back.

No one had moved, on the lawns or in the gardens around the house or on the bridge across the moat, all the time I had been kneeling here in the shadow of the great hedge, gazing my fill. The cows lay like stones, though now and again I saw a brown flank shudder off a fly, or the very tip of a tail twitch lazily. When I looked down I saw the little bee still on the clover blossom. I touched its wing curiously, wondering if it was dead. Its feelers shivered a little, but it did not stir. I looked back at the house, at the windows, and at the door – a side door – which I had first seen through the branches. I saw, without for some while knowing that I saw, that the two carved figures by the door were living men. They stood one on each side of the door as if in readiness for someone entering from the garden or the stables; one held a staff, the other a pike; and they were both leaning right back against the wall, sound asleep.

It did not surprise me. They're asleep, I thought. It seemed natural enough, here. I think I knew even then where I had come.

I do not mean that I knew the story, as you may know it. I did not know why they were asleep, how it had come about that they were asleep. I did not know the beginning of their story, nor the end. I did not know who was in the castle. But I knew already that they were all asleep. It was very strange, and I thought I should be afraid; but I could not feel any fear.

So even then, as I stood up, and went slowly down the sunny sward to the willows by the moat, I walked, not as if I were in a dream, but as if I were a dream. I didn't know who was dreaming me, if not myself, but it didn't matter. I knelt in the shade of the willows and put my sore hands down into the cool water of the moat. Just beyond my reach a golden-speckled carp floated, sleeping. A waterskater poised motionless on four tiny dimples in the skin of the water. Under the bridge, a swallow and her nestlings slept in their mud nest. A window was open, up in the castle wall; I saw a silky dark head pillowed on a pudgy arm on the window ledge.

I stripped, slow and quiet in my dream movements, and slid into the water. Though I could not swim, I had often bathed in shallow streams in the forest. The moat was deep, but I clung to the stone coping; presently I found a willow root that reached out from the stones, where I could sit with only my head out, and watch the golden-speckled carp hang in the clear, shadowed water.

I climbed out at last, refreshed and clean. I rinsed out my sweaty, winter-foul shirt and trousers, scrubbing them with stones, and spread them to dry in the hot sun on the grass above the willows. I had left my coat and my thick, straw-stuffed clogs up under the hedge. When my shirt and trousers were half dry I put them on – deliciously cool and wet-smelling – and combed my hair with my fingers. Then I stood up and walked to the end of the drawbridge.

I crossed it, always going slowly and quietly, without fear or hurry.

The old porter sat by the great door of the castle, his chin right down on his chest. He snored long, soft snores.

I pushed at the tall, iron-studded, oaken door. It opened with a little groan. Two boarhounds sprawled on the flag-stone floor just inside, huge dogs, sound asleep. One of them 'hunted' in his sleep, scrabbling his big legs, and then lay still again. The air inside the castle was still and shadowy, as the air outside was still and bright. There was no sound, inside or out. No bird sang, or woman; no voice spoke, or foot stirred, or bell struck the hour. The cooks slept over their cauldrons in the kitchen, the maids slept at their dusting and their mending, the king and his grooms slept by the sleeping horses in the stableyard, and the queen at her embroidery frame slept among her women. The cat slept by the mouse-hole, and the mice between the walls. The moth slept on the woollens, and the music slept in the strings of the minstrel's harp. There were no hours. The sun slept in the blue sky, and the shadows of the willows on the water never moved.

I know, I know it was not my enchantment. I had broken, hacked, chopped, forced my way into it. I know I am a poacher. I never learned how to be anything else. Even my forest, my domain as I had thought it, was never mine. It was the King's Forest, and the king slept here in his castle in the heart of his forest. But it had been a long time since anyone talked of the king. Petty barons held sway all round the forest; woodcutters stole wood from it, peasant boys snared rabbits in it; stray princes rode through it now and then, perhaps, hunting the red deer, not even knowing they were trespassing.

I knew I trespassed, but I could not see the harm. I did, of course, eat their food. The venison pastry that the chief cook had just taken out of the oven smelled so delicious that hungry flesh could not endure it. I arranged the chief cook in a more comfortable position on the slate floor of the kitchen, with his hat crumpled up for a pillow; and then I attacked the great pie, breaking off a corner with my hands and cramming it in my mouth. It was still warm, savoury, succulent. I ate my fill. Next time I came through the kitchen, the pastry was whole, unbroken. The enchantment held. Was it that as a dream, I could change nothing of this deep reality of sleep? I ate as I pleased, and always the cauldron of soup was full again and the loaves waited in the pantry, their brown crusts unbroken. The red wine brimmed the crystal goblet by the seneschal's hand, however many times I raised it, saluted him in thanks, and drank.

As I explored the castle and its grounds and outbuildings – always unhurriedly, wandering from room to room, pausing often, often lingering over some painted scene or fantastic tapestry or piece of fine workmanship in tool or fitting or furniture, often settling down on a soft, curtained bed or a sunny, grassy garden nook to sleep (for there was no night here, and I slept when I was tired and woke when I was refreshed) – as I wandered through all the rooms and offices and cellars and halls and barns and servants' quarters, I came to know, almost as if they were furniture too, the people who slept here and there, leaning or sitting or lying down, however they had chanced to be when the enchantment stole upon them and their eyes grew heavy, their breathing quiet, their limbs lax and still. A shepherd up on the hill had been pissing into a gopher's hole; he had settled down in a heap and slept contentedly, as no doubt the gopher was doing down in the dirt. The chief cook, as I have said, lay as if struck down unwilling in the heat of his art, and though I tried many times to pillow his head and arrange his limbs more comfortably, he always frowned, as if to say, 'Don't bother me now, I'm busy!' Up at the top of the old apple orchard lay a couple of lovers, peasants like me. He, his rough trousers pulled down, lay as he had slid off her, face buried in the blossom-littered grass, drowned in sleep and satisfaction. She, a short, buxom young woman with apple-red cheeks and nipples, lay sprawled right out, skirts hiked to her waist, legs parted and arms wide, smiling in her sleep. It was again more than hungry flesh could endure. I laid myself down softly on her, kissing those red nipples, and came into her honey sweetness. She smiled in her sleep again, whenever I did so, and sometimes made a little groaning grunt of pleasure. Afterwards I would lie beside her, a partner to her friend on the other side, and drowse, and wake to see the unfalling late blossoms on the apple boughs. When I slept, there inside the great hedge, I never dreamed.

What had I to dream of? Surely I had all I could desire. Still, while the time passed that did not pass, used as I was to solitude, I grew lonely; the company of the sleepers grew wearisome to me. Mild and harmless as they were, and dear as many of them became to me as I lived among them, they were no better companions to me than a child's wooden toys, to which he must lend his own voice and soul. I sought work, not only to repay them for their food and beds, but because I was, after all, used to working. I polished the silver, I swept and reswept the floors where the dust lay so still, I groomed

96

all the sleeping horses, I arranged the books on the shelves. And that led me to open a book, in mere idleness, and puzzle at the words in it.

I had not had a book in my hands since that primer of my stepmother's, nor seen any other but the priest's book in the church when we went to Mass at Yuletime. At first I looked only at the pictures, which were marvelous, and entertained me much. But I began to want to know what the words said about the pictures. When I came to study the shapes of the letters, they began to come back to me: *a* like a cat sitting, and the fatbellied *b* and *d*, and *t* the carpenter's square, and so on. And a-t was at, and c-a-t was cat, and so on. And time enough to learn to read, time enough and more than enough, slow as I might be. So I came to read, first the romances and histories in the queen's rooms, where I first had begun to read, and then the king's library of books about wars and kingdoms and travels and famous men, and finally the princess's books of fairy tales. So it is that I know now what a castle is, and a king, and a seneschal, and a story, and so can write my own.

But I was never happy going into the tower room, where the fairy tales were. I went there the first time; after the first time, I went there only for the books in the shelf beside the door. I would take a book, looking only at the shelf, and go away again at once, down the winding stair. I never looked at her but once, the first time, the one time.

She was alone in her room. She sat near the window, in a little straight chair. The thread she had been spinning lay across her lap and trailed to the floor. The thread was white; her dress was white and green. The spindle lay in her open hand. It had pricked her thumb, and the point of it still stuck just above the little thumb-joint. Her hands were small and delicate. She was younger even than I when I came there, hardly more than a child, and had never done any hard work at all. You could see that. She slept more sweetly than any of them, even the maid with the pudgy arm and the silky hair, even the rosy baby in the cradle in the gatekeeper's house, even the grandmother in the little south room, whom I loved best of all. I used to talk to the grandmother, when I was lonely. She sat so quietly as if looking out the window, and it was easy to believe that she was listening to me and only thinking before she answered.

But the princess's sleep was sweeter even than that. It was like a butterfly's sleep.

I knew, I knew as soon as I entered her room, that first time, that one time, as soon as I saw her I knew that she, she alone in all the castle, might wake at any moment. I knew that she, alone of all of them, all of us, was dreaming. I knew that if I spoke in that tower room she would hear me: maybe not waken, but hear me in her sleep, and her dreams would change. I knew that if I touched her or even came close to her I would trouble her dreams. If I so much as touched that spindle, moved it so that it did not pierce her thumb – and I longed to do that, for it was painful to see – but if I did that, if I moved the spindle, a drop of red blood would well up slowly on the delicate little cushion of flesh above the joint. And her eyes would open. Her eyes would open slowly; she would look at me. And the enchantment would be broken, the dream at an end.

I have lived here within the great hedge till I am older than my father ever was. I am as old as the grandmother in the south room, gray-haired. I have not climbed the winding stair for many years. I do not read the books of fairy tales any longer, nor visit the sweet orchard. I sit in the garden in the sunshine. When the prince comes riding, and strikes his way clear through the hedge of thorns – my two years' toil – with one blow of his privileged, bright sword, when he strides up the winding stair to the tower room, when he stoops to kiss her, and the spindle falls from her hand, and the drop of blood wells like a tiny ruby on the white skin, when she opens her eyes slowly and yawns, she will look up at him. As the castle begins to stir, the petals to fall, the little bee to move and buzz on the clover blossom, she will look up at him through the mists and tag-ends of dream, a hundred years of dreams; and I wonder if, for a moment, she will think, 'Is that the face I dreamed of seeing?' But by then I will be out by the midden heap, sleeping sounder than they ever did.

ISAK DINESEN

THE SAILOR-BOY'S TALE

THE BARQUE *CHARLOTTE* was on her way from Marseille to Athens, in grey weather, on a high sea, after three days' heavy gale. A small sailor-boy, named Simon, stood on the wet, swinging deck, held on to a shroud, and looked up towards the drifting clouds, and to the upper top-gallant yard of the main-mast.

A bird, that had sought refuge upon the mast, had got her feet entangled in some loose tackle-yarn of the halliard, and, high up there, struggled to get free. The boy on the deck could see her wings flapping and her head turning from side to side.

Through his own experience of life he had come to the conviction that in this world everyone must look after himself, and expect no help from others. But the mute, deadly fight kept him fascinated for more than an hour. He wondered what kind of bird it would be. These last days a number of birds had come to settle in the barque's rigging: swallows, quails, and a pair of peregrine falcons; he believed that this bird was a peregrine falcon. He remembered how, many years ago, in his own country and near his home, he had once seen a peregrine falcon quite close, sitting on a stone and flying straight up from it. Perhaps this was the same bird. He thought: 'That bird is like me. Then she was there, and now she is here.'

At that a fellow-feeling rose in him, a sense of common tragedy; he stood looking at the bird with his heart in his mouth. There were none of the sailors about to make fun of him; he began to think out how he might go up by the shrouds to help the falcon out. He brushed his hair back and pulled up his sleeves, gave the deck round him a great glance, and climbed up. He had to stop a couple of times in the swaying rigging.

It was indeed, he found when he got to the top of the mast, a peregrine falcon. As his head was on a level with hers, she gave up her struggle, and looked at him with a pair of angry, desperate yellow eyes. He had to take hold of her with one hand while he got his knife out, and cut off the tackle-yarn. He was scared as he looked down, but at the same time he felt that he had been ordered up by nobody, but that this was his own venture, and this gave him a proud, steadying sensation, as if the sea and the sky, the ship, the bird and himself were all one. Just as he had freed the falcon, she hacked him in the thumb, so that the blood ran, and he nearly let her go. He grew angry with her, and gave her a clout on the head, then he put her inside his jacket, and climbed down again.

When he reached the deck the mate and the cook were standing there, looking up; they roared to him to ask what he had had to do in the mast. He was so tired that the tears were in his eyes. He took the falcon out and showed her to them, and she kept still within his hands. They laughed and walked off. Simon set the falcon down, stood back and watched her. After a while he reflected that she might not be able to get up from the slippery deck, so he caught her once more, walked away with her and placed her upon a bolt of canvas. A little after she began to trim her feathers, made two or three sharp jerks forward, and then suddenly flew off. The boy could follow her flight above the troughs of the grey sea. He thought: 'There flies my falcon.'

When the *Charlotte* came home, Simon signed aboard another ship, and two years later he was a light hand on the schooner *Hebe* lying at Bodø, high up on the coast of Norway, to buy herrings.

To the great herring-markets of Bodø ships came together from all corners of the world; here were Swedish, Finnish and Russian boats, a forest of masts, and on shore a turbulent, irregular display of life, with many languages spoken, and mighty fights. On the shore booths had been set up, and the Lapps, small yellow people, noiseless in their movements, with watchful eyes, whom Simon had never seen before, came down to sell bead-embroidered leather-goods. It was April, the sky and the sea were so clear that it was difficult to hold one's eyes up against them – salt, infinitely wide, and filled with bird-shrieks – as if someone were incessantly whetting invisible knives, on all sides, high up in Heaven.

Simon was amazed at the lightness of these April evenings. He knew no geography, and did not assign it to the latitude, but he took it as a sign of an unwonted good-will in the Universe, a favour. Simon had been small for his age all his life, but this last winter he had grown, and had become strong of limb. That good luck, he felt, must spring from the very same source as the sweetness of the weather, from a new benevolence in the world. He had been in need of such encouragement, for he was timid by nature; now he asked for no more. The rest he felt to be his own affair. He went about slowly, and proudly.

One evening he was ashore with land-leave, and walked up to the booth of a small Russian trader, a Jew who sold gold watches. All the sailors knew that his watches were made from bad metal, and would not go, still they bought them, and paraded them about. Simon looked at these watches for a long time, but did not buy. The old Jew had divers goods in his shop, and amongst others a case of oranges. Simon had tasted oranges on his journeys; he bought one and took it with him. He meant to go up on a hill, from where he could see the sea, and suck it there.

As he walked on, and had got to the outskirts of the place, he saw a little girl in a blue frock, standing at the other side of a fence and looking at him. She was thirteen or fourteen years old, as slim as an eel, but with a round, clear, freckled face, and a pair of long plaits. The two looked at one another.

'Who are you looking out for?' Simon asked, to say something. The girl's face broke into an ecstatic, presumptuous smile. 'For the man I am going to marry, of course,' she said. Something in her countenance made the boy confident and happy; he grinned a little at her. 'That will perhaps be me,' he said. 'Ha, ha,' said the girl, 'he is a few years older than you, I can tell you.' 'Why,' said Simon, 'you are not grown up yourself.' The little girl shook her head solemnly. 'Nay,' she said, 'but when I grow up I will be exceedingly beautiful, and wear brown shoes with heels, and a hat.' 'Will you have an orange?' asked Simon, who could give her none of the things she had named. She looked at the orange and at him. 'They are very good to eat,' said he. 'Why do you not eat it yourself then?' she asked. 'I have eaten so many already,' said he, 'when I was in Athens. Here I had to pay a mark for it.' 'What is your name?' asked she. 'My name is Simon,' said he. 'What is yours?' 'Nora,' said the girl. 'What do you want for your orange now, Simon?'

When he heard his name in her mouth Simon grew bold. 'Will you give me a kiss for the orange?' he asked. Nora looked at him gravely for a moment. 'Yes,' she said, 'I should not mind giving you a kiss.' He grew as warm as if he had been running quickly. When she stretched out her hand for the orange he took hold of it. At that moment somebody in the house called out for her. 'That is my father,' said she, and tried to give him back the orange, but he would not take it. 'Then come again tomorrow,' she said quickly, 'then I will give you a kiss.' At that she slipped off. He stood and looked after her, and a little later went back to his ship.

Simon was not in the habit of making plans for the future, and now he did not know whether he would be going back to her or not.

The following evening he had to stay aboard, as the other sailors were going ashore, and he did not mind that either. He meant to sit on the deck with the ship's dog, Balthasar, and to practise upon a concertina that he had purchased some time ago. The pale evening was all round him, the sky was faintly roseate, the sea was quite calm, like milk-and-water, only in the wake of the boats going inshore it broke into streaks of vivid indigo. Simon sat and played; after a while his own music began to speak to him so strongly that he stopped, got up and looked upwards. Then he saw that the full moon was sitting high on the sky.

The sky was so light that she hardly seemed needed there; it was as if she had turned up by a caprice of her own. She was round, demure and presumptuous. At that he knew that he must go ashore, whatever it was to cost him. But he did not know how to get away, since the others had taken the yawl with them. He stood on the deck for a long time, a small lonely figure of a sailor-boy on a boat, when he caught sight of a yawl coming in from a ship farther out, and hailed her. He found that it was the Russian crew from a boat named *Anna*, going ashore. When he could make himself understood to them, they took him with them; they first asked him for money for his fare, then, laughing, gave it back to him. He thought: 'These people will be believing that I am going in to town, wenching.' And then he felt, with some pride, that they were right, although at the same time they were infinitely wrong, and knew nothing about anything.

When they came ashore they invited him to come in and drink in their company, and he would not refuse, because they had helped him. One of the Russians was a giant, as big as a bear; he told Simon that his name was Ivan. He got drunk at once, and then fell upon the boy with a bear-like affection, pawed him, smiled and laughed into his face, made him a present of a gold watch-chain, and kissed him on both cheeks. At that Simon reflected that he also ought to give Nora a present when they met again, and as soon as he could get away from the Russians he walked up to a booth that he knew of, and bought a small blue silk handkerchief, the same colour as her eyes.

It was Saturday evening, and there were many people amongst the houses; they came in long rows, some of them singing, all keen to have some fun that night. Simon, in the midst of this rich, bawling life under the clear moon, felt his head light with the flight from the ship and the strong drinks. He crammed the handkerchief in his pocket; it was silk, which he had never touched before, a present for his girl.

He could not remember the path up to Nora's house, lost his way, and came back to where he had started. Then he grew deadly afraid that he should be too late, and began to run. In a small passage between two wooden huts he ran straight into a big man, and found that it was Ivan once more. The Russian folded his arms round him and held him. 'Good! Good!' he cried in high glee, 'I have found you, my little chicken. I have looked for you everywhere, and poor Ivan has wept because he lost his friend.' 'Let me go, Ivan,' cried Simon. 'Oho,' said Ivan, 'I shall go with you and get you what you want. My heart and my money are all yours, all yours; I have been seventeen years old myself, a little lamb of God, and I want to be so again tonight.' 'Let me go,' cried Simon, 'I am in a hurry.' Ivan held him so that it hurt, and patted him with his other hand. 'I feel it, I feel it,' he said. 'Now trust to me, my little friend. Nothing shall part you and me. I hear the others coming; we will have such a night together as you will remember when you are an old grandpapa.'

Suddenly he crushed the boy to him, like a bear that carries off a sheep. The odious sensation of male bodily warmth and the bulk of a man close to him made the lean boy mad. He thought of Nora waiting, like a slender ship in the dim air, and of himself, here, in the hot embrace of a hairy animal. He struck Ivan with all his might. 'I shall kill you, Ivan,' he cried out, 'if you do not let me go.' 'Oh, you will be thankful to me later on,' said Ivan, and began to sing. Simon fumbled in his pocket for his knife, and got it opened. He could not lift his hand, but he drove the knife, furiously, in under the big man's arm. Almost immediately he felt the blood spouting out, and running down in his sleeve. Ivan stopped short in the song, let go his hold of the boy and gave two long deep grunts. The next second he tumbled down on his knees. 'Poor Ivan, poor Ivan,' he groaned. He fell straight on his face. At that moment Simon heard the other sailors coming along, singing, in the by-street.

He stood still for a minute, wiped his knife, and watched the blood spread into a dark pool underneath the big body. Then he ran. As he stopped for a second to choose his way, he heard the sailors behind him scream out over their dead comrade. He thought: 'I must get down to the sea, where I can wash my hand.' But at the same time he ran the other way. After a little while he found himself on the path that he had walked on the day before, and it seemed as familiar to him, as if he had walked it many hundred times in his life.

He slackened his pace to look round, and suddenly saw

Nora standing on the other side of the fence; she was quite close to him when he caught sight of her in the moonlight. Wavering and out of breath he sank down on his knees. For a moment he could not speak. The little girl looked down at him. 'Good evening, Simon,' she said in her small coy voice. 'I have waited for you a long time,' and after a moment she added: 'I have eaten your orange.'

'Oh, Nora,' cried the boy. 'I have killed a man.' She stared at him, but did not move. 'Why did you kill a man?' she asked after a moment. 'To get here,' said Simon. 'Because he tried to stop me. But he was my friend.' Slowly he got on to his feet. 'He loved me!' the boy cried out, and at that burst into tears. 'Yes,' said she slowly and thoughtfully. 'Yes, because you must be here in time.' 'Can you hide me?' he asked. 'For they are after me.' 'Nay,' said Nora, 'I cannot hide you. For my father is the parson here at Bodø, and he would be sure to hand you over to them, if he knew that you had killed a man.' 'Then,' said Simon, 'give me something to wipe my hands on.' 'What is the matter with your hands?' she asked, and took a little step forward. He stretched out his hands to her. 'Is that your own blood?' she asked. 'No,' said he, 'it is his.' She took the step back again. 'Do you hate me now?' he asked. 'No, I do not hate you,' said she. 'But do put your hands at your back.'

As he did so she came up close to him, at the other side of the fence, and clasped her arms round his neck. She pressed her young body to his, and kissed him tenderly. He felt her face, cool as the moonlight, upon his own, and when she released him, his head swam, and he did not know if the kiss had lasted a second or an hour. Nora stood up straight, her eyes wide open. 'Now,' she said slowly and proudly, 'I promise you that I will never marry anybody, as long as I live.' The boy kept standing with his hands on his back, as if she had tied them there. 'And now,' she said, 'you must run, for they are coming.' They looked at one another. 'Do not forget Nora,' said she. He turned and ran.

He leapt over a fence, and when he was down amongst the houses he walked. He did not know at all where to go. As he came to a house, from where music and noise streamed out, he slowly went through the door. The room was full of people; they were dancing in here. A lamp hung from the ceiling, and shone down on them; the air was thick and brown with the dust rising from the floor. There were some women in the room, but many of the men danced with each other, and gravely or laughingly stamped the floor. A moment after Simon had come in the crowd withdrew to the walls to clear the floor for two sailors, who were showing a dance from their own country.

Simon thought: 'Now, very soon, the men from the boat will come round to look for their comrade's murderer, and from my hands they will know that I have done it.' These five minutes during which he stood by the wall of the dancing-room, in the midst of the gay, sweating dancers, were of great significance to the boy. He himself felt it, as if during this time he grew up, and became like other people. He did not entreat his destiny, nor complain. Here he was, he had killed a man, and had kissed a girl. He did not demand any more from life, nor did life now demand more from him. He was Simon, a man like the men round him, and going to die, as all men are going to die.

He only became aware of what was going on outside him, when he saw that a woman had come in, and was standing in the midst of the cleared floor, looking round her. She was a short, broad old woman, in the clothes of the Lapps, and she took her stand with such majesty and fierceness as if she owned the whole place. It was obvious that most of the people knew her, and were a little afraid of her, although a few laughed; the din of the dancing-room stopped when she spoke.

'Where is my son?' she asked in a high shrill voice, like a bird's. The next moment her eyes fell on Simon himself, and she steered through the crowd, which opened up before her, stretched out her old skinny, dark hand, and took him by the elbow. 'Come home with me now,' she said. 'You need not dance here tonight. You may be dancing a high enough dance soon.'

Simon drew back, for he thought that she was drunk. But as she looked him straight in the face with her yellow eyes, it seemed to him that he had met her before, and that he might do well in listening to her. The old woman pulled him with her across the floor, and he followed her without a word. 'Do not birch your boy too badly, Sunniva,' one of the men in the room cried to her. 'He has done no harm, he only wanted to look at the dance.'

At the same moment as they came out through the door, there was an alarm in the street, a flock of people came running down it, and one of them, as he turned into the house, knocked against Simon, looked at him and the old woman, and ran on.

While the two walked along the street, the old woman lifted up her skirt, and put the hem of it into the boy's hand. 'Wipe your hand on my skirt,' she said. They had not gone far before they came to a small wooden house, and stopped; the door to it was so low that they must bend to get through it. As the Lapp-woman went in before Simon, still holding on to his arm, the boy looked up for a moment. The night had grown misty; there was a wide ring round the moon.

The old woman's room was narrow and dark, with but one small window to it; a lantern stood on the floor and lighted it up dimly. It was all filled with reindeer skins and wolf skins, and with reindeer horn, such as the Lapps use to make their carved buttons and knife-handles, and the air in here was rank and stifling. As soon as they were in, the woman turned to Simon, took hold of his head, and with her crooked fingers parted his hair and combed it down in Lapp fashion. She clapped a Lapp cap on him and stood back to glance at him. 'Sit down on my stool, now,' she said. 'But first take out your knife.' She was so commanding in voice and manner that the boy could not but choose to do as she told him; he sat down on the stool, and he could not take his eyes off her face, which was flat and brown, and as if smeared with dirt in its net of fine wrinkles. As he sat there he heard many people come along outside, and stop by the house; then someone knocked at the door, waited a moment and knocked again. The old woman stood and listened, as still as a mouse.

'Nay,' said the boy and got up. 'This is no good, for it is me that they are after. It will be better for you to let me go out to them.' 'Give me your knife,' said she. When he handed it to her, she stuck it straight into her thumb, so that the blood spouted out, and she let it drip all over her skirt. 'Come in, then,' she cried.

The door opened, and two of the Russian sailors came and stood in the opening; there were more people outside. 'Has anybody come in here?' they asked. 'We are after a man who has killed our mate, but he has run away from us. Have you seen or heard anybody this way?' The old Lapp-woman turned upon them, and her eyes shone like gold in the lamp-light. 'Have I seen or heard anyone?' she cried, 'I have heard you shriek murder all over the town. You frightened me, and my poor silly boy there, so that I cut my thumb as I was ripping the skin-rug that I sew. The boy is too scared to help me, and the rug is all ruined. I shall make you pay me for that. If you are looking for a murderer, come in and search my house for me, and I shall know you when we meet again.' She was so furious that she danced where she stood, and jerked her head like an angry bird of prey.

The Russian came in, looked round the room, and at her and her blood-stained hand and skirt. 'Do not put a curse on us now, Sunniva,' he said timidly. 'We know that you can do many things when you like. Here is a mark to pay you for the blood you have spilled.' She stretched out her hand, and he placed a piece of money in it. She spat on it. 'Then go, and there shall be no bad blood between us,' said Sunniva, and shut the door after them. She stuck her thumb in her mouth, and chuckled a little.

The boy got up from his stool, stood straight up before her and stared into her face. He felt as if he were swaying high up in the air, with but a small hold. 'Why have you helped me?' he asked her. 'Do you not know?' she answered. 'Have you not recognized me yet? But you will remember the peregrine falcon which was caught in the tackle-yarn of your boat, the *Charlotte*, as she sailed in the Mediterranean. That day you climbed up by the shrouds of the top-gallantmast to help her out, in a stiff wind, and with a high sea. That falcon was me. We Lapps often fly in such a manner, to see the world. When I first met you I was on my way to Africa, to see my younger sister and her children. She is a falcon too, when she chooses. By that time she was living at Takaunga, within an old ruined tower, which down there they call a minaret.' She swathed a corner of her skirt round her thumb, and bit at it. 'We do not forget,' she said. 'I hacked your thumb, when you took hold of me; it is only fair that I should cut my thumb for you tonight.'

She came close to him, and gently rubbed her two brown,

claw-like fingers against his forehead. 'So you are a boy,' she said, 'who will kill a man rather than be late to meet your sweetheart? We hold together, the females of this earth. I shall mark your forehead now, so that the girls will know of that, when they look at you, and they will like you for it.' She played with the boy's hair, and twisted it round her finger.

'Listen now, my little bird,' said she. 'My great grandson's brother-in-law is lying with his boat by the landing-place at this moment; he is to take a consignment of skins out to a Danish boat. He will bring you back to your boat, in time, before your mate comes. The *Hebe* is sailing tomorrow morning, is it not so? But when you are aboard, give him back my cap for me.' She took up his knife, wiped it in her skirt and handed it to him. 'Here is your knife,' she said. 'You will stick it into no more men; you will not need to, for from now you will sail the seas like a faithful seaman. We have enough trouble with our sons as it is.'

The bewildered boy began to stammer his thanks to her. 'Wait,' said she, 'I shall make you a cup of coffee, to bring back your wits, while I wash your jacket.' She went and rattled an old copper kettle upon the fireplace. After a while she handed him a hot, strong, black drink in a cup without a handle to it. 'You have drunk with Sunniva now,' she said; 'you have drunk down a little wisdom, so that in the future all your thoughts shall not fall like raindrops into the salt sea.'

When he had finished and set down the cup, she led him to the door and opened it for him. He was surprised to see that it was almost clear morning. The house was so high up that the boy could see the sea from it, and a milky mist about it. He gave her his hand to say good-bye.

She stared into his face. 'We do not forget,' she said. 'And you, you knocked me on the head there, high up in the mast. I shall give you that blow back.' With that she smacked him on the ear as hard as she could, so that his head swam. 'Now we are quits,' she said, gave him a great, mischievous, shining glance, and a little push down the doorstep, and nodded to him.

In this way the sailor-boy got back to his ship, which was to sail the next morning, and lived to tell the story.

ROBERT LOUIS STEVENSON

THE BOTTLE IMP

NOTE – Any student of that very unliterary product, the English drama of the early part of the century, will here recognize the name and the root idea of a piece once rendered popular by the redoubtable O. Smith. The root idea is there and identical, and yet I hope I have made it a new thing. And the fact that the tale has been designed and written for a Polynesian audience may lend it some extraneous interest nearer home.

R. L. S.

THERE WAS A MAN of the Island of Hawaii, whom I shall call Keawe; for the truth is, he still lives, and his name must be kept secret; but the place of his birth was not far from Honaunau, where the bones of Keawe the Great lie hidden in a cave. This man was poor, brave, and active; he could read and write like a schoolmaster; he was a first-rate mariner besides, sailed for some time in the island steamers, and steered a whaleboat on the Hamakua coast. At length it came in Keawe's mind to have a sight of the great world and foreign cities, and he shipped on a vessel bound to San Francisco.

This is a fine town, with a fine harbour, and rich people uncountable; and, in particular, there is one hill which is covered with palaces. Upon this hill Keawe was one day taking a walk with his pocket full of money, viewing the great houses upon either hand with pleasure. 'What fine houses these are!' he was thinking, 'and how happy must those people be who dwell in them, and take no care for the morrow!' The thought was in his mind when he came abreast of a house that was smaller than some others, but all finished and beautified like a toy; the steps of that house shone like silver, and the borders of the garden bloomed like garlands, and the windows were bright like diamonds; and Keawe stopped and wondered at the excellence of all he saw. So stopping, he was aware of a man that looked forth upon him through a window so clear that Keawe could see him as you see a fish in a pool upon the reef. The man was elderly, with a bald head and a black beard; and his face was heavy with sorrow, and he bitterly sighed. And the truth of it is, that as Keawe looked in upon the man, and the man looked out upon Keawe, each envied the other.

All of a sudden, the man smiled and nodded, and beckoned Keawe to enter, and met him at the door of the house.

'This is a fine house of mine,' said the man, and bitterly sighed. 'Would you not care to view the chambers?'

So he led Keawe all over it, from the cellar to the roof, and there was nothing there that was not perfect of its kind, and Keawe was astonished.

'Truly,' said Keawe, 'this is a beautiful house; if I lived in the like of it, I should be laughing all day long. How comes it, then, that you should be sighing?'

'There is no reason,' said the man, 'why you should not have a house in all points similar to this, and finer, if you wish. You have some money, I suppose?'

'I have fifty dollars,' said Keawe; 'but a house like this will cost more than fifty dollars.'

The man made a computation. 'I am sorry you have no more,' said he, 'for it may raise you trouble in the future; but it shall be yours at fifty dollars.'

'The house?' asked Keawe.

'No, not the house,' replied the man; 'but the bottle. For, I must tell you, although I appear to you so rich and fortunate, all my fortune, and this house itself and its garden, came out of a bottle not much bigger than a pint. This is it.'

And he opened a lockfast place, and took out a round-bellied bottle with a long neck; the glass of it was white like milk, with changing rainbow colours in the grain. Within-sides something obscurely moved, like a shadow and a fire.

'This is the bottle,' said the man; and, when Keawe laughed, 'You do not believe me?' he added. 'Try then, for yourself. See if you can break it.'

So Keawe took the bottle up and dashed it on the floor till he was weary; but it jumped on the floor like a child's ball, and was not injured.

'This is a strange thing,' said Keawe. 'For by the touch of it, as well as by the look, the bottle should be of glass.'

'Of glass it is,' replied the man, sighing more heavily than ever; 'but the glass of it was tempered in the flames of hell. An imp lives in it, and that is the shadow we behold there moving: or so I suppose. If any man buy this bottle the imp is at his command; all that he desires – love, fame, money, houses like this house, ay, or a city like this city – all are his at the word uttered. Napoleon had this bottle, and by it he grew to be the king of the world; but he sold it at the last, and fell. Captain Cook had this bottle, and by it he found his way to so many islands; but he, too, sold it, and was slain upon Hawaii. For, once it is sold, the power goes and the protection; and unless a man remain content with what he has, ill will befall him.'

'And yet you talk of selling it yourself?' Keawe said.

'I have all I wish, and I am growing elderly,' replied the man. 'There is one thing the imp cannot do – he cannot prolong life; and, it would not be fair to conceal from you, there is a drawback to the bottle; for if a man die before he sells it, he must burn in hell forever.'

'To be sure, that is a drawback and no mistake,' cried Keawe. 'I would not meddle with the thing. I can do without a house, thank God; but there is one thing I could not be doing with one particle, and that is to be damned.'

'Dear me, you must not run away with things,' returned the man. 'All you have to do is to use the power of the imp in moderation, and then sell it to someone else, as I do to you, and finish your life in comfort.'

'Well, I observe two things,' said Keawe. 'All the time you keep sighing like a maid in love, that is one; and, for the other, you sell this bottle very cheap.'

'I have told you already why I sigh,' said the man. 'It is because I fear my health is breaking up; and, as you said yourself, to die and go to the devil is a pity for anyone. As for why I sell so cheap, I must explain to you there is a peculiarity about the bottle. Long ago, when the devil brought it first upon earth, it was extremely expensive, and was sold first of all to Prester John for many millions of dollars; but it cannot be sold at all, unless sold at a loss. If you sell it for as much as you paid for it, back it comes to you again like a homing pigeon. It follows that the price has kept falling in these centuries, and the bottle is now remarkably cheap. I bought it myself from one of my great neighbours on this hill, and the price I paid was only ninety dollars. I could sell it for as high as eighty-nine dollars and ninety-nine cents, but not a penny dearer, or back the thing must come to me. Now, about this there are two bothers. First, when you offer a bottle so singular for eighty odd dollars, people suppose you to be jesting. And second – but there is no hurry about that – and I need not go into it. Only remember it must be coined money that you sell it for.'

'How am I to know that this is all true?' asked Keawe.

'Some of it you can try at once,' replied the man. 'Give me your fifty dollars, take the bottle, and wish your fifty dollars back into your pocket. If that does not happen, I pledge you my honour I will cry off the bargain and restore your money.'

'You are not deceiving me?' said Keawe.

The man bound himself with a great oath.

'Well, I will risk that much,' said Keawe, 'for that can do no harm.' And he paid over his money to the man, and the man handed him the bottle.

'Imp of the bottle,' said Keawe, 'I want my fifty dollars back.' And sure enough he had scarce said the word before his pocket was as heavy as ever.

'To be sure this is a wonderful bottle,' said Keawe.

'And now good-morning to you, my fine fellow, and the devil go with you for me!' said the man.

'Hold on,' said Keawe, 'I don't want any more of this fun. Here, take your bottle back.'

'You have bought it for less than I paid for it,' replied the man, rubbing his hands. 'It is yours now; and, for my part, I am only concerned to see the back of you.' And with that he rang for his Chinese servant, and had Keawe shown out of the house.

Now, when Keawe was in the street, with the bottle under his arm, he began to think. 'If all is true about this bottle, I may have made a losing bargain,' thinks he. 'But perhaps the man was only fooling me.' The first thing he did was to count his money; the sum was exact – forty-nine dollars American money, and one Chili piece. 'That looks like the truth,' said Keawe. 'Now I will try another part.'

The streets in that part of the city were as clean as a ship's decks, and though it was noon, there were no passengers.

Keawe set the bottle in the gutter and walked away. Twice he looked back, and there was the milky, round-bellied bottle where he left it. A third time he looked back, and turned a corner; but he had scarce done so, when something knocked upon his elbow, and behold! it was the long neck sticking up; and as for the round belly, it was jammed into the pocket of his pilot-coat.

'And that looks like the truth,' said Keawe.

The next thing he did was to buy a corkscrew in a shop, and go apart into a secret place in the fields. And there he tried to draw the cork, but as often as he put the screw in, out it came again, and the cork as whole as ever.

'This is some new sort of cork,' said Keawe, and all at once he began to shake and sweat, for he was afraid of that bottle.

On his way back to the port side, he saw a shop where a man sold shells and clubs from the wild islands, old heathen deities, old coined money, pictures from China and Japan, and all manner of things that sailors bring in their sea chests. And here he had an idea. So he went in and offered the bottle for a hundred dollars. The man of the shop laughed at him at the first, and offered him five; but, indeed, it was a curious bottle – such glass was never blown in any human glass-works, so prettily the colours shone under the milky white, and so strangely the shadow hovered in the midst; so, after he had disputed awhile after the manner of his kind, the shopman gave Keawe sixty silver dollars for the thing, and set it on a shelf in the midst of his window.

'Now,' said Keawe, 'I have sold that for sixty which I bought for fifty – or, to say truth, a little less, because one of my dollars was from Chili. Now I shall know the truth upon another point.'

So he went back on board his ship, and, when he opened his chest, there was the bottle, and had come more quickly than himself. Now Keawe had a mate on board whose name was Lopaka.

'What ails you?' said Lopaka, 'that you stare in your chest?'

They were alone in the ship's forecastle, and Keawe bound him to secrecy, and told all.

'This is a very strange affair,' said Lopaka; 'and I fear you will be in trouble about this bottle. But there is one point very clear – that you are sure of the trouble, and you had better have the profit in the bargain. Make up your mind what you want with it; give the order, and if it is done as you desire, I will buy the bottle myself; for I have an idea of my own to get a schooner, and go trading through the islands.'

'That is not my idea,' said Keawe; 'but to have a beautiful house and garden on the Kona Coast, where I was born, the sun shining in at the door, flowers in the garden, glass in the windows, pictures on the walls, and toys and fine carpets on the tables, for all the world like the house I was in this day – only a storey higher, and with balconies all about like the King's palace; and to live there without care and make merry with my friends and relatives.'

'Well,' said Lopaka, 'let us carry it back with us to Hawaii; and if all comes true, as you suppose, I will buy the bottle, as I said, and ask a schooner.'

Upon that they were agreed, and it was not long before the ship returned to Honolulu, carrying Keawe and Lopaka, and the bottle. They were scarce come ashore when they met a friend upon the beach, who began at once to condole with Keawe.

'I do not know what I am to be condoled about,' said Keawe.

'Is it possible you have not heard,' said the friend, 'your uncle – that good old man – is dead, and your cousin – that beautiful boy – was drowned at sea?'

Keawe was filled with sorrow, and, beginning to weep and to lament, he forgot about the bottle. But Lopaka was thinking to himself, and presently, when Keawe's grief was a little abated, 'I have been thinking,' said Lopaka. 'Had not your uncle lands in Hawaii, in the district of Kaü?'

'No,' said Keawe, 'not in Kaü: they are on the mountain-side – a little way south of Hookena.'

'These lands will now be yours?' asked Lopaka.

'And so they will,' says Keawe, and began again to lament for his relatives.

'No,' said Lopaka, 'do not lament at present. I have a thought in my mind. How if this should be the doing of the bottle? For here is the place ready for your house.'

'If this be so,' cried Keawe, 'it is a very ill way to serve me by killing my relatives. But it may be, indeed; for it was in just such a station that I saw the house with my mind's eye.'

'The house, however, is not yet built,' said Lopaka.

'No, nor like to be!' said Keawe; 'for though my uncle has some coffee and ava and bananas, it will not be more than will keep me in comfort; and the rest of that land is the black lava.'

'Let us go to the lawyer,' said Lopaka; 'I have still this idea in my mind.'

Now, when they came to the lawyer's, it appeared Keawe's uncle had grown monstrous rich in the last days, and there was a fund of money.

'And here is the money for the house!' cried Lopaka.

'If you are thinking of a new house,' said the lawyer, 'here is the card of a new architect, of whom they tell me great things.'

'Better and better!' cried Lopaka. 'Here is all made plain for us. Let us continue to obey orders.'

So they went to the architect, and he had drawings of houses on his table.

'You want something out of the way,' said the architect. 'How do you like this?' and he handed a drawing to Keawe.

Now, when Keawe set eyes on the drawing, he cried out aloud, for it was the picture of his thought exactly drawn.

'I am in for this house,' thought he. 'Little as I like the way it comes to me, I am in for it now, and I may as well take the good along with the evil.'

So he told the architect all that he wished, and how he would have that house furnished, and about the pictures on the wall and the knick-knacks on the tables; and he asked the man plainly for how much he would undertake the whole affair.

The architect put many questions, and took his pen and made a computation; and when he had done he named the very sum that Keawe had inherited.

Lopaka and Keawe looked at one another and nodded.

'It is quite clear,' thought Keawe, 'that I am to have this house, whether or no. It comes from the devil, and I fear I will get little good by that; and of one thing I am sure, I will make no more wishes as long as I have this bottle. But with the house I am saddled, and I may as well take the good along with the evil.'

So he made his terms with the architect, and they signed a paper; and Keawe and Lopaka took ship again and sailed to Australia; for it was concluded between them they should not interfere at all, but leave the architect and the bottle imp to build and to adorn that house at their own pleasure.

The voyage was a good voyage, only all the time Keawe was holding in his breath, for he had sworn he would utter no more wishes, and take no more favours from the devil. The time was up when they got back. The architect told them that the house was ready, and Keawe and Lopaka took a passage in the *Hall*, and went down Kona way to view the house, and see if all had been done fitly according to the thought that was in Keawe's mind.

Now, the house stood on the mountainside, visible to ships. Above, the forest ran up into the clouds of rain; below, the black lava fell in cliffs, where the kings of old lay buried. A garden bloomed about that house with every hue of flowers; and there was an orchard of papaia on the one hand and an orchard of breadfruit on the other, and right in front, toward the sea, a ship's mast had been rigged up and bore a flag. As for the house, it was three storeys high, with great chambers and broad balconies on each. The windows were of glass, so excellent that it was as clear as water and as bright as day. All manner of furniture adorned the chambers. Pictures hung upon the wall in golden frames: pictures of ships, and men fighting, and of the most beautiful women, and of singular places; nowhere in the world are there pictures of so bright a colour as those Keawe found hanging in his house. As for the knick-knacks, they were extraordinary fine; chiming clocks and musical boxes, little men with nodding heads, books filled with pictures, weapons of price from all quarters of the world, and the most elegant puzzles to entertain the leisure of a solitary man. And as no one would care to live in such chambers, only to walk through and view them, the balconies were made so broad that a whole town might have lived upon them in delight; and Keawe knew not which to prefer, whether the back porch, where you got the land breeze, and looked upon the orchards and the flowers, or the front balcony, where you could drink the wind of the sea, and look down the steep wall of the mountain and see the *Hall* going by once a week or so between Hookena and the hills of Pele, or the schooners plying up the coast for wood and ava and bananas.

When they had viewed all, Keawe and Lopaka sat on the porch.

'Well,' said Lopaka, 'is it all as you designed?'

'Words cannot utter it,' said Keawe. 'It is better than I dreamed, and I am sick with satisfaction.'

'There is but one thing to consider,' said Lopaka; 'all this may be quite natural, and the bottle imp have nothing whatever to say to it. If I were to buy the bottle, and got no schooner after all, I should have put my hand in the fire for nothing. I gave you my word, I know; but yet I think you would not grudge me one more proof.'

'I have sworn I would take no more favours,' said Keawe. 'I have gone already deep enough.'

'This is no favour I am thinking of,' replied Lopaka. 'It is only to see the imp himself. There is nothing to be gained by that, and so nothing to be ashamed of; and yet, if I once saw him, I should be sure of the whole matter. So indulge me so far, and let me see the imp; and, after that, here is the money in my hand, and I will buy it.'

'There is only one thing I am afraid of,' said Keawe. 'The imp may be very ugly to view; and if you once set eyes upon him you might be very undesirous of the bottle.'

'I am a man of my word,' said Lopaka. 'And here is the money betwixt us.'

'Very well,' replied Keawe. 'I have a curiosity myself. So come, let us have one look at you, Mr Imp.'

Now as soon as that was said, the imp looked out of the bottle, and in again, swift as a lizard; and there sat Keawe and Lopaka turned to stone. The night had quite come, before either found a thought to say or voice to say it with; and then Lopaka pushed the money over and took the bottle.

'I am a man of my word,' said he, 'and had need to be so, or I would not touch this bottle with my foot. Well, I shall get my schooner and a dollar or two for my pocket; and then I will be rid of this devil as fast as I can. For to tell you the plain truth, the look of him has cast me down.'

'Lopaka,' said Keawe, 'do not you think any worse of me than you can help; I know it is night, and the roads bad, and the pass by the tombs an ill place to go by so late, but I declare since I have seen that little face, I cannot eat or sleep or pray till it is gone from me. I will give you a lantern, and a basket to put the bottle in, and any picture or fine thing in all my house that takes your fancy; – and be gone at once, and go sleep at Hookena with Nahinu.'

'Keawe,' said Lopaka, 'many a man would take this ill; above all, when I am doing you a turn so friendly, as to keep my word and buy the bottle; and for that matter, the night and the dark, and the way by the tombs, must be all tenfold more dangerous to a man with such a sin upon his conscience, and such a bottle under his arm. But for my part, I am so extremely terrified myself, I have not the heart to blame you. Here I go then; and I pray God you may be happy in your house, and I fortunate with my schooner, and both get to heaven in the end in spite of the devil and his bottle.'

So Lopaka went down the mountain; and Keawe stood in his front balcony, and listened to the clink of the horse's shoes, and watched the lantern go shining down the path, and along the cliff of caves where the old dead are buried; and all the time he trembled and clasped his hands, and prayed for his friend, and gave glory to God that he himself was escaped out of that trouble.

But the next day came very brightly, and that new house of his was so delightful to behold that he forgot his terrors. One day followed another, and Keawe dwelt there in perpetual joy. He had his place on the back porch; it was there he ate and lived, and read the stories in the Honolulu newspapers; but when anyone came by they would go in and view the chambers and the pictures. And the fame of the house went far and wide; it was called *Ka-Hale Nui* – the Great House – in all Kona; and sometimes the Bright House, for Keawe kept a Chinaman, who was all day dusting and furbishing; and the glass, and the gilt, and the fine stuffs, and the pictures, shone as bright as the morning. As for Keawe himself, he could not walk in the chambers without singing, his heart was so enlarged; and when ships sailed by upon the sea, he would fly his colours on the mast.

So time went by, until one day Keawe went upon a visit as far as Kailua to certain of his friends. There he was well feasted; and left as soon as he could the next morning, and rode hard, for he was impatient to behold his beautiful house; and, besides, the night then coming on was the night in which the dead of old days go abroad in the sides of Kona; and having already meddled with the devil, he was the more chary of meeting with the dead. A little beyond Honaunau, looking far ahead, he was aware of a woman bathing in the edge of the sea; and she seemed a well-grown girl, but he thought no more of it. Then he saw her white shift flutter as she put it on, and then her red holoku; and by the time he came abreast of her she was done with her toilet, and had come up from the sea, and stood by the track side in her red holoku, and she was all freshened with the bath, and her eyes shone and were kind. Now Keawe no sooner beheld her than he drew rein.

'I thought I knew everyone in this country,' said he. 'How comes it that I do not know you?'

'I am Kokua, daughter of Kiano,' said the girl, 'and I have just returned from Oahu. Who are you?'

'I will tell you who I am in a little,' said Keawe, dismounting from his horse, 'but not now. For I have a thought in my mind, and if you knew who I was, you might have heard of me, and would not give me a true answer. But tell me, first of all, one thing: Are you married?'

At this Kokua laughed out aloud. 'It is you who ask questions,' she said. 'Are you married yourself?'

'Indeed, Kokua, I am not,' replied Keawe, 'and never thought to be until this hour. But here is the plain truth. I have met you here at the roadside, and I saw your eyes, which are like the stars, and my heart went to you as swift as a bird. And so now, if you want none of me, say so, and I will go on to my own place; but if you think me no worse than any other young man, say so, too, and I will turn aside to your father's for the night, and tomorrow I will talk with the good man.'

Kokua said never a word, but she looked at the sea and laughed.

'Kokua,' said Keawe, 'if you say nothing, I will take that for the good answer; so let us be stepping to your father's door.'

She went on ahead of him, still without speech; only sometimes she glanced back and glanced away again, and she kept the strings of her hat in her mouth.

Now, when they had come to the door, Kiano came out on his verandah, and cried out and welcomed Keawe by name. At that the girl looked over, for the fame of the great house had come to her ears; and, to be sure, it was a great temptation. All that evening they were very merry together; and the girl was as bold as brass under the eyes of her parents, and made a mock of Keawe, for she had a quick wit. The next day he had a word with Kiano, and found the girl alone.

'Kokua,' said he, 'you made a mock of me all the evening; and it is still time to bid me go. I would not tell you who I was, because I have so fine a house, and I feared you would think too much of that house and too little of the man that loves you. Now you know all, and if you wish to have seen the last of me, say so at once.'

'No,' said Kokua; but this time she did not laugh, nor did Keawe ask for more.

This was the wooing of Keawe; things had gone quickly; but so an arrow goes, and the ball of a rifle swifter still, and yet both may strike the target. Things had gone fast, but they had gone far also, and the thought of Keawe rang in the maiden's head; she heard his voice in the breach of the surf upon the lava, and for this young man that she had seen but twice she would have left father and mother and her native islands. As for Keawe himself, his horse flew up the path of the mountain under the cliff of tombs, and the sound of the hoofs, and the sound of Keawe singing to himself for pleasure, echoed in the caverns of the dead. He came to the Bright House, and still he was singing. He sat and ate in the broad balcony, and the Chinaman wondered at his master, to hear how he sang between the mouthfuls. The sun went down into the sea, and the night came; and Keawe walked the balconies by lamplight, high on the mountains, and the voice of his singing startled men on ships.

'Here am I now upon my high place,' he said to himself. 'Life may be no better; this is the mountain top; and all shelves about me toward the worse. For the first time I will light up the chambers, and bathe in my fine bath with the hot water and the cold, and sleep alone in the bed of my bridal chamber.'

So the Chinaman had word, and he must rise from sleep and light the furnaces; and as he wrought below, beside the boilers, he heard his master singing and rejoicing above him in the lighted chambers. When the water began to be hot the Chinaman cried to his master, and Keawe went into the bathroom; and the Chinaman heard him sing as he filled the marble basin; and heard him sing, and the singing broken, as he undressed; until of a sudden, the song ceased. The Chinaman listened, and listened; he called up the house to Keawe to ask if all were well, and Keawe answered him 'Yes,' and bade him to go bed; but there was no more singing in the Bright House; and all night long, the Chinaman heard his master's feet go round and round the balconies without repose.

Now the truth of it was this: as Keawe undressed for his bath, he spied upon his flesh a patch like a patch of lichen on a rock, and it was then that he stopped singing. For he knew the likeness of that patch, and knew that he was fallen in the Chinese Evil.

Now, it is a sad thing for any man to fall into this sickness. And it would be a sad thing for anyone to leave a house so beautiful and so commodious, and depart from all his friends to the north coast of Molokai, between the mighty cliff and the sea-breakers. But what was that to the case of the man Keawe, he who had met his love but yesterday, and won her but that morning, and now saw all his hopes break, in a moment, like a piece of glass?

Awhile he sat upon the edge of the bath; then sprang, with a cry, and ran outside; and to and fro, to and fro, along the balcony, like one despairing.

'Very willingly could I leave Hawaii, the home of my fathers,' Keawe was thinking. 'Very lightly could I leave my house, the high-placed, the many-windowed, here upon the mountains. Very bravely could I go to Molokai, to Kalaupapa by the cliffs, to live with the smitten and to sleep there, far from my fathers. But what wrong have I done, what sin lies upon my soul, that I should have encountered Kokua coming cool from the sea-water in the evening? Kokua, the soul ensnarer! Kokua, the light of my life! Her may I never wed, her may I look upon no longer, her may I no more handle with my loving hand; and it is for this, it is for you, O Kokua! that I pour my lamentations!'

Now you are to observe what sort of a man Keawe was, for he might have dwelt there in the Bright House for years, and no one been the wiser of his sickness; but he reckoned nothing of that, if he must lose Kokua. And again, he might have wed Kokua even as he was; and so many would have done, because they have the souls of pigs; but Keawe loved the maid manfully, and he would do her no hurt and bring her in no danger.

A little beyond the midst of the night, there came in his mind the recollection of that bottle. He went round to the back porch, and called to memory the day when the devil had looked forth; and at the thought ice ran in his veins.

'A dreadful thing is the bottle,' thought Keawe, 'and dreadful is the imp, and it is a dreadful thing to risk the flames of hell. But what other hope have I to cure my sickness or to wed Kokua? What!' he thought, 'would I beard the devil once, only to get me a house, and not face him again to win Kokua?'

Thereupon he called to mind it was the next day the *Hall* went by on her return to Honolulu. 'There must I go first,' he thought, 'and see Lopaka. For the best hope that I have now is to find that same bottle I was so pleased to be rid of.'

Never a wink could he sleep; the food stuck in his throat; but he sent a letter to Kiano, and about the time when the steamer would be coming, rode down beside the cliff of the tombs. It rained; his horse went heavily; he looked up at the black mouths of the caves, and he envied the dead that slept there and were done with trouble; and called to mind how he had galloped by the day before, and was astonished. So he came down to Hookena, and there was all the country gathered for the steamer as usual. In the shed before the store they sat and jested and passed the news; but there was no matter of speech in Keawe's bosom, and he sat in their midst and looked without on the rain falling on the houses, and the surf beating among the rocks, and the sighs arose in his throat.

'Keawe of the Bright House is out of spirits,' said one to another. Indeed, and so he was, and little wonder.

Then the *Hall* came, and the whaleboat carried him on board. The afterpart of the ship was full of Haoles who had been to visit the volcano, as their custom is; and the midst was crowded with Kanakas, and the forepart with wild bulls from Hilo and horses from Kaü; but Keawe sat apart from all in his sorrow, and watched for the house of Kiano. There it sat, low upon the shore in the black rocks, and shaded by the cocoa palms, and there by the door was a red holoku, no greater than a fly, and going to and fro with a fly's busyness. 'Ah, queen of my heart,' he cried, 'I'll venture my dear soul to win you!'

Soon after, darkness fell, and the cabins were lit up, and the Haoles sat and played at the cards and drank whiskey as their custom is; but Keawe walked the deck all night; and all the next day, as they steamed under the lee of Maui or of Molokai, he was still pacing to and fro like a wild animal in a menagerie.

Towards evening they passed Diamond Head, and came to the pier of Honolulu. Keawe stepped out among the crowd and began to ask for Lopaka. It seemed he had become the owner of a schooner – none better in the islands – and was gone upon an adventure as far as Pola-Pola or Kahiki; so there was no help to be looked for from Lopaka. Keawe called to mind a friend of his, a lawyer in the town (I must not tell his name), and inquired of him. They said he was grown suddenly rich, and had a fine new house upon Waikiki shore; and this put a thought in Keawe's head, and he called a hack and drove to the lawyer's house.

The house was all brand new, and the trees in the garden no greater than walking-sticks, and the lawyer, when he came, had the air of a man well pleased.

'What can I do to serve you?' said the lawyer.

'You are a friend of Lopaka's,' replied Keawe, 'and Lopaka purchased from me a certain piece of goods that I thought you might enable me to trace.'

The lawyer's face became very dark. 'I do not profess to misunderstand you, Mr Keawe,' said he, 'though this is an ugly business to be stirring in. You may be sure I know nothing, but yet I have a guess, and if you would apply in a certain quarter I think you might have news.'

And he named the name of a man, which, again, I had better not repeat. So it was for days, and Keawe went from one to another, finding everywhere new clothes and carriages, and fine new houses and men everywhere in great contentment, although, to be sure, when he hinted at his business their faces would cloud over.

'No doubt I am upon the track,' thought Keawe. 'These new clothes and carriages are all the gifts of the little imp, and these glad faces are the faces of men who have taken their profit and got rid of the accursed thing in safety. When I see pale cheeks and hear sighing, I shall know that I am near the bottle.'

So it befell at last that he was recommended to a Haole in Beritania Street. When he came to the door, about the hour of the evening meal, there were the usual marks of the new house, and the young garden, and the electric light shining in the windows; but when the owner came, a shock of hope and fear ran through Keawe; for here was a young man, white as a corpse, and black about the eyes, the hair shedding from his head, and such a look in his countenance as a man may have when he is waiting for the gallows.

'Here it is, to be sure,' thought Keawe, and so with this man he noways veiled his errand. 'I am come to buy the bottle,' said he.

At the word, the young Haole of Beritania Street reeled against the wall.

'The bottle!' he gasped. 'To buy the bottle!' Then he seemed to choke, and seizing Keawe by the arm carried him into a room and poured out wine in two glasses.

'Here is my respects,' said Keawe, who had been much about with Haoles in his time. 'Yes,' he added, 'I am come to buy the bottle. What is the price by now?'

At that word the young man let his glass slip through his fingers, and looked upon Keawe like a ghost.

'The price,' says he; 'the price! You do not know the price?'

'It is for that I am asking you,' returned Keawe. 'But why are you so much concerned? Is there anything wrong about the price?'

'It has dropped a great deal in value since your time, Mr Keawe,' said the young man, stammering.

'Well, well, I shall have the less to pay for it,' says Keawe. 'How much did it cost you?'

The young man was as white as a sheet. 'Two cents,' said he.

'What?' cried Keawe, 'two cents? Why, then, you can only sell it for one. And he who buys it—' The words died upon Keawe's tongue; he who bought it could never sell it again, the bottle and the bottle imp must abide with him until he died, and when he died must carry him to the red end of hell.

The young man of Beritania Street fell upon his knees. 'For God's sake buy it!' he cried. 'You can have all my fortune in the bargain. I was mad when I bought it at that price. I had embezzled money at my store; I was lost else; I must have gone to jail.'

'Poor creature,' said Keawe, 'you would risk your soul upon so desperate an adventure, and to avoid the proper punishment of your own disgrace; and you think I could hesitate with love in front of me. Give me the bottle, and the change which I make sure you have all ready. Here is a five-cent piece.'

It was as Keawe supposed; the young man had the change ready in a drawer; the bottle changed hands, and Keawe's fingers were no sooner clasped upon the stalk than he had breathed his wish to be a clean man. And, sure enough, when he got home to his room, and stripped himself before a glass, his flesh was whole like an infant's. And here was the strange thing: he had no sooner seen this miracle, than his mind was changed within him, and he cared naught for the Chinese Evil, and little enough for Kokua; and had but the one thought, that here he was bound to the bottle imp for time and for eternity, and had no better hope but to be a cinder for ever in the flames of hell. Away ahead of him he saw them blaze with his mind's eye, and his soul shrank, and darkness fell upon the light.

When Keawe came to himself a little, he was aware it was the night when the band played at the hotel. Thither he went, because he feared to be alone; and there, among happy faces, walked to and fro, and heard the tunes go up and down, and saw Berger beat the measure, and all the while he heard the flames crackle, and saw the red fire burning in the bottomless pit. Of a sudden the band played *Hiki-ao-ao*; that was a song that he had sung with Kokua, and at the strain courage returned to him.

'It is done now,' he thought, 'and once more let me take the good along with the evil.'

So it befell that he returned to Hawaii by the first steamer, and as soon as it could be managed he was wedded to Kokua, and carried her up the mountain side to the Bright House.

Now it was so with these two, that when they were together, Keawe's heart was stilled; but so soon as he was alone he fell into a brooding horror, and heard the flames crackle, and saw the red fire burn in the bottomless pit. The girl, indeed, had come to him wholly; her heart leapt in her side at sight of him, her hand clung to his; and she was so fashioned from the hair upon her head to the nails upon her toes that none could see her without joy. She was pleasant in her nature. She had the good word always. Full of song she was, and went to and fro in the Bright House, the brightest thing in its three storeys, carolling like the birds. And Keawe beheld and heard her with delight, and then must shrink upon one side, and weep and groan to think upon the price that he had paid for her; and then he must dry his eyes, and wash his face, and go and sit with her on the broad balconies, joining in her songs, and, with a sick spirit, answering her smiles.

There came a day when her feet began to be heavy and her songs more rare; and now it was not Keawe only that would weep apart, but each would sunder from the other and sit in opposite balconies with the whole width of the Bright House betwixt. Keawe was so sunk in his despair, he scarce observed the change, and was only glad he had more hours to sit alone and brood upon his destiny, and was not so frequently condemned to pull a smiling face on a sick heart. But one day, coming softly through the house, he heard the sound of a child sobbing, and there was Kokua rolling her face upon the balcony floor, and weeping like the lost.

'You do well to weep in this house, Kokua,' he said. 'And

yet I would give the head off my body that you (at least) might have been happy.'

'Happy!' she cried. 'Keawe, when you lived alone in your Bright House, you were the word of the island for a happy man; laughter and song were in your mouth, and your face was as bright as the sunrise. Then you wedded poor Kokua; and the good God knows what is amiss in her – but from that day you have not smiled. Oh!' she cried, 'what ails me? I thought I was pretty, and I knew I loved him. What ails me that I throw this cloud upon my husband?'

'Poor Kokua,' said Keawe. He sat down by her side, and sought to take her hand; but that she plucked away. 'Poor Kokua,' he said, again. 'My poor child – my pretty. And I had thought all this while to spare you! Well, you shall know all. Then, at least, you will pity poor Keawe; then you will understand how much he loved you in the past – that he dared hell for your possession – and how much he loves you still (the poor condemned one), that he can yet call up a smile when he beholds you.'

With that, he told her all, even from the beginning.

'You have done this for me?' she cried. 'Ah, well, then what do I care!' – and she clasped and wept upon him.

'Ah, child!' said Keawe, 'and yet, when I consider of the fire of hell, I care a good deal!'

'Never tell me,' said she; 'no man can be lost because he loved Kokua, and no other fault. I tell you, Keawe, I shall save you with these hands, or perish in your company. What! you loved me and gave your soul, and you think I will not die to save you in return?'

'Ah, my dear! you might die a hundred times, and what difference would that make?' he cried, 'except to leave me lonely till the time comes of my damnation?'

'You know nothing,' said she. 'I was educated in a school

in Honolulu; I am no common girl. And I tell you, I shall save my lover. What is this you say about a cent? But all the world is not American. In England they have a piece they call a farthing, which is about half a cent. Ah! sorrow!' she cried, 'that makes it scarcely better, for the buyer must be lost, and we shall find none so brave as my Keawe! But, then, there is France; they have a small coin there which they call a centime, and these go five to the cent or thereabout. We could not do better. Come, Keawe, let us go to the French islands; let us go to Tahiti, as fast as ships can bear us. There we have four centimes, three centimes, two centimes, one centime; four possible sales to come and go on; and two of us to push the bargain. Come, my Keawe! kiss me, and banish care. Kokua will defend you.'

'Gift of God!' he cried. 'I cannot think that God will punish me for desiring aught so good! Be it as you will, then; take me where you please: I put my life and my salvation in your hands.'

Early the next day Kokua was about her preparations. She took Keawe's chest that he went with sailoring; and first she put the bottle in a corner; and then packed it with the richest of their clothes and the bravest of the knick-knacks in the house. 'For,' said she, 'we must seem to be rich folks, or who will believe in the bottle?' All the time of her preparation she was as gay as a bird; only when she looked upon Keawe, the tears would spring in her eye, and she must run and kiss him. As for Keawe, a weight was off his soul; now that he had his secret shared, and some hope in front of him, he seemed like a new man, his feet went lightly on the earth, and his breath was good to him again. Yet was terror still at his elbow; and ever and again, as the wind blows out a taper, hope died in him, and he saw the flames toss and the red fire burn in hell.

It was given out in the country they were gone pleasuring

to the States, which was thought a strange thing, and yet not so strange as the truth, if any could have guessed it. So they went to Honolulu in the *Hall*, and thence in the *Umatilla* to San Francisco with a crowd of Haoles, and at San Francisco took their passage by the mail brigantine, the *Tropic Bird*, for Papeete, the chief place of the French in the south islands. Thither they came, after a pleasant voyage, on a fair day of the Trade Wind, and saw the reef with the surf breaking, and Motuiti with its palms, and the schooner riding within-side, and the white houses of the town low down along the shore among green trees, and overhead the mountains and the clouds of Tahiti, the wise island.

It was judged the most wise to hire a house, which they did accordingly, opposite the British Consul's, to make a great parade of money, and themselves conspicuous with carriages and horses. This it was very easy to do, so long as they had the bottle in their possession; for Kokua was more bold than Keawe, and, whenever she had a mind, called on the imp for twenty or a hundred dollars. At this rate they soon grew to be remarked in the town; and the strangers from Hawaii, their riding and their driving, the fine holokus and the rich lace of Kokua, became the matter of much talk.

They got on well after the first with the Tahitian language, which is indeed like to the Hawaiian, with a change of certain letters; and as soon as they had any freedom of speech, began to push the bottle. You are to consider it was not an easy subject to introduce; it was not easy to persuade people you were in earnest, when you offered to sell them for four centimes the spring of health and riches inexhaustible. It was necessary besides to explain the dangers of the bottle; and either people disbelieved the whole thing and laughed, or they thought the more of the darker part, became overcast with gravity, and drew away from Keawe and Kokua, as from persons who had dealings with the devil. So far from gaining ground, these two began to find they were avoided in the town; the children ran away from them screaming, a thing intolerable to Kokua; Catholics crossed themselves as they went by; and all persons began with one accord to disengage themselves from their advances.

Depression fell upon their spirits. They would sit at night in their new house, after a day's weariness, and not exchange one word, or the silence would be broken by Kokua bursting suddenly into sobs. Sometimes they would pray together; sometimes they would have the bottle out upon the floor, and sit all evening watching how the shadow hovered in the midst. At such times they would be afraid to go to rest. It was long ere slumber came to them, and, if either dozed off, it would be to wake and find the other silently weeping in the dark, or, perhaps, to wake alone, the other having fled from the house and the neighbourhood of that bottle, to pace under the bananas in the little garden, or to wander on the beach by moonlight.

One night it was so when Kokua awoke. Keawe was gone. She felt in the bed and his place was cold. Then fear fell upon her, and she sat up in bed. A little moonshine filtered through the shutters. The room was bright, and she could spy the bottle on the floor. Outside it blew high, the great trees of the avenue cried aloud, and the fallen leaves rattled in the verandah. In the midst of this Kokua was aware of another sound; whether of a beast or of a man she could scarce tell, but it was as sad as death, and cut her to the soul. Softly she arose, set the door ajar, and looked forth into the moonlit yard. There, under the bananas, lay Keawe, his mouth in the dust, and as he lay he moaned.

It was Kokua's first thought to run forward and console him; her second potently withheld her. Keawe had borne

144

himself before his wife like a brave man; it became her little in the hour of weakness to intrude upon his shame. With the thought she drew back into the house.

'Heaven!' she thought, 'how careless have I been – how weak! It is he, not I, that stands in this eternal peril; it was he, not I, that took the curse upon his soul. It is for my sake, and for the love of a creature of so little worth and such poor help, that he now beholds so close to him the flames of hell – ay, and smells the smoke of it, lying without there in the wind and moonlight. Am I so dull of spirit that never till now I have surmised my duty, or have I seen it before and turned aside? But now, at least, I take up my soul in both the hands of my affection; now I say farewell to the white steps of heaven and the waiting faces of my friends. A love for a love, and let mine be equalled with Keawe's! A soul for a soul, and be it mine to perish!'

She was a deft woman with her hands, and was soon apparelled. She took in her hands the change – the precious centimes they kept ever at their side, for this coin is little used, and they had made provision at a Government office. When she was forth in the avenue clouds came on the wind, and the moon was blackened. The town slept, and she knew not whither to turn till she heard one coughing in the shadow of the trees.

'Old man,' said Kokua, 'what do you here abroad in the cold night?'

The old man could scarce express himself for coughing, but she made out that he was old and poor, and a stranger in the island.

'Will you do me a service?' said Kokua. 'As one stranger to another, and as an old man to a young woman, will you help a daughter of Hawaii?'

'Ah,' said the old man. 'So you are the witch from the eight islands, and even my old soul you seek to entangle. But I have heard of you, and defy your wickedness.'

'Sit down here,' said Kokua, 'and let me tell you a tale.' And she told him the story of Keawe from the beginning to the end.

'And now,' said she, 'I am his wife, whom he bought with his soul's welfare. And what should I do? If I went to him myself and offered to buy it, he would refuse. But if you go, he will sell it eagerly; I will await you here; you will buy it for four centimes, and I will buy it again for three. And the Lord strengthen a poor girl!'

'If you meant falsely,' said the old man, 'I think God would strike you dead.'

'He would!' cried Kokua. 'Be sure he would. I could not be so treacherous – God would not suffer it.'

'Give me the four centimes and await me here,' said the old man.

Now, when Kokua stood alone in the street, her spirit died. The wind roared in the trees, and it seemed to her the rushing of the flames of hell; the shadows tossed in the light of the streetlamp, and they seemed to her the snatching hands of evil ones. If she had had the strength, she must have run away, and if she had had the breath she must have screamed aloud; but, in truth, she could do neither, and stood and trembled in the avenue, like an affrighted child.

Then she saw the old man returning, and he had the bottle in his hand.

'I have done your bidding,' said he, 'I left your husband weeping like a child; tonight he will sleep easy.' And he held the bottle forth.

'Before you give it me,' Kokua panted, 'take the good with the evil – ask to be delivered from your cough.'

'I am an old man,' replied the other, 'and too near the gate of the grave to take a favour from the devil. But what is this? Why do you not take the bottle? Do you hesitate?'

'Not hesitate!' cried Kokua. 'I am only weak. Give me a moment. It is my hand resists, my flesh shrinks back from the accursed thing. One moment only!'

The old man looked upon Kokua kindly. 'Poor child!' said he, 'you fear; your soul misgives you. Well, let me keep it. I am old, and can never more be happy in this world, and as for the next—'

'Give it me!' gasped Kokua. 'There is your money. Do you think I am so base as that? Give me the bottle.'

'God bless you, child,' said the old man.

Kokua concealed the bottle under her holoku, said farewell to the old man, and walked off along the avenue, she cared not whither. For all roads were now the same to her, and led equally to hell. Sometimes she walked, and sometimes ran; sometimes she screamed out loud in the night, and sometimes lay by the wayside in the dust and wept. All that she had heard of hell came back to her; she saw the flames blaze, and she smelt the smoke, and her flesh withered on the coals.

Near day she came to her mind again, and returned to the house. It was even as the old man said – Keawe slumbered like a child. Kokua stood and gazed upon his face.

'Now, my husband,' said she, 'it is your turn to sleep. When you wake it will be your turn to sing and laugh. But for poor Kokua, alas! that meant no evil – for poor Kokua no more sleep, no more singing, no more delight, whether in earth or heaven.'

With that she lay down in the bed by his side, and her misery was so extreme that she fell in a deep slumber instantly.

Late in the morning her husband woke her and gave her

the good news. It seemed he was silly with delight, for he paid no heed to her distress, ill though she dissembled it. The words stuck in her mouth, it mattered not; Keawe did the speaking. She ate not a bite, but who was to observe it? for Keawe cleared the dish. Kokua saw and heard him, like some strange thing in a dream; there were times when she forgot or doubted, and put her hands to her brow; to know herself doomed and hear her husband babble, seemed so monstrous.

All the while Keawe was eating and talking, and planning the time of their return, and thanking her for saving him, and fondling her, and calling her the true helper after all. He laughed at the old man that was fool enough to buy that bottle.

'A worthy old man he seemed,' Keawe said. 'But no one can judge by appearances. For why did the old reprobate require the bottle?'

'My husband,' said Kokua, humbly, 'his purpose may have been good.'

Keawe laughed like an angry man.

'Fiddle-de-dee!' cried Keawe. 'An old rogue, I tell you; and an old ass to boot. For the bottle was hard enough to sell at four centimes; and at three it will be quite impossible. The margin is not broad enough, the thing begins to smell of scorching – brr!' said he, and shuddered. 'It is true I bought it myself at a cent, when I knew not there were smaller coins. I was a fool for my pains; there will never be found another: and whoever has that bottle now will carry it to the pit.'

'O my husband!' said Kokua. 'Is it not a terrible thing to save oneself by the eternal ruin of another? It seems to me that I could not laugh. I would be humbled. I would be filled with melancholy. I would pray for the poor holder.'

Then Keawe, because he felt the truth of what she said, grew the more angry. 'Heighty-teighty!' cried he. 'You may be filled with melancholy if you please. It is not the mind of a good wife. If you thought at all of me, you would sit shamed.'

Thereupon he went out, and Kokua was alone.

What chance had she to sell that bottle at two centimes? None, she perceived. And if she had any, here was her husband hurrying her away to a country where there was nothing lower than a cent. And here – on the morrow of her sacrifice – was her husband leaving her and blaming her.

She would not even try to profit by what time she had, but sat in the house, and now had the bottle out and viewed it with unutterable fear, and now, with loathing, hid it out of sight.

By and by, Keawe came back, and would have her take a drive.

'My husband, I am ill,' she said. 'I am out of heart. Excuse me, I can take no pleasure.'

Then was Keawe more wroth than ever. With her, because he thought she was brooding over the case of the old man; and with himself, because he thought she was right, and was ashamed to be so happy.

'This is your truth,' cried he, 'and this your affection! Your husband is just saved from eternal ruin, which he encountered for the love of you – and you can take no pleasure! Kokua, you have a disloyal heart.'

He went forth again furious, and wandered in the town all day. He met friends, and drank with them; they hired a carriage and drove into the country, and there drank again. All the time Keawe was ill at ease, because he was taking this pastime while his wife was sad, and because he knew in his heart that she was more right than he; and the knowledge made him drink the deeper.

Now there was an old brutal Haole drinking with him,

149

one that had been a boatswain of a whaler, a runaway, a digger in gold mines, a convict in prisons. He had a low mind and a foul mouth; he loved to drink and to see others drunken; and he pressed the glass upon Keawe. Soon there was no more money in the company.

'Here, you!' says the boatswain, 'you are rich, you have been always saying. You have a bottle or some foolishness.'

'Yes,' says Keawe, 'I am rich; I will go back and get some money from my wife, who keeps it.'

'That's a bad idea, mate,' said the boatswain. 'Never you trust a petticoat with dollars. They're all as false as water; you keep an eye on her.'

Now, this word struck in Keawe's mind; for he was muddled with what he had been drinking.

'I should not wonder but she was false, indeed,' thought he. 'Why else should she be so cast down at my release? But I will show her I am not the man to be fooled. I will catch her in the act.'

Accordingly, when they were back in town, Keawe bade the boatswain wait for him at the corner, by the old calaboose, and went forward up the avenue alone to the door of his house. The night had come again; there was a light within, but never a sound; and Keawe crept about the corner, opened the back door softly, and looked in.

There was Kokua on the floor, the lamp at her side; before her was a milk-white bottle, with a round belly and a long neck; and as she viewed it, Kokua wrung her hands.

A long time Keawe stood and looked in the doorway. At first he was struck stupid; and then fear fell upon him that the bargain had been made amiss, and the bottle had come back to him as it came at San Francisco; and at that his knees were loosened, and the fumes of the wine departed from his head like mists off a river in the morning. And then he had another thought; and it was a strange one, that made his cheeks to burn.

'I must make sure of this,' thought he.

So he closed the door, and went softly round the corner again, and then came noisily in, as though he were but now returned. And, lo! by the time he opened the front door no bottle was to be seen; and Kokua sat in a chair and started up like one awakened out of sleep.

'I have been drinking all day and making merry,' said Keawe. 'I have been with good companions, and now I only come back for money, and return to drink and carouse with them again.'

Both his face and voice were as stern as judgment, but Kokua was too troubled to observe.

'You do well to use your own, my husband,' said she, and her words trembled.

'O, I do well in all things,' said Keawe, and he went straight to the chest and took out money. But he looked besides in the corner where they kept the bottle, and there was no bottle there.

At that the chest heaved upon the floor like a sea-billow, and the house span about him like a wreath of smoke, for he saw he was lost now, and there was no escape. 'It is what I feared,' he thought. 'It is she who has bought it.'

And then he came to himself a little and rose up; but the sweat streamed on his face as thick as the rain and as cold as the well-water.

'Kokua,' said he, 'I said to you today what ill became me. Now I return to carouse with my jolly companions,' and at that he laughed a little quietly. 'I will take more pleasure in the cup if you forgive me.'

She clasped his knees in a moment; she kissed his knees with flowing tears.

'O,' she cried, 'I asked but a kind word!'

'Let us never one think hardly of the other,' said Keawe, and was gone out of the house.

Now, the money that Keawe had taken was only some of that store of centime pieces they had laid in at their arrival. It was very sure he had no mind to be drinking. His wife had given her soul for him, now he must give his for hers; no other thought was in the world with him.

At the corner, by the old calaboose, there was the boatswain waiting.

'My wife has the bottle,' said Keawe, 'and, unless you help me to recover it, there can be no more money and no more liquor tonight.'

'You do not mean to say you are serious about that bottle?' cried the boatswain.

'There is the lamp,' said Keawe. 'Do I look as if I was jesting?'

'That is so,' said the boatswain. 'You look as serious as a ghost.'

'Well, then,' said Keawe, 'here are two centimes; you must go to my wife in the house, and offer her these for the bottle, which (if I am not much mistaken) she will give you instantly. Bring it to me here, and I will buy it back from you for one; for that is the law with this bottle, that it still must be sold for a less sum. But whatever you do, never breathe a word to her that you have come from me.'

'Mate, I wonder are you making a fool of me?' asked the boatswain.

'It will do you no harm if I am,' returned Keawe.

'That is so, mate,' said the boatswain.

'And if you doubt me,' added Keawe, 'you can try. As soon as you are clear of the house, wish to have your pocket full of money, or a bottle of the best rum, or what you please, and you will see the virtue of the thing.'

'Very well, Kanaka,' says the boatswain. 'I will try; but if you are having your fun out of me, I will take my fun out of you with a belaying pin.'

So the whaler-man went off up the avenue; and Keawe stood and waited. It was near the same spot where Kokua had waited the night before; but Keawe was more resolved, and never faltered in his purpose; only his soul was bitter with despair.

It seemed a long time he had to wait before he heard a voice singing in the darkness of the avenue. He knew the voice to be the boatswain's; but it was strange how drunken it appeared upon a sudden.

Next, the man himself came stumbling into the light of the lamp. He had the devil's bottle buttoned in his coat; another bottle was in his hand; and even as he came in view he raised it to his mouth and drank.

'You have it,' said Keawe. 'I see that.'

'Hands off!' cried the boatswain, jumping back. 'Take a step near me, and I'll smash your mouth. You thought you could make a cat's-paw of me, did you?'

'What do you mean?' cried Keawe.

'Mean?' cried the boatswain. 'This is a pretty good bottle, this is; that's what I mean. How I got it for two centimes I can't make out; but I'm sure you shan't have it for one.'

'You mean you won't sell?' gasped Keawe.

'No, *sir*!' cried the boatswain. 'But I'll give you a drink of the rum, if you like.'

'I tell you,' said Keawe, 'the man who has that bottle goes to hell.'

'I reckon I'm going anyway,' returned the sailor; 'and this

bottle's the best thing to go with I've struck yet. No, sir!' he cried again, 'this is my bottle now, and you can go and fish for another.'

'Can this be true?' Keawe cried. 'For your own sake, I beseech you, sell it me!'

'I don't value any of your talk,' replied the boatswain. 'You thought I was a liar; now you see I'm not; and there's an end. If you won't have a swallow of the rum, I'll have one myself. Here's your health, and good-night to you!'

So off he went down the avenue towards town, and there goes the bottle out of the story.

But Keawe ran to Kokua light as the wind; and great was their joy that night; and great, since then, has been the peace of all their days in the Bright House.

WILLIAM MAXWELL

THE INDUSTRIOUS
TAILOR

ONCE UPON A TIME, in the west of England, there was an industrious tailor who was always sitting cross-legged, plying his needle, when the sun came up over the hill, and all day long he drove himself, as if he were beating a donkey with a stick. 'I am almost through cutting out this velvet waistcoat,' he would tell himself, 'and when I am through cutting the velvet, I will cut the yellow satin lining. And then there is the buckram, and the collar and cuffs. The cuffs are to be thirteen inches wide, tapering to ten and a half – his lordship was very particular about that detail – and faced with satin. The basting should take me into the afternoon, and if all goes well, and I don't see why it shouldn't, I ought to be able to do all twenty-seven buttonholes before the light gives out.'

When snow lay deep on the ground and the sheep stayed in their pens, the shepherd came down to the tavern and in the conviviality he found there made up for the months of solitude on the moors. During the early part of the summer, when it was not yet time for anybody to be bringing wheat, barley, and rye to the mill to be ground into flour, the miller got out his hook and line and went fishing. In one way or another, everyone had some time that he called his own. On the first of May, lads and lasses went into the wood just before daybreak and came back wearing garlands of flowers and with their arms around each other. From his window the tailor saw them setting up the Maypole, but he did not lay aside his needle and thread to go join in the dancing. It is true that he was no longer young and, with his bald head and his bent back and his solemn manner, would have looked odd dancing around a Maypole, but that did not deter the miller's wife, who weighed seventeen stone and was as light on her feet as a fairy and didn't care who laughed at her as long as she was enjoying herself.

When the industrious tailor came to the end of all the work that he could expect for a while and his worktable was quite bare, he looked around for some lily that needed gilding. Sorting his pins, sharpening his scissors, and rearranging his patterns, he congratulated himself on keeping busy, though he might just as well have been sitting in his doorway enjoying the sun, for his scissors didn't need sharpening, and his patterns were not in disorder, and a pin is a pin, no matter what tray you put it in.

As with all of us, the tailor's upbringing had a good deal to do with the way he behaved. At the age of eight, he was apprenticed to his father, who was a master tailor and not only knew all there is to know about making clothes but also was full of native wisdom. While the boy was learning to sew a straight seam and how to cut cloth on the diagonal and that sort of thing, the father would from time to time raise his right hand, with the needle and thread in it, and, looking at the boy over the top of his spectacles, say 'A stitch in time saves nine,' or 'Waste makes want,' or some other bit of advice, which the boy took to his bosom and cherished. And he had never forgotten a wonderful story his father told about an ant and a grasshopper. Of all his father's sayings, the one that made the deepest impression on him was 'Never put off till tomorrow what you can do today,' though as a rule the industrious tailor had already done it yesterday and was hard at work on something that did not need to be done until the day after.

*   *   *

What is true of the day after tomorrow is equally true of the day after that, and the day after that, and the day after that, and so on, and in time a very curious thing happened. There was the past – there is always the past – and it was full of accomplishment, of things done well before they needed to be done, and the tailor regarded it with satisfaction. And there was the future, when things would have to be done, and bills would have to be made out and respectfully submitted and paid or not paid, as the case might be, and new work would be ordered, and so on. But it was never right now. The present had ceased to exist. When the industrious tailor looked out of the window and saw that it was raining, it was not raining today but on a day in the middle of next week, or the week after that, if he was that far ahead of himself, and he often was. You would have thought that he would sooner or later have realized that the time he was spending so freely was next month's, and that if he had already lived through the days of this month before it was well begun he was living beyond his means. But what is 'already'? What is 'now'? The words had lost their meaning. And this was not as serious as it sounds, because words are, after all, only words. 'I could kill you for doing that,' a man says to his wife and then they both cheerfully sit down to dinner. And many people live entirely in the past, without even noticing it. One day the tailor pushed his glasses up on his forehead and saw that he was in the middle of a lonely wood. He rubbed his poor tired eyes, but the trees didn't go away. He looked all around. No scissors and pins, no bolts of material, no patterns, no worktable, no shop. Only the needle and thread he had been sewing with. He listened anxiously. He had never been in a wood before. 'Wife?' he called out, but there was no answer.

159

He knew that it was late afternoon, and that he ought to get out of the wood before dark, so he stuck the needle in his vest and started walking along a path that constantly threatened to disappear, the way paths do in the wood. Sometimes the path divided, and he had to choose between the right and the left fork, without knowing which was the way that led out of the wood. The light began to fail even sooner than he had expected. When it was still daytime in the sky overhead, it was already so dark where he was that he could find the path only by the feel of the ground under his feet.

'I don't see why this should happen to me,' he said, and from the depths of the wood a voice said 'To *who?*' disconcertingly, but it was only an owl. So he kept on until he saw a light through the trees, and he made his way to it, through the underbrush and around fallen logs, until he came to a house in a clearing. At this time of night they'll be easily frightened, he thought. I must speak carefully or they'll close the door in my face. When the door opened in answer to his knock and a woman stood looking out at him from the lighted doorway, he said politely, 'It's all right, ma'am, I'm not a robber.'

'No,' the woman said, 'you're an industrious tailor.'

'Now, how did you know that?' he asked in amazement.

The woman did not seem to feel that this question needed answering, and there was something about her that made him uneasy, and so, though he would much rather that she invited him in and gave him a place by the fire and a bit of supper, he said, 'If you would be kind enough to show me the way out of the wood—'

'I don't know that I can,' the woman said.

'Isn't there a road of some kind?'

'There's a road,' the woman said doubtfully, 'but it wasn't built in your lifetime.'

'I beg pardon?'

'And anyway, you'd soon lose it in the dark. You'll have to wait until morning. How did you happen to—'

At that point a baby began to cry, and the woman said, 'I can't stand here talking. Come in.'

'Thank you,' he said. 'That's very kind of you, ma'am,' and as he stepped across the threshold there was suddenly no house, no lighted room, no woman. Nothing but a clearing in the wood.

In disappointment so acute that it brought tears to his eyes, he sat down on the ground and tucked his legs under him and tried to get used to the idea that he wasn't going to sit by a warm fire, under a snug roof, with a bit of supper by and by, and a place to lay his head at bedtime.

I will catch my death of pneumonia, he thought. He put his hand to his vest; the needle was still there. He felt his forehead, and then took his glasses off, folded them carefully, and put them in his vest pocket. Then he stretched out on the bare ground and, looking up through the trees, thought about his tailor shop, and about a greatcoat that he was working on. It was of French blue, part true cashmere and part Lincoln wool, with a three-tiered cape, and it wasn't promised until a fortnight, but he would have finished it and have given it to his wife to press if he hadn't suddenly found himself in this lonely wood. Then he thought about his wife, who would be wondering why he didn't come upstairs for his supper. And then about his father, who had a stroke and never recovered the use of his limbs or his speech. In the evening, after the day was over, the industrious tailor used to come and sit by his father's bed, and he would bring whatever he was working on – a waistcoat or a pair of knee breeches, or an embroidered vest – and spread it out on the counterpane, to show his father that the lessons had been well learned and that he needn't worry about the quality of work being turned out by the shop. And instead of being pleased with him, his father would push the work aside impatiently. There seemed to be something on his mind that he very much wanted to say, some final piece of wisdom, but when he tried to speak he could only utter meaningless sounds.

Now, through the tops of the bare trees, the tailor could see the stars, so bright and so far away . . . But how did it get to be autumn, he wondered. And why am I not cold? Why am I not hungry? He fell asleep and dreamed that he had more work to do than he could possibly manage, and woke up with the sun shining in his face.

'Wife?' he called out, before he remembered where he was or what had happened to him.

He sat up and looked around. There was no house in the clearing, and no sign that there ever had been, but there was a path leading off through the woods, and he followed it. At this time, more than half of England was forests, and so he knew that it might be days before he found his way out of the wood. 'I must be careful not to walk in a circle,' he told himself. 'That's what people always do when they are lost.' But one fallen tree, one sapling, one patch of dried fern, one bed of moss looked just like another, and he could not tell whether he was walking in a circle or not. Now and then, not far from the path, there would be a sudden dry rustle that made his heart race. Was it a poisonous viper? What was it? The rustle did not explain itself. Oddly enough, he himself, stepping on dry leaves and twigs, did not make a sound.

'I ought to be living on roots and berries,' he said to himself, and though there were plenty of both, he did not know which were edible and which were not, and he did not feel inclined to experiment. But when he came to a spring, he thought, I will drink, because this far from any house or pasture it cannot be contaminated. . . . He knelt down and put his face to the water and nothing happened. His throat was as dry as before. The water remained just out of reach. He leaned farther forward and again nothing happened. The water kept receding until his face touched dry gravel. He raised his head in surprise and there was the beautiful spring, glittering, jewel-like in the sunlight, pushing its way under logs and between boulders, murmuring as it went, but not to be drunk from. 'Can it be that I am dead?' the tailor asked himself. And then, 'If I am dead, why has nobody told me where to go, or what's expected of me?'

As he walked on, he tried to remember if in the old days, before he suddenly found himself in this wood, he had ever got down on his hands and knees to drink from a spring. All he remembered was that when the other boys were roaming the woods and bathing in the river, he was in his father's shop learning to be a master tailor.

'It is possible that I am dreaming,' he said to himself. But it did not seem like a dream. In dreams it is always – not twilight exactly, but the light is peculiar, comes from nowhere, and is never very bright. This was a blindingly beautiful sunny day.

'At all events,' he said to himself, 'I am a much better walker than I had any idea. I have been walking for hours and I don't feel in the least tired. And even if it should turn out that I have been walking in a circle—'

At that moment he saw, ahead of him, what seemed like a thinning out of trees, as if he was coming to the edge of the wood. It proved to be a small clearing with a house in it. Smoke was rising from the chimney, and as the tailor came nearer an unpleasant suspicion crossed his mind.

'Oh, it's you,' the woman said, when she opened the door and saw him standing there. She had a baby in her arms, and she didn't look particularly pleased to see him, or concerned that he had passed the whole night on the bare ground and the whole day walking in a circle.

'I'm sorry to trouble you, ma'am,' he said, 'but if you will be so kind as to show me that road you were speaking of—'

The baby began to fret, and the woman jounced it lightly on her shoulder. 'As you can see, I'm busy,' she said. 'And I don't see how you got here in the first place.'

'Neither do I,' he said.

'Did you come on a spring anywhere in the wood?'

He nodded.

'And did you drink from it?'

'I couldn't,' he said. 'When I put my face to the water, there wasn't any.'

'I'm afraid there's nothing I can do,' the woman said, and he saw that she was about to close the door in his face.

'Please, ma'am,' he said, 'if you'll just show me where that road begins I won't trouble you any further, I promise you.'

'Why you had to come today of all days, when the baby's cutting a tooth, and the fire in the stove has gone out, and I still have to do the churning. . . . You haven't murdered some-body? No, I can see you haven't. If the police are after you—'

'The police are not after me,' the tailor said with dignity, 'and I haven't committed any crime that I know of.'

'Well, that doesn't mean anything,' the woman said. 'Come, let me show you the road.'

He followed her across the clearing, and when she stopped they were standing in front of a clump of white birch trees. Beyond it the tangled underbrush began, and the big trees.

'I don't see any road,' the tailor said.

'That's what I mean,' the woman said. She stood looking at him and frowning thoughtfully.

'Even if there was only a path—' the tailor began, and the woman said, 'Oh, be quiet. If I let you go off into the woods again, you'll only end up here the way you did before. And I can't ask you into the house, because— Have you ever held a baby?'

'Oh, yes,' the tailor said. 'My children are grown now, but when they were little I often held them while my wife was busy doing something.'

As he was speaking, the woman put the baby in his arms. The baby turned its head on its weak neck and looked at him. Though the woman made him uneasy, the baby did not. The baby's face contorted, and he saw that it was about to cry. 'Hush-a,' he said, and jounced it gently against his shoulder, and felt the head wobble against his neck, and the down on the baby's head, softer than any material in his shop.

'This may not work,' the woman said, and started back across the clearing, and he followed her, still holding the baby.

At the door of the house she took a firm grip on the hem of the baby's garment and then she said, 'Go in, go in,' and after a last look over his shoulder at the clearing in the wood he stepped across the threshold, expecting to find himself outside again, and instead he was in his own shop, sitting cross-legged on his worktable.

He listened and heard the twittering of birds as they flitted from branch to branch in the elm tree outside, and then the miller's wife, laughing at some joke she had just made. He saw by the quality of the light outside that it was only the middle of the afternoon. A wagon came by, and the miller's wife called to whoever was in the wagon, and a man's voice said, 'Whoa, there … Whoa … Whoa.' The tailor listened with rapt attention to the conversation that followed, though he had heard it a hundred times. Or conversations just like it. All around him on the worktable were scraps of French-blue material, and he could see at a glance what was waiting to be stitched to what. Finally the man said, 'That's rich! That's a good one. Gee-up . . .' and the wheels turned again, and the slow plodding was resumed and grew fainter and was replaced by the sound of a child beating on a tin pan. The miller's wife went home, but there were other sounds – a dog, a door slamming, a child being scolded. Then it was quiet for a time, and without thinking the tailor put his hand to his vest and found the needle. Two boys went by, saying, 'I dare you to do it, I dare you, I double-dare you!' Do what, the tailor wondered, and went on sewing.

The quiet and the outbreaks of sound alternated in a way that was so regular that it almost seemed planned. A loud noise, such as a crow going caw, caw, caw, seemed to produce a deeper silence afterward. He studied the beautiful sound of footsteps approaching and receding, so like a piece of music.

The light began to fail and he hardly noticed it, because as the light went it was accompanied by all the sounds that mean the end of the day: men coming home from the fields, shops being closed, children being called in before dark.

When the tailor could not see any longer, he put his work aside and sat, listening and smiling to himself at what he heard, until his wife called him to supper.

VLADIMIR NABOKOV

THE DRAGON

HE LIVED IN RECLUSION in a deep, murky cave, in the very heart of a rocky mountain, feeding only on bats, rats, and mold. Occasionally, it is true, stalactite hunters or snoopy travelers would come peeking into the cave, and that was a tasty treat. Other pleasant memories included a brigand attempting to flee from justice, and two dogs that were once let loose to ascertain if the passage did not go clear through the mountain. The surrounding country was wild, porous snow lay here and there on the rock, and waterfalls rumbled with an icy roar. He had hatched some thousand years ago, and, perhaps because it had happened rather unexpectedly – the enormous egg was cracked open by a lightning bolt one stormy night – the dragon had turned out cowardly and not overly bright. Besides, he was strongly affected by his mother's death. . . . She had long terrorized the neighboring villages, had spat flames, and the king would get cross, and around her lair incessantly prowled knights, whom she would crunch to pieces like walnuts. But once, when she had swallowed a plump royal chef and dozed off on a sun-warmed rock, the great Ganon himself galloped up in iron armor, on a black steed under silver netting. The poor sleepy thing went rearing up, her green and red humps flashing like bonfires, and the charging knight thrust his swift lance into her smooth white breast. She crashed to the ground, and promptly, out of the pink wound, sidled the corpulent chef with her enormous, steaming heart under his arm.

The young dragon saw all this from a hiding place behind the rock and, forever after, could not think about knights without a shudder. He withdrew into the depths of a cave, whence he never emerged. Thus passed ten centuries, equivalent to twenty dragon years.

Then, suddenly, he fell prey to unbearable melancholy.... In fact, the spoiled food from the cave was provoking ferocious gastric alarms, revolting rumblings, and pain. He spent nine years making up his mind, and on the tenth, he did. Slowly and cautiously, gathering in and extending the rings of his tail, he clambered out of his cave.

Immediately he sensed that it was spring. The black rocks, washed by a recent downpour, were ashimmer; the sunlight boiled in the overflowing mountain torrent; the air was redolent of wild game. And the dragon, broadly inflating his flaming nostrils, started his descent into the valley. His satiny belly, white as a water lily, nearly touched the ground, crimson blotches stood out on his bloated green flanks, and the sturdy scales merged, on his back, into a jagged conflagration, a ridge of double ruddy humps, diminishing in size toward the potently, flexibly twitching tail. His head was smooth and greenish, bubbles of fiery mucus hung from his soft, warty underlip, and his giant, scaly paws left deep tracks, star-shaped concavities.

The first thing he saw upon descending into the valley was a railroad train traveling along rocky slopes. The dragon's first reaction was delight, since he mistook the train for a relative he could play with. Moreover, he thought that beneath that shiny, hard-looking shell there must surely be some tender meat. So he set off in pursuit, his feet slapping with a hollow, damp noise, but, just as he was about to gobble up the last car, the train sped into a tunnel. The dragon stopped, thrust his head into the black lair into which his quarry had vanished, but there was no way he could get in there. He dispatched a couple of torrid sneezes into the depths, then retracted his head, sat on his haunches, and began waiting – who knows, it might come running out again. After waiting some time he shook his head and moved on. At that instant a train did come scurrying out of the dark lair, gave a sly flash of window glass, and disappeared behind a curve. The dragon gave a hurt look over his shoulder and, raising his tail like a plume, resumed his journey.

Dusk was falling. Fog floated above the meadows. The gigantic beast, big as a live mountain, was seen by some homeward-bound peasants, who remained petrified with awe. A little auto speeding along the highway had all four of its tires blow out from fright, bounced, and ended up in the ditch. But the dragon walked on, noticing nothing; from afar came the hot scent of concentrated crowds of humans, and that is where he was headed. And, against the blue expanse of the night sky, there loomed before him black factory smokestacks, guardians of a large industrial town.

The main personages of this town were two: the owner of the Miracle Tobacco Company and that of the Big Helmet Tobacco Company. Between them raged age-old, subtle hostilities, about which one could write an entire epic poem. They were rivals in everything – the motley colors of their advertisements, their distribution techniques, pricing, and labor relations – but no one could say which had the upper hand. That memorable night, the owner of the Miracle Company stayed very late at his office. Nearby on his desk lay a stack of new, freshly printed advertisements that workmen from the cooperative were to plaster around the city at daybreak.

Suddenly a bell pierced the silence of the night and, a few moments later, entered a pale, haggard man with a burdock-like wart on his right cheek. The factory owner knew him: he was the proprietor of a model tavern the Miracle Company had set up on the outskirts.

'It's going on two in the morning, my friend. The only justification I can find for your visit is an event of unheard-of importance.'

'That's exactly the case,' said the tavern keeper in a calm voice, although his wart was twitching. This is what he reported:

He was bundling off five thoroughly soused old laborers. They must have seen something highly curious outdoors, for they all broke out laughing – 'Oh-ho-ho,' rumbled one of the voices, 'I must have had one glass too many, if I see, big as life, the hydra of counterrevo—'

He did not have time to finish, for there was a surge of terrifying, ponderous noise, and someone screamed. The tavern keeper stepped outside to have a look. A monster, glimmering in the murk like a moist mountain, was swallowing something large with its head thrown back, which made its whitish neck swell with alternating hillocks; it swallowed and licked its chops, its whole body rocked, and it gently lay down in the middle of the street.

'I think it must have dozed off,' finished the tavern keeper, restraining the twitching wart with his finger.

The factory owner got up. The robust fillings of his teeth flashed with the golden fire of inspiration. The arrival of a live dragon aroused in him no other feelings than the passionate desire that guided him in every instance – the desire to inflict a defeat on the rival firm.

'Eureka,' he exclaimed. 'Listen, my good man, are there any other witnesses?'

'I don't think so,' the other replied. 'Everybody was in bed, and I decided not to wake anyone and came straight to you. So as to avoid panic.'

The factory owner donned his hat.

'Splendid. Take this – no, not the whole pile, thirty or forty sheets will do – and bring along this can, and the brush too. There, now show me the way.'

They went out into the dark night and were soon at the quiet street at the end of which, according to the tavern keeper, reposed a monster. First, by the light of a lone, yellow streetlamp, they saw a policeman standing on his head in the middle of the pavement. It turned out later that, while making his nightly rounds, he had come upon the dragon and had such a fright that he turned upside down and remained petrified in that attitude. The factory owner, a man with the size and strength of a gorilla, turned him right side up and leaned him against the lightpost; then he approached the dragon. The dragon was asleep, and no wonder. The individuals he had devoured, it so happened, were totally impregnated with wine, and had popped succulently between his jaws. The alcohol on an empty stomach had gone straight to his head and he had lowered the pellicles of his eyelids with a blissful smile. He lay on his belly with his front paws folded under, and the glow of the streetlamp highlighted the glistening arcs of the double vertebral protuberances.

'Set up the ladder,' said the factory owner. 'I'll do the pasting myself.'

And, choosing flat spots on the slimy green flanks of the monster, he began unhurriedly brushing paste on the scaly skin and affixing ample advertising posters. When he had used all the sheets, he gave the brave tavern keeper a meaningful handshake and, chomping on his cigar, returned home.

Morning came, a magnificent spring morning softened by

a lilac haze. And suddenly the street came alive with a merry, excited din, doors and windows slammed, people poured into the street, mingling with those who were hurrying somewhere, laughing as they went. What they saw was a perfectly lifelike dragon, all covered with colorful advertisements, slapping listlessly along the asphalt. One poster was even stuck to the bald crown of his head. 'SMOKE ONLY MIRACLE BRAND,' rollicked the blue and crimson letters of the ads. 'ONLY FOOLS DON'T SMOKE MY CIGARETTES,' 'MIRACLE TOBACCO TURNS AIR INTO HONEY,' 'MIRACLE, MIRACLE, MIRACLE!'

It really is a miracle, laughed the crowd, and how is it done – is it a machine or are there people inside?

The dragon was feeling rotten after his involuntary binge. The cheap wine now made him sick to his stomach, his whole body felt weak, and the thought of breakfast was out of the question. Besides, he was now overcome by an acute sense of shame, the excruciating shyness of a creature that finds itself amid a crowd for the first time. Frankly speaking, he very much wished to return as soon as possible to his cave, but that would have been even more shameful – therefore, he continued his grim progress through the town. Several men with placards on their backs protected him from the curious and from urchins who wanted to slip under his white belly, clamber onto his lofty backbone, or touch his snout. Music played, people gaped from every window, behind the dragon automobiles drove single file, and in one of them slouched the factory owner, the hero of the day.

The dragon walked without looking at anybody, dismayed by the incomprehensible merriment that he aroused.

Meanwhile, in a sunlit office, along a carpet soft as moss, paced to and fro with clenched fists the rival manufacturer, owner of the Big Helmet Company. At an open window, observing the procession, stood his girlfriend, a diminutive tightrope dancer.

'This is an outrage,' croaked over and again the manufacturer, a middle-aged, bald man with blue-gray bags of flabby skin under his eyes. 'The police ought to put a stop to this scandal. . . . When did he manage to cobble together this stuffed dummy?'

'Ralph,' the dancer suddenly cried, clapping her hands. 'I know what you should do. We have a number at the circus called The Joust, and—'

In a torrid whisper, goggling her doll-like, mascara-lined eyes, she told him her plan. The manufacturer beamed. An instant later he was already on the phone with the circus manager.

'So,' said the manufacturer, hanging up. 'The dummy is made of inflated rubber. We'll see what's left of it if we give it a good prick.'

Meanwhile the dragon had crossed the bridge, passed the marketplace and the Gothic cathedral, which aroused some pretty repugnant memories, continued along the main boulevard, and was traversing a broad square when, parting the crowd, a knight unexpectedly came charging at him. The knight wore iron armor, visor lowered, a funereal plume on his helmet, and rode a ponderous black horse in silvery netting. Arms bearers – women dressed as pages – walked alongside, carrying picturesque, hastily devised banners heralding 'BIG HELMET,' 'SMOKE ONLY BIG HELMET,' 'BIG HELMET BEATS THEM ALL.' The circus rider impersonating the knight spurred his steed and clenched his lance. But the steed for some reason started backing, spurting foam, then suddenly reared up and sat heavily on its haunches. The knight tumbled to the asphalt, with such a clatter one might think someone had thrown all the dishes out the window. But the dragon did not see this. At the knight's first move he had stopped abruptly, then rapidly turned, knocking down a pair of curious old women standing on a balcony with his tail as he did so, and, squashing the scattering spectators, had taken flight. He was out of the town in a single bound, flew across the fields, scrambled up the rocky slopes, and dove into his bottomless cavern. There he collapsed onto his back, paws folded and showing his satiny, white, shuddering belly to the dark vaults, heaved a deep breath, closed his astonished eyes, and died.

GUY DE MAUPASSANT

NIGHT

A NIGHTMARE

Translated by Ernest Boyd

I LOVE NIGHT PASSIONATELY. I love it as one loves one's country or one's mistress. I love it with all my senses, with my eyes which see it, with my sense of smell which inhales it, with my ears which listen to its silence, with my whole body which is caressed by its shadows. The larks sing in the sunlight, in the blue heavens, in the warm air, in the light air of clear mornings. The owl flies at night, a sombre patch passing through black space, and, rejoicing in the black immensity that intoxicates him, he utters a vibrant and sinister cry.

In the day-time I am tired and bored. The day is brutal and noisy. I rarely get up, I dress myself languidly and I go out regretfully. Every movement, every gesture, every word, every thought, tires me as though I were raising a crushing load.

But when the sun goes down a confused joy invades my whole being. I awaken and become animated. As the shadows lengthen I feel quite different, younger, stronger, more lively, happier. I watch the great soft shadows falling from the sky and growing deeper. They envelop the city like an impenetrable and impalpable wave; they hide, efface and destroy colours and forms; they embrace houses, people and buildings in their imperceptible grasp. Then I would like to cry out with joy like the screech-owls, to run upon the roofs like the cats, and an impetuous, invincible desire to love burns in my veins. I go, I walk, sometimes in the darkened outskirts of Paris, sometimes in the neighbouring woods, where I hear my sisters, the beasts, and my brothers, the poachers, prowling.

One is killed at last by what one loves violently. But how shall I explain what happens to me? How can I ever make people understand that I am able to tell it? I do not know, I cannot tell. I only know that this is – that is all.

Well, yesterday – was it yesterday? – Yes, no doubt, unless it was earlier, a day, a month, a year earlier . . . I do not know, but it must have been yesterday, because since then no day has risen, no sun has dawned. But how long has it been night? How long? Who can tell? Who will ever know?

Yesterday, then, I went out after dinner, as I do every evening. It was very fine, very mild, very warm. As I went down towards the boulevards I looked above my head at the black streams full of stars, outlined in the sky between the roofs of the houses, which were turning round and causing this rolling stream of stars to undulate like a real river.

Everything was distinct in the clear air, from the planets to the gas-light. So many lights were burning above, in the city, that the shadows seemed luminous. Bright nights are more joyful than days of bright sunshine. The cafés on the boulevard were flaring; people were laughing, passing up and down, drinking. I went into a theatre for a few moments. Into what theatre, I cannot tell. There was so much light in there that I was depressed, and I came out again with my heart saddened by the clash of brutal light on the gold of the balcony, by the factitious glitter of the great crystal chandelier, by the glaring footlights, by the melancholy of this artificial and crude light. I arrived at the Champs-Élysées, where the open-air concerts look like conflagrations in the branches. The chestnut-trees, touched with yellow light, look as if they were painted, like phosphorescent trees. The electric bulbs, like pale dazzling moons, like eggs from the moon, fallen from heaven, like monstrous, living pearls, caused the streaks of gas-light, filthy, ugly gas-light and the garland of coloured, lighted glasses to grow pale beneath their pearly, mysterious and regal light.

I stopped beneath the Arc de Triomphe to look at the Avenue, the long and wonderful, starry Avenue, leading to Paris between two rows of fire and the stars! The stars above, the unknown stars, thrown haphazard through infinity, where they form those strange shapes which make us dream and think so much.

I entered the Bois de Boulogne, where I remained for a long, long time. I was seized by a strange thrill, a powerful and unforeseen emotion, an exaltation of mind which bordered on frenzy. I walked on and on, and then I returned. What time was it when I passed again beneath the Arc de Triomphe? I do not know. The city was sleeping, and clouds, great black clouds, were slowly spreading over the sky.

For the first time I felt that something strange was going to happen, something new.

It seemed to be getting cold, that the air was becoming thicker, that night, my beloved night, was weighing heavily upon my heart. The Avenue was deserted now. Two solitary policemen were walking near the cab-stand, and a string of vegetable carts was going to the Halles along the roadway, scarcely lit by the gas-jets, which seemed to be dying out. They moved along slowly, laden with carrots, turnips and cabbages. The invisible drivers were asleep, the horses were walking with an even step, following the carts in front of them, and making no noise on the wooden pavement. As they passed each lamp on the footpath, the carrots showed up red in the light, the turnips white, the cabbages green, and they passed one after another, these carts which were as red as fire, as white as silver, and as green as emeralds. I followed them, then I turned into the Rue Royale and returned to the boulevards. There was nobody to be seen, none of the cafés were open; only a few belated pedestrians hurried by. I had never seen Paris so dead and so deserted. I looked at my watch. It was two o'clock.

Some force was driving me, the desire to walk. So I went as far as the Bastille. There I became aware that I had never seen so dark a night, for I could not even see the Colonne de Juillet, whose Genius in gold was lost in the impenetrable obscurity. A curtain of clouds as dense as the ether had buried the stars and seemed to be descending upon the world to blot it out.

I retraced my steps. There was nobody about me. However, at the Place du Château d'Eau, a drunken man almost bumped into me, than disappeared. For some time I could hear his sonorous and uneven steps. I went on. At the top of the Faubourg Montmartre a cab passed, going in the direction of the Seine. I hailed it but the driver did not reply. Near the Rue Drouot a woman was loitering: 'Listen, dearie,' – I hastened my steps to avoid her outstretched hand. Then there was nothing more. In front of the Vaudeville Theatre a rag-picker was searching in the gutter. His little lantern was moving just above the ground. I said to him: 'What time is it, my good man?'

'How do I know?' he grumbled. 'I have no watch.'

Then I suddenly perceived that the lamps had all been extinguished. I know that at this time of year they are put out early, before dawn, for the sake of economy. But daylight was still far off, very far off indeed!

'Let us go to the Halles,' I said to myself; 'there at least I shall find life.'

I set off, but it was too dark even to see the way. I advanced slowly, as one does in a forest, recognizing the streets by counting them. In front of the Crédit Lyonnais a dog growled. I turned up the Rue de Grammont and lost my way. I wandered about, and then I recognized the Bourse by the iron railings around it. The whole of Paris was sleeping, a deep, terrifying sleep. In the distance a cab rumbled, one solitary cab, perhaps it was the one which had passed me a while back. I tried to reach it, going in the direction of the noise, through streets that were lonely and dark, dark and sombre as death. Again I lost my way. Where was I? What nonsense to put out the lights so soon! Not one person passing by. Not one late reveller, not one thief, not even the mewing of an amorous cat? Nothing.

'Where on earth were the police?' I said to myself: 'I will shout and they will come.' I shouted. There was no answer. I called more loudly. My voice vanished without an echo, weak, muffled, stifled by the night, the impenetrable night. I yelled: 'Help! Help! Help!' My desperate cry remained unanswered. What time was it? I pulled out my watch, but I had no matches. I listened to the gentle tick-tick of the little mechanism with a strange and unfamiliar pleasure. It seemed to be a living thing. I felt less lonely. What a mystery! I resumed my walk like a blind man, feeling my way along the wall with my stick, and every moment I raised my eyes to the heavens, hoping that day would dawn at last. But the sky was dark, all dark, more profoundly dark than the city.

What could the time be? It seemed to me I had been walking an infinite length of time, for my legs were giving way beneath me, my breast was heaving and I was suffering horribly from hunger. I decided to ring at the first street door. I pulled the copper bell and it rang sonorously through the house. It sounded strangely, as if that vibrating noise were alone in the house. I waited. There was no answer. The door did not open. I rang again. I waited again – nothing! I got frightened! I ran to the next house, and, twenty times in succession, I rang the bells in the dark corridors where the concierge was supposed to sleep, but he did not awake. I went on further, pulling the bells and the knockers with all my strength, kicking and knocking with my hand and stick on the doors, which remained obstinately closed.

Suddenly I perceived that I had reached the Halles. The market was deserted, not a sound, not a movement, not a cart, not a man, not a bundle of flowers or vegetables – it was empty, motionless, abandoned, dead. I was seized with a horrible terror. What was happening? Oh, my God, what was happening?

I set off again. But the time? The time? Who would tell me the time? Not a clock struck in the churches or the public buildings. I thought: 'I will open the glass of my watch and feel the hands with my fingers.' I pulled out my watch.... It was not going.... It had stopped. Nothing more, nothing more, not a ripple in the city, not a light, not the slightest suspicion of a sound in the air. Nothing! Nothing more! not even the distant rumbling of a cab! Nothing more. I had reached the quays, and a cold chill rose from the river. Was the Seine still flowing? I wanted to know, I found the steps and went down. I could not hear the current rushing under the bridge.... A few more steps.... Then sand.... Mud ... then water. I dipped my hand into it. It was flowing ... flowing ... cold ... cold ... cold ... almost frozen ... almost dried up ... almost dead.

I fully realized that I should never have the strength to come up, and that I was going to die there ... in my turn, of hunger, fatigue and cold.

LORD DUNSANY

WHERE THE TIDES
EBB AND FLOW

I DREAMT THAT I had done a horrible thing, so that burial was to be denied me either in soil or sea, neither could there be any hell for me.

I waited for some hours, knowing this. Then my friends came for me, and slew me secretly and with ancient rite, and lit great tapers, and carried me away.

It was all in London that the thing was done, and they went furtively at dead of night along grey streets and among mean houses until they came to the river. And the river and the tide of the sea were grappling with one another between the mud-banks, and both of them were black and full of lights. A sudden wonder came in to the eyes of each, as my friends came near to them with their glaring tapers. All these things I saw as they carried me dead and stiffening, for my soul was still among my bones, because there was no hell for it, and because Christian burial was denied me.

They took me down a stairway that was green with slimy things, and so came slowly to the terrible mud. There, in the territory of forsaken things, they dug a shallow grave. When they had finished they laid me in the grave, and suddenly they cast their tapers to the river. And when the water had quenched the flaring lights the tapers looked pale and small as they bobbed upon the tide, and at once the glamour of the calamity was gone, and I noticed then the approach of the huge dawn; and my friends cast their cloaks over their faces, and the solemn procession was turned into many fugitives that furtively stole away.

Then the mud came back wearily and covered all but my face. There I lay alone with quite forgotten things, with drifting things that the tides will take no farther, with useless things and lost things, and with the horrible unnatural bricks that are neither stone nor soil. I was rid of feeling, because I had been killed, but perception and thought were in my unhappy soul. The dawn widened, and I saw the desolate houses that crowded the marge of the river, and their dead windows peered into my dead eyes, windows with bales behind them instead of human souls. I grew so weary looking at these forlorn things that I wanted to cry out, but could not, because I was dead. Then I knew, as I had never known before, that for all the years that herd of desolate houses had wanted to cry out too, but, being dead, were dumb. And I knew then that it had yet been well with the forgotten drifting things if they had wept, but they were eyeless and without life. And I, too, tried to weep, but there were no tears in my dead eyes. And I knew then that the river might have cared for us, might have caressed us, might have sung to us, but he swept broadly onwards, thinking of nothing but the princely ships.

At last the tide did what the river would not, and came and covered me over, and my soul had rest in the green water, and rejoiced and believed that it had the Burial of the Sea. But with the ebb the water fell again, and left me alone again with the callous mud among the forgotten things that drift no more, and with the sight of all those desolate houses, and with the knowledge among all of us that each was dead.

In the mournful wall behind me, hung with green weeds, forsaken of the sea, dark tunnels appeared, and secret narrow passages that were clamped and barred. From these at last the stealthy rats came down to nibble me away, and my soul rejoiced thereat and believed that he would be free perforce from the accursed bones to which burial was refused. Very soon the rats ran away a little space and whispered among themselves. They never came any more. When I found that I was accursed even among the rats I tried to weep again.

Then the tide came swinging back and covered the dreadful mud, and hid the desolate houses, and soothed the forgotten things, and my soul had ease for a while in the sepulture of the sea. And then the tide forsook me again.

To and fro it came about me for many years. Then the County Council found me, and gave me decent burial. It was the first grave that I had ever slept in. That very night my friends came for me. They dug me up and put me back again in the shallow hold in the mud.

Again and again through the years my bones found burial, but always behind the funeral lurked one of those terrible men who, as soon as night fell, came and dug them up and carried them back again to the hole in the mud.

And then one day the last of those men died who once had done to me this terrible thing. I heard his soul go over the river at sunset.

And again I hoped.

A few weeks afterwards I was found once more, and once more taken out of that restless place and given deep burial in sacred ground, where my soul hoped that it should rest.

Almost at once men came with cloaks and tapers to give me back to the mud, for the thing had become a tradition and a rite. And all the forsaken things mocked me in their dumb hearts when they saw me carried back, for they were jealous of me because I had left the mud. It must be remembered that I could not weep.

And the years went by seawards where the black barges go, and the great derelict centuries became lost at sea, and still I lay there without any cause to hope, and daring not to hope without a cause, because of the terrible envy and the anger of the things that could drift no more.

Once a great storm rode up, even as far as London, out of the sea from the South; and he came curving into the river with the fierce East wind. And he was mightier than the dreary tides, and went with great leaps over the listless mud. And all the sad forgotten things rejoiced, and mingled with things that were haughtier than they, and rode once more amongst the lordly shipping that was driven up and down. And out of their hideous home he took my bones, never again, I hoped, to be vexed with the ebb and flow. And with the fall of the tide he went riding down the river and turned to the southwards, and so went to his home. And my bones he scattered among many isles and along the shores of happy alien mainlands. And for a moment, while they were far asunder, my soul was almost free.

Then there arose, at the will of the moon, the assiduous flow of the tide, and it undid at once the work of the ebb, and gathered my bones from the marge of sunny isles, and gleaned them all along the mainland's shores, and went rocking northwards till it came to the mouth of the Thames, and there turned westwards its relentless face, and so went up the river and came to the hole in the mud, and into it dropped my bones; and partly the mud covered them, and partly it left them white, for the mud cares not for its forsaken things.

Then the ebb came, and I saw the dead eyes of the houses and the jealousy of the other forgotten things that the storm had not carried thence.

And some more centuries passed over the ebb and flow and over the loneliness of things forgotten. And I lay there all the while in the careless grip of the mud, never wholly covered, yet never able to go free, and I longed for the great caress of the warm Earth or the comfortable lap of the Sea.

Sometimes men found my bones and buried them, but the tradition never died, and my friends' successors always brought them back. At last the barges went no more, and there were fewer lights; shaped timbers no longer floated down the fairway, and there came instead old wind-uprooted trees in all their natural simplicity.

At last I was aware that somewhere near me a blade of grass was growing, and the moss began to appear all over the dead houses. One day some thistledown went drifting over the river.

For some years I watched these signs attentively, until I became certain that London was passing away. Then I hoped once more, and all along both banks of the river there was anger among the lost things that anything should dare to hope upon the forsaken mud. Gradually the horrible houses crumbled, until the poor dead things that never had had life got decent burial among the weeds and moss. At last the may appeared and the convolvulus. Finally, the wild rose stood up over mounds that had been wharves and warehouses. Then I knew that the cause of Nature had triumphed, and London had passed away.

The last man in London came to the wall by the river, in an ancient cloak that was one of those that once my friends had worn, and peered over the edge to see that I still was there. Then he went, and I never saw men again: they had passed away with London.

A few days after the last man had gone the birds came into London, all the birds that sing. When they first saw me they all looked sideways at me, then they went away a little and spoke among themselves.

'He only sinned against Man,' they said; 'it is not our quarrel.'

'Let us be kind to him,' they said.

Then they hopped nearer me and began to sing. It was the time of the rising of the dawn, and from both banks of the river, and from the sky, and from the thickets that were once the streets, hundreds of birds were singing. As the light increased the birds sang more and more; they grew thicker and thicker in the air above my head, till there were thousands of them singing there, and then millions, and at last I could see nothing but a host of flickering wings with the sunlight on them, and little gaps of sky. Then when there was nothing to be heard in London but the myriad notes of that exultant song, my soul rose up from the bones in the hole in the mud and began to climb heavenwards. And it seemed that a lane-way opened amongst the wings of the birds, and it went up and up, and one of the smaller gates of Paradise stood ajar at the end of it. And then I knew by a sign that the mud should receive me no more, for suddenly I found that I could weep.

At this moment I opened my eyes in bed in a house in London, and outside some sparrows were twittering in a tree in the light of the radiant morning; and there were tears still wet upon my face, for one's restraint is feeble while one sleeps. But I arose and opened the window wide, and stretching my hands out over the little garden, I blessed the birds whose song had woken me up from the troubled and terrible centuries of my dream.

JULIO CORTÁZAR

THE NIGHT
FACE UP

Translated by Paul Blackburn

HALFWAY DOWN THE long hotel vestibule, he thought that probably he was going to be late, and hurried on into the street to get out his motorcycle from the corner where the next-door superintendent let him keep it. On the jewelry store at the corner he read that it was ten to nine; he had time to spare. The sun filtered through the tall downtown buildings, and he – because for himself, for just going along thinking, he did not have a name – he swung onto the machine, savoring the idea of the ride. The motor whirred between his legs, and a cool wind whipped his pantslegs.

He let the ministries zip past (the pink, the white), and a series of stores on the main street, their windows flashing. Now he was beginning the most pleasant part of the run, the real ride: a long street bordered with trees, very little traffic, with spacious villas whose gardens rambled all the way down to the sidewalks, which were barely indicated by low hedges. A bit inattentive perhaps, but tooling along on the right side of the street, he allowed himself to be carried away by the freshness, by the weightless contraction of this hardly begun day. This involuntary relaxation, possibly, kept him from preventing the accident. When he saw that the woman standing on the corner had rushed into the crosswalk while

N.B. The war of the blossom was the name the Aztecs gave to a ritual war in which they took prisoners for sacrifice. It is metaphysics to say that the gods see men as flowers, to be so uprooted, trampled, cut down. – ED.

195

he still had the green light, it was already somewhat too late for a simple solution. He braked hard with foot and hand, wrenching himself to the left; he heard the woman scream, and at the collision his vision went. It was like falling asleep all at once.

He came to abruptly. Four or five young men were getting him out from under the cycle. He felt the taste of salt and blood, one knee hurt, and when they hoisted him up he yelped, he couldn't bear the presssure on his right arm. Voices which did not seem to belong to the faces hanging above him encouraged him cheerfully with jokes and assurances. His single solace was to hear someone else confirm that the lights indeed had been in his favor. He asked about the woman, trying to keep down the nausea which was edging up into his throat. While they carried him face up to a nearby pharmacy, he learned that the cause of the accident had gotten only a few scrapes on the legs. 'Nah, you barely got her at all, but when ya hit, the impact made the machine jump and flop on its side . . .' Opinions, recollections of other smash-ups, take it easy, work him in shoulders first, there, that's fine, and someone in a dustcoat giving him a swallow of something soothing in the shadowy interior of the small local pharmacy.

Within five minutes the police ambulance arrived, and they lifted him onto a cushioned stretcher. It was a relief for him to be able to lie out flat. Completely lucid, but realizing that he was suffering the effects of a terrible shock, he gave his information to the officer riding in the ambulance with him. The arm almost didn't hurt; blood dripped down from a cut over the eyebrow all over his face. He licked his lips once or twice to drink it. He felt pretty good, it had been an accident, tough luck; stay quiet a few weeks, nothing worse. The guard said that the motorcycle didn't seem badly racked up. 'Why should it,' he replied. 'It all landed on top of me.' They both laughed, and when they got to the hospital, the guard shook his hand and wished him luck. Now the nausea was coming back little by little; meanwhile they were pushing him on a wheeled stretcher toward a pavilion further back, rolling along under trees full of birds, he shut his eyes and wished he were asleep or chloroformed. But they kept him for a good while in a room with that hospital smell, filling out a form, getting his clothes off, and dressing him in a stiff, grayish smock. They moved his arm carefully, it didn't hurt him. The nurses were constantly making wisecracks, and if it hadn't been for the stomach contractions he would have felt fine, almost happy.

They got him over to X-ray, and twenty minutes later, with the still-damp negative lying on his chest like a black tombstone, they pushed him into surgery. Someone tall and thin in white came over and began to look at the X-rays. A woman's hands were arranging his head, he felt that they were moving him from one stretcher to another. The man in white came over to him again, smiling, something gleamed in his right hand. He patted his cheek and made a sign to someone stationed behind.

It was unusual as a dream because it was full of smells, and he never dreamt smells. First a marshy smell, there to the left of the trail the swamps began already, the quaking bogs from which no one ever returned. But the reek lifted, and instead there came a dark, fresh composite fragrance, like the night under which he moved, in flight from the Aztecs. And it was all so natural, he had to run from the Aztecs who had set out on their manhunt, and his sole chance was to find a place to hide in the deepest part of the forest, taking care not to lose the narrow trail which only they, the Motecas, knew.

What tormented him the most was the odor, as though, notwithstanding the absolute acceptance of the dream, there was something which resisted that which was not habitual, which until that point had not participated in the game. 'It smells of war,' he thought, his hand going instinctively to the stone knife which was tucked at an angle into his girdle of woven wool. An unexpected sound made him crouch suddenly stock-still and shaking. To be afraid was nothing strange, there was plenty of fear in his dreams. He waited, covered by the branches of a shrub and the starless night. Far off, probably on the other side of the big lake, they'd be lighting the bivouac fires; that part of the sky had a reddish glare. The sound was not repeated. It had been like a broken limb. Maybe an animal that, like himself, was escaping from the smell of war. He stood erect slowly, sniffing the air. Not a sound could be heard, but the fear was still following, as was the smell, that cloying incense of the war of the blossom. He had to press forward, to stay out of the bogs and get to the heart of the forest. Groping uncertainly through the dark, stooping every other moment to touch the packed earth of the trail, he took a few steps. He would have liked to have broken into a run, but the gurgling fens lapped on either side of him. On the path and in darkness, he took his bearings. Then he caught a horrible blast of that foul smell he was most afraid of, and leaped forward desperately.

'You're going to fall off the bed,' said the patient next to him. 'Stop bouncing around, old buddy.'

He opened his eyes and it was afternoon, the sun already low in the oversized windows of the long ward. While trying to smile at his neighbor, he detached himself almost physically from the final scene of the nightmare. His arm, in a plaster cast, hung suspended from an apparatus with weights and pulleys. He felt thirsty, as though he'd been running for miles, but they didn't want to give him much water, barely enough to moisten his lips and make a mouthful. The fever was winning slowly and he would have been able to sleep again, but he was enjoying the pleasure of keeping awake, eyes half-closed, listening to the other patients' conversation, answering a question from time to time. He saw a little white pushcart come up beside the bed, a blond nurse rubbed the front of his thigh with alcohol and stuck him with a fat needle connected to a tube which ran up to a bottle filled with a milky, opalescent liquid. A young intern arrived with some metal and leather apparatus which he adjusted to fit onto the good arm to check something or other. Night fell, and the fever went along dragging him down softly to a state in which things seemed embossed as through opera glasses, they were real and soft and, at the same time, vaguely distasteful; like sitting in a boring movie and thinking that, well, still, it'd be worse out in the street, and staying.

A cup of a marvelous golden broth came, smelling of leeks, celery and parsley. A small hunk of bread, more precious than a whole banquet, found itself crumbling little by little. His arm hardly hurt him at all, and only in the eyebrow where they'd taken stitches a quick, hot pain sizzled occasionally. When the big windows across the way turned to smudges of dark blue, he thought it would not be difficult for him to sleep. Still on his back so a little uncomfortable, running his tongue out over his hot, too-dry lips, he tasted the broth still, and with a sigh of bliss, he let himself drift off.

First there was a confusion, as of one drawing all his sensations, for that moment blunted or muddled, into himself. He realized that he was running in pitch darkness, although, above, the sky criss-crossed with treetops was less black than the rest. 'The trail,' he thought, 'I've gotten off the trail.' His feet sank into a bed of leaves and mud, and then he couldn't

199

take a step that the branches of shrubs did not whiplash against his ribs and legs. Out of breath, knowing despite the darkness and silence that he was surrounded, he crouched down to listen. Maybe the trail was very near, with the first daylight he would be able to see it again. Nothing now could help him to find it. The hand that had unconsciously gripped the haft of the dagger climbed like a fen scorpion up to his neck where the protecting amulet hung. Barely moving his lips, he mumbled the supplication of the corn which brings about the beneficent moons, and the prayer to Her Very Highness, to the distributor of all Motecan possessions. At the same time he felt his ankles sinking deeper into the mud, and the waiting in the darkness of the obscure grove of live oak grew intolerable to him. The war of the blossom had started at the beginning of the moon and had been going on for three days and three nights now. If he managed to hide in the depths of the forest, getting off the trail further up past the marsh country, perhaps the warriors wouldn't follow his track. He thought of the many prisoners they'd already taken. But the number didn't count, only the consecrated period. The hunt would continue until the priests gave the sign to return. Everything had its number and its limit, and it was within the sacred period, and he on the other side from the hunters.

He heard the cries and leaped up, knife in hand. As if the sky were aflame on the horizon, he saw torches moving among the branches, very near him. The smell of war was unbearable, and when the first enemy jumped him, leaped at his throat, he felt an almost-pleasure in sinking the stone blade flat to the haft into his chest. The lights were already around him, the happy cries. He managed to cut the air once or twice, then a rope snared him from behind.

'It's the fever,' the man in the next bed said. 'The same

thing happened to me when they operated on my duo-
denum. Take some water, you'll see, you'll sleep all right.'

Laid next to the night from which he came back, the tepid
shadow of the ward seemed delicious to him. A violet lamp
kept watch high on the far wall like a guardian eye. You could
hear coughing, deep breathing, once in a while a conversation in whispers. Everything was pleasant and secure, without the chase, no ... But he didn't want to go on thinking
about the nightmare. There were lots of things to amuse
himself with. He began to look at the cast on his arm, and
the pulleys that held it so comfortably in the air. They'd left
a bottle of mineral water on the night table beside him. He
put the neck of the bottle to his mouth and drank it like a
precious liqueur. He could now make out the different
shapes in the ward, the thirty beds, the closets with glass
doors. He guessed that his fever was down, his face felt cool.
The cut over the eyebrow barely hurt at all, like a recollection. He saw himself leaving the hotel again, wheeling out
the cycle. Who'd have thought that it would end like this?
He tried to fix the moment of the accident exactly, and it
got him very angry to notice that there was a void there, an
emptiness he could not manage to fill. Between the impact
and the moment that they picked him up off the pavement,
the passing out or what went on, there was nothing he could
see. And at the same time he had the feeling that this void,
this nothingness, had lasted an eternity. No, not even time,
more as if, in this void, he had passed across something, or
had run back immense distances. The shock, the brutal dashing against the pavement. Anyway, he had felt an immense
relief in coming out of the black pit while the people were
lifting him off the ground. With pain in the broken arm,
blood from the split eyebrow, contusion on the knee; with
all that, a relief in returning to daylight, to the day, and to

feel sustained and attended. That was weird. Someday he'd ask the doctor at the office about that. Now sleep began to take over again, to pull him slowly down. The pillow was so soft, and the coolness of the mineral water in his fevered throat. The violet light of the lamp up there was beginning to get dimmer and dimmer.

As he was sleeping on his back, the position in which he came to did not surprise him, but on the other hand the damp smell, the smell of oozing rock, blocked his throat and forced him to understand. Open the eyes and look in all directions, hopeless. He was surrounded by an absolute darkness. Tried to get up and felt ropes pinning his wrists and ankles. He was staked to the ground on a floor of dank, icy stone slabs. The cold bit into his naked back, his legs. Dully, he tried to touch the amulet with his chin and found they had stripped him of it. Now he was lost, no prayer could save him from the final . . . From afar off, as though filtering through the rock of the dungeon, he heard the great kettledrums of the feast. They had carried him to the temple, he was in the underground cells of Teocalli itself, awaiting his turn.

He heard a yell, a hoarse yell that rocked off the walls. Another yell, ending in a moan. It was he who was screaming in the darkness, he was screaming because he was alive, his whole body with that cry fended off what was coming, the inevitable end. He thought of his friends filling up the other dungeons, and of those already walking up the stairs of the sacrifice. He uttered another choked cry, he could barely open his mouth, his jaws were twisted back as if with a rope and a stick, and once in a while they would open slowly with an endless exertion, as if they were made of rubber. The creaking of the wooden latches jolted him like a whip. Rent, writhing, he fought to rid himself of the cords sinking into his flesh. His right arm, the strongest, strained until the pain became unbearable and he had to give up. He watched the double door open, and the smell of the torches reached him before the light did. Barely girdled by the ceremonial loincloths, the priests' acolytes moved in his direction, looking at him with contempt. Lights reflected off the sweaty torsos and off the black hair dressed with feathers. The cords went slack, and in their place the grappling of hot hands, hard as bronze; he felt himself lifted, still face up, and jerked along by the four acolytes who carried him down the passageway. The torchbearers went ahead, indistinctly lighting up the corridor with its dripping walls and a ceiling so low that the acolytes had to duck their heads. Now they were taking him out, taking him out, it was the end. Face up, under a mile of living rock which, for a succession of moments, was lit up by a glimmer of torchlight. When the stars came out up there instead of the roof and the great terraced steps rose before him, on fire with cries and dances, it would be the end. The passage was never going to end, but now it was beginning to end, he would see suddenly the open sky full of stars, but not yet, they trundled him along endlessly in the reddish shadow, hauling him roughly along and he did not want that, but how to stop it if they had torn off the amulet, his real heart, the life-center.

In a single jump he came out into the hospital night, to the high, gentle, bare ceiling, to the soft shadow wrapping him round. He thought he must have cried out, but his neighbors were peacefully snoring. The water in the bottle on the night table was somewhat bubbly, a translucent shape against the dark azure shadow of the windows. He panted, looking for some relief for his lungs, oblivion for those images still glued to his eyelids. Each time he shut his eyes he saw them take shape instantly, and he sat up, completely wrung out, but savoring at the same time the surety that now he was awake, that the night nurse would answer if he rang, that soon it would be daybreak, with the good, deep sleep he usually had at that hour, no images, no nothing ... It was difficult to keep his eyes open, the drowsiness was more powerful than he. He made one last effort, he sketched a gesture toward the bottle of water with his good hand and did not manage to reach it, his fingers closed again on a black emptiness, and the passageway went on endlessly, rock after rock, with momentary ruddy flares, and face up he choked out a dull moan because the roof was about to end, it rose, was opening like a mouth of shadow, and the acolytes straightened up, and from on high a waning moon fell on a face whose eyes wanted not to see it, were closing and opening desperately, trying to pass to the other side, to find again the bare, protecting ceiling of the ward. And every time they opened, it was night and the moon, while they climbed the great terraced steps, his head hanging down backward now, and up at the top were the bonfires, red columns of perfumed smoke, and suddenly he saw the red stone, shiny with the blood dripping off it, and the spinning arcs cut by the feet of the victim whom they pulled off to throw him rolling down the north steps. With a last hope he shut his lids tightly, moaning to wake up. For a second he thought he had gotten there, because once more he was immobile in the bed, except that his head was hanging down off it, swinging. But he smelled death, and when he opened his eyes he saw the blood-soaked figure of the executioner-priest coming toward him with the stone knife in his hand. He managed to close his eyelids again, although he knew now he was not going to wake up, that he was awake, that the marvelous dream had been the other, absurd as all dreams are – a dream in which he was going through the strange avenues of an astonishing city, with green and red lights that burned without fire or

204

smoke, on an enormous metal insect that whirred away between his legs. In the infinite lie of the dream, they had also picked him up off the ground, someone had approached him also with a knife in his hand, approached him who was lying face up, face up with his eyes closed between the bonfires on the steps.

AMBROSE BIERCE

AN OCCURRENCE AT OWL CREEK BRIDGE

I

A MAN STOOD upon a railroad bridge in northern Alabama, looking down into the swift water twenty feet below. The man's hands were behind his back, the wrists bound with a cord. A rope closely encircled his neck. It was attached to a stout cross-timber above his head and the slack fell to the level of his knees. Some loose boards laid upon the ties supporting the rails of the railway supplied a footing for him and his executioners – two private soldiers of the Federal army, directed by a sergeant who in civil life may have been a deputy sheriff. At a short remove upon the same temporary platform was an officer in the uniform of his rank, armed. He was a captain. A sentinel at each end of the bridge stood with his rifle in the position known as 'support', that is to say, vertical in front of the left shoulder, the hammer resting on the forearm thrown straight across the chest – a formal and unnatural position, enforcing an erect carriage of the body. It did not appear to be the duty of these two men to know what was occurring at the center of the bridge; they merely blockaded the two ends of the foot planking that traversed it.

Beyond one of the sentinels nobody was in sight; the railroad ran straight away into a forest for a hundred yards, then, curving, was lost to view. Doubtless there was an outpost farther along. The other bank of the stream was open ground – a gentle slope topped with a stockade of vertical tree trunks, loopholed for rifles, with a single embrasure through which protruded the muzzle of a brass cannon commanding the bridge. Midway up the slope between the bridge and fort were the spectators – a single company of infantry in line, at 'parade rest', the butts of their rifles on the ground, the barrels inclining slightly backward against the right shoulder, the hands crossed upon the stock. A lieutenant stood at the right of the line, the point of his sword upon the ground, his left hand resting upon his right. Excepting the group of four at the center of the bridge, not a man moved. The company faced the bridge, staring stonily, motionless. The sentinels, facing the banks of the stream, might have been statues to adorn the bridge. The captain stood with folded arms, silent, observing the work of his subordinates, but making no sign. Death is a dignitary who when he comes announced is to be received with formal manifestations of respect, even by those most familiar with him. In the code of military etiquette silence and fixity are forms of deference.

The man who was engaged in being hanged was apparently about thirty-five years of age. He was a civilian, if one might judge from his habit, which was that of a planter. His features were good – a straight nose, firm mouth, broad forehead, from which his long, dark hair was combed straight back, falling behind his ears to the collar of his well fitting frock coat. He wore a moustache and pointed beard, but no whiskers; his eyes were large and dark gray, and had a kindly expression which one would hardly have expected in one whose neck was in the hemp. Evidently this was no vulgar assassin. The liberal military code makes provision for hanging many kinds of persons, and gentlemen are not excluded.

The preparations being complete, the two private soldiers stepped aside and each drew away the plank upon which he had been standing. The sergeant turned to the captain, saluted and placed himself immediately behind that officer, who in turn moved apart one pace. These movements left the condemned man and the sergeant standing on the two ends of the same plank, which spanned three of the cross-ties of the bridge. The end upon which the civilian stood almost, but not quite, reached a fourth. This plank had been held in place by the weight of the captain; it was now held by that of the sergeant. At a signal from the former the latter would step aside, the plank would tilt and the condemned man go down between two ties. The arrangement commended itself to his judgement as simple and effective. His face had not been covered nor his eyes bandaged. He looked a moment at his 'unsteadfast footing', then let his gaze wander to the swirling water of the stream racing madly beneath his feet. A piece of dancing driftwood caught his attention and his eyes followed it down the current. How slowly it appeared to move! What a sluggish stream!

He closed his eyes in order to fix his last thoughts upon his wife and children. The water, touched to gold by the early sun, the brooding mists under the banks at some distance down the stream, the fort, the soldiers, the piece of drift – all had distracted him. And now he became conscious of a new disturbance. Striking through the thought of his dear ones was a sound which he could neither ignore nor understand, a sharp, distinct, metallic percussion like the stroke of a blacksmith's hammer upon the anvil; it had the same ringing quality. He wondered what it was, and whether immeasurably distant or near by – it seemed both. Its recurrence was regular, but as slow as the tolling of a death knell. He awaited each new stroke with impatience and – he knew not why – apprehension. The intervals of silence grew progressively longer; the delays became maddening. With their greater infrequency the sounds increased in strength and sharpness. They hurt his ear like the thrust of a knife; he feared he would shriek. What he heard was the ticking of his watch.

He unclosed his eyes and saw again the water below him. 'If I could free my hands,' he thought, 'I might throw off the noose and spring into the stream. By diving I could evade the bullets and, swimming vigorously, reach the bank, take to the woods and get away home. My home, thank God, is as yet outside their lines; my wife and little ones are still beyond the invader's farthest advance.'

As these thoughts, which have here to be set down in words, were flashed into the doomed man's brain rather than evolved from it the captain nodded to the sergeant. The sergeant stepped aside.

II

Peyton Fahrquhar was a well-to-do planter, of an old and highly respected Alabama family. Being a slave owner and like other slave owners a politician, he was naturally an original secessionist and ardently devoted to the Southern cause. Circumstances of an imperious nature, which it is unnecessary to relate here, had prevented him from taking service with that gallant army which had fought the disastrous campaigns ending with the fall of Corinth, and he chafed under the inglorious restraint, longing for the release of his energies, the larger life of the soldier, the opportunity for distinction. That opportunity, he felt, would come, as it comes to all in wartime. Meanwhile he did what he could. No service was too humble for him to perform in the aid of the South, no adventure too perilous for him to undertake if consistent with the character of a civilian who was at heart a soldier, and who in good faith and without too much qualification assented to at least a part of the frankly villainous dictum that all is fair in love and war.

One evening while Fahrquhar and his wife were sitting on

a rustic bench near the entrance to his grounds, a gray-clad soldier rode up to the gate and asked for a drink of water. Mrs Fahrquhar was only too happy to serve him with her own white hands. While she was fetching the water her husband approached the dusty horseman and inquired eagerly for news from the front.

'The Yanks are repairing the railroads,' said the man, 'and are getting ready for another advance. They have reached the Owl Creek bridge, put it in order and built a stockade on the north bank. The commandant has issued an order, which is posted everywhere, declaring that any civilian caught interfering with the railroad, its bridges, tunnels, or trains will be summarily hanged. I saw the order.'

'How far is it to the Owl Creek bridge?' Fahrquhar asked.

'About thirty miles.'

'Is there no force on this side of the creek?'

'Only a picket post half a mile out, on the railroad, and a single sentinel at this end of the bridge.'

'Suppose a man – a civilian and student of hanging – should elude the picket post and perhaps get the better of the sentinel,' said Fahrquhar, smiling, 'what could he accomplish?'

The soldier reflected. 'I was there a month ago,' he replied. 'I observed that the flood of last winter had lodged a great quantity of driftwood against the wooden pier at this end of the bridge. It is now dry and would burn like tinder.'

The lady had now brought the water, which the soldier drank. He thanked her ceremoniously, bowed to her husband and rode away. An hour later, after nightfall, he repassed the plantation, going northward in the direction from which he had come. He was a Federal scout.

III

As Peyton Fahrquhar fell straight downward through the bridge he lost consciousness and was as one already dead. From this state he was awakened – ages later, it seemed to him – by the pain of a sharp pressure upon his throat, followed by a sense of suffocation. Keen, poignant agonies seemed to shoot from his neck downward through every fiber of his body and limbs. These pains appeared to flash along well defined lines of ramification and to beat with an inconceivably rapid periodicity. They seemed like streams of pulsating fire heating him to an intolerable temperature. As to his head, he was conscious of nothing but a feeling of fullness – of congestion. These sensations were unaccompanied by thought. The intellectual part of his nature was already effaced; he had power only to feel, and feeling was torment. He was conscious of motion. Encompassed in a luminous cloud, of which he was now merely the fiery heart, without material substance, he swung through unthinkable arcs of oscillation, like a vast pendulum. Then all at once, with terrible suddenness, the light about him shot upward with the noise of a loud splash; a frightful roaring was in his ears, and all was cold and dark. The power of thought was restored; he knew that the rope had broken and he had fallen into the stream. There was no additional strangulation; the noose about his neck was already suffocating him and kept the water from his lungs. To die of hanging at the bottom of a river! – the idea seemed to him ludicrous. He opened his eyes in the darkness and saw above him a gleam of light, but how distant, how inaccessible! He was still sinking, for the light became fainter and fainter until it was a mere glimmer. Then it began to grow and brighten, and he knew that he was rising toward the surface – knew it with reluctance, for he was now very comfortable. 'To be hanged and drowned,' he thought, 'that is not so bad; but I do not wish to be shot. No; I will not be shot; that is not fair.'

He was not conscious of an effort, but a sharp pain in his wrist apprised him that he was trying to free his hands. He gave the struggle his attention, as an idler might observe the feat of a juggler, without interest in the outcome. What splendid effort! – what magnificent, what superhuman strength! Ah, that was a fine endeavor! Bravo! The cord fell away; his arms parted and floated upward, the hands dimly seen on each side in the growing light. He watched them with a new interest as first one and then the other pounced upon the noose at his neck. They tore it away and thrust it fiercely aside, its undulations resembling those of a water snake. 'Put it back, put it back!' He thought he shouted these words to his hands, for the undoing of the noose had been succeeded by the direst pang that he had yet experienced. His neck ached horribly; his brain was on fire, his heart, which had been fluttering faintly, gave a great leap, trying to force itself out at his mouth. His whole body was racked and wrenched with an insupportable anguish! But his disobedient hands gave no heed to the command. They beat the water vigorously with quick, downward strokes, forcing him to the surface. He felt his head emerge; his eyes were blinded by the sunlight; his chest expanded convulsively, and with a supreme and crowning agony his lungs engulfed a great draught of air, which instantly he expelled in a shriek!

He was now in full possession of his physical senses. They were, indeed, preternaturally keen and alert. Something in the awful disturbance of his organic system had so exalted and refined them that they made record of things never before perceived. He felt the ripples upon his face and heard their separate sounds as they struck. He looked at the forest on the bank of the stream, saw the individual trees, the leaves and the veining of each leaf – he saw the very insects upon them: the locusts, the brilliant bodied flies, the gray spiders stretching their webs from twig to twig. He noted the prismatic colors in all the dewdrops upon a million blades of grass. The humming of the gnats that danced above the eddies of the stream, the beating of the dragon flies' wings, the strokes of the water spiders' legs, like oars which had lifted their boat – all these made audible music. A fish slid along beneath his eyes and he heard the rush of its body parting the water.

He had come to the surface facing down the stream; in a moment the visible world seemed to wheel slowly round, himself the pivotal point, and he saw the bridge, the fort, the soldiers upon the bridge, the captain, the sergeant, the two privates, his executioners. They were in silhouette against the blue sky. They shouted and gesticulated, pointing at him. The captain had drawn his pistol, but did not fire; the others were unarmed. Their movements were grotesque and horrible, their forms gigantic.

Suddenly he heard a sharp report and something struck the water smartly within a few inches of his head, spattering his face with spray. He heard a second report, and saw one of the sentinels with his rifle at his shoulder, a light cloud of blue smoke rising from the muzzle. The man in the water saw the eye of the man on the bridge gazing into his own through the sights of the rifle. He observed that it was a gray eye and remembered having read that gray eyes were keenest, and that all famous marksmen had them. Nevertheless, this one had missed.

A counter-swirl had caught Fahrquhar and turned him half round; he was again looking at the forest on the bank

opposite the fort. The sound of a clear, high voice in a monotonous singsong now rang out behind him and came across
the water with a distinctness that pierced and subdued all
other sounds, even the beating of the ripples in his ears.
Although no soldier, he had frequented camps enough to
know the dread significance of that deliberate, drawling,
aspirated chant; the lieutenant on shore was taking a part in
the morning's work. How coldly and pitilessly – with what
an even, calm intonation, presaging, and enforcing tran-
quility in the men – with what accurately measured interval
fell those cruel words:

'Company! . . . Attention! . . . Shoulder arms! . . . Ready!
. . . Aim! . . . Fire!'

Fahrquhar dived – dived as deeply as he could. The water
roared in his ears like the voice of Niagara, yet he heard
the dull thunder of the volley and, rising again toward the
surface, met shining bits of metal, singularly flattened,
oscillating slowly downward.

Some of them touched him on the face and hands, then
fell away, continuing their descent. One lodged between his
collar and neck; it was uncomfortably warm and he snatched
it out.

As he rose to the surface, gasping for breath, he saw that
he had been a long time under water; he was perceptibly
farther downstream – nearer to safety. The soldiers had
almost finished reloading; the metal ramrods flashed all at
once in the sunshine as they were drawn from the barrels,
turned in the air, and thrust into their sockets. The two
sentinels fired again, independently and ineffectually.

The hunted man saw all this over his shoulder; he was now
swimming vigorously with the current. His brain was as
energetic as his arms and legs; he thought with the rapidity
of lightning:

'The officer,' he reasoned, 'will not make that martinet's error a second time. It is as easy to dodge a volley as a single shot. He has probably already given the command to fire at will. God help me, I cannot dodge them all!'

An appalling splash within two yards of him was followed by a loud, rushing sound, *diminuendo*, which seemed to travel back through the air to the fort and died in an explosion which stirred the very river to its deeps! A rising sheet of water curved over him, fell down upon him, blinded him, strangled him! The cannon had taken a hand in the game. As he shook his head free from the commotion of the smitten water he heard the deflected shot humming through the air ahead, and in an instant it was cracking and smashing the branches in the forest beyond.

'They will not do that again,' he thought; 'the next time they will use a charge of grape. I must keep my eye upon the gun; the smoke will apprise me – the report arrives too late; it lags behind the missile. That is a good gun.'

Suddenly he felt himself whirled round and round – spinning like a top. The water, the banks, the forests, the now distant bridge, fort and men, all were commingled and blurred. Objects were represented by their colors only; circular horizontal streaks of color – that was all he saw. He had been caught in a vortex and was being whirled on with a velocity of advance and gyration that made him giddy and sick. In a few moments he was flung upon the gravel at the foot of the left bank of the stream – the southern bank – and behind a projecting point which concealed him from his enemies. The sudden arrest of his motion, the abrasion of one of his hands on the gravel, restored him, and he wept with delight. He dug his fingers into the sand, threw it over himself in handfuls and audibly blessed it. It looked like diamonds, rubies, emeralds; he could think of nothing beautiful which it did not resemble. The trees upon the bank were giant garden plants; he noted a definite order in their arrangement, inhaled the fragrance of their blooms. A strange roseate light shone through the spaces among their trunks and the wind made in their branches the music of æolian harps. He had no wish to perfect his escape – he was content to remain in that enchanting spot until retaken.

A whiz and a rattle of grapeshot among the branches high above his head roused him from his dream. The baffled cannoneer had fired him a random farewell. He sprang to his feet, rushed up the sloping bank, and plunged into the forest.

All that day he traveled, laying his course by the rounding sun. The forest seemed interminable; nowhere did he discover a break in it, not even a woodman's road. He had not known that he lived in so wild a region. There was something uncanny in the revelation.

By nightfall he was fatigued, footsore, famished. The thought of his wife and children urged him on. At last he found a road which led him in what he knew to be the right direction. It was as wide and straight as a city street, yet it seemed untraveled. No fields bordered it, no dwelling anywhere. Not so much as the barking of a dog suggested human habitation. The black bodies of the trees formed a straight wall on both sides, terminating on the horizon in a point, like a diagram in a lesson in perspective. Overhead, as he looked up through this rift in the wood, shone great golden stars looking unfamiliar and grouped in strange constellations. He was sure they were arranged in some order which had a secret and malign significance. The wood on either side was full of singular noises, among which – once, twice, and again – he distinctly heard whispers in an unknown tongue.

His neck was in pain and lifting his hand to it found it horribly swollen. He knew that it had a circle of black where the rope had bruised it. His eyes felt congested; he could no longer close them. His tongue was swollen with thirst; he relieved its fever by thrusting it forward from between his teeth into the cold air. How softly the turf had carpeted the untraveled avenue – he could no longer feel the roadway beneath his feet!

Doubtless, despite his suffering, he had fallen asleep while walking, for now he sees another scene – perhaps he has merely recovered from a delirium. He stands at the gate of his own home. All is as he left it, and all bright and beautiful in the morning sunshine. He must have traveled the entire night. As he pushes open the gate and passes up the wide white walk, he sees a flutter of female garments; his wife, looking fresh and cool and sweet, steps down from the veranda to meet him. At the bottom of the steps she stands waiting, with a smile of ineffable joy, an attitude of matchless grace and dignity. Ah, how beautiful she is! He springs forwards with extended arms. As he is about to clasp her he feels a stunning blow upon the back of the neck; a blinding white light blazes all about him with a sound like the shock of a cannon – then all is darkness and silence!

Peyton Fahrquhar was dead; his body, with a broken neck, swung gently from side to side beneath the timbers of the Owl Creek bridge.

H. G. WELLS

THE COUNTRY OF
THE BLIND

THREE HUNDRED MILES and more from Chimborazo, one hundred from the snows of Cotopaxi, in the wildest wastes of Ecuador's Andes, there lies that mysterious mountain valley, cut off from all the world of men, the Country of the Blind. Long years ago that valley lay so far open to the world that men might come at last through frightful gorges and over an icy pass into its equable meadows, and thither indeed men came, a family or so of Peruvian half-breeds fleeing from the lust and tyranny of an evil Spanish ruler. Then came the stupendous outbreak of Mindobamba, when it was night in Quito for seventeen days, and the water was boiling at Yaguachi and all the fish floating dying even as far as Guayaquil; everywhere along the Pacific slopes there were land-slips and swift thawings and sudden floods, and one whole side of the old Arauca crest slipped and came down in thunder, and cut off the Country of the Blind for ever from the exploring feet of men. But one of these early settlers had chanced to be on the hither side of the gorges when the world had so terribly shaken itself, and he perforce had to forget his wife and his child and all the friends and possessions he had left up there, and start life over again in the lower world. He started it again but ill, blindness overtook him, and he died of punishment in the mines; but the story he told begot a legend that lingers along the length of the Cordilleras of the Andes to this day.

He told of his reason for venturing back from that

fastness, into which he had first been carried lashed to a llama, beside a vast bale of gear, when he was a child. The valley, he said, had in it all that the heart of man could desire – sweet water, pasture, an even climate, slopes of rich brown soil with tangles of a shrub that bore an excellent fruit, and on one side great hanging forests of pine that held the avalanches high. Far overhead, on three sides, vast cliffs of grey-green rock were capped by cliffs of ice; but the glacier stream came not to them, but flowed away by the farther slopes, and only now and then huge ice masses fell on the valley side. In this valley it neither rained nor snowed, but the abundant springs gave a rich green pasture, that irrigation would spread over all the valley space. The settlers did well indeed there. Their beasts did well and multiplied, and but one thing marred their happiness. Yet it was enough to mar it greatly. A strange disease had come upon them and had made all the children born to them there – and, indeed, several older children also – blind. It was to seek some charm or antidote against this plague of blindness that he had with fatigue and danger and difficulty returned down the gorge. In those days, in such cases, men did not think of germs and infections, but of sins, and it seemed to him that the reason of this affliction must be in the negligence of these priestless immigrants to set up a shrine so soon as they entered the valley. He wanted a shrine – a handsome, cheap, effectual shrine – to be erected in the valley; he wanted relics and such-like potent things of faith, blessed objects and mysterious medals and prayers. In his wallet he had a bar of native silver for which he would not account; he insisted there was none in the valley with something of the insistence of an inexpert liar. They had all clubbed their money and ornaments together, having little need for such treasure up there, he said, to buy them holy help against their ill. I figure this dim-eyed young mountaineer, sunburnt, gaunt, and anxious, hat brim clutched feverishly, a man all unused to the ways of the lower world, telling this story to some keen-eyed, attentive priest before the great convulsion; I can picture him presently seeking to return with pious and infallible remedies against that trouble, and the infinite dismay with which he must have faced the tumbled vastness where the gorge had once come out. But the rest of his story of mischances is lost to me, save that I know of his evil death after several years. Poor stray from that remoteness! The stream that had once made the gorge now bursts from the mouth of a rocky cave, and the legend his poor, ill-told story set going developed into the legend of a race of blind men somewhere 'over there' one may still hear today.

And amidst the little population of that now isolated and forgotten valley the disease ran its course. The old became groping, the young saw but dimly, and the children that were born to them never saw at all. But life was very easy in that snow-rimmed basin, lost to all the world, with neither thorns nor briers, with no evil insects nor any beasts save the gentle breed of llamas they had lugged and thrust and followed up the beds of the shrunken rivers in the gorges up which they had come. The seeing had become purblind so gradually that they scarcely noticed their loss. They guided the sightless youngsters hither and thither until they knew the whole valley marvellously, and when at last sight died out among them the race lived on. They had even time to adapt themselves to the blind control of fire, which they made carefully in stoves of stone. They were a simple strain of people at the first, unlettered, only slightly touched with the Spanish civilization, but with something of a tradition of the arts of old Peru and of its lost philosophy. Generation followed generation. They forgot many things; they devised many things.

Their tradition of the greater world they came from became mythical in colour and uncertain. In all things save sight they were strong and able, and presently chance sent one who had an original mind and who could talk and persuade among them, and then afterwards another. These two passed, leaving their effects, and the little community grew in numbers and in understanding, and met and settled social and economic problems that arose. Generation followed generation. Generation followed generation. There came a time when a child was born who was fifteen generations from that ancestor who went out of the valley with a bar of silver to seek God's aid, and who never returned. Thereabout it chanced that a man came into this community from the outer world. And this is the story of that man.

He was a mountaineer from the country near Quito, a man who had been down to the sea and had seen the world, a reader of books in an original way, an acute and enterprising man, and he was taken on by a party of Englishmen who had come out to Ecuador to climb mountains, to replace one of their three Swiss guides who had fallen ill. He climbed here and he climbed there, and then came the attempt on Parascotopetl, the Matterhorn of the Andes, in which he was lost to the outer world. The story of that accident has been written a dozen times. Pointer's narrative is the best. He tells how the little party worked their difficult and almost vertical way up to the very foot of the last and greatest precipice, and how they built a night shelter amidst the snow upon a little shelf of rock, and, with a touch of real dramatic power, how presently they found Nunez had gone from them. They shouted, and there was no reply; shouted and whistled, and for the rest of that night they slept no more.

As the morning broke they saw the traces of his fall. It seems impossible he could have uttered a sound. He had slipped eastward towards the unknown side of the mountain; far below he had struck a steep slope of snow, and ploughed his way down it in the midst of a snow avalanche. His track went straight to the edge of a frightful precipice, and beyond that everything was hidden. Far, far below, and hazy with distance, they could see trees rising out of a narrow, shut-in valley – the lost Country of the Blind. But they did not know it was the lost Country of the Blind, nor distinguish it in any way from any other narrow streak of upland valley. Unnerved by this disaster, they abandoned their attempt in the afternoon, and Pointer was called away to the war before he could make another attack. To this day Parascotopetl lifts an unconquered crest, and Pointer's shelter crumbles unvisited amidst the snows.

And the man who fell survived.

At the end of the slope he fell a thousand feet, and came down in the midst of a cloud of snow upon a snow-slope even steeper than the one above. Down this he was whirled, stunned and insensible, but without a bone broken in his body; and then at last came to gentler slopes, and at last rolled out and lay still, buried amidst a softening heap of the white masses that had accompanied and saved him. He came to himself with a dim fancy that he was ill in bed; then realized his position with a mountaineer's intelligence and worked himself loose and, after a rest or so, out until he saw the stars. He rested flat upon his chest for a space, wondering where he was and what had happened to him. He explored his limbs, and discovered that several of his buttons were gone and his coat turned over his head. His knife had gone from his pocket and his hat was lost, though he had tied it under his chin. He recalled that he had been looking for loose stones to raise his piece of the shelter wall. His ice-axe had disappeared.

He decided he must have fallen, and looked up to see, exaggerated by the ghastly light of the rising moon, the tremendous flight he had taken. For a while he lay, gazing blankly at the vast, pale cliff towering above, rising moment by moment out of a subsiding tide of darkness. Its phantasmal, mysterious beauty held him for a space, and then he was seized with a paroxysm of sobbing laughter. . . .

After a great interval of time he became aware that he was near the lower edge of the snow. Below, down what was now a moon-lit and practicable slope, he saw the dark and broken appearance of rock-strewn turf. He struggled to his feet, aching in every joint and limb, got down painfully from the heaped loose snow about him, went downward until he was on the turf, and there dropped rather than lay beside a boulder, drank deep from the flask in his inner pocket, and instantly fell asleep. . . .

He was awakened by the singing of birds in the trees far below.

He sat up and perceived he was on a little alp at the foot of a vast precipice that sloped only a little in the gully down which he and his snow had come. Over against him another wall of rock reared itself against the sky. The gorge between these precipices ran east and west and was full of the morning sunlight, which lit to the westward the mass of fallen mountain that closed the descending gorge. Below him it seemed there was a precipice equally steep, but behind the snow in the gully he found a sort of chimney-cleft dripping with snow-water, down which a desperate man might venture. He found it easier than it seemed, and came at last to another desolate alp, and then after a rock climb of no particular difficulty, to a steep slope of trees. He took his bearings and turned his face up the gorge, for he saw it opened out above upon green meadows, among which he now glimpsed quite distinctly a cluster of stone huts of unfamiliar fashion. At times his progress was like clambering along the face of a wall, and after a time the rising sun ceased to strike along the gorge, the voices of the singing birds died away, and the air grew cold and dark about him. But the distant valley with its houses was all the brighter for that. He came presently to talus, and among the rocks he noted – for he was an observant man – an unfamiliar fern that seemed to clutch out of the crevices with intense green hands. He picked a frond or so and gnawed its stalk, and found it helpful.

About midday he came at last out of the throat of the gorge into the plain and the sunlight. He was stiff and weary; he sat down in the shadow of a rock, filled up his flask with water from a spring and drank it down, and remained for a time, resting before he went on to the houses.

They were very strange to his eyes, and indeed the whole aspect of that valley became, as he regarded it, queerer and more unfamiliar. The greater part of its surface was lush green meadow, starred with many beautiful flowers, irrigated with extraordinary care, and bearing evidence of systematic cropping piece by piece. High up and ringing the valley about was a wall, and what appeared to be a circumferential water channel, from which the little trickles of water that fed the meadow plants came, and on the higher slopes above this flocks of llamas cropped the scanty herbage. Sheds, apparently shelters or feeding-places for the llamas, stood against the boundary wall here and there. The irrigation streams ran together into a main channel down the centre of the valley, and this was enclosed on either side by a wall breast high. This gave a singularly urban quality to this secluded place, a quality that was greatly enhanced by the fact that a number of paths paved with black and white stones, and each with a curious little kerb at the side, ran hither and thither in an orderly manner. The houses of the central village were quite unlike the casual and higgledy-piggledy agglomeration of the mountain villages he knew; they stood in a continuous row on either side of a central street of astonishing cleanness, here and there their parti-coloured facade was pierced by a door, and not a solitary window broke their even frontage. They were parti-coloured with extraordinary irregularity, smeared with a sort of plaster that was sometimes grey, sometimes drab, sometimes slate-coloured or dark brown; and it was the sight of this wild plastering first brought the word 'blind' into the thoughts of the explorer. 'The good man who did that,' he thought, 'must have been as blind as a bat.'

He descended a steep place, and so came to the wall and channel that ran about the valley, near where the latter spouted out its surplus contents into the deeps of the gorge in a thin and wavering thread of cascade. He could now see a number of men and women resting on piled heaps of grass, as if taking a siesta, in the remoter part of the meadow, and nearer the village a number of recumbent children, and then nearer at hand three men carrying pails on yokes along a little path that ran from the encircling wall towards the houses. These latter were clad in garments of llama cloth and boots and belts of leather, and they wore caps of cloth with back and ear flaps. They followed one another in single file, walking slowly and yawning as they walked, like men who have been up all night. There was something so reassuringly prosperous and respectable in their bearing that after a moment's hesitation Nunez stood forward as conspicuously as possible upon his rock, and gave vent to a mighty shout that echoed round the valley.

The three men stopped, and moved their heads as though they were looking about them. They turned their faces this way and that, and Nunez gesticulated with freedom. But they did not appear to see him for all his gestures, and after a time, directing themselves towards the mountains far away to the right, they shouted as if in answer. Nunez bawled again, and then once more, and as he gestured ineffectually the word 'blind' came up to the top of his thoughts. 'The fools must be blind,' he said.

When at last, after much shouting and wrath, Nunez crossed the stream by a little bridge, came through a gate in the wall, and approached them, he was sure that they were blind. He was sure that this was the Country of the Blind of which the legends told. Conviction had sprung upon him, and a sense of great and rather enviable adventure. The three stood side by side, not looking at him, but with their ears directed towards him, judging him by his unfamiliar steps. They stood close together like men a little afraid, and he could see their eyelids closed and sunken, as though the very balls beneath had shrunk away. There was an expression near awe on their faces.

'A man,' one said, in hardly recognizable Spanish. 'A man it is – a man or a spirit – coming down from the rocks.'

But Nunez advanced with the confident steps of a youth who enters upon life. All the old stories of the lost valley and the Country of the Blind had come back to his mind, and through his thoughts ran this old proverb, as if it were a refrain:

'In the Country of the Blind the One-Eyed Man is King.'

'In the Country of the Blind the One-Eyed Man is King.'

And very civilly he gave them greeting. He talked to them and used his eyes.

'Where does he come from, brother Pedro?' asked one.

'Down out of the rocks.'

'Over the mountains I come,' said Nunez, 'out of the country beyond there – where men can see. From near Bogota –

where there are a hundred thousands of people, and where the city passes out of sight.'

'Sight?' muttered Pedro. 'Sight?'

'He comes,' said the second blind man, 'out of the rocks.'

The cloth of their coats, Nunez saw, was curious fashioned, each with a different sort of stitching.

They startled him by a simultaneous movement towards him, each with a hand outstretched. He stepped back from the advance of these spread fingers.

'Come hither,' said the third blind man, following his motion and clutching him neatly.

And they held Nunez and felt him over, saying no word further until they had done so.

'Carefully,' he cried, with a finger in his eye, and found they thought that organ, with its fluttering lids, a queer thing in him. They went over it again.

'A strange creature, Correa,' said the one called Pedro. 'Feel the coarseness of his hair. Like a llama's hair.'

'Rough he is as the rocks that begot him,' said Correa, investigating Nunez's unshaven chin with a soft and slightly moist hand. 'Perhaps he will grow finer.'

Nunez struggled a little under their examination, but they gripped him firm.

'Carefully,' he said again.

'He speaks,' said the third man. 'Certainly he is a man.'

'Ugh!' said Pedro, at the roughness of his coat.

'And you have come into the world?' asked Pedro.

'*Out* of the world. Over mountains and glaciers; right over above there, half-way to the sun. Out of the great, big world that goes down, twelve days' journey to the sea.'

They scarcely seemed to heed him. 'Our fathers have told us men may be made by the forces of Nature,' said Correa.

'It is the warmth of things, and moisture, and rottenness – rottenness.'

'Let us lead him to the elders,' said Pedro.

'Shout first,' said Correa, 'lest the children be afraid. This is a marvellous occasion.'

So they shouted, and Pedro went first and took Nunez by the hand to lead him to the houses.

He drew his hand away. 'I can see,' he said.

'See?' said Correa.

'Yes; see,' said Nunez, turning towards him, and stumbled against Pedro's pail.

'His senses are still imperfect,' said the third blind man. 'He stumbles, and talks unmeaning words. Lead him by the hand.'

'As you will,' said Nunez, and was led along laughing.

It seemed they knew nothing of sight.

Well, all in good time he would teach them.

He heard people shouting, and saw a number of figures gathering together in the middle roadway of the village.

He found it tax his nerve and patience more than he had anticipated, that first encounter with the population of the Country of the Blind. The place seemed larger as he drew near to it, and the smeared plasterings queerer, and a crowd of children and men and women (the women and girls he was pleased to note had, some of them, quite sweet faces, for all that their eyes were shut and sunken) came about him, holding on to him, touching him with soft, sensitive hands, smelling at him, and listening at every word he spoke. Some of the maidens and children, however, kept aloof as if afraid, and indeed his voice seemed coarse and rude beside their softer notes. They mobbed him. His three guides kept close to him with an effect of proprietorship, and said again and again, 'A wild man out of the rocks.'

'Bogota,' he said. 'Bogota. Over the mountain crests.'

'A wild man – using wild words,' said Pedro. 'Did you hear that— *Bogota*? His mind has hardly formed yet. He has only the beginnings of speech.'

A little boy nipped his hand. 'Bogota!' he said mockingly.

'Aye! A city to your village. I come from the great world – where men have eyes and see.'

'His name's Bogota,' they said.

'He stumbled,' said Correa – 'stumbled twice as we came hither.'

'Bring him in to the elders.'

And they thrust him suddenly through a doorway into a room as black as pitch, save at the end there faintly glowed a fire. The crowd closed in behind him and shut out all but the faintest glimmer of day, and before he could arrest himself he had fallen headlong over the feet of a seated man. His arm, outflung, struck the face of someone else as he went down; he felt the soft impact of features and heard a cry of anger, and for a moment he struggled against a number of hands that clutched him. It was a one-sided fight. An inkling of the situation came to him and he lay quiet.

'I fell down,' he said; 'I couldn't see in this pitchy darkness.'

There was a pause as if the unseen persons about him tried to understand his words. Then the voice of Correa said: 'He is but newly formed. He stumbles as he walks and mingles words that mean nothing with his speech.'

Others also said things about him that he heard or understood imperfectly.

'May I sit up?' he asked, in a pause. 'I will not struggle against you again.'

They consulted and let him rise.

The voice of an older man began to question him, and

234

Nunez found himself trying to explain the great world out of which he had fallen, and the sky and mountains and suchlike marvels, to these elders who sat in darkness in the Country of the Blind. And they would believe and understand nothing whatever that he told them, a thing quite outside his expectation. They would not even understand many of his words. For fourteen generations these people had been blind and cut off from all the seeing world; the names for all the things of sight had faded and changed; the story of the outer world was faded and changed to a child's story; and they had ceased to concern themselves with anything beyond the rocky slopes above their circling wall. Blind men of genius had arisen among them and questioned the shreds of belief and tradition they had brought with them from their seeing days, and had dismissed all these things as idle fancies and replaced them with new and saner explanations. Much of their imagination had shrivelled with their eyes, and they had made for themselves new imaginations with their ever more sensitive ears and finger-tips. Slowly Nunez realized this: that his expectation of wonder and reverence at his origin and his gifts was not to be borne out; and after his poor attempt to explain sight to them had been set aside as the confused version of a new-made being describing the marvels of his incoherent sensations, he subsided, a little dashed, into listening to their instruction. And the eldest of the blind men explained to him life and philosophy and religion, how that the world (meaning their valley) had been first an empty hollow in the rocks, and then had come first inanimate things without the gift of touch, and llamas and a few other creatures that had little sense, and then men, and at last angels, whom one could hear singing and making fluttering sounds, but whom no one could touch at all, which puzzled Nunez greatly until he thought of the birds.

He went on to tell Nunez how this time had been divided into the warm and the cold, which are the blind equivalents of day and night, and how it was good to sleep in the warm and work during the cold, so that now, but for his advent, the whole town of the blind would have been asleep. He said Nunez must have been specially created to learn and serve the wisdom they had acquired, and that for all his mental incoherency and stumbling behaviour he must have courage and do his best to learn, and at that all the people in the door-way murmured encouragingly. He said the night – for the blind call their day night – was now far gone, and it behooved everyone to go back to sleep. He asked Nunez if he knew how to sleep, and Nunez said he did, but that before sleep he wanted food. They brought him food, llama's milk in a bowl and rough salted bread, and led him into a lonely place to eat out of their hearing, and afterwards to slumber until the chill of the mountain evening roused them to begin their day again. But Nunez slumbered not at all.

Instead, he sat up in the place where they had left him, resting his limbs and turning the unanticipated circum- stances of his arrival over and over in his mind.

Every now and then he laughed, sometimes with amuse- ment and sometimes with indignation.

'Unformed mind!' he said. 'Got no senses yet! They little know they've been insulting their Heaven-sent King and master. . . .

'I see I must bring them to reason.'

'Let me think.'

'Let me think.'

He was still thinking when the sun set.

Nunez had an eye for all beautiful things, and it seemed to him that the glow upon the snow-fields and glaciers that rose about the valley on every side was the most beautiful thing he had ever seen. His eyes went from that inaccessible glory to the village and irrigated fields, fast sinking into the twilight, and suddenly a wave of emotion took him, and he thanked God from the bottom of his heart that the power of sight had been given him.

He heard a voice calling to him from out of the village.

'Yaho there, Bogota! Come hither!'

At that he stood up, smiling. He would show these people once and for all what sight would do for a man. They would seek him, but not find him.

'You move not, Bogota,' said the voice.

He laughed noiselessly and made two stealthy steps aside from the path.

'Trample not on the grass, Bogota; that is not allowed.'

Nunez had scarcely heard the sound he made himself. He stopped, amazed.

The owner of the voice came running up the piebald path towards him.

He stepped back into the pathway. 'Here I am,' he said.

'Why did you not come when I called you?' said the blind man. 'Must you be led like a child? Cannot you hear the path as you walk?'

Nunez laughed. 'I can see it,' he said.

'There is no such word as *see*,' said the blind man, after a pause. 'Cease this folly and follow the sound of my feet.'

Nunez followed, a little annoyed.

'My time will come,' he said.

'You'll learn,' the blind man answered. 'There is much to learn in the world.'

'Has no one told you, "In the Country of the Blind the One-Eyed Man is King?"'

'What is blind?' asked the blind man, carelessly, over his shoulder.

Four days passed and the fifth found the King of the Blind still incognito, as a clumsy and useless stranger among his subjects.

It was, he found, much more difficult to proclaim himself than he had supposed, and in the meantime, while he meditated his coup d'état, he did what he was told and learnt the manners and customs of the Country of the Blind. He found working and going about at night a particularly irksome thing, and he decided that that should be the first thing he would change.

They led a simple, laborious life, these people, with all the elements of virtue and happiness as these things can be understood by men. They toiled, but not oppressively; they had food and clothing sufficient for their needs; they had days and seasons of rest; they made much of music and singing, and there was love among them and little children.

It was marvellous with what confidence and precision they went about their ordered world. Everything, you see, had been made to fit their needs; each of the radiating paths of the valley area had a constant angle to the others, and was distinguished by a special notch upon its kerbing; all obstacles and irregularities of path or meadow had long since been cleared away; all their methods and procedure arose naturally from their special needs. Their senses had become marvellously acute; they could hear and judge the slightest gesture of a man a dozen paces away – could hear the very beating of his heart. Intonation had long replaced expression with them, and touches gesture, and their work with hoe and spade and fork was as free and confident as garden work can be. Their sense of smell was extraordinarily fine; they could distinguish individual differences as readily as a dog can, and they went about the tending of llamas, who lived among the rocks above and came to the wall for food and shelter, with ease and confidence. It was only when at last Nunez sought to assert himself that he found how easy and confident their movements could be.

He rebelled only after he had tried persuasion.

He tried at first on several occasions to tell them of sight. 'Look you here, you people,' he said. 'There are things you do not understand in me.'

Once or twice one or two of them attended to him; they sat with faces downcast and ears turned intelligently towards him, and he did his best to tell them what it was to see. Among his hearers was a girl, with eyelids less red and sunken than the others, so that one could almost fancy she was hiding eyes, whom especially he hoped to persuade. He spoke of the beauties of sight, of watching the mountains, of the sky and the sunrise, and they heard him with amused incredulity that presently became condemnatory. They told him there were indeed no mountains at all, but that the end of the rocks where the llamas grazed was indeed the end of the world; thence sprang a cavernous roof of the universe, from which the dew and the avalanches fell; and when he maintained stoutly the world had neither end nor roof such as they supposed, they said his thoughts were wicked. So far as he could describe sky and clouds and stars to them it seemed to them a hideous void, a terrible blankness in the place of the smooth roof to things in which they believed – it was an article of faith with them that the cavern roof was exquisitely smooth to the touch. He saw that in some manner he shocked them, and gave up that aspect of the matter altogether, and tried to show them the practical value of sight. One morning he saw Pedro in the path called Seventeen and coming towards the central houses, but still too far off for hearing or scent, and he told them as much. 'In a little while,' he prophesied, 'Pedro will be here.' An old man remarked that Pedro had no business on path Seventeen, and then, as if in confirmation, that individual as he drew near turned and went transversely into path Ten, and so back with nimble paces towards the outer wall. They mocked Nunez when Pedro did not arrive, and afterwards, when he asked Pedro questions to clear his character, Pedro denied and out-faced him, and was afterwards hostile to him.

Then he induced them to let him go a long way up the sloping meadows towards the wall with one complaisant individual, and to him he promised to describe all that hap-pened among the houses. He noted certain goings and com-ings, but the things that really seemed to signify to these people happened inside of or behind the windowless houses – the only things they took note of to test him by – and of those he could see or tell nothing; and it was after the failure of this attempt, and the ridicule they could not repress, that he resorted to force. He thought of seizing a spade and sud-denly smiting one or two of them to earth, and so in fair combat showing the advantage of eyes. He went so far with that resolution as to seize his spade, and then he discovered a new thing about himself, and that was that it was impos-sible for him to hit a blind man in cold blood.

He hesitated, and found them all aware that he had snatched up the spade. They stood all alert, with their heads on one side, and bent ears towards him for what he would do next.

'Put that spade down,' said one, and he felt a sort of help-less horror. He came near obedience.

Then he had thrust one backwards against a house wall, and fled past him and out of the village.

He went athwart one of their meadows, leaving a track of trampled grass behind his feet, and presently sat down by the side of one of their ways. He felt something of the buoyancy that comes to all men in the beginning of a fight, but more perplexity. He began to realize that you cannot even fight happily with creatures who stand upon a different mental basis to yourself. Far away he saw a number of men carrying spades and sticks come out of the street of houses and advance in a spreading line along the several paths towards him. They advanced slowly, speaking frequently to one another, and ever and again the whole cordon would halt and sniff the air and listen.

The first time they did this Nunez laughed. But afterwards he did not laugh.

One struck his trail in the meadow grass and came stooping and feeling his way along it.

For five minutes he watched the slow extension of the cordon, and then his vague disposition to do something forthwith became frantic. He stood up, went a pace or so towards the circumferential wall, turned, and went back a little way. There they all stood in a crescent, still and listening.

He also stood still, gripping his spade very tightly in both hands. Should he charge them?

The pulse in his ears ran into the rhythm of 'In the Country of the Blind the One-Eyed Man is King.'

Should he charge them?

He looked back at the high and unclimbable wall behind – unclimbable because of its smooth plastering, but withal pierced with many little doors – and at the approaching line of seekers. Behind these others were now coming out of the street of houses.

Should he charge them?

'Bogota!' called one. 'Bogota! where are you?'

He gripped his spade still tighter and advanced down the meadows towards the place of habitations, and directly he moved they converged upon him. 'I'll hit them if they touch me,' he swore; 'by Heaven, I will. I'll hit.' He called aloud, 'Look here, I'm going to do what I like in this valley! Do you hear? I'm going to do what I like and go where I like.'

They were moving in upon him quickly, groping, yet moving rapidly. It was like playing blind man's buff with everyone blindfolded except one. 'Get hold of him!' cried one. He found himself in the arc of a loose curve of pursuers. He felt suddenly he must be active and resolute.

'You don't understand,' he cried, in a voice that was meant to be great and resolute, and which broke. 'You are blind and I can see. Leave me alone!'

'Bogota! Put down that spade and come off the grass!'

The last order, grotesque in its urban familiarity, produced a gust of anger. 'I'll hurt you,' he said, sobbing with emotion. 'By Heaven, I'll hurt you! Leave me alone!'

He began to run – not knowing clearly where to run. He ran from the nearest blind man, because it was a horror to hit him. He stopped, and then made a dash to escape from their closing ranks. He made for where a gap was wide, and the men on either side, with a quick perception of the approach of his paces, rushed in on one another. He sprang forward, and then saw he must be caught, and *swish*! the spade had struck. He felt the soft thud of hand and arm, and the man was down with a yell of pain, and he was through.

Through! And then he was close to the street of houses again, and blind men, whirling spades and stakes, were running with a reasoned swiftness hither and thither.

He heard steps behind him just in time, and found a tall man rushing forward and swiping at the sound of him. He lost his nerve, hurled his spade a yard wide of this antagonist, and whirled about and fled, fairly yelling as he dodged another.

He was panic-stricken. He ran furiously to and fro, dodging when there was no need to dodge, and, in his anxiety to see on every side of him at once, stumbling. For a moment he was down and they heard his fall. Far away in the circumferential wall a little doorway looked like Heaven, and he set off in a wild rush for it. He did not even look round at his pursuers until it was gained, and he had stumbled across the bridge, clambered a little way among the rocks, to the surprise and dismay of a young llama, who went leaping out of sight, and lay down sobbing for breath.

And so his coup d'état came to an end.

He stayed outside the wall of the valley of the blind for two nights and days without food or shelter, and meditated upon the Unexpected. During these meditations he repeated very frequently and always with a profounder note of derision the exploded proverb: 'In the Country of the Blind the One-Eyed Man is King.' He thought chiefly of ways of fighting and conquering these people, and it grew clear that for him no practicable way was possible. He had no weapons, and now it would be hard to get one.

The canker of civilization had got to him even in Bogota, and he could not find it in himself to go down and assassinate a blind man. Of course, if he did that, he might then dictate terms on the threat of assassinating them all. But – sooner or later he must sleep! . . .

He tried also to find food among the pine trees, to be comfortable under pine boughs while the frost fell at night, and – with less confidence – to catch a llama by artifice in order to try to kill it – perhaps by hammering it with a stone – and so finally, perhaps, to eat some of it. But the llamas had a doubt of him and regarded him with distrustful brown eyes and spat when he drew near. Fear came on him the second day and fits of shivering. Finally he crawled down to the wall of the Country of the Blind and tried to make his terms. He crawled along by the stream, shouting, until two blind men came out to the gate and talked to him.

'I was mad,' he said. 'But I was only newly made.'

They said that was better.

He told them he was wiser now, and repented of all he had done.

Then he wept without intention, for he was very weak and ill now, and they took that as a favourable sign.

They asked him if he still thought he could *see*.

'No,' he said. 'That was folly. The word means nothing. Less than nothing!'

They asked him what was overhead.

'About ten times ten the height of a man there is a roof above the world – of rock – and very, very smooth. So smooth – so beautifully smooth. . . .' He burst again into hysterical tears. 'Before you ask me any more, give me some food or I shall die!'

He expected dire punishments, but these blind people were capable of toleration. They regarded his rebellion as but one more proof of his general idiocy and inferiority, and after they had whipped him they appointed him to do the simplest and heaviest work they had for anyone to do, and he, seeing no other way of living, did submissively what he was told.

He was ill for some days and they nursed him kindly. That refined his submission. But they insisted on his lying in the dark, and that was a great misery. And blind philosophers came and talked to him of the wicked levity of his mind, and reproved him so impressively for his doubts about the lid of rock that covered their cosmic casserole that he almost doubted whether indeed he was not the victim of hallucination in not seeing it overhead.

So Nunez became a citizen of the Country of the Blind, and these people ceased to be a generalized people and became individualities to him, and familiar to him, while the world beyond the mountains became more and more remote and unreal. There was Yacob, his master, a kindly man when not annoyed; there was Pedro, Yacob's nephew; and there was Medina-sarote, who was the youngest daughter of Yacob. She was little esteemed in the world of the blind, because she had a clear-cut face and lacked that satisfying, glossy smoothness that is the blind man's ideal of feminine beauty, but Nunez thought her beautiful at first, and presently the most beautiful thing in the whole creation. Her closed eyelids were not sunken and red after the common way of the valley, but lay as though they might open again at any moment; and she had long eyelashes, which were considered a grave disfigurement. And her voice was weak and did not satisfy the acute hearing of the valley swains. So that she had no lover.

There came a time when Nunez thought that, could he win her, he would be resigned to live in the valley for all the rest of his days.

He watched her; he sought opportunities of doing her little services and presently he found that she observed him. Once at a rest-day gathering they sat side by side in the dim starlight, and the music was sweet. His hand came upon hers and he dared to clasp it. Then very tenderly she returned his pressure. And one day, as they were at their meal in the darkness, he felt her hand very softly seeking him, and as it chanced the fire leapt then, and he saw the tenderness of her face.

He sought to speak to her.

He went to her one day when she was sitting in the

summer moonlight spinning. The light made her a thing of silver and mystery. He sat down at her feet and told her he loved her, and told her how beautiful she seemed to him. He had a lover's voice, he spoke with a tender reverence that came near to awe, and she had never before been touched by adoration. She made him no definite answer, but it was clear his words pleased her.

After that he talked to her whenever he could take an opportunity. The valley became the world for him, and the world beyond the mountains where men lived by day seemed no more than a fairy tale he would some day pour into her ears. Very tentatively and timidly he spoke to her of sight.

Sight seemed to her the most poetical of fancies, and she listened to his description of the stars and the mountains and her own sweet white-lit beauty as though it was a guilty indulgence. She did not believe, she could only half understand, but she was mysteriously delighted, and it seemed to him that she completely understood.

His love lost its awe and took courage. Presently he was for demanding her of Yacob and the elders in marriage, but she became fearful and delayed. And it was one of her elder sisters who first told Yacob that Medina-sarote and Nunez were in love.

There was from the first very great opposition to the marriage of Nunez and Medina-sarote; not so much because they valued her as because they held him as a being apart, an idiot, incompetent thing below the permissible level of a man. Her sisters opposed it bitterly as bringing discredit on them all; and old Yacob, though he had formed a sort of liking for his clumsy, obedient serf, shook his head and said the thing could not be. The young men were all angry at the idea of corrupting the race, and one went so far as to revile and strike Nunez. He struck back. Then for the first time he found an advantage in seeing, even by twilight, and after that fight was over no one was disposed to raise a hand against him. But they still found his marriage impossible.

Old Yacob had a tenderness for his last little daughter, and was grieved to have her weep upon his shoulder.

'You see, my dear, he's an idiot. He has delusions; he can't do anything right.'

'I know,' wept Medina-sarote. 'But he's better than he was. He's getting better. And he's strong, dear father, and kind – stronger and kinder than any other man in the world. And he loves me – and, father, I love him.'

Old Yacob was greatly distressed to find her inconsolable, and, besides – what made it more distressing – he liked Nunez for many things. So he went and sat in the windowless council-chamber with the other elders and watched the trend of the talk, and said, at the proper time, 'He's better than he was. Very likely, some day, we shall find him as sane as ourselves.'

Then afterwards one of the elders, who thought deeply, had an idea. He was a great doctor among these people, their medicine-man, and he had a very philosophical and inventive mind, and the idea of curing Nunez of his peculiarities appealed to him. One day when Yacob was present he returned to the topic of Nunez. 'I have examined Nunez,' he said, 'and the case is clearer to me. I think very probably he might be cured.'

'This is what I have always hoped,' said old Yacob.

'His brain is affected,' said the blind doctor.

The elders murmured assent.

'Now, *what* affects it?'

'Ah!' said old Yacob.

'*This*,' said the doctor, answering his own question. 'Those queer things that are called the eyes, and which exist

247

to make an agreeable depression in the face, are diseased, in the case of Nunez, in such a way as to affect his brain. They are greatly distended, he has eyelashes, and his eyelids move, and consequently his brain is in a state of constant irritation and distraction.'

'Yes?' said old Yacob. 'Yes?'

'And I think I may say with reasonable certainty that, in order to cure him completely, all that we need to do is a simple and easy surgical operation – namely, to remove these irritant bodies.'

'And then he will be sane?'

'Then he will be perfectly sane, and a quite admirable citizen.'

'Thank Heaven for science!' said old Yacob, and went forth at once to tell Nunez of his happy hopes.

But Nunez's manner of receiving the good news struck him as being cold and disappointing.

'One might think,' he said, 'from the tone you take that you did not care for my daughter.'

It was Medina-sarote who persuaded Nunez to face the blind surgeons.

'*You* do not want me,' he said, 'to lose my gift of sight?'

She shook her head.

'My world is sight.'

Her head drooped lower.

'There are the beautiful things, the beautiful little things – the flowers, the lichens amidst the rocks, the light and soft-ness on a piece of fur, the far sky with its drifting dawn of clouds, the sunsets and the stars. And there is *you*. For you alone it is good to have sight, to see your sweet, serene face, your kindly lips, your dear, beautiful hands folded together. . . . It is these eyes of mine you won, these eyes that hold me to you, that these idiots seek. Instead, I must touch you, hear you, and never see you again. I must come under that roof of rock and stone and darkness, that horrible roof under which your imaginations stoop ... *no*; *you* would not have me do that?'

A disagreeable doubt had arisen in him. He stopped and left the thing a question.

'I wish,' she said, 'sometimes—' She paused.

'Yes?' he said, a little apprehensively.

'I wish sometimes – you would not talk like that.'

'Like what?'

'I know it's pretty – it's your imagination. I love it, but *now*—'

He felt cold. '*Now?*' he said, faintly.

She sat quite still.

'You mean – you think – I should be better, better perhaps—'

He was realizing things very swiftly. He felt anger perhaps, anger at the dull course of fate, but also sympathy for her lack of understanding – a sympathy near akin to pity.

'*Dear,*' he said, and he could see by her whiteness how tensely her spirit pressed against the things she could not say. He put his arms about her, he kissed her ear, and they sat for a time in silence.

'If I were to consent to this?' he said at last, in a voice that was very gentle.

She flung her arms about him, weeping wildly. 'Oh, if you would,' she sobbed, 'if only you would!'

For a week before the operation that was to raise him from his servitude and inferiority to the level of a blind citizen Nunez knew nothing of sleep, and all through the warm, sunlit hours, while the others slumbered happily, he sat brooding or wandered aimlessly, trying to bring his mind to bear on his dilemma. He had given his answer, he had given his consent, and still he was not sure. And at last work-time was over, the sun rose in splendour over the golden crests, and his last day of vision began for him. He had a few minutes with Medina-sarote before she went apart to sleep.

'To-morrow,' he said, 'I shall see no more.'

'Dear heart!' she answered, and pressed his hands with all her strength.

'They will hurt you but little,' she said; 'and you are going through this pain, you are going through it, dear lover, for *me*. . . . Dear, if a woman's heart and life can do it, I will repay you. My dearest one, my dearest with the tender voice, I will repay.'

He was drenched in pity for himself and her.

He held her in his arms, and pressed his lips to hers and looked on her sweet face for the last time. 'Good-bye!' he whispered to that dear sight, 'good-bye!'

And then in silence he turned away from her.

She could hear his slow retreating footsteps, and something in the rhythm of them threw her into a passion of weeping.

He walked away.

He had fully meant to go to a lonely place where the meadows were beautiful with white narcissus, and there remain until the hour of his sacrifice should come, but as he walked he lifted up his eyes and saw the morning, the morning like an angel in golden armour, marching down the steeps. . . .

It seemed to him that before this splendour he and this blind world in the valley, and his love and all, were no more than a pit of sin.

He did not turn aside as he had meant to do, but went on and passed through the wall of the circumference and out upon the rocks, and his eyes were always upon the sunlit ice and snow.

He saw their infinite beauty, and his imagination soared over them to the things beyond he was now to resign for ever!

He thought of that great free world that he was parted from, the world that was his own, and he had a vision of those further slopes, distance beyond distance, with Bogota, a place of multitudinous stirring beauty, a glory by day, a luminous mystery by night, a place of palaces and fountains and statues and white houses, lying beautifully in the middle distance. He thought how for a day or so one might come down through passes drawing ever nearer and nearer to its busy streets and ways. He thought of the river journey, day by day, from great Bogota to the still vaster world beyond, through towns and villages, forest and desert places, the rushing river day by day, until its banks receded, and the big steamers came splashing by and one had reached the sea – the limitless sea, with its thousand islands, its thousands of islands, and its ships seen dimly far away in their incessant journeyings round and about that greater world. And there, unpent by mountains, one saw the sky – the sky, not such a disc as one saw it here, but an arch of immeasurable blue, a deep of deeps in which the circling stars were floating. . . .

His eyes began to scrutinize the great curtain of the mountains with a keener inquiry.

For example; if one went so, up that gully and to that chimney there, then one might come out high among those stunted pines that ran round in a sort of shelf and rose still higher and higher as it passed above the gorge. And then? That talus might be managed. Thence perhaps a climb might be found to take him up to the precipice that came below the snow; and if that chimney failed, then another farther to the east might serve his purpose better. And then? Then one would be out upon the amber-lit snow there, and half-way up to the crest of those beautiful desolations. And suppose one had good fortune!

He glanced back at the village, then turned right round and regarded it with folded arms.

He thought of Medina-sarote, and she had become small and remote.

He turned again towards the mountain wall down which the day had come to him.

Then very circumspectly he began his climb.

When sunset came he was no longer climbing, but he was far and high. His clothes were torn, his limbs were blood-stained, he was bruised in many places, but he lay as if he were at his ease, and there was a smile on his face.

From where he rested the valley seemed as if it were in a pit and nearly a mile below. Already it was dim with haze and shadow, though the mountain summits around him were things of light and fire. The mountain summits around him were things of light and fire, and the little things in the rocks near at hand were drenched with light and beauty, a vein of green mineral piercing the grey, a flash of small crystal here and there, a minute, minutely-beautiful orange lichen close beside his face. There were deep, mysterious shadows in the gorge, blue deepening into purple, and purple into a luminous darkness, and overhead was the illimitable vastness of the sky. But he heeded these things no longer, but lay quite still there, smiling as if he were content now merely to have escaped from the valley of the Blind, in which he had thought to be King. And the glow of the sunset passed, and the night came, and still he lay there, under the cold, clear stars.

WASHINGTON IRVING

THE LEGEND OF
SLEEPY HOLLOW

A pleasing land of drowsy head it was,
  Of dreams that wave before the half-shut eye;
And of gay castles in the clouds that pass,
  For ever flushing round a summer sky.

                    CASTLE OF INDOLENCE.

IN THE BOSOM of one of those spacious coves which indent
the eastern shore of the Hudson, at that broad expansion of
the river denominated by the ancient Dutch navigators the
Tappan Zee, and where they always prudently shortened sail,
and implored the protection of St Nicholas when they
crossed, there lies a small market-town or rural port, which
by some is called Greensburgh, but which is more generally
and properly known by the name of Tarry Town. This name
was given, we are told, in former days, by the good housewives of the adjacent country, from the inveterate propensity
of their husbands to linger about the village tavern on market
days. Be that as it may, I do not vouch for the fact, but merely
advert to it, for the sake of being precise and authentic. Not
far from this village, perhaps about two miles, there is a little
valley, or rather lap of land, among high hills, which is one of
the quietest places in the whole world. A small brook glides
through it, with just murmur enough to lull one to repose;

and the occasional whistle of a quail, or tapping of a wood-pecker, is almost the only sound that ever breaks in upon the uniform tranquillity.

I recollect that, when a stripling, my first exploit in squirrel-shooting was in a grove of tall walnut-trees that shades one side of the valley. I had wandered into it at noon time, when all nature is peculiarly quiet, and was startled by the roar of my own gun, as it broke the Sabbath stillness around, and was prolonged and reverberated by the angry echoes. If ever I should wish for a retreat, whither I might steal from the world and its distractions, and dream quietly away the remnant of a troubled life, I know of none more promising than this little valley.

From the listless repose of the place, and the peculiar character of its inhabitants, who are descendants from the original Dutch settlers, this sequestered glen has long been known by the name of SLEEPY HOLLOW, and its rustic lads are called the Sleepy Hollow Boys throughout all the neigh-boring country. A drowsy, dreamy influence seems to hang over the land, and to pervade the very atmosphere. Some say that the place was bewitched by a high German doctor, during the early days of the settlement; others, that an old Indian chief, the prophet or wizard of his tribe, held his pow-wows there before the country was discovered by Master Hendrick Hudson. Certain it is, the place still continues under the sway of some witching power, that holds a spell over the minds of the good people, causing them to walk in a continual reverie. They are given to all kinds of marvellous beliefs; are subject to trances and visions; and frequently see strange sights, and hear music and voices in the air. The whole neighborhood abounds with local tales, haunted spots, and twilight superstitions; stars shoot and meteors glare oftener across the valley than in any other part of the country, and the nightmare, with her whole nine fold, seems to make it the favorite scene of her gambols.

The dominant spirit, however, that haunts this enchanted region, and seems to be commander-in-chief of all the powers of the air, is the apparition of a figure on horseback without a head. It is said by some to be the ghost of a Hessian trooper, whose head had been carried away by a cannon-ball, in some nameless battle during the revolutionary war; and who is ever and anon seen by the country folk hurrying along in the gloom of night, as if on the wings of the wind. His haunts are not confined to the valley, but extend at times to the adjacent roads, and especially to the vicinity of a church at no great distance. Indeed, certain of the most authentic historians of those parts, who have been careful in collecting and collating the floating facts concerning this spectre, allege that the body of the trooper, having been buried in the church-yard, the ghost rides forth to the scene of battle in nightly quest of his head; and that the rushing speed with which he sometimes passes along the Hollow, like a midnight blast, is owing to his being belated, and in a hurry to get back to the church-yard before daybreak.

Such is the general purport of this legendary superstition, which has furnished materials for many a wild story in that region of shadows; and the spectre is known, at all the country firesides, by the name of the Headless Horseman of Sleepy Hollow.

It is remarkable that the visionary propensity I have mentioned is not confined to the native inhabitants of the valley, but is unconsciously imbibed by every one who resides there for a time. However wide awake they may have been before they entered that sleepy region, they are sure, in a little time, to inhale the witching influence of the air, and begin to grow imaginative – to dream dreams, and see apparitions.

I mention this peaceful spot with all possible laud; for it is in such little retired Dutch valleys, found here and there embosomed in the great State of New York, that population, manners, and customs, remain fixed; while the great torrent of migration and improvement, which is making such incessant changes in other parts of this restless country, sweeps by them unobserved. They are like those little nooks of still water which border a rapid stream; where we may see the straw and bubble riding quietly at anchor, or slowly revolving in their mimic harbor, undisturbed by the rush of the passing current. Though many years have elapsed since I trod the drowsy shades of Sleepy Hollow, yet I question whether I should not still find the same trees and the same families vegetating in its sheltered bosom.

In this by-place of nature, there abode, in a remote period of American history, that is to say, some thirty years since, a worthy wight of the name of Ichabod Crane; who sojourned, or, as he expressed it, 'tarried', in Sleepy Hollow, for the purpose of instructing the children of the vicinity. He was a native of Connecticut; a State which supplies the Union with pioneers for the mind as well as for the forest, and sends forth yearly its legions of frontier woodsmen and country schoolmasters. The cognomen of Crane was not inapplicable to his person. He was tall, but exceedingly lank, with narrow shoulders, long arms and legs, hands that dangled a mile out of his sleeves, feet that might have served for shovels, and his whole frame most loosely hung together. His head was small, and flat at top, with huge ears, large green glassy eyes, and a long snipe nose, so that it looked like a weather-cock, perched upon his spindle neck, to tell which way the wind blew. To see him striding along the profile of a hill on a windy day, with his clothes bagging and fluttering about him, one might have mistaken him for the genius of famine descending upon the earth, or some scare-crow eloped from a cornfield.

His school-house was a low building of one large room, rudely constructed of logs; the windows partly glazed, and partly patched with leaves of old copy-books. It was most ingeniously secured at vacant hours, by a withe twisted in the handle of the door, and stakes set against the window shutters; so that, though a thief might get in with perfect ease, he would find some embarrassment in getting out; an idea most probably borrowed by the architect, Yost Van Houton, from the mystery of an eel-pot. The school-house stood in a rather lonely but pleasant situation just at the foot of a woody hill, with a brook running close by, and a formidable birch tree growing at one end of it. From hence the low murmur of his pupils' voices, conning over their lessons, might be heard in a drowsy summer's day, like the hum of a bee-hive; interrupted now and then by the authoritative voice of the master, in the tone of menace or command; or, peradventure, by the appalling sound of the birch, as he urged some tardy loiterer along the flowery path of knowledge. Truth to say, he was a conscientious man, and ever bore in mind the golden maxim, 'Spare the rod and spoil the child.' Ichabod Crane's scholars certainly were not spoiled.

I would not have it imagined, however, that he was one of those cruel potentates of the school, who joy in the smart of their subjects; on the contrary, he administered justice with discrimination rather than severity; taking the burthen off the backs of the weak, and laying it on those of the strong. Your mere puny stripling, that winced at the least flourish of the rod, was passed by with indulgence; but the claims of justice were satisfied by inflicting a double portion on some little, tough, wrong-headed, broad-skirted Dutch urchin, who sulked and swelled and grew dogged and sullen beneath the birch. All this he called 'doing his duty by their parents'; and he never inflicted a chastisement without following it by the assurance, so consolatory to the smarting urchin, that 'he would remember it, and thank him for it the longest day he had to live'.

When school hours were over, he was even the companion and playmate of the larger boys; and on holiday afternoons would convoy some of the smaller ones home, who happened to have pretty sisters, or good housewives for mothers, noted for the comforts of the cupboard. Indeed it behooved him to keep on good terms with his pupils. The revenue arising from his school was small, and would have been scarcely sufficient to furnish him with daily bread, for he was a huge feeder, and though lank, had the dilating powers of an anaconda; but to help out his maintenance, he was, according to country custom in those parts, boarded and lodged at the houses of the farmers, whose children he instructed. With these he lived successively a week at a time; thus going the rounds of the neighborhood, with all his worldly effects tied up in a cotton handkerchief.

That all this might not be too onerous on the purses of his rustic patrons, who are apt to consider the costs of schooling a grievous burden, and schoolmasters as mere drones, he had various ways of rendering himself both useful and agreeable. He assisted the farmers occasionally in the lighter labors of their farms; helped to make hay; mended the fences; took the horses to water; drove the cows from pasture; and cut wood for the winter fire. He laid aside, too, all the dominant dignity and absolute sway with which he lorded it in his little empire, the school, and became wonderfully gentle and ingratiating. He found favor in the eyes of the mothers, by petting the children, particularly the youngest; and like the lion bold, which whilom so magnanimously the lamb did hold, he would sit with a child on one knee, and rock a cradle with his foot for whole hours together.

In addition to his other vocations, he was the singing-master of the neighborhood, and picked up many bright shillings by instructing the young folks in psalmody. It was a matter of no little vanity to him, on Sundays, to take his station in front of the church gallery, with a band of chosen singers; where, in his own mind, he completely carried away the palm from the parson. Certain it is, his voice resounded far above all the rest of the congregation; and there are peculiar quavers still to be heard in that church, and which may even be heard half a mile off, quite to the opposite side of the mill-pond, on a still Sunday morning, which are said to be legitimately descended from the nose of Ichabod Crane. Thus, by divers little makeshifts in that ingenious way which is commonly denominated 'by hook and by crook', the worthy pedagogue got on tolerably enough, and was thought, by all who understood nothing of the labor of headwork, to have a wonderfully easy life of it.

The schoolmaster is generally a man of some importance in the female circle of a rural neighborhood; being considered a kind of idle gentlemanlike personage, of vastly superior taste and accomplishments to the rough country swains, and, indeed, inferior in learning only to the parson. His appearance, therefore, is apt to occasion some little stir at the tea-table of a farmhouse, and the addition of a supernumerary dish of cakes or sweetmeats, or, peradventure, the parade of a silver tea-pot. Our man of letters, therefore, was peculiarly happy in the smiles of all the country damsels. How he would figure among them in the church-yard, between services on Sundays! gathering grapes for them from the wild vines that overrun the surrounding trees; reciting for their amusement all the epitaphs on the tombstones; or sauntering, with a whole bevy of them, along the banks of the adjacent mill-pond; while the more bashful country bumpkins hung sheepishly back, envying his superior elegance and address.

From his half itinerant life, also, he was a kind of travelling gazette, carrying the whole budget of local gossip from house to house; so that his appearance was always greeted with satisfaction. He was, moreover, esteemed by the women as a man of great erudition, for he had read several books quite through, and was a perfect master of Cotton Mather's history of New England Witchcraft, in which, by the way, he most firmly and potently believed.

He was, in fact, an odd mixture of small shrewdness and simple credulity. His appetite for the marvellous, and his powers of digesting it, were equally extraordinary; and both had been increased by his residence in this spellbound region. No tale was too gross or monstrous for his capacious swallow. It was often his delight, after his school was dismissed in the afternoon, to stretch himself on the rich bed of clover, bordering the little brook that whimpered by his school-house, and there con over old Mather's direful tales, until the gathering dusk of the evening made the printed page a mere mist before his eyes. Then, as he wended his way, by swamp and stream and awful woodland, to the farmhouse where he happened to be quartered, every sound of nature, at that witching hour, fluttered his excited imagination: the moan of the whip-poor-will from the hill-side; the boding cry of the tree-toad, that harbinger of storm; the dreary hooting of the screech-owl, or the sudden rustling in the thicket of birds frightened from their roost. The fire-flies, too, which sparkled most vividly in the darkest places, now and then startled him, as one of uncommon brightness would stream across his path; and if, by chance, a huge blockhead of a beetle came winging his blundering flight against him, the poor varlet was ready to give up the ghost, with the idea that he was struck with a witch's token. His only resource on such occasions, either to drown thought, or drive away evil spirits, was to sing psalm tunes; – and the good people of Sleepy Hollow, as they sat by their doors of an evening, were often filled with awe, at hearing his nasal melody, 'in linked sweetness long drawn out', floating from the distant hill, or along the dusky road.

Another of his sources of fearful pleasure was, to pass long winter evenings with the old Dutch wives, as they sat spinning by the fire, with a row of apples roasting and spluttering along the hearth, and listen to their marvellous tales of ghosts and goblins, and haunted fields, and haunted brooks, and haunted bridges, and haunted houses, and particularly of the headless horseman, or galloping Hessian of the Hollow, as they sometimes called him. He would delight them equally by his anecdotes of witchcraft, and of the direful omens and portentous sights and sounds in the air, which prevailed in the earlier times of Connecticut; and would frighten them wofully with speculations upon comets and shooting stars; and with the alarming fact that the world did absolutely turn round, and that they were half the time topsy turvy!

But if there was a pleasure in all this, while snugly cuddling in the chimney corner of a chamber that was all of a ruddy glow from the crackling wood fire, and where, of course, no spectre dared to show his face, it was dearly purchased by the terrors of his subsequent walk homewards. What fearful shapes and shadows beset his path amidst the dim and ghastly glare of a snowy night! – With what wistful look did he eye every trembling ray of light streaming across the waste fields from some distant window! – How often was he appalled by some shrub covered with snow, which, like a sheeted spectre, beset his very path! – How often did he shrink with curdling awe at the sound of his own steps on the frosty crust beneath his feet; and dread to look over his shoulder, lest he should behold some uncouth being tramping close behind him! – and how often was he thrown into complete dismay by some rushing blast, howling among the trees, in the idea that it was the Galloping Hessian on one of his nightly scourings!

All these, however, were mere terrors of the night, phantoms of the mind that walk in darkness; and though he had seen many spectres in his time, and been more than once beset by Satan in divers shapes, in his lonely perambulations, yet daylight put an end to all these evils; and he would have passed a pleasant life of it, in despite of the devil and all his works, if his path had not been crossed by a being that causes more perplexity to mortal man than ghosts, goblins, and the whole race of witches put together, and that was – a woman.

Among the musical disciples who assembled, one evening in each week, to receive his instructions in psalmody, was Katrina Van Tassel, the daughter and only child of a substantial Dutch farmer. She was a blooming lass of fresh eighteen; plump as a partridge; ripe and melting and rosy cheeked as one of her father's peaches, and universally famed, not merely for her beauty, but her vast expectations. She was withal a little of a coquette, as might be perceived even in her dress, which was a mixture of ancient and modern fashions, as most suited to set off her charms. She wore the ornaments of pure yellow gold, which her great-great-grandmother had brought over from Saardam, the tempting stomacher of the olden time; and withal a provokingly short petticoat, to display the prettiest foot and ankle in the country round.

Ichabod Crane had a soft and foolish heart towards the sex; and it is not to be wondered at, that so tempting a morsel soon found favor in his eyes; more especially after he had visited her in her paternal mansion. Old Baltus Van Tassel was a perfect picture of a thriving, contented, liberal-hearted farmer. He seldom, it is true, sent either his eyes or his thoughts beyond the boundaries of his own farm; but within those every thing was snug, happy, and well-conditioned. He was satisfied with his wealth, but not proud of it; and piqued himself upon the hearty abundance, rather than the style in which he lived. His stronghold was situated on the banks of the Hudson, in one of those green, sheltered, fertile nooks, in which the Dutch farmers are so fond of nestling. A great elm-tree spread its broad branches over it; at the foot of which bubbled up a spring of the softest and sweetest water, in a little well, formed of a barrel; and then stole sparkling away through the grass, to a neighboring brook, that bubbled along among alders and dwarf willows. Hard by the farmhouse was a vast barn, that might have served for a church; every window and crevice of which seemed bursting forth with the treasures of the farm; the flail was busily resounding within it from morning to night; swallows and martins skimmed twittering about the eaves; and rows of pigeons, some with one eye turned up, as if watching the weather, some with their heads under their wings, or buried in their bosoms, and others swelling, and cooing, and bowing about their dames, were enjoying the sunshine on the roof. Sleek unwieldy porkers were grunting in the repose and abundance of their pens; whence sallied forth, now and then, troops of sucking pigs, as if to snuff the air. A stately squadron of snowy geese were riding in an adjoining pond, convoying whole fleets of ducks; regiments of turkeys were gobbling through the farmyard, and guinea fowls fretting about it, like ill-tempered housewives, with their peevish dis-contented cry. Before the barn door strutted the gallant cock, that pattern of a husband, a warrior, and a fine gentleman, clapping his burnished wings, and crowing in the pride and gladness of his heart – sometimes tearing up the earth with his feet, and then generously calling his ever-hungry family of wives and children to enjoy the rich morsel which he had discovered.

The pedagogue's mouth watered, as he looked upon this sumptuous promise of luxurious winter fare. In his devour-ing mind's eye, he pictured to himself every roasting-pig run-ning about with a pudding in his belly, and an apple in his mouth; the pigeons were snugly put to bed in a comfortable pie, and tucked in with a coverlet of crust; the geese were swimming in their own gravy; and the ducks pairing cosily in dishes, like snug married couples, with a decent compe-tency of onion sauce. In the porkers he saw carved out the future sleek side of bacon, and juicy relishing ham; not a turkey but he beheld daintily trussed up, with its gizzard under its wing, and, peradventure, a necklace of savory saus-ages; and even bright chanticleer himself lay sprawling on his back, in a side-dish, with uplifted claws, as if craving that quarter which his chivalrous spirit disdained to ask while living.

As the enraptured Ichabod fancied all this, and as he rolled his great green eyes over the fat meadow-lands, the rich fields of wheat, of rye, of buckwheat, and Indian corn, and the orchards burthened with ruddy fruit, which surrounded the warm tenement of Van Tassel, his heart yearned after the damsel who was to inherit these domains, and his imagina-tion expanded with the idea, how they might be readily turned into cash, and the money invested in immense tracts of wild land, and shingle palaces in the wilderness. Nay, his busy fancy already realized his hopes, and presented to him the blooming Katrina, with a whole family of children, mounted on the top of a wagon loaded with household trumpery, with pots and kettles dangling beneath; and he beheld himself bestriding a pacing mare, with a colt at her heels, setting out for Kentucky, Tennessee, or the Lord knows where.

When he entered the house the conquest of his heart was complete. It was one of those spacious farmhouses, with high-ridged, but lowly-sloping roofs, built in the style handed down from the first Dutch settlers; the low projecting eaves forming a piazza along the front, capable of being closed up in bad weather. Under this were hung flails, harness, various utensils of husbandry, and nets for fishing in the neighboring river. Benches were built along the sides for summer use; and a great spinning-wheel at one end, and a churn at the other, showed the various uses to which this important porch might be devoted. From this piazza the wondering Ichabod entered the hall, which formed the centre of the mansion and the place of usual residence. Here, rows of resplendent pewter, ranged on a long dresser, dazzled his eyes. In one corner stood a huge bag of wool ready to be spun; in another a quantity of linsey-woolsey just from the loom; ears of Indian corn, and strings of dried apples and peaches, hung in gay festoons along the walls, mingled with the gaud of red peppers; and a door left ajar gave him a peep into the best parlor, where the claw-footed chairs, and dark mahogany tables, shone like mirrors; and irons, with their accompanying shovel and tongs, glistened from their covert of asparagus tops; mock-oranges and conch-shells decorated the mantelpiece; strings of various colored birds' eggs were suspended above it: a great ostrich egg was hung from the centre of the room, and a corner cupboard, knowingly left open, displayed immense treasures of old silver and well-mended china.

From the moment Ichabod laid his eyes upon these regions of delight, the peace of his mind was at an end, and his only study was how to gain the affections of the peerless daughter of Van Tassel. In this enterprise, however, he had more real difficulties than generally fell to the lot of a knight-errant of yore, who seldom had any thing but giants, enchanters, fiery dragons, and such like easily-conquered adversaries, to contend with; and had to make his way merely through gates of iron and brass, and walls of adamant, to the castle keep, where the lady of his heart was confined; all which he achieved as easily as a man would carve his way to the centre of a Christmas pie; and then the lady gave him her hand as a matter of course. Ichabod, on the contrary, had to win his way to the heart of a country coquette, beset with a labyrinth of whims and caprices, which were for ever presenting new difficulties and impediments; and he had to encounter a host of fearful adversaries of real flesh and blood, the numerous rustic admirers, who beset every portal to her heart; keeping a watchful and angry eye upon each other, but ready to fly out in the common cause against any new competitor.

Among these the most formidable was a burly, roaring, roystering blade, of the name of Abraham, or, according to the Dutch abbreviation, Brom Van Brunt, the hero of the country round, which rang with his feats of strength and hardihood. He was broad-shouldered and double-jointed, with short curly black hair, and a bluff, but not unpleasant countenance, having a mingled air of fun and arrogance. From his Herculean frame and great powers of limb, he had received the nickname of BROM BONES, by which he was universally known. He was famed for great knowledge and skill in horsemanship, being as dexterous on horseback as a Tartar.

He was foremost at all races and cock-fights; and, with the ascendency which bodily strength acquires in rustic life, was the umpire in all disputes, setting his hat on one side, and giving his decisions with an air and tone admitting of no gainsay or appeal. He was always ready for either a fight or a frolic; but had more mischief than ill-will in his composition; and, with all his overbearing roughness, there was a strong dash of waggish good humor at bottom. He had three or four boon companions, who regarded him as their model, and at the head of whom he scoured the country, attending every scene of feud or merriment for miles round. In cold weather he was distinguished by a fur cap, surmounted with a flaunting fox's tail; and when the folks at a country gathering descried this well-known crest at a distance, whisking about among a squad of hard riders, they always stood by for a squall. Sometimes his crew would be heard dashing along past the farmhouses at midnight, with whoop and halloo, like a troop of Don Cossacks; and the old dames, startled out of their sleep, would listen for a moment till the hurry-scurry had clattered by, and then exclaim, 'Ay, there goes Brom Bones and his gang!' The neighbors looked upon him with a mixture of awe, admiration, and good will; and when any madcap prank, or rustic brawl, occurred in the vicinity, always shook their heads, and warranted Brom Bones was at the bottom of it.

This rantipole hero had for some time singled out the blooming Katrina for the object of his uncouth gallantries, and though his amorous toyings were something like the gentle caresses and endearments of a bear, yet it was whispered that she did not altogether discourage his hopes. Certain it is, his advances were signals for rival candidates to retire, who felt no inclination to cross a lion in his amours; insomuch, that when his horse was seen tied to Van Tassel's paling, on a Sunday night, a sure sign that his master was courting, or, as it is termed 'sparking', within, all other suitors passed by in despair, and carried the war into other quarters.

Such was the formidable rival with whom Ichabod Crane had to contend, and, considering all things, a stouter man than he would have shrunk from the competition, and a wiser man would have despaired. He had, however, a happy mixture of pliability and perseverance in his nature; he was in form and spirit like a supple-jack – yielding, but tough; though he bent, he never broke; and though he bowed beneath the slightest pressure, yet, the moment it was away – jerk! he was as erect, and carried his head as high as ever.

To have taken the field openly against his rival would have been madness; for he was not a man to be thwarted in his amours, any more than that stormy lover, Achilles. Ichabod, therefore, made his advances in a quiet and gently-insinuating manner. Under cover of his character of singing-master, he made frequent visits at the farmhouse; not that he had any thing to apprehend from the meddlesome inter-ference of parents, which is so often a stumbling-block in the path of lovers. Balt Van Tassel was an easy indulgent soul; he loved his daughter better even than his pipe, and, like a reasonable man and an excellent father, let her have her way in every thing. His notable little wife, too, had enough to do to attend to her housekeeping and manage her poultry; for, as she sagely observed, ducks and geese are foolish things, and must be looked after, but girls can take care of them-selves. Thus while the busy dame bustled about the house, or plied her spinning-wheel at one end of the piazza, honest Balt would sit smoking his evening pipe at the other, watch-ing the achievements of a little wooden warrior, who, armed with a sword in each hand, was most valiantly fighting the wind on the pinnacle of the barn. In the mean time, Ichabod would carry on his suit with the daughter by the side of the spring under the great elm, or sauntering along in the twilight, that hour so favorable to the lover's eloquence.

I profess not to know how women's hearts are wooed and won. To me they have always been matters of riddle and admiration. Some seem to have but one vulnerable point, or door of access; while others have a thousand avenues, and may be captured in a thousand different ways. It is a great triumph of skill to gain the former, but a still greater proof of generalship to maintain possession of the latter, for the man must battle for his fortress at every door and window. He who wins a thousand common hearts is therefore entitled to some renown; but he who keeps undisputed sway over the heart of a coquette, is indeed a hero. Certain it is, this was not the case with the redoubtable Brom Bones; and from the moment Ichabod Crane made his advances, the interests of the former evidently declined; his horse was no longer seen tied at the palings on Sunday nights, and a deadly feud gradually arose between him and the preceptor of Sleepy Hollow.

Brom, who had a degree of rough chivalry in his nature, would fain have carried matters to open warfare, and have settled their pretensions to the lady, according to the mode of those most concise and simple reasoners, the knights-errant of yore – by single combat; but Ichabod was too conscious of the superior might of his adversary to enter the lists against him: he had overheard a boast of Bones, that he would 'double the schoolmaster up, and lay him on a shelf of his own school-house'; and he was too wary to give him an opportunity. There was something extremely provoking in this obstinately pacific system; it left Brom no alternative but to draw upon the funds of rustic waggery in his disposition, and to play off boorish practical jokes upon his rival. Ichabod became the object of whimsical persecution to Bones, and his gang of rough riders. They harried his hitherto peaceful domains; smoked out his singing school, by stopping up the chimney; broke into the school-house at night, in spite of its formidable fastenings of withe and window stakes, and turned every thing topsy-turvy: so that the poor schoolmaster began to think all the witches in the country held their meetings there. But what was still more annoying, Brom took all opportunities of turning him into ridicule in presence of his mistress, and had a scoundrel dog whom he taught to whine in the most ludicrous manner, and introduced as a rival of Ichabod's to instruct her in psalmody.

In this way matters went on for some time, without producing any material effect on the relative situation of the contending powers. On a fine autumnal afternoon, Ichabod, in pensive mood, sat enthroned on the lofty stool whence he usually watched all the concerns of his little literary realm. In his hand he swayed a ferule, that sceptre of despotic power; the birch of justice reposed on three nails, behind the throne, a constant terror to evil doers; while on the desk before him might be seen sundry contraband articles and prohibited weapons, detected upon the persons of idle urchins; such as half-munched apples, popguns, whirligigs, fly-cages, and whole legions of rampant little paper gamecocks. Apparently there had been some appalling act of justice recently inflicted, for his scholars were all busily intent upon their books, or slyly whispering behind them with one eye kept upon the master; and a kind of buzzing stillness reigned throughout the school-room. It was suddenly interrupted by the appearance of a negro, in tow-cloth jacket and trowsers, a round-crowned fragment of a hat, like the cap of Mercury, and mounted on the back of a ragged, wild, half-broken colt, which he managed with a rope by way of halter. He came clattering up to the school door with an invitation to Ichabod to attend a merry-making or 'quilting frolic', to be held that evening at Mynheer Van Tassel's; and having delivered his message with that air of importance, and effort at fine language, which a negro is apt to display on petty embassies of that kind, he dashed over the brook, and was seen scampering away up the hollow, full of the importance and hurry of his mission.

All was now bustle and hubbub in the late quiet school-room. The scholars were hurried through their lessons, without stopping at trifles; those who were nimble skipped over half with impunity, and those who were tardy, had a smart application now and then in the rear, to quicken their speed, or help them over a tall word. Books were flung aside without being put away on the shelves, inkstands were overturned, benches thrown down, and the whole school was turned loose an hour before the usual time, bursting forth like a legion of young imps, yelping and racketing about the green, in joy at their early emancipation.

The gallant Ichabod now spent at least an extra half hour at his toilet, brushing and furbishing up his best, and indeed only suit of rusty black, and arranging his looks by a bit of broken looking-glass, that hung up in the school-house. That he might make his appearance before his mistress in the true style of a cavalier, he borrowed a horse from the farmer with whom he was domiciliated, a choleric old Dutchman, of the name of Hans Van Ripper, and, thus gallantly mounted, issued forth, like a knight-errant in quest of adventures. But it is meet I should, in the true spirit of romantic story, give some account of the looks and equipments of my hero and his steed. The animal he bestrode was a broken-down plough-horse, that had outlived almost every thing but his viciousness. He was gaunt and shagged, with a ewe neck and a head like a hammer; his rusty mane and tail were tangled and knotted with burrs; one eye had lost its pupil, and was glaring and spectral; but the other had the gleam of a genuine devil in it. Still he must have had fire and mettle in his day, if we may judge from the name he bore of Gunpowder. He had, in fact, been a favorite steed of his master's, the choleric Van Ripper, who was a furious rider, and had infused, very probably, some of his own spirit into the animal; for, old and broken-down as he looked, there was more of the lurking devil in him than in any young filly in the country.

Ichabod was a suitable figure for such a steed. He rode with short stirrups, which brought his knees nearly up to the pommel of the saddle; his sharp elbows stuck out like grasshoppers'; he carried his whip perpendicularly in his hand, like a sceptre, and, as his horse jogged on, the motion of his arms was not unlike the flapping of a pair of wings. A small wool hat rested on the top of his nose, for so his scanty strip of forehead might be called; and the skirts of his black coat fluttered out almost to the horse's tail. Such was the appearance of Ichabod and his steed, as they shambled out of the gate of Hans Van Ripper, and it was altogether such an apparition as is seldom to be met with in broad daylight.

It was, as I have said, a fine autumnal day, the sky was clear and serene, and nature wore that rich and golden livery which we always associate with the idea of abundance. The forests had put on their sober brown and yellow, while some trees of the tenderer kind had been nipped by the frosts into brilliant dyes of orange, purple, and scarlet. Streaming files of wild ducks began to make their appearance high in the air; the bark of the squirrel might be heard from the groves of beech and hickory nuts, and the pensive whistle of the quail at intervals from the neighboring stubble-field.

The small birds were taking their farewell banquets. In the fulness of their revelry, they fluttered, chirping and frolicking, from bush to bush, and tree to tree, capricious from the very profusion and variety around them. There was the honest cock-robin, the favorite game of stripling sportsmen, with its loud querulous note; and the twittering blackbirds flying in sable clouds; and the golden-winged woodpecker, with his crimson crest, his broad black gorget, and splendid plumage; and the cedar bird, with its red-tipt wings and yellow-tipt tail, and its little monteiro cap of feathers; and the blue-jay, that noisy coxcomb, in his gay light-blue coat and white underclothes; screaming and chattering, nodding and bobbing and bowing, and pretending to be on good terms with every songster of the grove.

As Ichabod jogged slowly on his way, his eye, ever open to every symptom of culinary abundance, ranged with delight over the treasures of jolly autumn. On all sides he beheld vast store of apples; some hanging in oppressive opulence on the trees; some gathered into baskets and barrels for the market; others heaped up in rich piles for the cider-press. Farther on he beheld great fields of Indian corn, with its golden ears peeping from their leafy coverts, and holding out the promise of cakes and hasty pudding; and the yellow pumpkins lying beneath them, turning up their fair round bellies to the sun, and giving ample prospects of the most luxurious of pies; and anon he passed the fragrant buckwheat fields, breathing the odor of the beehive, and as he beheld them, soft anticipations stole over his mind of dainty slapjacks, well buttered, and garnished with honey or treacle, by the delicate little dimpled hand of Katrina Van Tassel.

Thus feeding his mind with many sweet thoughts and

'sugared suppositions', he journeyed along the sides of a range of hills which look out upon some of the goodliest scenes of the mighty Hudson. The sun gradually wheeled his broad disk down into the west. The wide bosom of the Tappan Zee lay motionless and glassy, excepting that here and there a gentle undulation waved and prolonged the blue shadow of the distant mountain. A few amber clouds floated in the sky, without a breath of air to move them. The horizon was of a fine golden tint, changing gradually into a pure apple green, and from that into the deep blue of the mid-heaven. A slanting ray lingered on the woody crests of the precipices that overhung some parts of the river, giving greater depth to the dark-gray and purple of their rocky sides. A sloop was loitering in the distance, dropping slowly down with the tide, her sail hanging uselessly against the mast; and as the reflection of the sky gleamed along the still water, it seemed as if the vessel was suspended in the air.

It was toward evening that Ichabod arrived at the castle of the Heer Van Tassel, which he found thronged with the pride and flower of the adjacent country. Old farmers, a spare leathern-faced race, in homespun coats and breeches, blue stockings, huge shoes, and magnificent pewter buckles. Their brisk withered little dames, in close crimped caps, long-waisted short-gowns, home-spun petticoats, with scissors and pincushions, and gay calico pockets hanging on the outside. Buxom lasses, almost as antiquated as their mothers, excepting where a straw hat, a fine ribbon, or perhaps a white frock, gave symptoms of city innovation. The sons, in short square-skirted coats with rows of stupendous brass buttons, and their hair generally queued in the fashion of the times, especially if they could procure an eel-skin for the purpose, it being esteemed, throughout the country, as a potent nourisher and strengthener of the hair.

Brom Bones, however, was the hero of the scene, having come to the gathering on his favorite steed Daredevil, a creature, like himself, full of mettle and mischief, and which no one but himself could manage. He was, in fact, noted for preferring vicious animals, given to all kinds of tricks, which kept the rider in constant risk of his neck, for he held a tractable well-broken horse as unworthy of a lad of spirit.

Fain would I pause to dwell upon the world of charms that burst upon the enraptured gaze of my hero, as he entered the state parlor of Van Tassel's mansion. Not those of the bevy of buxom lasses, with their luxurious display of red and white; but the ample charms of a genuine Dutch country tea-table, in the sumptuous time of autumn. Such heaped-up platters of cakes of various and almost indescribable kinds, known only to experienced Dutch housewives! There was the doughty dough-nut, the tenderer oly koek, and the crisp and crumbling cruller; sweet cakes and short cakes, ginger cakes and honey cakes, and the whole family of cakes. And then there were apple pies and peach pies and pumpkin pies; besides slices of ham and smoked beef; and moreover delectable dishes of preserved plums, and peaches, and pears, and quinces; not to mention broiled shad and roasted chickens; together with bowls of milk and cream, all mingled higgledy-piggledly, pretty much as I have enumerated them, with the motherly tea-pot sending up its clouds of vapor from the midst – Heaven bless the mark! I want breath and time to discuss this banquet as it deserves, and am too eager to get on with my story. Happily, Ichabod Crane was not in so great a hurry as his historian, but did ample justice to every dainty.

He was a kind and thankful creature, whose heart dilated in proportion as his skin was filled with good cheer; and whose spirits rose with eating as some men's do with drink.

He could not help, too, rolling his large eyes round him as he ate, and chuckling with the possibility that he might one day be lord of all this scene of almost unimaginable luxury and splendor. Then, he thought, how soon he'd turn his back upon the old school-house; snap his fingers in the face of Hans Van Ripper, and every other niggardly patron, and kick any itinerant pedagogue out of doors that should dare to call him comrade!

Old Baltus Van Tassel moved about among his guests with a face dilated with content and good humor, round and jolly as the harvest moon. His hospitable attentions were brief, but expressive, being confined to a shake of the hand, a slap on the shoulder, a loud laugh, and a pressing invitation to 'fall to, and help themselves'.

And now the sound of the music from the common room, or hall, summoned to the dance. The musician was an old gray-headed negro, who had been the itinerant orchestra of the neighborhood for more than half a century. His instrument was as old and battered as himself. The greater part of the time he scraped on two or three strings, accompanying every movement of the bow with a motion of the head; bowing almost to the ground, and stamping with his foot whenever a fresh couple were to start.

Ichabod prided himself upon his dancing as much as upon his vocal powers. Not a limb, not a fibre about him was idle; and to have seen his loosely hung frame in full motion, and clattering about the room, you would have thought Saint Vitus himself, that blessed patron of the dance, was figuring before you in person. He was the admiration of all the negroes; who, having gathered, of all ages and sizes, from the farm and the neighborhood, stood forming a pyramid of shining black faces at every door and window, gazing with delight at the scene, rolling their white eye-balls, and showing grinning rows of ivory from ear to ear. How could the flogger of urchins be otherwise than animated and joyous? the lady of his heart was his partner in the dance, and smiling graciously in reply to all his amorous oglings; while Brom Bones, sorely smitten with love and jealousy, sat brooding by himself in one corner.

When the dance was at an end, Ichabod was attracted to a knot of the sager folks, who, with old Van Tassel, sat smoking at one end of the piazza, gossiping over former times, and drawing out long stories about the war.

This neighborhood, at the time of which I am speaking, was one of those highly-favored places which abound with chronicle and great men. The British and American line had run near it during the war; it had, therefore, been the scene of marauding, and infested with refugees, cowboys, and all kinds of border chivalry. Just sufficient time had elapsed to enable each story-teller to dress up his tale with a little becoming fiction, and, in the indistinctness of his recollection, to make himself the hero of every exploit.

There was the story of Doffue Martling, a large blue-bearded Dutchman, who had nearly taken a British frigate with an old iron nine-pounder from a mud breastwork, only that his gun burst at the sixth discharge. And there was an old gentleman who shall be nameless, being too rich a mynheer to be lightly mentioned, who, in the battle of White-plains, being an excellent master of defence, parried a musket ball with a small sword, insomuch that he absolutely felt it whiz round the blade, and glance off at the hilt: in proof of which, he was ready at any time to show the sword, with the hilt a little bent. There were several more that had been equally great in the field, not one of whom but was persuaded that he had a considerable hand in bringing the war to a happy termination.

But all these were nothing to the tales of ghosts and apparitions that succeeded. The neighborhood is rich in legendary treasures of the kind. Local tales and superstitions thrive best in these sheltered long-settled retreats; but are trampled under foot by the shifting throng that forms the populations of most of our country places. Besides, there is no encouragement for ghosts in most of our villages, for, they have scarcely had time to finish their first nap, and turn themselves in their graves, before their surviving friends have travelled away from the neighborhood; so that when they turn out at night to walk their rounds, they have no acquaintance left to call upon. This is perhaps the reason why we so seldom hear of ghosts except in our long-established Dutch communities.

The immediate cause, however, of the prevalence of supernatural stories in these parts, was doubtless owing to the vicinity of Sleepy Hollow. There was a contagion in the very air that blew from that haunted region; it breathed forth an atmosphere of dreams and fancies infecting all the land. Several of the Sleepy Hollow people were present at Van Tassel's, and, as usual, were doling out their wild and wonderful legends. Many dismal tales were told about funeral trains, and mourning cries and wailing heard and seen about the great tree where the unfortunate Major André was taken, and which stood in the neighborhood. Some mention was made also of the woman in white, that haunted the dark glen at Raven Rock, and was often heard to shriek on winter nights before a storm, having perished there in the snow. The chief part of the stories, however, turned upon the favorite spectre of Sleepy Hollow, the headless horseman, who had been heard several times of late, patrolling the country; and, it was said, tethered his horse nightly among the graves in the church-yard.

The sequestered situation of this church seems always to

have made it a favorite haunt of troubled spirits. It stands on a knoll, surrounded by locust-trees and lofty elms, from among which its decent whitewashed walls shine modestly forth, like Christian purity beaming through the shades of retirement. A gentle slope descends from it to a silver sheet of water, bordered by high trees, between which, peeps may be caught at the blue hills of the Hudson. To look upon its grass-grown yard, where the sunbeams seem to sleep so quietly, one would think that there at least the dead might rest in peace. On one side of the church extends a wide woody dell, along which raves a large brook among broken rocks and trunks of fallen trees. Over a deep black part of the stream, not far from the church, was formerly thrown a wooden bridge; the road that led to it, and the bridge itself, were thickly shaded by overhanging trees, which cast a gloom about it, even in the daytime; but occasioned a fearful darkness at night. This was one of the favorite haunts of the headless horseman; and the place where he was most frequently encountered. The tale was told of old Brouwer, a most heretical disbeliever in ghosts, how he met the horseman returning from his foray into Sleepy Hollow, and was obliged to get up behind him; how they galloped over bush and brake, over hill and swamp, until they reached the bridge; when the horseman suddenly turned into a skeleton, threw old Brouwer into the brook, and sprang away over the tree-tops with a clap of thunder.

This story was immediately matched by a thrice marvellous adventure of Brom Bones, who made light of the galloping Hessian as an arrant jockey. He affirmed that, on returning one night from the neighboring village of Sing Sing, he had been overtaken by this midnight trooper; that he had offered to race with him for a bowl of punch, and should have won it too, for Daredevil beat the goblin horse all hollow, but, just as they came to the church bridge, the Hessian bolted, and vanished in a flash of fire.

All these tales, told in that drowsy undertone with which men talk in the dark, the countenances of the listeners only now and then receiving a casual gleam from the glare of a pipe, sank deep in the mind of Ichabod. He repaid them in kind with large extracts from his invaluable author, Cotton Mather, and added many marvellous events that had taken place in his native State of Connecticut, and fearful sights which he had seen in his nightly walks about Sleepy Hollow.

The revel now gradually broke up. The old farmers gathered together their families in their wagons, and were heard for some time rattling along the hollow roads, and over the distant hills. Some of the damsels mounted on pillions behind their favorite swains, and their light-hearted laughter, mingling with the clatter of hoofs, echoed along the silent woodlands, sounding fainter and fainter until they gradually died away – and the late scene of noise and frolic was all silent and deserted. Ichabod only lingered behind, according to the custom of country lovers, to have a tête-à-tête with the heiress, fully convinced that he was now on the high road to success. What passed at this interview I will not pretend to say, for in fact I do not know. Something, however, I fear me, must have gone wrong, for he certainly sallied forth, after no very great interval, with an air quite desolate and chop-fallen. – Oh these women! these women! Could that girl have been playing off any of her coquettish tricks? – Was her encouragement of the poor pedagogue all a mere sham to secure her conquest of his rival? – Heaven only knows, not I! – Let it suffice to say, Ichabod stole forth with the air of one who had been sacking a hen-roost, rather than a fair lady's heart. Without looking to the right or left to notice the scene of rural wealth, on which he had so often gloated, he went straight to the stable, and with several hearty cuffs and kicks, roused his steed most uncourteously from the comfortable quarters in which he was soundly sleeping, dreaming of mountains of corn and oats, and whole valleys of timothy and clover.

It was the very witching time of night that Ichabod, heavy-hearted and crest-fallen, pursued his travel homewards, along the sides of the lofty hills which rise above Tarry Town, and which he had traversed so cheerily in the afternoon. The hour was dismal as himself. Far below him, the Tappan Zee spread its dusky and indistinct waste of waters, with here and there the tall mast of a sloop, riding quietly at anchor under the land. In the dead hush of midnight, he could even hear the barking of the watch dog from the opposite shore of the Hudson; but it was so vague and faint as only to give an idea of his distance from this faithful companion of man. Now and then, too, the long drawn crowing of a cock, accidentally awakened, would sound far, far off from some farmhouse away among the hills – but it was like a dreaming sound in his ear. No signs of life occurred near him, but occasionally the melancholy chirp of a cricket, or perhaps the guttural twang of a bull-frog, from a neighboring marsh, as if sleeping uncomfortably, and turning suddenly in his bed.

All the stories of ghosts and goblins that he had heard in the afternoon, now came crowding upon his recollection. The night grew darker and darker; the stars seemed to sink deeper in the sky, and driving clouds occasionally hid them from his sight. He had never felt so lonely and dismal. He was, moreover, approaching the very place where many of the scenes of the ghost stories had been laid. In the centre of the road stood an enormous tulip-tree, which towered like a giant above all the other trees of the neighborhood, and formed a kind of landmark. Its limbs were gnarled, and fantastic, large enough to form trunks for ordinary trees, twisting down almost to the earth, and rising again into the air.

It was connected with the tragical story of the unfortunate André, who had been taken prisoner hard by; and was universally known by the name of Major André's tree. The common people regarded it with a mixture of respect and superstition, partly out of sympathy for the fate of its ill-starred namesake, and partly from the tales of strange sights and doleful lamentations told concerning it.

As Ichabod approached this fearful tree, he began to whistle: he thought his whistle was answered – it was but a blast sweeping sharply through the dry branches. As he approached a little nearer, he thought he saw something white, hanging in the midst of the tree – he paused and ceased whistling; but on looking more narrowly, perceived that it was a place where the tree had been scathed by lightning, and the white wood laid bare. Suddenly he heard a groan – his teeth chattered and his knees smote against the saddle: it was but the rubbing of one huge bough upon another, as they were swayed about by the breeze. He passed the tree in safety, but new perils lay before him.

About two hundred yards from the tree a small brook crossed the road, and ran into a marshy and thickly-wooded glen, known by the name of Wiley's swamp. A few rough logs, laid side by side, served for a bridge over this stream. On that side of the road where the brook entered the wood, a group of oaks and chestnuts, matted thick with wild grapevines, threw a cavernous gloom over it. To pass this bridge was the severest trial. It was at this identical spot that the unfortunate André was captured, and under the covert of those chestnuts and vines were the sturdy yeomen concealed who surprised him. This has ever since been considered a haunted stream, and fearful are the feelings of the schoolboy who has to pass it alone after dark.

As he approached the stream his heart began to thump; he summoned up, however, all his resolution, gave his horse half a score of kicks in the ribs, and attempted to dash briskly across the bridge; but instead of starting forward, the perverse old animal made a lateral movement, and ran broadside against the fence. Ichabod, whose fears increased with the delay, jerked the reins on the other side, and kicked lustily with the contrary foot: it was all in vain; his steed started, it is true, but it was only to plunge to the opposite side of the road into a thicket of brambles and alder bushes. The schoolmaster now bestowed both whip and heel upon the starveling ribs of old Gunpowder, who dashed forward, snuffling and snorting, but came to a stand just by the bridge, with a suddenness that had nearly sent his rider sprawling over his head. Just at this moment a plashy tramp by the side of the bridge caught the sensitive ear of Ichabod. In the dark shadow of the grove, on the margin of the brook, he beheld something huge, misshapen, black and towering. It stirred not, but seemed gathered up in the gloom, like some gigantic monster ready to spring upon the traveller.

The hair of the affrighted pedagogue rose upon his head with terror. What was to be done? To turn and fly was now too late; and besides, what chance was there of escaping ghost or goblin, if such it was, which could ride upon the wings of the wind? Summoning up, therefore, a show of courage, he demanded in stammering accents – 'Who are you?' He received no reply. He repeated his demand in a still more agitated voice. Still there was no answer. Once more he cudgelled the sides of the inflexible Gunpowder, and, shutting his eyes, broke forth with involuntary fervor into a psalm tune. Just then the shadowy object of alarm put itself in motion, and, with a scramble and a bound, stood at once in the middle of the road. Though the night was dark and dismal, yet the form of the unknown might now in some degree be ascertained. He appeared to be a horseman of large dimensions, and mounted on a black horse of powerful frame. He made no offer of molestation or sociability, but kept aloof on one side of the road, jogging along on the blind side of old Gunpowder, who had now got over his fright and waywardness.

Ichabod, who had no relish for this strange midnight companion, and bethought himself of the adventure of Brom Bones with the Galloping Hessian, now quickened his steed, in hopes of leaving him behind. The stranger, however, quickened his horse to an equal pace. Ichabod pulled up, and fell into a walk, thinking to lag behind – the other did the same. His heart began to sink within him; he endeavored to resume his psalm tune, but his parched tongue clove to the roof of his mouth, and he could not utter a stave. There was something in the moody and dogged silence of this pertinacious companion, that was mysterious and appalling. It was soon fearfully accounted for. On mounting a rising ground, which brought the figure of his fellow-traveller in relief against the sky, gigantic in height, and muffled in a cloak, Ichabod was horror-struck, on perceiving that he was headless! – but his horror was still more increased, on observing that the head, which should have rested on his shoulders, was carried before him on the pommel of the saddle; his terror rose to desperation; he rained a shower of kicks and blows upon Gunpowder; hoping, by a sudden movement, to give his companion the slip – but the spectre started full jump with him. Away then they dashed, through thick and thin; stones flying, and sparks flashing at every bound. Ichabod's flimsy garments fluttered in the air, as he stretched his long lanky body away over his horse's head, in the eagerness of his flight.

They had now reached the road which turns off to Sleepy Hollow; but Gunpowder, who seemed possessed with a demon, instead of keeping up it, made an opposite turn, and plunged headlong down hill to the left. This road leads through a sandy hollow, shaded by trees for about a quarter of a mile, where it crosses the bridge famous in goblin story, and just beyond swells the green knoll on which stands the whitewashed church.

As yet the panic of the steed had given his unskilful rider an apparent advantage in the chase; but just as he had got half way through the hollow, the girths of the saddle gave way, and he felt it slipping from under him. He seized it by the pommel, and endeavored to hold it firm, but in vain; and had just time to save himself by clasping old Gunpowder round the neck, when the saddle fell to the earth, and he heard it trampled under foot by his pursuer. For a moment the terror of Hans Van Ripper's wrath passed across his mind—for it was his Sunday saddle; but this was no time for petty fears; the goblin was hard on his haunches; and (unskilful rider that he was!) he had much ado to maintain his seat; sometimes slipping on one side, sometimes on another, and sometimes jolted on the high ridge of his horse's backbone, with a violence that he verily feared would cleave him asunder.

An opening in the trees now cheered him with the hopes that the church bridge was at hand. The wavering reflection of a silver star in the bosom of the brook told him that he was not mistaken. He saw the walls of the church dimly glaring under the trees beyond. He recollected the place where Brom Bones's ghostly competitor had disappeared. 'If I can but reach that bridge,' thought Ichabod, 'I am safe.' Just then he heard the black steed panting and blowing close behind him; he even fancied that he felt his hot breath. Another convulsive kick in the ribs, and old Gunpowder sprang upon the bridge; he thundered over the resounding planks; he gained the opposite side; and now Ichabod cast a look behind to see if his pursuer should vanish, according to rule, in a flash of fire and brimstone. Just then he saw the goblin rising in his stirrups, and in the very act of hurling his head at him. Ichabod endeavored to dodge the horrible missile, but too late. It encountered his cranium with a tremendous crash – he was tumbled headlong into the dust, and Gunpowder, the black steed, and the goblin rider, passed by like a whirlwind.

The next morning the old horse was found without his saddle, and with the bridle under his feet, soberly cropping the grass at his master's gate. Ichabod did not make his appearance at breakfast – dinner-hour came, but no Ichabod. The boys assembled at the school-house, and strolled idly about the banks of the brook; but no schoolmaster. Hans Van Ripper now began to feel some uneasiness about the fate of poor Ichabod, and his saddle. An inquiry was set on foot, and after diligent investigation they came upon his traces. In one part of the road leading to the church was found the saddle trampled in the dirt; the tracks of horses' hoofs deeply dented in the road, and evidently at furious speed, were traced to the bridge, beyond which, on the bank of a broad part of the brook, where the water ran deep and black, was found the hat of the unfortunate Ichabod, and close beside it a shattered pumpkin.

The brook was searched, but the body of the school-master was not to be discovered. Hans Van Ripper, as executor of his estate, examined the bundle which contained all his worldly effects. They consisted of two shirts and a half; two stocks for the neck; a pair or two of worsted stockings;

an old pair of corduroy small-clothes; a rusty razor; a book of psalm tunes, full of dogs' ears; and a broken pitchpipe. As to the books and furniture of the school-house, they belonged to the community, excepting Cotton Mather's History of Witchcraft, a New England Almanac, and a book of dreams and fortune-telling; in which last was a sheet of foolscap much scribbled and blotted in several fruitless attempts to make a copy of verses in honor of the heiress of Van Tassel. These magic books and the poetic scrawls were forthwith consigned to the flames by Hans Van Ripper; who from that time forward determined to send his children no more to school; observing, that he never knew any good come of this same reading and writing. Whatever money the schoolmaster possessed, and he had received his quarter's pay but a day or two before, he must have had about his person at the time of his disappearance.

The mysterious event caused much speculation at the church on the following Sunday. Knots of gazers and gossips were collected in the church-yard, at the bridge, and at the spot where the hat and pumpkin had been found. The stories of Brouwer, of Bones, and a whole budget of others, were called to mind; and when they had diligently considered them all, and compared them with the symptoms of the present case, they shook their heads, and came to the conclusion that Ichabod had been carried off by the galloping Hessian. As he was a bachelor, and in nobody's debt, nobody troubled his head any more about him. The school was removed to a different quarter of the hollow, and another pedagogue reigned in his stead.

It is true, an old farmer, who had been down to New York on a visit several years after, and from whom this account of the ghostly adventure was received, brought home the intelligence that Ichabod Crane was still alive; that he had left the neighborhood, partly through fear of the goblin and Hans Van Ripper, and partly in mortification at having been suddenly dismissed by the heiress; that he had changed his quarters to a distant part of the country; had kept school and studied law at the same time, had been admitted to the bar, turned politician, electioneered, written for the newspapers, and finally had been made a justice of the Ten Pound Court. Brom Bones too, who shortly after his rival's disappearance conducted the blooming Katrina in triumph to the altar, was observed to look exceedingly knowing whenever the story of Ichabod was related, and always burst into a hearty laugh at the mention of the pumpkin; which led some to suspect that he knew more about the matter than he chose to tell.

The old country wives, however, who are the best judges of these matters, maintain to this day that Ichabod was spirited away by supernatural means; and it is a favorite story often told about the neighborhood round the winter evening fire. The bridge became more than ever an object of superstitious awe, and that may be the reason why the road has been altered of late years, so as to approach the church by the border of the mill-pond. The school-house being deserted, soon fell to decay, and was reported to be haunted by the ghost of the unfortunate pedagogue; and the ploughboy, loitering homeward of a still summer evening, has often fancied his voice at a distance, chanting a melancholy psalm tune among the tranquil solitudes of Sleepy Hollow.

F. SCOTT FITZGERALD

THE CURIOUS
CASE OF BENJAMIN
BUTTON

I

AS LONG AGO as 1860 it was the proper thing to be born at home. At present, so I am told, the high gods of medicine have decreed that the first cries of the young shall be uttered upon the anesthetic air of a hospital, preferably a fashionable one. So young Mr and Mrs Roger Button were fifty years ahead of style when they decided, one day in the summer of 1860, that their first baby should be born in a hospital. Whether this anachronism had any bearing upon the astonishing history I am about to set down will never be known.

I shall tell you what occurred, and let you judge for yourself.

The Roger Buttons held an enviable position, both social and financial, in ante-bellum Baltimore. They were related to the This Family and the That Family, which, as every Southerner knew, entitled them to membership in that enormous peerage which largely populated the Confederacy. This was their first experience with the charming old custom of having babies – Mr Button was naturally nervous. He hoped it would be a boy so that he could be sent to Yale College in Connecticut, at which institution Mr Button himself had been known for four years by the somewhat obvious nickname of 'Cuff'.

On the September morning consecrated to the enormous

event he arose nervously at six o'clock, dressed himself, adjusted an impeccable stock, and hurried forth through the streets of Baltimore to the hospital, to determine whether the darkness of the night had borne in new life upon its bosom.

When he was approximately a hundred yards from the Maryland Private Hospital for Ladies and Gentlemen he saw Doctor Keene, the family physician, descending the front steps, rubbing his hands together with a washing movement – as all doctors are required to do by the unwritten ethics of their profession.

Mr Roger Button, the president of Roger Button & Co., Wholesale Hardware, began to run toward Doctor Keene with much less dignity than was expected from a Southern gentleman of that picturesque period. 'Doctor Keene!' he called. 'Oh, Doctor Keene!'

The doctor heard him, faced around, and stood waiting, a curious expression settling on his harsh, medicinal face as Mr Button drew near.

'What happened?' demanded Mr Button, as he came up in a gasping rush. 'What was it? How is she? A boy? Who is it? What—'

'Talk sense!' said Doctor Keene sharply. He appeared somewhat irritated.

'Is the child born?' begged Mr Button.

Doctor Keene frowned. 'Why, yes, I suppose so – after a fashion.' Again he threw a curious glance at Mr Button.

'Is my wife all right?'

'Yes.'

'Is it a boy or a girl?'

'Here now!' cried Doctor Keene in a perfect passion of irritation, 'I'll ask you to go and see for yourself. Outrageous!' He snapped the last word out in almost one syllable, then he turned away muttering: 'Do you imagine a case like this will help my professional reputation? One more would ruin me – ruin anybody.'

'What's the matter?' demanded Mr Button, appalled. 'Triplets?'

'No, not triplets!' answered the doctor cuttingly. 'What's more, you can go and see for yourself. And get another doctor. I brought you into the world, young man, and I've been physician to your family for forty years, but I'm through with you! I don't want to see you or any of your relatives ever again! Good-bye!'

Then he turned sharply, and without another word climbed into his phaeton, which was waiting at the curbstone, and drove severely away.

Mr Button stood there upon the sidewalk, stupefied and trembling from head to foot. What horrible mishap had occurred? He had suddenly lost all desire to go into the Maryland Private Hospital for Ladies and Gentlemen – it was with the greatest difficulty that, a moment later, he forced himself to mount the steps and enter the front door.

A nurse was sitting behind a desk in the opaque gloom of the hall. Swallowing his shame, Mr Button approached her.

'Good-morning,' she remarked, looking up at him pleasantly.

'Good-morning. I – I am Mr Button.'

At this a look of utter terror spread itself over the girl's face. She rose to her feet and seemed about to fly from the hall, restraining herself only with the most apparent difficulty.

'I want to see my child,' said Mr Button.

The nurse gave a little scream. 'Oh – of course!' she cried hysterically. 'Up-stairs. Right up-stairs. Go – *up*!'

She pointed the direction, and Mr Button, bathed in a cool perspiration, turned falteringly, and began to mount to the second floor. In the upper hall he addressed another nurse who approached him, basin in hand. 'I'm Mr Button,' he managed to articulate. 'I want to see my—'

Clank! The basin clattered to the floor and rolled in the direction of the stairs. Clank! Clank! It began a methodical descent as if sharing in the general terror which this gentleman provoked.

'I want to see my child!' Mr Button almost shrieked. He was on the verge of collapse.

Clank! The basin had reached the first floor. The nurse regained control of herself, and threw Mr Button a look of hearty contempt.

'All *right*, Mr Button,' she agreed in a hushed voice. 'Very *well*! But if you *knew* what state it's put us all in this morning! It's perfectly outrageous! The hospital will never have the ghost of a reputation after—'

'Hurry!' he cried hoarsely. 'I can't stand this!'

'Come this way, then, Mr Button.'

He dragged himself after her. At the end of a long hall they reached a room from which proceeded a variety of howls – indeed, a room which, in later parlance, would have been known as the 'crying-room'. They entered. Ranged around the walls were half a dozen white-enameled rolling cribs, each with a tag tied at the head.

'Well,' gasped Mr Button, 'which is mine?'

'There!' said the nurse.

Mr Button's eyes followed her pointing finger, and this is what he saw. Wrapped in a voluminous white blanket, and partially crammed into one of the cribs, there sat an old man apparently about seventy years of age. His sparse hair was almost white, and from his chin dripped a long smoke-colored beard, which waved absurdly back and forth, fanned by the breeze coming in at the window. He looked up at

Mr Button with dim, faded eyes in which lurked a puzzled question.

'Am I mad?' thundered Mr Button, his terror resolving into rage. 'Is this some ghastly hospital joke?'

'It doesn't seem like a joke to us,' replied the nurse severely. 'And I don't know whether you're mad or not – but that is most certainly your child.'

The cool perspiration redoubled on Mr Button's forehead. He closed his eyes, and then, opening them, looked again. There was no mistake – he was gazing at a man of threescore and ten – a *baby* of threescore and ten, a baby whose feet hung over the sides of the crib in which it was reposing.

The old man looked placidly from one to the other for a moment, and then suddenly spoke in a cracked and ancient voice. 'Are you my father?' he demanded.

Mr Button and the nurse started violently.

'Because if you are,' went on the old man querulously, 'I wish you'd get me out of this place – or, at least, get them to put a comfortable rocker in here.'

'Where in God's name did you come from? Who are you?' burst out Mr Button frantically.

'I can't tell you *exactly* who I am,' replied the querulous whine, 'because I've only been born a few hours – but my last name is certainly Button.'

'You lie! You're an impostor!'

The old man turned wearily to the nurse. 'Nice way to welcome a new-born child,' he complained in a weak voice. 'Tell him he's wrong, why don't you?'

'You're wrong, Mr Button,' said the nurse severely. 'This is your child, and you'll have to make the best of it. We're going to ask you to take him home with you as soon as possible – some time today.'

'Home?' repeated Mr Button incredulously.

'Yes, we can't have him here. We really can't, you know?'

'I'm right glad of it,' whined the old man. 'This is a fine place to keep a youngster of quiet tastes. With all this yelling and howling, I haven't been able to get a wink of sleep. I asked for something to eat' – here his voice rose to a shrill note of protest – 'and they brought me a bottle of milk!'

Mr Button sank down upon a chair near his son and concealed his face in his hands. 'My heavens!' he murmured, in an ecstasy of horror. 'What will people say? What must I do?'

'You'll have to take him home,' insisted the nurse – 'immediately!'

A grotesque picture formed itself with dreadful clarity before the eyes of the tortured man – a picture of himself walking through the crowded streets of the city with this appalling apparition stalking by his side. 'I can't. I can't,' he moaned.

People would stop to speak to him, and what was he going to say? He would have to introduce this – this septuagenarian: 'This is my son, born early this morning.' And then the old man would gather his blanket around him and they would plod on, past the bustling stores, the slave market – for a dark instant Mr Button wished passionately that his son was black – past the luxurious houses of the residential district, past the home for the aged. . . .

'Come! Pull yourself together,' commanded the nurse.

'See here,' the old man announced suddenly, 'if you think I'm going to walk home in this blanket, you're entirely mistaken.'

'Babies always have blankets.'

With a malicious cackle the old man held up a small white swaddling garment. 'Look!' he quavered. '*This* is what they had ready for me.'

'Babies always wear those,' said the nurse primly.

'Well,' said the old man, 'this baby's not going to wear anything in about two minutes. This blanket itches. They might at least have given me a sheet.'

'Keep it on! Keep it on!' said Mr Button hurriedly. He turned to the nurse. 'What'll I do?'

'Go down town and buy your son some clothes.'

Mr Button's son's voice followed him down into the hall: 'And a cane, father. I want to have a cane.'

Mr Button banged the outer door savagely. . . .

II

'Good-morning,' Mr Button said, nervously, to the clerk in the Chesapeake Dry Goods Company. 'I want to buy some clothes for my child.'

'How old is your child, sir?'

'About six hours,' answered Mr Button, without due consideration.

'Babies' supply department in the rear.'

'Why, I don't think – I'm not sure that's what I want. It's – he's an unusually large-size child. Exceptionally – ah – large.'

'They have the largest child's sizes.'

'Where is the boys' department?' inquired Mr Button, shifting his ground desperately. He felt that the clerk must surely scent his shameful secret.

'Right here.'

'Well—' He hesitated. The notion of dressing his son in men's clothes was repugnant to him. If, say, he could only find a *very* large boy's suit, he might cut off that long and awful beard, dye the white hair brown, and thus manage to conceal the worst, and to retain something of his own self-respect – not to mention his position in Baltimore society.

But a frantic inspection of the boys' department revealed

no suits to fit the new-born Button. He blamed the store, of course – in such cases it is the thing to blame the store.

'How old did you say that boy of yours was?' demanded the clerk curiously.

'He's – sixteen.'

'Oh, I beg your pardon. I thought you said six *hours*. You'll find the youths' department in the next aisle.'

Mr Button turned miserably away. Then he stopped, brightened, and pointed his finger toward a dressed dummy in the window display. 'There!' he exclaimed. 'I'll take that suit, out there on the dummy.'

The clerk stared. 'Why,' he protested, 'that's not a child's suit. At least it *is*, but it's for fancy dress. You could wear it yourself!'

'Wrap it up,' insisted his customer nervously. 'That's what I want.'

The astonished clerk obeyed.

Back at the hospital Mr Button entered the nursery and almost threw the package at his son. 'Here's your clothes,' he snapped out.

The old man untied the package and viewed the contents with a quizzical eye.

'They look sort of funny to me,' he complained. 'I don't want to be made a monkey of—'

'You've made a monkey of me!' retorted Mr Button fiercely. 'Never you mind how funny you look. Put them on – or I'll – or I'll *spank* you.' He swallowed uneasily at the penultimate word, feeling nevertheless that it was the proper thing to say.

'All right, father' – this with a grotesque simulation of filial respect – 'you've lived longer; you know best. Just as you say.'

As before, the sound of the word 'father' caused Mr Button to start violently.

'And hurry.'

'I'm hurrying, father.'

When his son was dressed Mr Button regarded him with depression. The costume consisted of dotted socks, pink pants, and a belted blouse with a wide white collar. Over the latter waved the long whitish beard, drooping almost to the waist. The effect was not good.

'Wait!'

Mr Button seized some hospital shears and with three quick snaps amputated a large section of the beard. But even with this improvement the ensemble fell far short of perfection. The remaining brush of scraggly hair, the watery eyes, the ancient teeth, seemed oddly out of tone with the gayety of the costume. Mr Button, however, was obdurate – he held out his hand. 'Come along!' he said sternly.

His son took the hand trustingly. 'What are you going to call me, dad?' he quavered as they walked from the nursery – 'just "baby" for a while? till you think of a better name?'

Mr Button grunted. 'I don't know,' he answered harshly. 'I think we'll call you Methuselah.'

III

Even after the new addition to the Button family had had his hair cut short and then dyed to a sparse unnatural black, had had his face shaved so close that it glistened, and had been attired in small-boy clothes made to order by a flabbergasted tailor, it was impossible for Mr Button to ignore the fact that his son was a poor excuse for a first family baby. Despite his aged stoop, Benjamin Button – for it was by this name they called him instead of by the appropriate but invidious Methuselah – was five feet eight inches tall. His clothes did not conceal this, nor did the clipping and dyeing of his eyebrows disguise the fact that the eyes underneath were faded and watery and tired. In fact, the baby-nurse who had been engaged in advance left the house after one look, in a state of considerable indignation.

But Mr Button persisted in his unwavering purpose. Benjamin was a baby, and a baby he should remain. At first he declared that if Benjamin didn't like warm milk he could go without food altogether, but he was finally prevailed upon to allow his son bread and butter, and even oatmeal by way of a compromise. One day he brought home a rattle and, giving it to Benjamin, insisted in no uncertain terms that he should 'play with it', whereupon the old man took it with a weary expression and could be heard jingling it obediently at intervals throughout the day.

There can be no doubt, though, that the rattle bored him, and that he found other and more soothing amusements when he was left alone. For instance, Mr Button discovered one day that during the preceding week he had smoked more cigars than ever before – a phenomenon which was explained a few days later when, entering the nursery unexpectedly, he found the room full of faint blue haze and Benjamin, with a guilty expresssion on his face, trying to conceal the butt of a dark Havana. This, of course, called for a severe spanking but Mr Button found that he could not bring himself to administer it. He merely warned his son that he would 'stunt his growth'.

Nevertheless he persisted in his attitude. He brought home lead soldiers, he brought toy trains, he brought large pleasant animals made of cotton, and, to perfect the illusion which he was creating – for himself at least – he passionately demanded of the clerk in the toy-store whether 'the paint would come off the pink duck if the baby put it in his mouth'. But, despite all his father's efforts, Benjamin refused to be interested. He would steal down the back stairs and return to the nursery with a volume of the 'Encyclopædia Britannica', over which he would pore through an afternoon, while his cotton cows and his Noah's ark were left neglected on the floor. Against such a stubbornness Mr Button's efforts were of little avail.

The sensation created in Baltimore was, at first, prodigious. What the mishap would have cost the Buttons and their kinsfolk socially cannot be determined, for the out break of the Civil War drew the city's attention to other things. A few people who were unfailingly polite racked their brains for compliments to give to the parents – and finally hit upon the ingenious device of declaring that the baby resembled his grandfather, a fact which, due to the standard state of decay common to all men of seventy, could not be denied. Mr and Mrs Roger Button were not pleased and Benjamin's grandfather was furiously insulted.

Benjamin, once he left the hospital, took life as he found it. Several small boys were brought to see him, and he spent a stiff jointed afternoon trying to work up an interest in tops and marbles – he even managed, quite accidentally, to break a kitchen window with a stone from a sling shot, a feat which secretly delighted his father.

Thereafter Benjamin contrived to break something every day, but he did these things only because they were expected of him, and because he was by nature obliging.

When his grandfather's initial antagonism wore off, Benjamin and that gentleman took enormous pleasure in one another's company. They would sit for hours, these two so far apart in age and experience, and, like old cronies, discuss with tireless monotony the slow events of the day. Benjamin felt more at ease in his grandfather's presence than in his parents' – they seemed always somewhat in awe of him and, despite the dictatorial authority they exercised over him, frequently addressed him as 'Mr'.

He was as puzzled as any one else at the apparently advanced age of his mind and body at birth. He read up on it in the medical journal, but found that no such case had been previously recorded. At his father's urging he made an honest attempt to play with other boys, and frequently he joined in the milder games – football shook him up too much, and he feared that in case of a fracture his ancient bones would refuse to knit.

When he was five he was sent to kindergarten, where he was initiated into the art of pasting green paper on orange paper, of weaving colored maps and manufacturing eternal cardboard necklaces. He was inclined to drowse off to sleep in the middle of these tasks, a habit which both irritated and frightened his young teacher. To his relief she complained to his parents, and he was removed from the school. The Roger Buttons told their friends that they felt he was too young.

By the time he was twelve years old his parents had grown used to him. Indeed, so strong is the force of custom that they no longer felt that he was different from any other child – except when some curious anomaly reminded them of the fact. But one day a few weeks after his twelfth birthday, while looking in the mirror, Benjamin made, or thought he made, an astonishing discovery. Did his eyes deceive him, or had his hair turned in the dozen years of his life from white to iron-gray under its concealing dye? Was the network of wrinkles on his face becoming less pronounced? Was his skin healthier and firmer, with even a touch of ruddy winter color? He could not tell. He knew that he no longer stooped and that his physical condition had improved since the early days of his life.

'Can it be—?' he thought to himself, or, rather, scarcely dared to think.

He went to his father. 'I am grown,' he announced determinedly. 'I want to put on long trousers.'

His father hesitated. 'Well,' he said finally, 'I don't know. Fourteen is the age for putting on long trousers – and you are only twelve.'

'But you'll have to admit,' protested Benjamin, 'that I'm big for my age.'

His father looked at him with illusory speculation. 'Oh, I'm not so sure of that,' he said. 'I was as big as you when I was twelve.'

This was not true – it was all part of Roger Button's silent agreement with himself to believe in his son's normality.

Finally a compromise was reached. Benjamin was to continue to dye his hair. He was to make a better attempt to play with boys of his own age. He was not to wear his spectacles or carry a cane in the street. In return for these concessions he was allowed his first suit of long trousers. . . .

IV

Of the life of Benjamin Button between his twelfth and twenty-first year I intend to say little. Suffice to record that they were years of normal ungrowth. When Benjamin was eighteen he was erect as a man of fifty; he had more hair and it was of a dark gray; his step was firm, his voice had lost its cracked quaver and descended to a healthy baritone. So his father sent him up to Connecticut to take examinations for entrance to Yale College. Benjamin passed his examination and became a member of the freshman class.

On the third day following his matriculation he received

a notification from Mr Hart, the college registrar, to call at his office and arrange his schedule. Benjamin, glancing in the mirror, decided that his hair needed a new application of its brown dye, but an anxious inspection of his bureau drawer disclosed that the dye bottle was not there. Then he remembered – he had emptied it the day before and thrown it away.

He was in a dilemma. He was due at the registrar's in five minutes. There seemed to be no help for it – he must go as he was. He did.

'Good-morning,' said the registrar politely. 'You've come to inquire about your son.'

'Why, as a matter of fact, my name's Button—' began Benjamin, but Mr Hart cut him off.

'I'm very glad to meet you, Mr Button. I'm expecting your son here any minute.'

'That's me!' burst out Benjamin. 'I'm a freshman.'

'What!'

'I'm a freshman.'

'Surely you're joking.'

'Not at all.'

The registrar frowned and glanced at a card before him. 'Why, I have Mr Benjamin Button's age down here as eighteen.'

'That's my age,' asserted Benjamin, flushing slightly.

The registrar eyed him wearily. 'Now surely, Mr Button, you don't expect me to believe that.'

Benjamin smiled wearily. 'I am eighteen,' he repeated.

The registrar pointed sternly to the door. 'Get out,' he said. 'Get out of college and get out of town. You are a dangerous lunatic.'

'I am eighteen.'

Mr Hart opened the door. 'The idea!' he shouted. 'A man

306

of your age trying to enter here as a freshman. Eighteen years old, are you? Well, I'll give you eighteen minutes to get out of town.'

Benjamin Button walked with dignity from the room, and half a dozen undergraduates, who were waiting in the hall, followed him curiously with their eyes. When he had gone a little way he turned around, faced the infuriated registrar, who was still standing in the doorway, and repeated in a firm voice: 'I am eighteen years old.'

To a chorus of titters which went up from the group of undergraduates, Benjamin walked away.

But he was not fated to escape so easily. On his melancholy walk to the railroad station he found that he was being followed by a group, then by a swarm, and finally by a dense mass of undergraduates. The word had gone around that a lunatic had passed the entrance examinations for Yale and attempted to palm himself off as a youth of eighteen. A fever of excitement permeated the college. Men ran hatless out of classes, the football team abandoned its practice and joined the mob, professors' wives with bonnets awry and bustles out of position, ran shouting after the procession, from which proceeded a continual succession of remarks aimed at the tender sensibilities of Benjamin Button.

'He must be the Wandering Jew!'

'He ought to go to prep school at his age!'

'Look at the infant prodigy!'

'He thought this was the old men's home.'

'Go up to Harvard!'

Benjamin increased his gait, and soon he was running. He would show them! He *would* go to Harvard, and then they would regret these ill-considered taunts!

Safely on board the train for Baltimore, he put his head from the window. 'You'll regret this!' he shouted.

'Ha-ha!' the undergraduates laughed. 'Ha-ha-ha!' It was the biggest mistake that Yale College had ever made. . . .

V

In 1880 Benjamin Button was twenty years old, and he signalized his birthday by going to work for his father in Roger Button & Co., Wholesale Hardware. It was in that same year that he began 'going out socially' – that is, his father insisted on taking him to several fashionable dances. Roger Button was now fifty, and he and his son were more and more companionable – in fact, since Benjamin had ceased to dye his hair (which was still grayish) they appeared about the same age, and could have passed for brothers.

One night in August they got into the phaeton attired in their full-dress suits and drove out to a dance at the Shevlins' country house, situated just outside of Baltimore. It was a gorgeous evening. A full moon drenched the road to the lustreless color of platinum, and late-blooming harvest flowers breathed into the motionless air aromas that were like low, half-heard laughter. The open country, carpeted for rods around with bright wheat, was translucent as in the day. It was almost impossible not to be affected by the sheer beauty of the sky – almost.

'There's a great future in the dry-goods business,' Roger Button was saying. He was not a spiritual man – his esthetic sense was rudimentary.

'Old fellows like me can't learn new tricks,' he observed profoundly. 'It's you youngsters with energy and vitality that have the great future before you.'

Far up the road the lights of the Shevlins' country house drifted into view, and presently there was a sighing sound that crept persistently toward them – it might have been the fine plaint of violins or the rustle of the silver wheat under the moon.

They pulled up behind a handsome brougham whose passengers were disembarking at the door. A lady got out, then an elderly gentleman, then another young lady, beautiful as sin. Benjamin started; an almost chemical change seemed to dissolve and recompose the very elements of his body. A rigor passed over him, blood rose into his cheeks, his forehead, and there was a steady thumping in his ears. It was first love.

The girl was slender and frail, with hair that was ashen under the moon and honey-colored under the sputtering gas-lamps of the porch. Over her shoulders was thrown a Spanish mantilla of softest yellow, butterflied in black; her feet were glittering buttons at the hem of her bustled dress.

Roger Button leaned over to his son. 'That,' he said, 'is young Hildegarde Moncrief, the daughter of General Moncrief.'

Benjamin nodded coldly. 'Pretty little thing,' he said indifferently. But when the negro boy had led the buggy away, he added: 'Dad, you might introduce me to her.'

They approached a group of which Miss Moncrief was the center. Reared in the old tradition, she courtesied low before Benjamin. Yes, he might have a dance. He thanked her and walked away – staggered away.

The interval until the time for his turn should arrive dragged itself out interminably. He stood close to the wall, silent, inscrutable, watching with murderous eyes the young bloods of Baltimore as they eddied around Hildegarde Moncrief, passionate admiration in their faces. How obnoxious they seemed to Benjamin; how intolerably rosy! Their curling brown whiskers aroused in him a feeling equivalent to indigestion.

But when his own time came, and he drifted with her out upon the changing floor to the music of the latest waltz from Paris, his jealousies and anxieties melted from him like a mantle of snow. Blind with enchantment, he felt that life was just beginning.

'You and your brother got here just as we did, didn't you?' asked Hildegarde, looking up at him with eyes that were like bright blue enamel.

Benjamin hesitated. If she took him for his father's brother, would it be best to enlighten her? He remembered his experience at Yale, so he decided against it. It would be rude to contradict a lady; it would be criminal to mar this exquisite occasion with the grotesque story of his origin. Later, perhaps. So he nodded, smiled, listened, was happy.

'I like men of your age,' Hildegarde told him. 'Young boys are so idiotic. They tell me how much champagne they drink at college, and how much money they lose playing cards. Men of your age know how to appreciate women.'

Benjamin felt himself on the verge of a proposal – with an effort he choked back the impulse.

'You're just the romantic age,' she continued – 'fifty. Twenty-five is too worldly-wise; thirty is apt to be pale from overwork; forty is the age of long stories that take a whole cigar to tell; sixty is – oh, sixty is too near seventy; but fifty is the mellow age. I love fifty.'

Fifty seemed to Benjamin a glorious age. He longed passionately to be fifty.

'I've always said,' went on Hildegarde, 'that I'd rather marry a man of fifty and be taken care of than marry a man of thirty and take care of *him*.'

For Benjamin the rest of the evening was bathed in a honey-colored mist. Hildegarde gave him two more dances, and they discovered that they were marvellously in accord on all the questions of the day. She was to go driving with him on the following Sunday, and then they would discuss all these questions further.

Going home in the phaeton just before the crack of dawn, when the first bees were humming and the fading moon glimmered in the cool dew, Benjamin knew vaguely that his father was discussing wholesale hardware.

'...And what do you think should merit our biggest attention after hammers and nails?' the elder Button was saying.

'Love,' replied Benjamin absent-mindedly.

'Lugs?' exclaimed Roger Button. 'Why, I've just covered the question of lugs.'

Benjamin regarded him with dazed eyes just as the eastern sky was suddenly cracked with light, and an oriole yawned piercingly in the quickening trees....

VI

When, six months later, the engagement of Miss Hildegarde Moncrief to Mr Benjamin Button was made known (I say 'made known', for General Moncrief declared he would rather fall upon his sword than announce it), the excitement in Baltimore society reached a feverish pitch. The almost forgotten story of Benjamin's birth was remembered and sent out upon the winds of scandal in picaresque and incredible forms. It was said that Benjamin was really the father of Roger Button, that he was his brother who had been in prison for forty years, that he was John Wilkes Booth in disguise – and, finally, that he had two small conical horns sprouting from his head.

The Sunday supplements of the New York papers played up the case with fascinating sketches which showed the head of Benjamin Button attached to a fish, to a snake, and, finally, to a body of solid brass. He became known, journalistically, as the Mystery Man of Maryland. But the true story, as is usually the case, had a very small circulation.

However, every one agreed with General Moncrief that it was 'criminal' for a lovely girl who could have married any beau in Baltimore to throw herself into the arms of a man who was assuredly fifty. In vain Mr Roger Button published his son's birth certificate in large type in the Baltimore *Blaze*. No one believed it. You had only to look at Benjamin and see.

On the part of the two people most concerned there was no wavering. So many of the stories about her fiancé were false that Hildegarde refused stubbornly to believe even the true one. In vain General Moncrief pointed out to her the high mortality among men of fifty – or, at least, among men who looked fifty; in vain he told her of the instability of the wholesale hardware business. Hildegarde had chosen to marry for mellowness – and marry she did. . . .

VII

In one particular, at least, the friends of Hildegarde Moncrief were mistaken. The wholesale hardware business prospered amazingly. In the fifteen years between Benjamin Button's marriage in 1880 and his father's retirement in 1895, the family fortune was doubled – and this was due largely to the younger member of the firm.

Needless to say, Baltimore eventually received the couple to its bosom. Even old General Moncrief became reconciled to his son-in-law when Benjamin gave him the money to bring out his 'History of the Civil War' in twenty volumes, which had been refused by nine prominent publishers.

In Benjamin himself fifteen years had wrought many

changes. It seemed to him that the blood flowed with new vigor through his veins. It began to be a pleasure to rise in the morning, to walk with an active step along the busy, sunny street, to work untiringly with his shipments of hammers and his cargoes of nails. It was in 1890 that he executed his famous business coup: he brought up the suggestion that *all nails used in nailing up the boxes in which nails are shipped are the property of the shippee,* a proposal which became a statute, was approved by Chief Justice Fossile, and saved Roger Button and Company, Wholesale Hardware, more than *six hundred nails every year.*

In addition, Benjamin discovered that he was becoming more and more attracted by the gay side of life. It was typical of his growing enthusiasm for pleasure that he was the first man in the city of Baltimore to own and run an automobile. Meeting him on the street, his contemporaries would stare enviously at the picture he made of health and vitality.

'He seems to grow younger every year,' they would remark. And if old Roger Button, now sixty-five years old, had failed at first to give a proper welcome to his son he atoned at last by bestowing on him what amounted to adulation.

And here we come to an unpleasant subject which it will be well to pass over as quickly as possible. There was only one thing that worried Benjamin Button: his wife had ceased to attract him.

At that time Hildegarde was a woman of thirty-five, with a son, Roscoe, fourteen years old. In the early days of their marriage Benjamin had worshipped her. But, as the years passed, her honey-colored hair became an unexciting brown, the blue enamel of her eyes assumed the aspect of cheap crockery – moreover, and most of all, she had become too settled in her ways, too placid, too content, too anemic in her excitements, and too sober in her taste. As a bride it had been she who had 'dragged' Benjamin to dances and dinners – now conditions were reversed. She went out socially with him, but without enthusiasm, devoured already by that eternal inertia which comes to live with each of us one day and stays with us to the end.

Benjamin's discontent waxed stronger. At the outbreak of the Spanish–American War in 1898 his home had for him so little charm that he decided to join the army. With his business influence he obtained a commission as captain, and proved so adaptable to the work that he was made a major, and finally a lieutenant-colonel just in time to participate in the celebrated charge up San Juan Hill. He was slightly wounded, and received a medal.

Benjamin had become so attached to the activity and excitement of army life that he regretted to give it up, but his business required attention, so he resigned his commission and came home. He was met at the station by a brass band and escorted to his house.

VIII

Hildegarde, waving a large silk flag, greeted him on the porch, and even as he kissed her he felt with a sinking of the heart that these three years had taken their toll. She was a woman of forty now, with a faint skirmish line of gray hairs in her head. The sight depressed him.

Up in his room he saw his reflection in the familiar mirror – he went closer and examined his own face with anxiety, comparing it after a moment with a photograph of himself in uniform taken just before the war.

'Good Lord!' he said aloud. The process was continuing. There was no doubt of it – he looked now like a man of thirty. Instead of being delighted, he was uneasy – he was growing younger. He had hitherto hoped that once he reached a bodily age equivalent to his age in years, the grotesque phenomenon which had marked his birth would cease to function. He shuddered. His destiny seemed to him awful, incredible.

When he came down-stairs Hildegarde was waiting for him. She appeared annoyed, and he wondered if she had at last discovered that there was something amiss. It was with an effort to relieve the tension between them that he broached the matter at dinner in what he considered a delicate way.

'Well,' he remarked lightly, 'everybody says I look younger than ever.'

Hildegarde regarded him with scorn. She sniffed. 'Do you think it's anything to boast about?'

'I'm not boasting,' he asserted uncomfortably.

She sniffed again. 'The idea,' she said, and after a moment: 'I should think you'd have enough pride to stop it.'

'How can I?' he demanded.

'I'm not going to argue with you,' she retorted. 'But there's a right way of doing things and a wrong way. If you've made up your mind to be different from everybody else, I don't suppose I can stop you, but I really don't think it's very considerate.'

'But, Hildegarde, I can't help it.'

'You can too. You're simply stubborn. You think you don't want to be like any one else. You always have been that way, and you always will be. But just think how it would be if every one else looked at things as you do — what would the world be like?'

As this was an inane and unanswerable argument Benjamin made no reply, and from that time on a chasm began to widen between them. He wondered what possible fascination she had ever exercised over him.

To add to the breach, he found, as the new century

gathered headway, that his thirst for gayety grew stronger. Never a party of any kind in the city of Baltimore but he was there, dancing with the prettiest of the young married women, chatting with the most popular of the débutantes, and finding their company charming, while his wife, a dowager of evil omen, sat among the chaperons, now in haughty disapproval, and now following him with solemn, puzzled, and reproachful eyes.

'Look!' people would remark. 'What a pity! A young fellow that age tied to a woman of forty-five. He must be twenty years younger than his wife.' They had forgotten – as people inevitably forget – that back in 1880 their mammas and papas had also remarked about this same ill-matched pair.

Benjamin's growing unhappiness at home was compensated for by his many new interests. He took up golf and made a great success of it. He went in for dancing: in 1906 he was an expert at 'The Boston', and in 1908 he was considered proficient at the 'Maxixe', while in 1909 his 'Castle Walk' was the envy of every young man in town.

His social activities, of course, interfered to some extent with his business, but then he had worked hard at wholesale hardware for twenty-five years and felt that he could soon hand it on to his son, Roscoe, who had recently graduated from Harvard.

He and his son were, in fact, often mistaken for each other. This pleased Benjamin – he soon forgot the insidious fear which had come over him on his return from the Spanish–American War, and grew to take a naïve pleasure in his appearance. There was only one fly in the delicious ointment – he hated to appear in public with his wife. Hildegarde was almost fifty, and the sight of her made him feel absurd. . . .

IX

One September day in 1910 – a few years after Roger Button & Co., Wholesale Hardware, had been handed over to young Roscoe Button – a man, apparently about twenty years old, entered himself as a freshman at Harvard University in Cambridge. He did not make the mistake of announcing that he would never see fifty again nor did he mention the fact that his son had been graduated from the same institution ten years before.

He was admitted, and almost immediately attained a prominent position in the class, partly because he seemed a little older than the other freshmen, whose average age was about eighteen.

But his success was largely due to the fact that in the football game with Yale he played so brilliantly, with so much dash and with such a cold, remorseless anger that he scored seven touchdowns and fourteen field goals for Harvard, and caused one entire eleven of Yale men to be carried singly from the field, unconscious. He was the most celebrated man in college.

Strange to say, in his third or junior year he was scarcely able to 'make' the team. The coaches said that he had lost weight, and it seemed to the more observant among them that he was not quite as tall as before. He made no touchdowns – indeed, he was retained on the team chiefly in hope that his enormous reputation would bring terror and disorganization to the Yale team.

In his senior year he did not make the team at all. He had grown so slight and frail that one day he was taken by some sophomores for a freshman, an incident which humiliated him terribly. He became known as something of a prodigy – a senior who was surely no more than sixteen – and he was often shocked at the worldliness of some of his classmates. His studies seemed harder to him – he felt that they were too advanced. He had heard his classmates speak of St Midas', the famous preparatory school, at which so many of them had prepared for college, and he determined after his graduation to enter himself at St Midas', where the sheltered life among boys his own size would be more congenial to him.

Upon his graduation in 1914 he went home to Baltimore with his Harvard diploma in his pocket. Hildegarde was now residing in Italy, so Benjamin went to live with his son, Roscoe. But though he was welcomed in a general way, there was obviously no heartiness in Roscoe's feeling toward him – there was even perceptible a tendency on his son's part to think that Benjamin, as he moped about the house in adolescent mooniness, was somewhat in the way. Roscoe was married now and prominent in Baltimore life, and he wanted no scandal to creep out in connection with his family.

Benjamin, no longer persona grata with the débutantes and younger college set, found himself left much alone, except for the companionship of three or four fifteen-year-old boys in the neighborhood. His idea of going to Midas' school recurred to him.

'Say,' he said to Roscoe one day, 'I've told you over and over that I want to go to prep school.'

'Well, go, then,' replied Roscoe shortly. The matter was distasteful to him, and he wished to avoid a discussion.

'I can't go alone,' said Benjamin helplessly. 'You'll have to enter me and take me up there.'

'I haven't got time,' declared Roscoe abruptly. His eyes narrowed and he looked uneasily at his father. 'As a matter of fact,' he added, 'you'd better not go on with this business much longer. You better pull up short. You better – you better' – he paused and his face crimsoned as he sought for words – 'you better turn right around and start back the other way. This has gone too far to be a joke. It isn't funny any longer. You – you behave yourself!'

Benjamin looked at him, on the verge of tears.

'And another thing,' continued Roscoe, 'when visitors are in the house I want you to call me "Uncle" – not "Roscoe", but "Uncle", do you understand? It looks absurd for a boy of fifteen to call me by my first name. Perhaps you'd better call me "Uncle" *all* the time, so you'll get used to it.'

With a harsh look at his father, Roscoe turned away. . . .

X

At the termination of this interview, Benjamin wandered dismally up-stairs and stared at himself in the mirror. He had not shaved for three months, but he could find nothing on his face but a faint white down with which it seemed unnecessary to meddle. When he had first come home from Harvard, Roscoe had approached him with the proposition that he should wear eye-glasses and imitation whiskers glued to his cheeks, and it had seemed for a moment that the farce of his early years was to be repeated. But whiskers had itched and made him ashamed. He wept and Roscoe had reluctantly relented.

Benjamin opened a book of boys' stories, 'The Boy Scouts in Bimini Bay', and began to read. But he found himself thinking persistently about the war. America had joined the Allied cause during the preceding month, and Benjamin wanted to enlist, but, alas, sixteen was the minimum age, and he did not look that old. His true age, which was fifty-seven, would have disqualified him, anyway.

There was a knock at his door, and the butler appeared with a letter bearing a large official legend in the corner and addressed to Mr Benjamin Button. Benjamin tore it open eagerly, and read the enclosure with delight. It informed him that many reserve officers who had served in the Spanish–American War were being called back into service with a higher rank, and it enclosed his commission as brigadier-general in the United States army with orders to report immediately.

Benjamin jumped to his feet fairly quivering with enthusiasm. This was what he had wanted. He seized his cap and ten minutes later he had entered a large tailoring establishment on Charles Street, and asked in his uncertain treble to be measured for a uniform.

'Want to play soldier, sonny?' demanded a clerk, casually.

Benjamin flushed. 'Say! Never mind what I want!' he retorted angrily. 'My name's Button and I live on Mt Vernon Place, so you know I'm good for it.'

'Well,' admitted the clerk, hesitantly, 'if you're not, I guess your daddy is, all right.'

Benjamin was measured, and a week later his uniform was completed. He had difficulty in obtaining the proper general's insignia because the dealer kept insisting to Benjamin that a nice Y.W.C.A. badge would look just as well and be much more fun to play with.

Saying nothing to Roscoe, he left the house one night and proceeded by train to Camp Mosby, in South Carolina, where he was to command an infantry brigade. On a sultry April day he approached the entrance to the camp, paid off the taxicab which had brought him from the station, and turned to the sentry on guard.

'Get some one to handle my luggage!' he said briskly.

The sentry eyed him reproachfully. 'Say,' he remarked, 'where you goin' with the general's duds, sonny?'

Benjamin, veteran of the Spanish–American War, whirled

upon him with fire in his eye, but with, alas, a changing treble voice.

'Come to attention!' he tried to thunder; he paused for breath – then suddenly he saw the sentry snap his heels together and bring his rifle to the present. Benjamin concealed a smile of gratification, but when he glanced around his smile faded. It was not he who had inspired obedience, but an imposing artillery colonel who was approaching on horseback.

'Colonel!' called Benjamin shrilly.

The colonel came up, drew rein, and looked coolly down at him with a twinkle in his eyes. 'Whose little boy are you?' he demanded kindly.

'I'll soon darn well show you whose little boy I am!' retorted Benjamin in a ferocious voice. 'Get down off that horse!'

The colonel roared with laughter.

'You want him, eh, general?'

'Here!' cried Benjamin desperately. 'Read this.' And he thrust his commission toward the colonel.

The colonel read it, his eyes popping from their sockets.

'Where'd you get this?' he demanded, slipping the document into his own pocket.

'I got it from the Government, as you'll soon find out!'

'You come along with me,' said the colonel with a peculiar look. 'We'll go up to headquarters and talk this over. Come along.'

The colonel turned and began walking his horse in the direction of headquarters. There was nothing for Benjamin to do but follow with as much dignity as possible – meanwhile promising himself a stern revenge.

But this revenge did not materialize. Two days later, however, his son Roscoe materialized from Baltimore, hot and cross from a hasty trip, and escorted the weeping general, *sans* uniform, back to his home.

XI

In 1920 Roscoe Button's first child was born. During the attendant festivities, however, no one thought it 'the thing' to mention that the little grubby boy, apparently about ten years of age who played around the house with lead soldiers and a miniature circus, was the new baby's own grandfather.

No one disliked the little boy whose fresh, cheerful face was crossed with just a hint of sadness, but to Roscoe Button his presence was a source of torment. In the idiom of his generation Roscoe did not consider the matter 'efficient'. It seemed to him that his father, in refusing to look sixty, had not behaved like a 'red-blooded he-man' – this was Roscoe's favorite expression – but in a curious and perverse manner. Indeed, to think about the matter for as much as a half an hour drove him to the edge of insanity. Roscoe believed that 'live wires' should keep young, but carrying it out on such a scale was – was – was inefficient. And there Roscoe rested.

Five years later Roscoe's little boy had grown old enough to play childish games with little Benjamin under the supervision of the same nurse. Roscoe took them both to kindergarten on the same day and Benjamin found that playing with little strips of colored paper, making mats and chains and curious and beautiful designs, was the most fascinating game in the world. Once he was bad and had to stand in the corner – then he cried – but for the most part there were gay hours in the cheerful room, with the sunlight coming in the windows and Miss Bailey's kind hand resting for a moment now and then in his tousled hair.

Roscoe's son moved up into the first grade after a year, but

Benjamin stayed on in the kindergarten. He was very happy. Sometimes when other tots talked about what they would do when they grew up a shadow would cross his little face as if in a dim, childish way he realized that those were things in which he was never to share.

The days flowed on in monotonous content. He went back a third year to the kindergarten, but he was too little now to understand what the bright shining strips of paper were for. He cried because the other boys were bigger than he and he was afraid of them. The teacher talked to him, but though he tried to understand he could not understand at all.

He was taken from the kindergarten. His nurse, Nana, in her starched gingham dress, became the center of his tiny world. On bright days they walked in the park; Nana would point at a great gray monster and say 'elephant', and Benjamin would say it after her, and when he was being undressed for bed that night he would say it over and over aloud to her: 'Elyphant, elyphant, elyphant.' Sometimes Nana let him jump on the bed, which was fun, because if you sat down exactly right it would bounce you up on your feet again, and if you said 'Ah' for a long time while you jumped you got a very pleasing broken vocal effect.

He loved to take a big cane from the hatrack and go around hitting chairs and tables with it and saying: 'Fight, fight, fight.' When there were people there the old ladies would cluck at him, which interested him, and the young ladies would try to kiss him, which he submitted to with mild boredom. And when the long day was done at five o'clock he would go up-stairs with Nana and be fed oatmeal and nice soft mushy foods with a spoon.

There were no troublesome memories in his childish sleep; no token came to him of his brave days at college, of the glittering years when he flustered the hearts of many girls.

There were only the white, safe walls of his crib and Nana and a man who came to see him sometimes, and a great big orange ball that Nana pointed at just before his twilight bed hour and called 'sun'. When the sun went his eyes were sleepy – there were no dreams, no dreams to haunt him.

The past – the wild charge at the head of his men up San Juan Hill; the first years of his marriage when he worked late into the summer dusk down in the busy city for young Hildegarde whom he loved; the days before that when he sat smoking far into the night in the gloomy old Button house on Monroe Street with his grandfather – all these had faded like unsubstantial dreams from his mind as though they had never been.

He did not remember. He did not remember clearly whether the milk was warm or cool at his last feeding or how the days passed – there was only his crib and Nana's familiar presence. And then he remembered nothing. When he was hungry he cried – that was all. Through the noons and nights he breathed and over him there were soft mumblings and murmurings that he scarcely heard, and faintly differentiated smells, and light and darkness.

Then it was all dark, and his white crib and the dim faces that moved above and the warm sweet aroma of the milk, faded out altogether from his mind.

STEVEN MILLHAUSER

A VISIT

ALTHOUGH I HAD not heard from my friend in nine years, I wasn't surprised, not really, to receive a short letter from him dashed off in pencil, announcing that he had 'taken a wife', and summoning me to visit him in some remote up-state town I had never heard of. 'Come see me on the 16th and 17th' was what he had actually written. 'Be here for lunch.' The offhand peremptory tone was Albert all over. He had scribbled a map, with a little black circle marked 'Village' and a little white square marked 'My house'. A wavy line con-nected the two. Under the line were the words '$3\frac{1}{2}$ miles, more or less'. Over the line were the words 'County Road 39'. I knew those desolate little upstate villages, consisting of one Baptist church, three bars, and a gas station with a single pump, and I imagined Albert living at an ironic distance, with his books and his manias. What I couldn't imagine was his wife. Albert had never struck me as the marrying kind, though women had always liked him. I had plans for the weekend, but I canceled them and headed north.

I still considered Albert my friend, in a way my best friend, even though I hadn't heard from him in nine years. He had once been my best friend and it was hard to think of him in any other way. Even in the flourishing time of our friendship, in the last two years of college and the year after, when we saw each other daily, he had been a difficult and exacting friend, scornful of convention though quiet in his own habits, subject to sudden flare-ups and silences, earnest but with an edge of mockery, intolerant of mediocrity, and cursed with an unfailing scent for the faintly fraudulent in a gesture or a phrase or a face. He was handsome in a sharp-featured New England way – his family, as he put it, had lived in Connecticut since the fall of the Roman Empire – but despite the inviting smiles of girls in his classes he confined himself to brisk affairs with leather-jacketed town girls with whom he had nothing in common. After graduating, we roomed together for a year in a little college town full of cafés and bookstores, sharing the rent and drifting from one part-time job to another, as I put off the inevitable suit-and-tie life that awaited me while he mocked my conventional fear of becoming conventional, defended business as America's only source of originality, and read his Plato and his *Modern Chess Openings* and tootled his flute. One day he left, just like that, to start what he called a new life. In the next year I received postcards from small towns all over America, showing pictures of Main Streets and quaint village railroad stations. They bore messages such as 'Still looking' or 'Have you seen my razor? I think I left it on the bathtub'. Then there was nothing for six months, and then a sudden postcard from Eugene, Oregon, on which he described in minute detail a small unknown wooden object that he had found in the top drawer of the bureau in his rented bedroom, and then nine years of silence. During that time I had settled into a job and almost married an old girlfriend. I had bought a house on a pleasant street lined with porches and maples, thought quite a bit about my old friend Albert, and wondered whether this was what I had looked forward to, this life I was now leading, in the old days, the days when I still looked forward to things.

The town was even worse than I had imagined. Slowly I passed its crumbling brick paper mill with boarded-up windows, its rows of faded and flaking two-family houses with sagging front porches where guys in black T-shirts sat drinking beer, its tattoo parlor and its sluggish stream. County Road 39 wound between fields of Queen Anne's lace and yellow ragweed, with now and then a melancholy house or a patch of sun-scorched corn. Once I passed a rotting barn with a caved-in roof. At 3.2 miles on the odometer I came to a weathered house near the edge of the road. A bicycle lay in the high grass of the front yard and an open garage was entirely filled with old furniture. Uncertainly I turned onto the unpaved drive, parked with the motor running, and walked up to the front door. There was no bell. I knocked on the wooden screen door, which banged loudly against the frame, and a tall, barefoot, and very pale woman with sleepy eyes came to the door, wearing a long rumpled black skirt and a lumberjack shirt over a T-shirt. When I asked for Albert she looked at me suspiciously, shook her head quickly twice, and slammed the inner door. As I walked back to the car I saw her pale face looking out at me past a pushed-aside pink curtain. It occurred to me that perhaps Albert had married this woman and that she was insane. It further occurred to me, as I backed out of the drive, that I really ought to turn back now, right now, away from this misguided adventure in the wilderness. After all, I hadn't seen him for nine long years, things were bound to be different. At 4.1 miles on the odometer I rounded a bend of rising road and saw a shadowy house set back in a cluster of dusty-looking trees. I turned in to the unknown dirt drive, deep-rutted and sprouting weeds, and as I stepped on the brake with a sharp sense of desolation and betrayal, for here I was, in the god-forsaken middle of nauseating nowhere, prowling around like a fool and a criminal, the front door opened and Albert came out, one hand in his pocket and one hand waving.

He looked the same, nearly the same, though browner and leatherier than I remembered, as if he had lived all those years in the sun, his face a little longer and leaner – a handsome man in jeans and a dark shirt. 'I wondered if you'd show up,' he said when he reached the car, and suddenly seemed to study me. 'You look just the way you ought to,' he then said.

I let the words settle in me. 'It depends what I ought to look like,' I answered, glancing at him sharply, but he only laughed.

'Isn't this a great place?' he said, throwing out one arm as he began carrying my traveling bag toward the house. 'Ten acres and they're practically giving it away. First day after I bought the place I go walking around and bingo! what do you think I found? Grapes. Billions of grapes. An old fallen-down grape arbor, grapes growing all over the ground. Italy in New York. Wait till you see the pond.'

We stepped into the shade of the high trees, a little thicket of pines and maples, that grew close to the house. Big bushes climbed halfway up the windows. It struck me that the house was well protected from view, a private place, a shadowy isle in a sea of fields. 'And yet,' I said, looking around for his wife, 'somehow I never thought of you as getting married, somehow.'

'Not back then,' he said. 'Watch that rail.'

We had climbed onto the steps of the long, deep-shaded front porch, and I had grasped a wobbly iron handrail that needed to be screwed into the wood. A coil of old garden hose hung over the porch rail. A few hornets buzzed about the ceiling light. On the porch stood a sunken chaise longue, an old three-speed bicycle, a metal garbage can containing a rusty snow shovel, and a porch swing on which sat an empty flowerpot.

He opened the wooden screen door and with a little

flourish urged me in. 'Humble,' he said, 'but mine own.' He looked at me with a kind of excitement, an excitement I couldn't entirely account for, but which reminded me of the old excitement, and I wondered, as I entered the house, whether that was what I had been looking for, back then. The house was cool and almost dark, the dark of deep shade lightened by streaks of sun. Under the half-drawn window-shades I saw bush-branches growing against the glass. We had entered the living room, where I noticed a rocking chair that leaned too far back and a couch with one pillow. Ancient wallpaper showed faded scenes of some kind repeating themselves all over the room. Albert, who seemed more and more excited, led me up the creaking worn-edged stairs to my room – a bed with a frilly pink spread, a lamp table on which lay a screwdriver with a transparent yellow handle – and quickly back down.

'You must be starving,' he said, with that odd quiver of excitement, as he led me through an open doorway into a dining room that was almost dark. At a big round table there were three place settings, which glowed whitely in the gloom. One of the round-backed chairs appeared to be occupied. Only as I drew closer through the afternoon darkness did I see that the occupant was a large frog, perhaps two feet high, which sat with its throat resting on the table edge. 'My wife,' Albert said, looking at me fiercely, as if he were about to spring at my face. I felt I was being tested in some fiendish way. 'Pleased to meet you,' I said harshly, and sat down across from her. The table lay between us like a lake. I had thought she might be something else, maybe a stuffed toy of some sort, but even in the dark daylight I could see the large moist eyes looking here and there, I could see her rapid breathing and smell her marshy odor. I thought Albert must be making fun of me in some fashion, trying to trick me into exposing what he took to be my hideous bourgeois soul, but whatever his game I wasn't going to give myself away.

'Help yourself,' Albert said, pushing toward me a bread-board with a round loaf and a hunk of cheese on it. A big-bladed knife lay on the table and I began cutting the bread. 'And if you'd cut just a little piece of cheese for Alice.' I immediately cut a little piece of cheese for Alice. Albert disappeared into the kitchen and in the room's dusk I stared across the round table at Alice before looking away uncomfortably. Albert returned with a wax carton of orange juice and a small brown bottle of beer, both of which he set before me. 'The choice,' he said with a little bow, 'is yours entirely.' He picked up the piece of cheese I had cut for Alice, placed it on her plate, and broke it into smaller pieces. Alice looked at him – it seemed to me that she looked at him – with those moist and heavy-lidded eyes, and flicked up her cheese. Then she placed her throat on the table edge and sat very still.

Albert sat down and cut himself a piece of bread. 'After lunch I want to show you the place. Take you down to the pond and so on.' He looked at me, tilting his head in a way I suddenly remembered. 'And you? It's been a while.'

'Oh, still a roving bachelor,' I said, and immediately disliked my fatuous tone. I had a sudden urge to talk seriously to Albert, as we'd done in the old days, watching the night turn slowly gray through our tall, arched windows. But I felt constrained, it had been too long a time, and though he had summoned me after all these years, though he had shown me his wife, it was all askew somehow, as if he hadn't shown me anything, as if he'd kept himself hidden away. And I remembered that even then, in the time of our friendship, he had seemed intimate and secretive at the same time, as if even his revelations were forms of concealment. 'Not that I have any fixed plan,' I continued. 'I see women, but they're not the right one. You know, I was always sure I'd be the one to get married, not you.'

'It wasn't something I planned. But when the moment comes, you'll know.' He looked at Alice with tenderness and suddenly leaned over and touched the side of her head lightly with his fingertips.

'How did you,' I began, and stopped. I felt like bursting into screams of wild laughter, or of outrage, pure outrage, but I held myself down, I pretended everything was fine. 'I mean, how did you meet? You two. If I may ask.'

'So formal! If you may ask! Down by the pond – if I may answer. I saw her in the reeds one day. I'd never seen her before, but she was always there, after that. I'll show you the exact place after lunch.'

His little mocking rebuke irritated me, and I recalled how he had always irritated me, and made me retreat more deeply into myself, because of some little reproach, some little ironic look, and it seemed strange to me that someone who irritated me and made me retreat into myself was also someone who released me into a freer version of myself, a version superior to the constricted one that had always felt like my own hand on my throat. But who was Albert, after all, that he should have the power to release me or constrict me – this man I no longer knew, with his run-down house and his ludicrous frog-wife. Then I ate for a while in sullen silence, looking only at my food, and when I glanced up I saw him looking at me kindly, almost affectionately.

'It's all right,' he said quietly, as if he understood, as if he knew how difficult it was for me, this journey, this wife, this life. And I was grateful, as I had always been, for we had been close, he and I, back then.

After lunch he insisted on showing me his land – his domain, as he called it. I had hoped that Alice might stay

333

behind, so that I could speak with him alone, but it was clear that he wanted her to come with us. So as we made our way out the back door and into his domain she followed along, taking hops about two strides in length, always a little behind us or a little before. At the back of the house a patch of overgrown lawn led to a vegetable garden on both sides of a grassy path. There were vines of green peas and string-beans climbing tall sticks, clusters of green peppers, rows of carrots and radishes identified by seed packets on short sticks, fat heads of lettuce and flashes of yellow squash – a rich and well-tended oasis, as if the living center of the house were here, on the outside, hidden in back. At the end of the garden grew a scattering of fruit trees, pear and cherry and plum. An old wire fence with a broken wooden gate separated the garden from the land beyond.

We walked along a vague footpath through fields of high grass, passed into thickets of oak and maple, crossed a stream. Alice kept up the pace. Alice in sunlight, Alice in the open air, no longer seemed a grotesque pet, a monstrous mistake of Nature, a nightmare frog and freakish wife, but rather a companion of sorts, staying alongside us, resting when we rested – Albert's pal. And yet it was more than that. For when she emerged from high grass or tree-shade into full sunlight, I saw or sensed for a moment, with a kind of inner start, Alice as she was, Alice in the sheer brightness and fullness of her being, as if the dark malachite sheen of her skin, the pale shimmer of her throat, the moist warmth of her eyes, were as natural and mysterious as the flight of a bird. Then I would tumble back into myself and realize that I was walking with my old friend beside a monstrous lumbering frog who had somehow become his wife, and a howl of inward laughter and rage would erupt in me, calmed almost at once by the rolling meadows, the shady thickets, the black crow rising from a tree with slowly lifted and lowered wings, rising higher and higher into the pale blue sky touched here and there with delicate fernlike clouds.

The pond appeared suddenly, on the far side of a low rise. Reeds and cattails grew in thick clusters at the marshy edge. We sat down on flat-topped boulders and looked out at the green-brown water, where a few brown ducks floated, out past fields to a line of low hills. There was a desolate beauty about the place, as if we had come to the edge of the world. 'It was over there I first saw her,' Albert said, pointing to a cluster of reeds. Alice sat off to one side, low to the ground, in a clump of grass at the water's edge. She was still as a rock, except for her sides moving in and out as she breathed. I imagined her growing in the depths of the pond, under a mantle of lilypads and mottled scum, down below the rays of green sunlight, far down, at the silent bottom of the world.

Albert leaned back on both elbows, a pose I remembered well, and stared out at the water. For a long while we sat in a silence that struck me as uncomfortable, though he himself seemed at ease. It wasn't so much that I felt awkward in Alice's presence as that I didn't know what I had come all this way to say. Did I really want to speak at all? Then Albert said, 'Tell me about your life.' And I was grateful to him, for that was exactly what I wanted to talk about, my life. I told him about my almost-marriage, my friendships that lacked excitement, my girlfriends who lacked one thing or another, my good job that somehow wasn't exactly what I had been looking for, back then, my feeling that things were all right but not as all right as they might be, that I was not un-happy but not really happy either, but caught in some inter-mediate place, looking both ways. And as I spoke it seemed to me that I was looking in one direction toward a happiness that was growing vaguer, and in the other direction toward an unhappiness that was emerging more clearly, without yet revealing itself completely.

'It's hard,' Albert then said, in the tone of someone who knew what I was talking about, and though I was soothed by his words, which were spoken gently, I was disappointed that he didn't say more, that he didn't show himself to me.

And I said, 'Why did you write to me, after all this time?' which was only another way of saying, why didn't you write to me, in all this time.

'I waited,' he said, 'until I had something to show you.' That was what he said: something to show me. And it seemed to me then that if all he had to show me after nine years was his run-down house and his marshy frog-wife, then I wasn't so badly off, in my own way, not really.

After that we continued walking about his domain, with Alice always at our side. He showed me things, and I looked. He showed me the old grape arbor that he had put back up; unripe green grapes, hard as nuts, hung in bunches from the decaying slats. 'Try one,' he said, but it was bitter as a tiny lemon. He laughed at my grimace. 'We like 'em this way,' he said, plucking a few into his palm, then tossing them into his mouth. He pulled off another handful and held them down to Alice, who devoured them swiftly: flick flick flick. He showed me a woodpecker's nest, and a slope of wild tiger lilies, and an old toolshed containing a rusty hoe and a rusty rake. Suddenly, from a nearby field, a big bird rose up with a loud beating of wings. 'Did you see that!' cried Albert, seizing my arm. 'A pheasant! Protecting her young. Over there.' In the high grass six fuzzy little ducklike creatures walked in a line, their heads barely visible.

At dinner Alice sat in her chair with her throat resting on the edge of the table while Albert walked briskly in and out of the kitchen. I was pleased to see a fat bottle of red wine, which he poured into two juice glasses. The glasses had pictures of Winnie-the-Pooh and Eeyore on them. 'Guy gave them to me at a gas station,' Albert said. He frowned suddenly, pressed his fingertips against his forehead, looked up with a radiant smile. 'I've got it. The more it *snows*, tiddely-pom, the more it *goes*, tiddely-pom.' He poured a little wine into a cereal bowl and placed it near Alice.

Dinner was a heated-up supermarket chicken, fresh squash from his garden, and big bowls of garden salad. Albert was in high spirits, humming snatches of songs, lighting a stub of candle in a green wine bottle, filling our wineglasses and Alice's bowl again and again, urging me to drink up, crunching lustily into his salad. The cheap wine burned my tongue but I kept drinking, taken by Albert's festive spirit, eager to carry myself into his mood. Even Alice kept finishing the wine he put in her cereal bowl. The candleflame seemed to grow brighter in the darkening air of the room; through bush-branches in the window I saw streaks of sunset. A line of wax ran down the bottle and stopped. Albert brought in his bread-board, more salad, another loaf of bread. And as the meal continued I had the sense that Alice, sitting there with her throat resting on the table edge, flicking up her wine, was looking at Albert with those large eyes of hers, moist and dark in the flame-light. She was looking at him and trying to attract his attention. Albert was leaning back in his chair, laughing, throwing his arm about as he talked, but it seemed to me that he was darting glances back at her. Yes, they were exchanging looks, there at the darkening dinner table, looks that struck me as amorous. And as I drank I was filled with a warm, expansive feeling, which took in the room, the meal, the Winnie-the-Pooh glasses, the large moist eyes, the reflection of the candleflame in the black window, the glances of Albert and his wife; for after all, she was the one he had chosen, up here in the wilderness, and who was I to say what was right, in such matters.

Albert leaped up and returned with a bowl of pears and cherries from his fruit trees, and filled my glass again. I was settling back with my warm, expansive feeling, looking forward to the night of talk stretching lazily before me, when Albert announced that it was getting late, he and Alice would be retiring. I had the run of the house. Just be sure to blow out the candle. Nighty night. Through the roar of wine I was aware of my plunging disappointment. He pulled back her chair and she hopped to the floor. Together they left the dining room and disappeared into the dark living room, where he turned on a lamp so dim that it was like lighting a candle. I heard him creaking up the stairs and thought I heard a dull thumping sound, as I imagined Alice lumbering her way up beside him.

I sat listening to the thumps and creaks of the upper hall, a sudden sharp rush of water in the bathroom sink, a squeak – what was that squeak? – a door shutting. In the abrupt silence, which seemed to spread outward from the table in widening ripples, I felt abandoned, there with the wine and the candle and the glimmering dishes. Yet I saw that it was bound to be this way, and no other way, for I had watched their amorous looks, it was only to be expected. And hadn't he, back then, been in the habit of unexpected departures? Then I began to wonder whether they had ever taken place, those talks stretching into the gray light of dawn, or whether I had only desired them. Then I imagined Alice hopping onto the white sheets. And I tried to imagine frog-love, its possible pleasures, its oozy raptures, but I turned my mind violently away, for in the imagining I felt something petty and cruel, something in the nature of a violation.

I drank down the last of the wine and blew out the

candle. From the dark room where I sat I could see a ghostly corner of refrigerator in the kitchen and a dim-lit reddish couch-arm in the living room, like a moonlit dead flower. A car passed on the road. Then I became aware of the crickets, whole fields and meadows of them, the great hum that I had always heard rising from back yards and vacant lots in childhood summers, the long sound of summer's end. And yet it was only the middle of summer, was it not, just last week I had spent a day at the beach. So for a long time I sat at the dark table, in the middle of a decaying house, listening to the sound of summer's end. Then I picked up my empty glass, silently saluted Albert and his wife, and went up to bed.

But I could not sleep. Maybe it was the wine, or the mashed mattress, or the early hour, but I lay there twisting in my sheets, and as I turned restlessly, the day's adventures darkened in my mind and I saw only a crazed friend, a ruined house, an ugly and monstrous frog. And I saw myself, weak and absurd, wrenching my mind into grotesque shapes of sympathy and understanding. At some point I began to slide in and out of dreams, or perhaps it was a single long dream broken by many half-wakings. I was walking down a long hall with a forbidden door at the end. With a sense of mournful excitement I opened the door and saw Albert standing with his arms crossed, looking at me sternly. He began to shout at me, his face became very red, and bending over he bit me on the hand. Tears ran down my face. Behind him someone rose from a chair and came toward us. 'Here,' said the newcomer, who was somehow Albert, 'use this.' He held up a handkerchief draped over his fist, and when I pulled off the handkerchief a big frog rose angrily into the air with wild flappings of its wings.

I woke tense and exhausted in a sun-streaked room.

Through a dusty window I saw tree branches with big three-lobed leaves and between the leaves pieces of blue sky. It was nearly nine. I had three separate headaches: one behind my left eye, one in my right temple, and one at the back of my head. I washed and dressed quickly and made my way down the darkening stairs, through a dusk that deepened as I drew toward the bottom. On the faded wallpaper I could make out two scenes repeating themselves into the distance: a faded boy in blue lying against a faded yellow haystack with a horn at his side, and a girl in white drawing water from a faded well.

The living room was empty. The whole house appeared to be deserted. On the round table in the twilight of the dining room the dishes still sat from dinner. All I wanted was a cup of coffee before leaving. In the slightly less gloomy kitchen I found an old jar of instant coffee and a chipped blue teapot decorated with a little decal picturing an orange brontosaurus. I heard sharp sounds, and through the leaves and branches in the kitchen window I saw Albert with his back to me, digging in the garden. Outside the house it was a bright, sunny day. Beside him, on the dirt, sat Alice.

I brought my cup of harsh-tasting, stale coffee into the dining room and drank it at the table while I listened to the sounds of Albert's shovel striking the soil. It was peaceful in the darkish room, at the round brown table. A thin slant of sun glittered in the open kitchen. The sun-slant mingled with the whistle of a bird, leaves in the window, the brown dusk, the sound of the shovel striking loam, turning it over. It occurred to me that I could simply pack my things now, and glide away without the awkwardness of a leave-taking.

I finished the dismal coffee and carried the cup into the kitchen, where the inner back door stood slightly open. There I paused, holding the empty cup in my hand. Obeying a sudden impulse, I opened the door a little more and slipped between it and the wooden screen door.

Through the buckled screen I could see Albert some ten feet away. His sleeves were rolled up and his foot was pressing down on the blade of the shovel. He was digging up grassy dirt at the edge of the garden, turning it over, breaking up the soil, tossing away clumps of grass roots. Nearby sat Alice, watching him. From time to time, as he moved along the edge of the garden, he would look over at her. Their looks seemed to catch for a moment, before he returned to his garden. Standing in the warm shade of the half-open door, looking through the rippling screen at the garden quivering with sunlight, I sensed a mysterious rhythm trembling between Albert and his wife, a kind of lightness or buoyancy, a quivering sunlit harmony. It was as if both of them had shed their skins and were mingling in air, or dissolving into light and as I felt that airy mingling, that tender dissolution, as I sensed that hidden harmony, clear as the ringing of a distant bell, it came over me that what I lacked, in my life, was exactly that harmony. It was as if I were composed of some hard substance that could never dissolve in anything, whereas Albert had discovered the secret of air. But my throat was beginning to hurt, the bright light burned my eyes, and setting down my cup on the counter, which sounded like the blow of a hammer, I pushed open the door and went out.

Albert turned around in the sun. 'Sleep well?' he said, running the back of his hand slowly across his dripping forehead.

'Well enough. But you know, I've got to be getting back. A million things to do! You know how it is.'

'Sure,' Albert said. He rested both hands on the top of the long shovel handle and placed his chin on his hands. 'I know how it is.' His tone struck me as brilliantly poised between understanding and mockery.

He brought my bag down from my room and loaded it in the car. Alice had hopped through the dining room and living room and had come to rest in the deep shade of the front porch. It struck me that she kept carefully out of sight of the road. Albert bent over the driver's window and crossed his arms on the door. 'If you're ever up this way,' he said, but who would ever be up that way, 'drop in.' 'I'll do that,' I said. Albert stood up and stretched out an elbow, rubbed his shoulder. 'Take care,' he said, and gave a little wave and stepped away.

As I backed up the dirt driveway and began edging onto County Road 39, I had the sense that the house was withdrawing into its trees and shadows, fading into its island of shade. Albert had already vanished. From the road I could see only a stand of high trees clustered about a dark house. A few moments later, at the bend of the road, I glanced back again. I must have waited a second too long, because the road was already dipping, the house had sunk out of sight, and in the bright sunshine I saw only a scattering of roadside trees, a cloudless sky, fields of Queen Anne's lace stretching away.

ANGELA CARTER

THE TIGER'S
BRIDE

MY FATHER LOST me to The Beast at cards.

There's a special madness strikes travellers from the North when they reach the lovely land where the lemon trees grow. We come from countries of cold weather; at home, we are at war with nature but here, ah! you think you've come to the blessed plot where the lion lies down with the lamb. Everything flowers; no harsh wind stirs the voluptuous air. The sun spills fruit for you. And the deathly, sensual lethargy of the sweet South infects the starved brain; it gasps: 'Luxury! more luxury!' But then the snow comes, you cannot escape it, it followed us from Russia as if it ran behind our carriage, and in this dark, bitter city has caught up with us at last, flocking against the window-panes to mock my father's expectations of perpetual pleasure as the veins in his forehead stand out and throb, his hands shake as he deals the Devil's picture books.

The candles dropped hot, acrid gouts of wax on my bare shoulders. I watched with the furious cynicism peculiar to women whom circumstances force mutely to witness folly, while my father, fired in his desperation by more and yet more draughts of the firewater they call 'grappa', rids himself of the last scraps of my inheritance. When we left Russia, we owned black earth, blue forest with bear and wild boar, serfs, cornfields, farmyards, my beloved horses, white nights of cool summer, the fireworks of the northern lights. What a burden all those possessions must have been to him, because he laughs as if with glee as he beggars himself; he is in such a passion to donate all to The Beast.

Everyone who comes to this city must play a hand with the *grande seigneur*; few come. They did not warn us at Milan, or, if they did, we did not understand them – my limping Italian, the bewildering dialect of the region. Indeed, I myself spoke up in favour of this remote, provincial place, out of fashion two hundred years, because, oh irony, it boasted no casino. I did not know that the price of a stay in its Decembral solitude was a game with Milord.

The hour was late. The chill damp of this place creeps into the stones, into your bones, into the spongy pith of the lungs; it insinuated itself with a shiver into our parlour, where Milord came to play in the privacy essential to him. Who could refuse the invitation his valet brought to our lodging? Not my profligate father, certainly; the mirror above the table gave me back his frenzy, my impassivity, the withering candles, the emptying bottles, the coloured tide of the cards as they rose and fell, the still mask that concealed all the features of The Beast but for the yellow eyes that strayed, now and then, from his unfurled hand towards myself.

'*La Bestia!*' said our landlady, gingerly fingering an envelope with his huge crest of a tiger rampant on it, something of fear, something of wonder in her face. And I could not ask her why they called the master of the place, *La Bestia* – was it to do with the heraldic signature – because her tongue was so thickened by the phlegmy, bronchitic speech of the region I scarcely managed to make out a thing she said except, when she saw me: '*Che bella!*'

Since I could toddle, always the pretty one, with my glossy, nut-brown curls, my rosy cheeks. And born on Christmas Day – her 'Christmas rose', my English nurse called me. The peasants said: 'The living image of her mother,' crossing themselves out of respect for the dead. My mother did not blossom long; bartered for her dowry to such a feckless sprig of the Russian nobility that she soon died of his gaming, his whoring, his agonizing repentances. And The Beast gave me the rose from his own impeccable if outmoded button-hole when he arrived, the valet brushing the snow off his black cloak. This white rose, unnatural, out of season, that now my nervous fingers ripped, petal by petal, apart as my father magnificently concluded the career he had made of catastrophe.

This is a melancholy, introspective region; a sunless, fea-tureless landscape, the sullen river sweating fog, the shorn, hunkering willows. And a cruel city; the sombre piazza, a place uniquely suited to public executions, under the beet-ling shadow of that malign barn of a church. They used to hang condemned men in cages from the city walls; un-kindness comes naturally to them, their eyes are set so close together, they have thin lips. Poor food, pasta soaked in oil, boiled beef with sauce of bitter herbs. A funereal hush about the place, the inhabitants huddled up against the cold so you can hardly see their faces. And they lie to you and cheat you, innkeepers, coachmen, everybody. God, how they fleeced us.

The treacherous South, where you think there is no winter but forget you take it with you.

My senses were increasingly troubled by the fuddling perfume of Milord, far too potent a reek of purplish civet at such close quarters in so small a room. He must bathe him-self in scent, soak his shirts and underlinen in it; what can he smell of, that needs so much camouflage?

I never saw a man so big look so two-dimensional, in spite of the quaint elegance of The Beast, in the old-fashioned tailcoat that might, from its looks, have been bought in those distant years before he imposed seclusion on himself;

347

he does not feel he need keep up with the times. There is a crude clumsiness about his outlines, that are on the ungainly, giant side; and he has an odd air of self-imposed restraint, as if fighting a battle with himself to remain upright when he would far rather drop down on all fours. He throws our human aspirations to the godlike sadly awry, poor fellow; only from a distance would you think The Beast not much different from any other man, although he wears a mask with a man's face painted most beautifully on it. Oh, yes, a beautiful face; but one with too much formal symmetry of feature to be entirely human: one profile of his mask is the mirror image of the other, too perfect, uncanny. He wears a wig, too, false hair tied at the nape with a bow, a wig of the kind you see in old-fashioned portraits. A chaste silk stock stuck with a pearl hides his throat. And gloves of blond kid that are yet so huge and clumsy they do not seem to cover hands.

He is a carnival figure made of papier-mâché and crêpe hair; and yet he has the Devil's knack at cards.

His masked voice echoes as from a great distance as he stoops over his hand and he has such a growling impediment in his speech that only his valet, who understands him, can interpret for him, as if his master were the clumsy doll and he the ventriloquist.

The wick slumped in the eroded wax, the candles guttered. By the time my rose had lost all its petals, my father, too, was left with nothing.

'Except the girl.'

Gambling is a sickness. My father said he loved me yet he staked his daughter on a hand of cards. He fanned them out; in the mirror, I saw wild hope light up his eyes. His collar was unfastened, his rumpled hair stood up on end, he had the anguish of a man in the last stages of debauchery. The draughts came out of the old walls and bit me, I was colder than I'd ever been in Russia, when nights are coldest there.

A queen, a king, an ace. I saw them in the mirror. Oh, I know he thought he could not lose me; besides, back with me would come all he had lost, the unravelled fortunes of our family at one blow restored. And would he not win, as well, The Beast's hereditary palazzo outside the city; his immense revenues; his lands around the river; his rents, his treasure chest, his Mantegnas, his Giulio Romanos, his Cellini salt-cellars, his titles . . . the very city itself.

You must not think my father valued me at less than a king's ransom; but at *no more* than a king's ransom.

It was cold as hell in the parlour. And it seemed to me, child of the severe North, that it was not my flesh but, truly, my father's soul that was in peril.

My father, of course, believed in miracles; what gambler does not? In pursuit of just such a miracle as this, had we not travelled from the land of bears and shooting stars?

So we teetered on the brink.

The Beast bayed; laid down all three remaining aces.

The indifferent servants now glided smoothly forward as on wheels to douse the candles one by one. To look at them you would think that nothing of any moment had occurred. They yawned a little resentfully; it was almost morning. We had kept them out of bed. The Beast's man brought his cloak. My father sat amongst these preparations for departure, staring on at the betrayal of his cards upon the table.

The Beast's man informed me crisply that he, the valet, would call for me and my bags tomorrow, at ten, and conduct me forthwith to The Beast's palazzo. *Capisco?* So shocked was I that I scarcely did *capisco*; he repeated my orders patiently, he was a strange, thin, quick little man who walked with an irregular jolting rhythm upon splayed feet in curious, wedge-shaped shoes.

Where my father had been red as fire, now he was white as the snow that caked the window-pane. His eyes swam; soon he would cry.

' "Like the base Indian," ' he said; he loved rhetoric. ' "One whose hand,/Like the base Indian, threw a pearl away/Richer than all his tribe . . ." I have lost my pearl, my pearl beyond price.'

At that, The Beast made a sudden, dreadful noise, halfway between a growl and a roar; the candles flared. The quick valet, the prim hypocrite, interpreted unblinkingly: 'My master says: If you are so careless of your treasures, you should expect them to be taken from you.'

He gave us the bow and smile his master could not offer us and they departed.

I watched the snow until, just before dawn, it stopped falling; a hard frost settled, next morning there was a light like iron.

The Beast's carriage, of an elegant if antique design, was black as a hearse and it was drawn by a dashing black gelding who blew smoke from his nostrils and stamped upon the packed snow with enough sprightly appearance of life to give me some hope that not all the world was locked in ice, as I was. I had always held a little towards Gulliver's opinion, that horses are better than we are, and, that day, I would have been glad to depart with him to the kingdom of horses, if I'd been given the chance.

The valet sat up on the box in a natty black and gold livery, clasping, of all things, a bunch of his master's damned white roses as if a gift of flowers would reconcile a woman to any humiliation. He sprang down with preternatural agility to place them ceremoniously in my reluctant hand. My tear-beslobbered father wants a rose to show that I forgive him. When I break off a stem, I prick my finger and so he gets his rose all smeared with blood.

The valet crouched at my feet to tuck the rugs about me with a strange kind of unflattering obsequiousness yet he forgot his station sufficiently to scratch busily beneath his white periwig with an over-supple index finger as he offered me what my old nurse would have called an 'old-fashioned look', ironic, sly, a smidgen of disdain in it. And pity? No pity. His eyes were moist and brown, his face seamed with the innocent cunning of an ancient baby. He had an irritating habit of chattering to himself under his breath all the time as he packed up his master's winnings. I drew the curtains to conceal the sight of my father's farewell; my spite was sharp as broken glass.

Lost to The Beast! And what, I wondered, might be the exact nature of his 'beastliness'? My English nurse once told me about a tiger-man she saw in London, when she was a little girl, to scare me into good behaviour, for I was a wild wee thing and she could not tame me into submission with a frown or the bribe of a spoonful of jam. If you don't stop plaguing the nursemaids, my beauty, the tiger-man will come and take you away. They'd brought him from Sumatra, in the Indies, she said; his hinder parts were all hairy and only from the head downwards did he resemble a man.

And yet The Beast goes always masked; it cannot be his face that looks like mine.

But the tiger-man, in spite of his hairiness, could take a glass of ale in his hand like a good Christian and drink it down. Had she not seen him do so, at the sign of The George, by the steps of Upper Moor Fields when she was just as high as me and lisped and toddled, too. Then she would sigh for London, across the North Sea of the lapse of years. But, if this young lady was not a good little girl and did not eat her boiled beetroot, then the tiger-man would put on his big black travelling cloak lined with fur, just like your daddy's, and hire the Erl-King's galloper of wind and ride through the night straight to the nursery and –

Yes, my beauty! GOBBLE YOU UP!

How I'd squeal in delighted terror, half believing her, half knowing that she teased me. And there were things I knew that I must not tell her. In our lost farmyard, where the giggling nursemaids initiated me into the mysteries of what the bull did to the cows, I heard about the waggoner's daughter. Hush, hush, don't let on to your nursie we said so; the waggoner's lass, hare-lipped, squint-eyed, ugly as sin, who would have taken her? Yet, to her shame, her belly swelled amid the cruel mockery of the ostlers and her son was born of a bear, they whispered. Born with a full pelt and teeth; that proved it. But, when he grew up, he was a good shepherd, although he never married, lived in a hut outside the village and could make the wind blow any way he wanted to besides being able to tell which eggs would become cocks, which hens.

The wondering peasants once brought my father a skull with horns four inches long on either side of it and would not go back to the field where their poor plough disturbed it until the priest went with them; for this skull had the jawbone of a *man*, had it not?

Old wives' tales, nursery fears! I knew well enough the reason for the trepidation I cosily titillated with superstitious marvels of my childhood on the day my childhood ended. For now my own skin was my sole capital in the world and today I'd make my first investment.

We had left the city far behind us and were now traversing

a wide, flat dish of snow where the mutilated stumps of the willows flourished their ciliate heads athwart frozen ditches; mist diminished the horizon, brought down the sky until it seemed no more than a few inches above us. As far as eye could see, not one thing living. How starveling, how bereft the dead season of this spurious Eden in which all the fruit was blighted by cold! And my frail roses, already faded. I opened the carriage door and tossed the defunct bouquet into the rucked, frost-stiff mud of the road. Suddenly a sharp, freezing wind arose and pelted my face with a dry rice of powdered snow. The mist lifted sufficiently to reveal before me an acreage of half-derelict façades of sheer red brick, the vast man-trap, the megalomaniac citadel of his palazzo.

It was a world in itself but a dead one, a burned-out planet. I saw The Beast bought solitude, not luxury, with his money.

The little black horse trotted smartly through the figured bronze doors that stood open to the weather like those of a barn and the valet handed me out of the carriage on to the scarred tiles of the great hall itself, into the odorous warmth of a stable, sweet with hay, acrid with horse dung. An equine chorus of neighings and soft drummings of hooves broke out beneath the tall roof, where the beams were scabbed with last summer's swallows' nests; a dozen gracile muzzles lifted from their mangers and turned towards us, ears erect. The Beast had given his horses the use of the dining room. The walls were painted, aptly enough, with a fresco of horses, dogs and men in a wood where fruit and blossom grew on the bough together.

The valet tweaked politely at my sleeve. Milord is waiting.

Gaping doors and broken windows let the wind in everywhere. We mounted one staircase after another, our feet clopping on the marble. Through archways and open doors, I glimpsed suites of vaulted chambers opening one out of another like systems of Chinese boxes into the infinite complexity of the innards of the place. He and I and the wind were the only things stirring; and all the furniture was under dust sheets, the chandeliers bundled up in cloth, pictures taken from their hooks and propped with their faces to the walls as if their master could not bear to look at them. The palace was dismantled, as if its owner were about to move house or had never properly moved in; The Beast had chosen to live in an uninhabited place.

The valet darted me a reassuring glance from his brown, eloquent eyes, yet a glance with so much queer superciliousness in it that it did not comfort me, and went bounding ahead of me on his bandy legs, softly chattering to himself. I held my head high and followed him; but for all my pride, my heart was heavy.

Milord has his eyrie high above the house, a small, stifling, darkened room; he keeps his shutters locked at noon. I was out of breath by the time we reached it and returned to him the silence with which he greeted me. I will not smile. He cannot smile.

In his rarely disturbed privacy, The Beast wears a garment of Ottoman design, a loose, dull purple gown with gold embroidery round the neck that falls from his shoulders to conceal his feet. The feet of the chair he sits in are handsomely clawed. He hides his hands in his ample sleeves. The artificial masterpiece of his face appals me. A small fire in a small grate. A rushing wind rattles the shutters.

The valet coughed. To him fell the delicate task of transmitting to me his master's wishes.

'My master—'

A stick fell in the grate. It made a mighty clatter in that dreadful silence, the valet started, lost his place in his speech, began again.

'My master has but one desire.'

The thick, rich, wild scent with which Milord had soaked himself the previous evening hangs all about us, ascends in cursive blue from the smoke hole of a precious Chinese pot.

'He wishes only—'

Now, in the face of my impassivity, the valet twittered, his ironic composure gone, for the desire of a master, however trivial, may yet sound unbearably insolent in the mouth of a servant and his role of go-between clearly caused him a good deal of embarrassment. He gulped; he swallowed, at last contrived to unleash an unpunctuated flood.

'My master's sole desire is to see the pretty young lady unclothed nude without her dress and that only for the one time after which she will be returned to her father undamaged with bankers' orders for the sum which he lost to my master at cards and also a number of fine presents such as furs, jewels and horses—'

I remained standing. During this interview, my eyes were level with those inside the mask that now evaded mine as if, to his credit, he was ashamed of his own request even as his mouthpiece made it for him. *Agitato, molto agitato*, the valet wrung his white-gloved hands.

'Desnuda—'

I could scarcely believe my ears. I let out a raucous guffaw; no young lady laughs like that! my old nurse used to remonstrate. But I did. And do. At the clamour of my heartless mirth, the valet danced backwards with perturbation, palpitating his fingers as if attempting to wrench them off, expostulating, wordlessly pleading. I felt that I owed it to him to make my reply in as exquisite a Tuscan as I could master.

'You may put me in a windowless room, sir, and I promise you I will pull my skirt up to my waist, ready for you. But there must be a sheet over my face, to hide it; though the sheet must be laid over me so lightly that it will not choke me. So I shall be covered completely from the waist upwards, and no lights. There you can visit me once, sir, and only the once. After that I must be driven directly to the city and deposited in the public square, in front of the church. If you wish to give me money, then I should be pleased to receive it. But I must stress that you should give me only the same amount of money that you would give to any other woman in such circumstances. However, if you choose not to give me a present, then that is your right.'

How pleased I was to see I struck The Beast to the heart! For, after a baker's dozen heart-beats, one single tear swelled, glittering, at the corner of the masked eye. A tear! A tear, I hoped, of shame. The tear trembled for a moment on an edge of painted bone, then tumbled down the painted cheek to fall, with an abrupt tinkle, on the tiled floor.

The valet, ticking and clucking to himself, hastily ushered me out of the room. A mauve cloud of his master's perfume billowed out into the chill corridor with us and dissipated itself on the spinning winds.

A cell had been prepared for me, a veritable cell, window-less, airless, lightless, in the viscera of the palace. The valet lit a lamp for me; a narrow bed, a dark cupboard with fruit and flowers carved on it bulked out of the gloom.

'I shall twist a noose out of my bed linen and hang myself with it,' I said.

'Oh, no,' said the valet, fixing upon me wide and suddenly melancholy eyes. 'Oh, no, you will not. You are a woman of honour.'

And what was *he* doing in my bedroom, this jigging caricature of a man? Was he to be my warder until I submit-ted to The Beast's whim or he to mine? Am I in such reduced circumstances that I may not have a lady's maid?

As if in reply to my unspoken demand, the valet clapped his hands.

'To assuage your loneliness, madame . . .'

A knocking and clattering behind the door of the cupboard; the door swings open and out glides a soubrettte from an operetta, with glossy, nut-brown curls, rosy cheeks, blue, rolling eyes; it takes me a moment to recognize her, in her little cap, her white stockings, her frilled petticoats. She carries a looking glass in one hand and a powder puff in the other and there is a musical box where her heart should be; she tinkles as she rolls towards me on her tiny wheels.

'Nothing human lives here,' said the valet.

My maid halted, bowed; from a split seam at the side of her bodice protrudes the handle of a key. She is a marvellous machine, the most delicately balanced system of cords and pulleys in the world.

'We have dispensed with servants,' the valet said. 'We surround ourselves instead, for utility and pleasure, with simulacra and find it no less convenient than do most gentlemen.'

This clockwork twin of mine halted before me, her bowels churning out a settecento minuet, and offered me the bold carnation of her smile. Click, click – she raises her arm and busily dusts my cheeks with pink, powdered chalk that makes me cough, then thrusts towards me her little mirror.

I saw within it not my own face but that of my father, as if I had put on his face when I arrived at The Beast's palace as the discharge of his debt. What, you self-deluding fool, are you crying still? And drunk, too. He tossed back his grappa and hurled the tumbler away.

Seeing my astonished fright, the valet took the mirror away from me, breathed on it, polished it with the ham of his gloved fist, handed it back to me. Now all I saw was myself, haggard from a sleepless night, pale enough to need my maid's supply of rouge.

I heard the key turn in the heavy door and the valet's footsteps patter down the stone passage. Meanwhile, my double continued to powder the air, emitting her jangling tune but, as it turned out, she was not inexhaustible; soon she was powdering more and yet more languorously, her metal heart slowed in imitation of fatigue, her musical box ran down until the notes separated themselves out of the tune and plopped like single raindrops and, as if sleep had overtaken her, at last she moved no longer. As she succumbed to sleep, I had no option but to do so too. I dropped on the narrow bed as if felled.

Time passed but I do not know how much; then the valet woke me with rolls and honey. I gestured the tray away but he set it down firmly beside the lamp and took from it a little shagreen box, which he offered to me.

I turned away my head.

'Oh, my lady!' Such hurt cracked his high-pitched voice! He dextrously unfastened the gold clasp; on a bed of crimson velvet lay a single diamond earring, perfect as a tear.

I snapped the box shut and tossed it into a corner. This sudden, sharp movement must have disturbed the mechanism of the doll; she jerked her arm almost as if to reprimand me, letting out a rippling fart of gavotte. Then she was still again.

'Very well,' said the valet, put out. And indicated it was time for me to visit my host again. He did not let me wash or comb my hair. There was so little natural light in the interior of the palace that I could not tell whether it was day or night.

You would not think The Beast had budged an inch since I last saw him; he sat in his huge chair, with his hands in his

358

sleeves, and the heavy air never moved. I might have slept an hour, a night, or a month, but his sculptured calm, the stifling air remained just as it had been. The incense rose from the pot, still traced the same signature on the air. The same fire burned.

Take off my clothes for you, like a ballet girl? Is that all you want of me?

'The sight of a young lady's skin that no man has seen before—' stammered the valet.

I wished I'd rolled in the hay with every lad on my father's farm, to disqualify myself from this humiliating bargain. That he should want so little was the reason why I could not give it; I did not need to speak for The Beast to understand me.

A tear came from his other eye. And then he moved; he buried his cardboard carnival head with its ribboned weight of false hair in, I would say, his arms; he withdrew his, I might say, hands from his sleeves and I saw his furred pads, his excoriating claws.

The dropped tear caught upon his fur and shone. And in my room for hours I heard those paws pad back and forth outside my door.

When the valet arrived again with his silver salver, I had a pair of diamond earrings of the finest water in the world; I threw the other into the corner where the first one lay. The valet twittered with aggrieved regret but did not offer to lead me to The Beast again. Instead, he smiled ingratiatingly and confided: 'My master, he say: invite the young lady to go riding.'

'What's this?'

He briskly mimicked the action of a gallop and, to my amazement, tunelessly croaked: 'Tantivy! tantivy! a-hunting we will go!'

'I'll run away, I'll ride to the city.'

'Oh, no,' he said. 'Are you not a woman of honour?'

He clapped his hands and my maidservant clicked and jangled into the imitation of life. She rolled towards the cupboard where she had come from and reached inside it to fetch out over her synthetic arm my riding habit. Of all things. My very own riding habit, that I'd left behind me in a trunk in a loft in the country house outside Petersburg that we'd lost long ago, before, even, we set out on this wild pilgrimage to the cruel South. Either the very riding habit my old nurse had sewn for me or else a copy of it perfect to the lost button on the right sleeve, the ripped hem held up with a pin. I turned the worn cloth about in my hands, looking for a clue. The wind that sprinted through the palace made the door tremble in its frame; had the north wind blown my garments across Europe to me? At home, the bear's son directed the winds at his pleasure; what democracy of magic held this palace and the fir forest in common? Or, should I be prepared to accept it as proof of the axiom my father had drummed into me: that, if you have enough money, anything is possible?

'Tantivy,' suggested the now twinkling valet, evidently charmed at the pleasure mixed with my bewilderment. The clockwork maid held my jacket out to me and I allowed myself to shrug into it as if reluctantly, although I was half mad to get out into the open air, away from this deathly palace, even in such company.

The doors of the hall let the bright day in; I saw that it was morning. Our horses, saddled and bridled, beasts in bondage, were waiting for us, striking sparks from the tiles with their impatient hooves while their stablemates lolled at ease among the straw, conversing with one another in the mute speech of horses. A pigeon or two, feathers puffed to keep out the cold, strutted about, pecking at ears of corn. The little black gelding who had brought me here greeted me with a ringing neigh that resonated inside the mist roof as in a sounding box and I knew he was meant for me to ride.

I always adored horses, noblest of creatures, such wounded sensitivity in their wise eyes, such rational restraint of energy at their high-strung hindquarters. I lirruped and hurrumphed to my shining black companion and he acknowledged my greeting with a kiss on the forehead from his soft lips. There was a little shaggy pony nuzzling away at the *trompe l'oeil* foliage beneath the hooves of the painted horses on the wall, into whose saddle the valet sprang with a flourish as of the circus. Then The Beast, wrapped in a black fur-lined cloak, came to heave himself aloft a grave grey mare. No natural horseman he; he clung to her mane like a ship-wrecked sailor to a spar.

Cold, that morning, yet dazzling with the sharp winter sunlight that wounds the retina. There was a scurrying wind about that seemed to go with us, as if the masked, immense one who did not speak carried it inside his cloak and let it out at his pleasure, for it stirred the horses' manes but did not lift the lowland mists.

A bereft landscape in the sad browns and sepias of winter lay all about us, the marshland drearily protracting itself towards the wide river. Those decapitated willows. Now and then, the swoop of a bird, its irreconcilable cry.

A profound sense of strangeness slowly began to possess me. I knew my two companions were not, in any way, as other men, the simian retainer and the master for whom he spoke, the one with clawed forepaws who was in a plot with the witches who let the winds out of their knotted handkerchiefs up towards the Finnish border. I knew they lived according to a different logic than I had done until my father abandoned

361

me to the wild beasts by his human carelessness. This knowledge gave me a certain fearfulness still; but, I would say, not much … I was a young girl, a virgin, and therefore men denied me rationality just as they denied it to all those who were not exactly like themselves, in all their unreason. If I could see not one single soul in that wilderness of desolation all around me, then the six of us – mounts and riders, both – could boast amongst us not one soul, either, since all the best religions in the world state categorically that not beasts nor women were equipped with the flimsy, insubstantial things when the good Lord opened the gates of Eden and let Eve and her familiars tumble out. Understand, then, that though I would not say I privately engaged in metaphysical speculation as we rode through the reedy approaches to the river, I certainly meditated on the nature of my own state, how I had been bought and sold, passed from hand to hand. That clockwork girl who powdered my cheeks for me; had I not been allotted only the same kind of imitative life amongst men that the doll-maker had given her?

Yet, as to the true nature of the being of this clawed magus who rode his pale horse in a style that made me recall how Kublai Khan's leopards went out hunting on horseback, of that I had no notion.

We came to the bank of the river that was so wide we could not see across it, so still with winter that it scarcely seemed to flow. The horses lowered their heads to drink. The valet cleared his throat, about to speak; we were in a place of perfect privacy, beyond a brake of winter-bare rushes, a hedge of reeds.

'If you will not let him see you without your clothes—'

I involuntarily shook my head—

'—you must, then, prepare yourself for the sight of my master, naked.'

The river broke on the pebbles with a diminishing sigh. My composure deserted me; all at once I was on the brink of panic. I did not think that I could bear the sight of him, whatever he was. The mare raised her dripping muzzle and looked at me keenly, as if urging me. The river broke again at my feet. I was far from home.

'You,' said the valet, 'must.'

When I saw how scared he was I might refuse, I nodded.

The reed bowed down in a sudden snarl of wind that brought with it a gust of the heavy odour of his disguise. The valet held out his master's cloak to screen him from me as he removed the mask. The horses stirred.

The tiger will never lie down with the lamb; he acknowledges no pact that is not reciprocal. The lamb must learn to run with the tigers.

A great, feline, tawny shape whose pelt was barred with a savage geometry of bars the colour of burned wood. His domed, heavy head, so terrible he must hide it. How subtle the muscles, how profound the tread. The annihilating vehemence of his eyes, like twin suns.

I felt my breast ripped apart as if I suffered a marvellous wound.

The valet moved forward as if to cover up his master now the girl had acknowledged him, but I said: 'No.' The tiger sat still as a heraldic beast, in the pact he had made with his own ferocity to do me no harm. He was far larger than I could have imagined. From the poor, shabby things I'd seen once, in the Czar's menagerie at Petersburg, the golden fruit of their eyes dimming, withering in the far North of captivity. Nothing about him reminded me of humanity.

I therefore, shivering, now unfastened my jacket, to show him I would do him no harm. Yet I was clumsy and blushed a little, for no man had seen me naked and I was a proud girl. Pride it was, not shame, that thwarted my fingers so; and a certain trepidation lest this frail little article of human upholstery before him might not be, in itself, grand enough to satisfy his expectations of us, since those, for all I knew, might have grown infinite during the endless time he had been waiting. The wind clattered in the rushes, purled and eddied in the river.

I showed his grave silence my white skin, my red nipples, and the horses turned their heads to watch me, also, as if they, too, were courteously curious as to the fleshly nature of women. Then The Beast lowered his massive head; Enough! said the valet with a gesture. The wind died down. All was still again.

Then they went off together, the valet on his pony, the tiger running before him like a hound, and I walked along the river bank for a while. I felt I was at liberty for the first time in my life. Then the winter sun began to tarnish, a few flakes of snow drifted from the darkening sky and, when I returned to the horses, I found The Beast mounted again on his grey mare, cloaked and masked and once more, to all appearances, a man, while the valet had a fine catch of waterfowl dangling from his hand and the corpse of a young roebuck slung behind his saddle. I climbed up on the black gelding in silence and so we returned to the palace as the snow fell more and more heavily, obscuring the tracks that we had left behind us.

The valet did not return me to my cell but, instead, to an elegant, if old-fashioned boudoir with sofas of faded pink brocade, a jinn's treasury of Oriental carpets, tintinnabula-tion of cut-glass chandeliers. Candles in antlered holders struck rainbows from the prismatic hearts of my diamond earrings, that lay on my new dressing table at which my attentive maid stood ready with her powder puff and mirror.

Intending to fix the ornaments in my ears, I took the looking glass from her hand, but it was in the midst of one of its magic fits again and I did not see my own face in it but that of my father; at first I thought he smiled at me. Then I saw he was smiling with pure gratification.

He sat, I saw, in the parlour of our lodgings, at the very table where he had lost me, but now he was busily engaged in counting out a tremendous pile of banknotes. My father's circumstances had changed already; well-shaven, neatly barbered, smart new clothes. A frosted glass of sparkling wine sat convenient to his hand beside an ice bucket. The Beast had clearly paid cash on the nail for his glimpse of my bosom and paid up promptly, as if it had not been a sight I might have died of showing. Then I saw my father's trunks were packed, ready for departure. Could he so easily leave me here?

There was a note on the table with the money, in a fine hand. I could read it quite clearly. 'The young lady will arrive immediately.' Some harlot with whom he'd briskly negotiated a liaison on the strength of his spoils? Not at all. For, at that moment, the valet knocked at my door to announce that I might leave the palace at any time hereafter, and he bore over his arm a handsome sable cloak, my very own little gratuity, The Beast's morning gift, in which he proposed to pack me up and send me off.

When I looked at the mirror again, my father had disappeared and all I saw was a pale, hollow-eyed girl whom I scarcely recognized. The valet asked politely when he should prepare the carriage, as if he did not doubt that I would leave with my booty at the first opportunity while my maid, whose face was no longer the spit of my own, continued bonnily to beam. I will dress her in my own clothes, wind her up, send her back to perform the part of my father's daughter.

'Leave me alone,' I said to the valet.

He did not need to lock the door, now. I fixed the earrings in my ears. They were very heavy. Then I took off my riding habit, left it where it lay on the floor. But, when I got down to my shift, my arms dropped to my sides. I was unaccustomed to nakedness. I was so unused to my own skin that to take off all my clothes involved a kind of flaying. I thought The Beast had wanted a little thing compared with what I was prepared to give him; but it is not natural for humankind to go naked, not since first we hid our loins with fig leaves. He had demanded the abominable. I felt as much atrocious pain as if I was stripping off my own underpelt and the smiling girl stood poised in the oblivion of her balked simulation of life, watching me peel down to the cold, white meat of contract and, if she did not see me, then so much more like the market place, where the eyes that watch you take no account of your existence.

And it seemed my entire life, since I had left the North, had passed under the indifferent gaze of eyes like hers.

Then I was flinching stark, except for his irreproachable tears.

I huddled in the furs I must return to him, to keep me from the lacerating winds that raced along the corridors. I knew the way to his den without the valet to guide me.

No response to my tentative rap on his door.

Then the wind blew the valet whirling along the passage. He must have decided that, if one should go naked, then all should go naked; without his livery, he revealed himself, as I had suspected, a delicate creature, covered with silken moth-grey fur, brown fingers supple as leather, chocolate muzzle, the gentlest creature in the world. He gibbered a little to see my fine furs and jewels as if I were dressed up for the opera and, with a great deal of tender ceremony, removed the sables from my shoulders. The sables thereupon resolved themselves into a pack of black squeaking rats that rattled immediately down the stairs on their hard little feet and were lost to sight.

The valet bowed me inside The Beast's room.

The purple dressing gown, the mask, the wig, were laid out on his chair; a glove was planted on each arm. The empty house of his appearance was ready for him but he had abandoned it. There was a reek of fur and piss; the incense pot lay broken in pieces on the floor. Half-burned sticks were scattered from the extinguished fire. A candle stuck by its own grease to the mantelpiece lit two narrow flames in the pupils of the tiger's eyes.

He was pacing backwards and forwards, backwards and forwards, the tip of his heavy tail twitching as he paced out the length and breadth of his imprisonment between the gnawed and bloody bones.

He will gobble you up.

Nursery fears made flesh and sinew; earliest and most archaic of fears, fear of devourment. The beast and his carnivorous bed of bone and I, white, shaking, raw, approaching him as if offering, in myself, the key to a peaceable kingdom in which his appetite need not be my extinction.

He went still as stone. He was far more frightened of me than I was of him.

I squatted on the wet straw and stretched out my hand. I was now within the field of force of his golden eyes. He growled at the back of his throat, lowered his head, sank on to his forepaws, snarled, showed me his red gullet, his yellow teeth. I never moved. He snuffled the air, as if to smell my fear; he could not.

Slowly, slowly he began to drag his heavy, gleaming weight across the floor towards me.

A tremendous throbbing, as of the engine that makes the earth turn, filled the little room; he had begun to purr.

The sweet thunder of this purr shook the old walls, made the shutters batter the windows until they burst apart and let in the white light of the snowy moon. Tiles came crashing down from the roof; I heard them fall into the courtyard far below. The reverberations of his purring rocked the foundations of the house, the walls began to dance. I thought: 'It will all fall, everything will disintegrate.'

He dragged himself closer and closer to me, until I felt the harsh velvet of his head against my hand, then a tongue, abrasive as sandpaper. 'He will lick the skin off me!'

And each stroke of his tongue ripped off skin after successive skin, all the skins of a life in the world, and left behind a nascent patina of shiny hairs. My earrings turned back to water and trickled down my shoulders; I shrugged the drops off my beautiful fur.

HARUKI MURAKAMI

THE DANCING DWARF

Translated by Jay Rubin

A DWARF CAME into my dream and asked me to dance.

I knew this was a dream, but I was just as tired in my dream as in real life at the time. So, very politely, I declined. The dwarf was not offended but danced alone instead.

He set a portable record player on the ground and danced to the music. Records were spread all around the player. I picked up a few from different spots in the pile. They comprised a genuine musical miscellany, as if the dwarf had chosen them with his eyes closed, grabbing whatever his hand happened to touch. And none of the records was in the right jacket. The dwarf would take half-played records off the turntable, throw them onto the pile without returning them to their jackets, lose track of which went with which, and afterward put records in jackets at random. There would be a Rolling Stones record in a Glenn Miller jacket, a recording of the Mitch Miller chorus in the jacket for Ravel's *Daphnis and Chloé*.

But none of this confusion seemed to matter to the dwarf. As long as he could dance to whatever was playing, he was satisfied. At the moment, he was dancing to a Charlie Parker record that had been in a jacket labeled *Great Selections for the Classical Guitar*. His body whirled like a tornado, sucking up the wild flurry of notes that poured from Charlie Parker's saxophone. Eating grapes, I watched him dance.

The sweat poured out of him. Each swing of his head sent drops of sweat flying from his face; each wave of an arm shot streams of sweat from his fingertips. But nothing could stop him. When a record ended, I would set my bowl of grapes down and put on a new one. And on he would go.

'You're a great dancer,' I cried out to him. 'You're music itself.'

'Thank you,' he answered with a hint of affectation.

'Do you always go at it like this?'

'Pretty much,' he said.

Then the dwarf did a beautiful twirl on tiptoe, his soft, wavy hair flowing in the wind. I applauded. I had never seen such accomplished dancing in my life. The dwarf gave a respectful bow as the song ended. He stopped dancing and toweled himself down. The needle was clicking in the inner groove of the record. I lifted the tonearm and turned the player off. I put the record into the first empty jacket that came to hand.

'I guess you haven't got time to hear my story,' said the dwarf, glancing at me. 'It's a long one.'

Unsure how to answer, I took another grape. Time was no problem for me, but I wasn't that eager to hear the long life story of a dwarf. And besides, this was a dream. It could evaporate at any moment.

Rather than wait for me to answer, the dwarf snapped his fingers and started to speak. 'I'm from the north country,' he said. 'Up north, they don't dance. Nobody knows how. They don't even realize that it's something you can do. But I wanted to dance. I wanted to stamp my feet and wave my arms, shake my head and spin around. Like this.'

The dwarf stamped his feet, waved his arms, shook his head, and spun around. Each movement was simple enough in itself, but in combination the four produced an almost incredible beauty of motion, erupting from the dwarf's body all at once, as when a globe of light bursts open.

'I wanted to dance like this. And so I came south. I danced in the taverns. I became famous, and danced in the presence of the king. That was before the revolution, of course. Once the revolution broke out, the king passed away, as you know, and I was banished from the town to live in the forest.'

The dwarf went to the middle of the clearing and began to dance again. I put a record on. It was an old Frank Sinatra record. The dwarf danced, singing 'Night and Day' along with Sinatra. I pictured him dancing before the throne. Glittering chandeliers and beautiful ladies-in-waiting, exotic fruits and the long spears of the royal guard, portly eunuchs, the young king in jewel-bedecked robes, the dwarf drenched in sweat but dancing with unbroken concentration: As I imagined the gorgeous scene, I felt that at any moment the roar of the revolution's cannon would echo from the distance.

The dwarf went on dancing, and I ate my grapes. The sun set, covering the earth in the shadows of the forest. A huge black butterfly the size of a bird cut across the clearing and vanished into the depths of the forest. I felt the chill of the evening air. It was time for my dream to melt away, I knew.

'I guess I have to go now,' I said to the dwarf.

He stopped dancing and nodded in silence.

'I enjoyed watching you dance,' I said. 'Thanks a lot.'

'Anytime,' said the dwarf.

'We may never meet again,' I said. 'Take care of yourself.'

'Don't worry,' said the dwarf. 'We will meet again.'

'Are you sure?'

'Oh, yes. You'll be coming back here,' he said with a snap of his fingers. 'You'll live in the forest. And every day you'll dance with me. You'll become a really good dancer yourself before long.'

'How do you know?' I asked, taken aback.

'It's been decided,' he answered. 'No one has the power to

change what has been decided. I know that you and I will meet again soon enough.'

The dwarf looked right up at me as he spoke. The deepening darkness had turned him the deep blue of water at night.

'Well, then,' he said. 'Be seeing you.'

He turned his back to me and began dancing again, alone.

I woke up alone. Facedown in bed, I was drenched in sweat. There was a bird outside my window. It seemed different from the bird I was used to seeing there.

I washed my face with great care, shaved, put some bread in the toaster, and boiled water for coffee. I fed the cat, changed its litter, put on a necktie, and tied my shoes. Then I took a bus to the elephant factory.

Needless to say, the manufacture of elephants is no easy matter. They're big, first of all, and very complex. It's not like making hairpins or colored pencils. The factory covers a huge area, and it consists of several buildings. Each building is big, too, and the sections are color-coded. Assigned to the ear section that month, I worked in the building with the yellow ceiling and posts. My helmet and pants were also yellow. All I did there was make ears. The month before, I had been assigned to the green building, where I wore a green helmet and pants and made heads. We moved from section to section each month, like Gypsies. It was company policy. That way, we could all form a complete picture of what an elephant looked like. No one was permitted to spend his whole life making just ears, say, or just toenails. The executives put together the chart that controlled our movements, and we followed the chart.

Making elephant heads is tremendously rewarding work. It requires enormous attention to detail, and at the end of the day you're so tired you don't want to talk to anybody. I've lost as much as six pounds working there for a month, but it does give me a great sense of accomplishment. By comparison, making ears is a breeze. You just make these big, flat, thin things, put a few wrinkles in them, and you're done. We call working in the ear section 'taking an ear break'. After a monthlong ear break, I go to the trunk section, where the work is again very demanding. A trunk has to be flexible, and its nostrils must be unobstructed for its entire length. Otherwise, the finished elephant will go on a rampage. Which is why making the trunk is nerve-racking work from beginning to end.

We don't make elephants from nothing, of course. Properly speaking, we reconstitute them. First we saw a single elephant into six distinct parts: ears, trunk, head, abdomen, legs, and tail. These we then recombine to make five elephants, which means that each new elephant is in fact only one-fifth genuine and four-fifths imitation. This is not obvious to the naked eye, nor is the elephant itself aware of it. We're that good.

Why must we artificially manufacture – or, should I say, reconstitute – elephants? It is because we are far less patient than they are. Left to their own devices, elephants would give birth to no more than one baby in four or five years. And because we love elephants, of course, it makes us terribly impatient to see this custom – or habitual behavior – of theirs. This is what led us to begin reconstituting them ourselves.

To protect the newly reconstituted elephants against improper use, they are initially purchased by the Elephant Supply Corporation, a publicly owned monopoly, which keeps them for two weeks and subjects them to a battery of highly exacting tests, after which the sole of one foot is stamped with the corporation's logo before the elephant is released into the jungle. We make fifteen elephants in a normal week. Though in the pre-Christmas season we can increase that to as many as twenty-five by running the machinery at full speed, I think that fifteen is just about right.

As I mentioned earlier, the ear section is the easiest single phase in the elephant-manufacturing process. It demands little physical exertion on the part of workers, it requires no close concentration, and it employs no complex machinery. The number of actual operations involved is limited, as well. Workers can either work at a relaxed pace all day or exert themselves to meet their quota in the morning so as to have the afternoon free.

My partner and I in the ear shop liked the second approach. We'd finish up in the morning and spend the afternoon talking or reading or amusing ourselves separately. The afternoon following my dream of the dancing dwarf, all we had to do was hang ten freshly wrinkled ears on the wall, after which we sat on the floor enjoying the sunshine.

I told my partner about the dwarf. I remembered the dream in vivid detail and described everything about it to him, no matter how trivial. Where description was difficult, I demonstrated by shaking my head or swinging my arms or stamping my feet. He listened with frequent grunts of interest, sipping his tea. He was five years my senior, a strongly built fellow with a dark beard and a penchant for silence. He had this habit of thinking with his arms folded. Judging by the expression on his face, you would guess that he was a serious thinker, looking at things from all angles, but usually he'd just come up straight after a while and say, 'That's a tough one.' Nothing more.

He sat there thinking for a long time after I told him about my dream – so long that I started polishing the control panel of the electric bellows to kill time. Finally, he came up straight, as always, and said, 'That's a tough one. Hmmm. A dancing dwarf. That's a tough one.'

This came as no great disappointment to me. I hadn't been expecting him to say any more than he usually did. I had just wanted to tell someone about it. I put the electric bellows back and drank my now-lukewarm tea.

He went on thinking, though, for a much longer time than he normally devoted to such matters.

'What gives?' I asked.

'I'm pretty sure I once heard about that dwarf.'

This caught me off guard.

'I just can't remember who told me.'

'Please try,' I urged him.

'Sure,' he said, and gave it another go.

He finally managed to recall what he knew about the dwarf three hours later, as the sun was going down near quitting time.

'That's it!' he exclaimed. 'The old guy in Stage Six! You know, the one who plants hairs. C'mon, you know: long white hair down to his shoulders, hardly any teeth. Been working here since before the revolution.'

'Oh,' I said. 'Him.' I had seen him in the tavern any number of times.

'Yeah. He told me about the dwarf way back when. Said it was a good dancer. I didn't pay much attention to him, figured he was senile. But now I don't know. Maybe he wasn't crazy after all.'

'So, what did he tell you?'

'Gee, I'm not so sure. It was a long time ago.' He folded his arms and fell to thinking again. But it was hopeless. After a while, he straightened up and said, 'Can't remember. Go ask him yourself.'

*　*　*

As soon as the bell rang at quitting time, I went to the Stage Six area, but there was no sign of the old man. I found only two young girls sweeping the floor. The thin girl told me he had probably gone to the tavern, 'the older one'. Which is exactly where I found him, sitting very erect at the bar, drinking, with his lunch box beside him.

The tavern was an old, old place. It had been there since long before I was born, before the revolution. For generations now, the elephant craftsmen had been coming here to drink, play cards, and sing. The walls were lined with photographs of the old days at the elephant factory. There was a picture of the first president of the company inspecting a tusk, a photo of an old-time movie queen visiting the factory, shots taken at summer dances, that kind of thing. The revolutionary guards had burned all pictures of the king and the royal family and anything else that was deemed to be royalist. There were pictures of the revolution, of course: the revolutionary guards occupying the factory and the revolutionary guards stringing up the plant superintendent.

I found the old fellow drinking Mecatol beneath an old, discolored photo labeled THREE FACTORY BOYS POLISHING TUSKS. When I took the stool next to him, the old man pointed to the photo and said, 'This one is me.'

I squinted hard at the photo. The young boy on the right, maybe twelve or thirteen years old, did appear to be this old man in his youth. You would never notice the resemblance on your own, but once it had been pointed out to you, you could see that both had the same sharp nose and flat lips. Apparently, the old guy always sat here, and whenever he noticed an unfamiliar customer come in he'd say, 'This one is me.'

'Looks like a real old picture,' I said, hoping to draw him out.

'Fore the revolution,' he said matter-of-factly. 'Even an old guy like me was still a kid back then. We all get old, though. You'll look like me before too long. Just you wait, sonny boy!'

He let out a great cackle, spraying spit from a wide-open mouth missing half its teeth.

Then he launched into stories about the revolution. Obviously, he hated both the king and the revolutionary guards. I let him talk all he wanted, bought him another glass of Mecatol, and when the time was right asked him if, by any chance, he happened to know about a dancing dwarf.

'Dancing dwarf?' he said. 'You wanna hear about the dancing dwarf?'

'I'd like to.'

His eyes glared into mine. 'What the hell for?' he asked.

'I don't know,' I lied. 'Somebody told me about him. Sounded interesting.'

He continued to look hard at me until his eyes reverted to the special mushy look that drunks have. 'Awright,' he said. 'Why not? Ya bought me a drink. But just one thing,' he said, holding a finger in my face, 'don't tell anybody. The revolution was a hell of a long time ago, but you're still not supposed to talk about the dancing dwarf. So, whatever I tell you, keep it to yourself. And don't mention my name. Okay?'

'Okay.'

'Now, order me another drink and let's go to a booth.'

I ordered two Mecatols and brought them to the booth, away from the bartender. The table had a green lamp in the shape of an elephant.

'It was before the revolution,' said the old man. 'The dwarf came from the north country. What a great dancer he was! Nah, he wasn't just great *at* dancing. He *was* dancing. Nob'dy could touch 'im. Wind and light and fragrance and shadow: It was all there bursting inside him. That dwarf could do that, y'know. It was somethin' to see.'

He clicked his glass against his few remaining teeth.

'Did you actually see him dance?' I asked.

'Did I see him?' The old fellow stared at me, spreading the fingers of both hands out atop the table. 'Of *course* I saw him. Every day. Right here.'

'Here?'

'You heard me. Right here. He used to dance here every day. Before the revolution.'

The old man went on to tell me how the dwarf had arrived from the north country without a penny in his pocket. He holed up in this tavern, where the elephant-factory workers gathered, doing odd jobs until the manager realized what a good dancer he was and hired him to dance full-time. At first, the workers grumbled because they wanted to have a dancing girl, but that didn't last long. With their drinks in their hands, they were practically hypnotized watching him dance. And he danced like nobody else. He could draw feelings out of his audience, feelings they hardly ever used or didn't even know they had. He'd bare these feelings to the light of day the way you'd pull out a fish's guts.

The dwarf danced at this tavern for close to half a year. The place overflowed with customers who wanted to see him dance. And as they watched him, they would steep themselves in boundless happiness or be overcome with boundless grief. Soon, the dwarf had the power to manipulate people's emotions with a mere choice of dance step.

Talk of the dancing dwarf eventually reached the ears of the chief of the council of nobles, a man who had deep ties with the elephant factory and whose fief lay nearby. From this nobleman – who, as it turned out, would be captured by the revolutionary guard and flung, still living, into a boiling pot of glue – word of the dwarf reached the young king. A lover of music, the king was determined to see the dwarf dance. He dispatched the vertical-induction ship with the royal crest to the tavern, and the royal guards carried the dwarf to the palace with the utmost respect. The owner of the tavern was compensated for his loss, almost too generously. The customers grumbled over *their* loss, but they knew better than to grumble to the king. Resigned, they drank their beer and Mecatol and went back to watching the dances of young girls.

Meanwhile, the dwarf was given a room in the palace, where the ladies-in-waiting washed him and dressed him in silk and taught him the proper etiquette for appearing before the king. The next night, he was taken to the great hall, where the king's orchestra, upon cue, performed a polka that the king had composed. The dwarf danced to the polka, sedately at first, as if allowing his body to absorb the music, then gradually increasing the speed of his dance until he was whirling with the force of a tornado. People watched him, breathless. No one could speak. Several of the noble ladies fainted to the floor, and from the king's own hand fell a crystal goblet containing gold dust wine, but not a single person noticed the sound of it shattering.

At this point in his story, the old man set his glass on the table and wiped his mouth with the back of his hand, then reached out for the elephant-shaped lamp and began to fiddle with it. I waited for him to continue, but he remained silent for several minutes. I called to the bartender and ordered more beer and Mecatol. The tavern was slowly filling up, and onstage a young woman singer was tuning her guitar.

'Then what happened?' I asked.

'Then?' he said. 'Then the revolution started. The king was killed, and the dwarf ran away.'

I set my elbows on the table and, cradling my mug, took a long swallow of beer. I looked at the old man and asked, 'You mean the revolution occurred just after the dwarf entered the palace?'

'Not long after. 'Bout a year, I'd say.' The old man let out a huge burp.

'I don't get it,' I said. 'Before, you said that you weren't supposed to talk about the dwarf. Why is that? Is there some connection between the dwarf and the revolution?'

'Ya got me there. One thing's sure, though. The revolutionary guard wanted to bring that dwarf in somethin' terrible. Still do. The revolution's an old story already, but they're still lookin' for the dancing dwarf. Even so, I don't know what the connection is between the dwarf and the revolution. All you hear is rumors.'

'What kind of rumors?'

I could see that he was having trouble deciding whether to tell me any more. 'Rumors are just rumors,' he said finally. 'You never know what's true. But some folks say the dwarf used a kind of evil power on the palace, and that's what caused the revolution. Anyhow, that's all I know about the dwarf. Nothin' else.'

The old man let out one long hiss of a sigh, and then he drained his glass in a single gulp. The pink liquid oozed out at the corners of his mouth, dripping down into the sagging collar of his undershirt.

I didn't dream about the dwarf again. I went to the elephant factory every day as usual and continued making ears, first softening an ear with steam, then flattening it with a press hammer, cutting out five ear shapes, adding the ingredients to make five full-size ears, drying them, and finally, adding wrinkles. At noon, my partner and I would break to eat our pack lunches and talk about the new girl in Stage Eight.

There were lots of girls working at the elephant factory, most of them assigned to splicing nervous systems or machine stitching or cleanup. We'd talk about them whenever we had free time. And whenever they had free time, they'd talk about us.

'Great-looking girl,' my partner said. 'All the guys've got their eye on her. But nobody's nailed her yet.'

'Can she really be that good-looking?' I asked. I had my doubts. Any number of times I had made a point of going to see the latest 'knockout', who turned out to be nothing much. This was one kind of rumor you could never trust.

'No lie,' he said. 'Check her out yourself. If you don't think she's a beauty, go to Stage Six and get a new pair of eyes. Wish I didn't have a wife, I'd get her. Or die tryin'.'

Lunch break was almost over, but as usual my section had almost no work left for the afternoon so I cooked up an excuse to go to Stage Eight. To get there, you had to go through a long underground tunnel. There was a guard at the tunnel entrance, but he knew me from way back, so I had no trouble getting in.

The far end of the tunnel opened on a riverbank, and the Stage Eight building was a little ways downstream. Both the roof and the smokestack were pink. Stage Eight made elephant legs. Having worked there just four months earlier, I knew the layout well. The young guard at the entrance was a newcomer I had never seen before, though.

'What's your business?' he demanded. In his crisp uniform, he looked like a typical new-broom type, determined to enforce the rules.

'We ran out of nerve cable,' I said, clearing my throat. 'I'm here to borrow some.'

'That's weird,' he said, glaring at my uniform. 'You're in the ear section. Cable from the ear and leg sections shouldn't be interchangeable.'

'Well, let me try to make a long story short. I was originally planning to borrow cable from the trunk section, but they didn't have any extra. And *they* were out of leg cable, so they said if I could get them a reel of that, they'd let me have a reel of the fine stuff. When I called here, they said they have extra leg cable, so that's why I'm here.'

The guard flipped through the pages of his clipboard. 'I haven't heard anything about this,' he said. 'These things are supposed to be arranged beforehand.'

'That's strange. It has been. Somebody goofed. I'll tell the guys inside to straighten it out.'

The guard just stood there whining. I warned him that he was slowing down production and that I would hold him responsible if somebody from upstairs got on my back. Finally, still grumbling, he let me in.

Stage Eight – the leg shop – was housed in a low-set, spacious building, a long, narrow place with a partially sunken sandy floor. Inside, your eyes were at ground level, and narrow glass windows were the only source of illumination. Suspended from the ceiling were movable rails from which hung dozens of elephant legs. If you squinted up at them, it looked as if a huge herd of elephants was winging down from the sky.

The whole shop had no more than thirty workers altogether, both men and women. Everybody had on hats and masks and goggles, so in the gloom it was impossible to tell which one was the new girl. I recognized one guy I used to work with and asked him where I could find her.

'She's the girl at Bench Fifteen attaching toenails,' he said. 'But if you're planning to put the make on her, forget it. She's hard as nails. You haven't got a chance.'

'Thanks for the advice,' I said.

The girl at Bench Fifteen was a slim little thing. She looked like a boy in a medieval painting.

'Excuse me,' I said. She looked at me, at my uniform, at my shoes, and then up again. Then she took her hat off, and her goggles. She was incredibly beautiful. Her hair was long and curly; her eyes were as deep as the ocean.

'Yes?'

'I was wondering if you'd like to go out dancing with me tomorrow night. Saturday. If you're free.'

'Well, I *am* free tomorrow night, and I *am* going to go dancing, but not with you.'

'Have you got a date with someone else?'

'Not at all,' she said. Then she put her goggles and hat back on, picked up an elephant toenail from her bench, and held it against a foot, checking the fit. The nail was just a little too wide, so she filed it down with a few quick strokes.

'C'mon,' I said. 'If you haven't got a date, go with me. It's more fun than going alone. And I know a good restaurant we could go to.'

'That's all right. I want to dance by myself. If you want to dance, too, there's nothing stopping you from coming.'

'I will,' I said.

'It's up to you,' she said.

Ignoring me, she continued to work. Now she pressed the filed nail into the hollow at the front of the foot. This time, it fit perfectly.

'Pretty good for a beginner,' I said.

She didn't answer me.

*   *   *

That night, the dwarf came into my dream again, and again I knew it was a dream. He was sitting on a log in the middle of the clearing in the forest, smoking a cigarette. This time he had neither record player nor records. There were signs of weariness in his face that made him look a little more advanced in years than he had when I first saw him – though in no way could he be taken for someone who had been born before the revolution. He looked perhaps two or three years older than me, but it was hard to tell. That's the way it is with dwarfs.

For lack of anything better to do, I strolled around the dwarf, looked up at the sky, and finally sat down beside him. The sky was gray and overcast, and black clouds were drifting westward. It might have begun to rain at any time. The dwarf had probably put away the records and player to keep them from being rained on.

'Hi,' I said to the dwarf.

'Hi,' he answered.

'Not dancing today?' I asked.

'No, not today,' he said.

When he wasn't dancing, the dwarf was a feeble, sad-looking creature. You would never guess that he had once been a proud figure of authority in the royal palace.

'You look a little sick,' I said.

'I am,' he replied. 'It can be very cold in the forest. When you live alone for a long time, different things start to affect your health.'

'That's terrible,' I said.

'I need energy. I need a new source of energy flowing in my veins – energy that will enable me to dance and dance, to get wet in the rain without catching cold, to run through the fields and hills. That's what I need.'

'Gosh,' I said.

We sat on the log for a long time, saying nothing. From far overhead, I heard the wind in the branches. Flitting among the trunks of the trees, a huge butterfly would appear and disappear.

'Anyhow,' he said, 'you wanted me to do something for you.'

'I did?' I had no idea what he was talking about.

The dwarf picked up a branch and drew a star on the ground. 'The girl,' he said. 'You want the girl, don't you?'

He meant the pretty new girl in Stage Eight. I was amazed that he knew so much. Of course, this was a dream, so anything could happen.

'Sure, I want her. But I can't ask you to help me get her. I'll have to do it myself.'

'You can't.'

'What makes you so sure?'

'I know,' he said 'Go ahead and get angry, but the fact is you can't do it yourself.'

He might be right, I thought. I was so ordinary. I had nothing to be proud of – no money, no good looks, no special way with words, even – nothing special at all. True, I wasn't a bad guy, and I worked hard. The people at the factory liked me. I was strong and healthy. But I wasn't the type that girls go crazy over at first sight. How could a guy like me ever hope to get his hands on a beauty like that?

'You know,' the dwarf whispered, 'if you let me help you, it just might work out.'

'Help me? How?' He had aroused my curiosity.

'By dancing. She likes dancing. Show her you're a good dancer and she's yours. Then you just stand beneath the tree and wait for the fruit to fall into your hands.'

'You mean you'll teach me to dance?'

'I don't mind,' he said. 'But a day or two of practice won't

387

do you any good. It takes six months at least, and then only if you work at it all day, every day. That's what it takes to capture someone's heart by dancing.'

I shook my head. 'It's no use, then,' I said. 'If I have to wait six months, some other guy will get her for sure.'

'When do you go dancing?'

'Tomorrow night. Saturday. She'll be going to the dance hall, and I will, too. I'll ask her to dance with me.'

The dwarf used the branch to draw a number of vertical lines in the dirt. Then he bridged them with a horizontal line to make a strange diagram. Silent, I followed the movement of his hand. The dwarf spit the butt of his cigarette on the ground and crushed it with his foot.

'There's a way to do it – if you really want her,' he said. 'You want her, don't you?'

'Sure I do.'

'Want me to tell you how it can be done?'

'Please. I'd like to know.'

'It's simple, really. I just get inside you. I use your body to dance. You're healthy and strong: You should be able to manage a little dancing.'

'I *am* in good shape. Nobody better,' I said. 'But can you really do such a thing – get inside me and dance?'

'Absolutely. And then she's yours. I guarantee it. And not just her. You can have any girl.'

I licked my lips. It sounded too good to be true. If I let the dwarf get inside me, he might never come out. My body could be taken over by this dwarf. As much as I wanted the girl, I was not willing to let that happen.

'You're scared,' he said, as if reading my mind. 'You think I'll take possession of your body.'

'I've heard things about you,' I said.

'Bad things, I suppose.'

'Yes, bad things.'

He gave me a sly smile. 'Don't worry. I may have power, but I can't just take over a person's body once and for all. An agreement is required for that. I can't do it unless both parties agree. *You* don't want your body permanently taken over, do you?'

'No, of course not,' I said with a shiver.

'And *I* don't want to help you get your girl without any kind of compensation.' The dwarf raised a finger. 'But I'll do it on one condition. It's not such a difficult condition, but it is a condition nonetheless.'

'What is it?'

'I get into your body. We go to the dance hall. You ask her to join you and you captivate her with your dancing. Then you take her. But you're not allowed to say a word from beginning to end. You can't make a sound until you've gone all the way with her. That's the one condition.'

'How am I supposed to seduce her if I can't say a word to her?' I protested.

'Don't worry,' said the dwarf, shaking his head. 'As long as you have me dancing for you, you can get any woman without opening your mouth. So, from the time you set foot in the dance hall to the moment you make her yours, you are absolutely forbidden to use your voice.'

'And if I do?'

'Then your body is mine,' he said, as if stating the obvious.

'And if I do the whole thing without making a sound?'

'Then the girl is yours, and I leave your body and go back to the forest.'

I released a deep, deep sigh. What was I to do? While I wrestled with the question, the dwarf scratched another strange diagram into the earth. A butterfly came and rested on it, exactly in the center. I confess I was afraid. I could not say for certain that I would be able to keep silent from beginning to end. But I knew it was the only way for me to hold that gorgeous girl in my arms. I pictured her in Stage Eight, filing the elephant toenail. I had to have her.

'All right,' I said. 'I'll do it.'

'That's it,' said the dwarf. 'We've got our agreement.'

THE DANCE FLOOR stood by the main factory gate, its floor always packed on a Saturday night with the young men and women who worked at the elephant factory. Virtually all of us unattached workers, both male and female, would come here every week to dance and drink and talk with our friends. Couples would eventually slip out to make love in the woods.

How I've missed this! the dwarf sighed within me. *This is what dancing is all about – the crowd, the drinks, the lights, the smell of sweat, the girls' perfume. Oh, it takes me back!*

I cut through the crowd, searching for her. Friends who noticed me would clap me on the shoulder and call out to me. I responded to each with a big, friendly smile but said nothing. Before long, the band started playing, but still there was no sign of her.

Take it slow, said the dwarf. *The night is young. You've got plenty to look forward to.*

The dance floor was a large, motorized circle that rotated very slowly. Chairs and tables were set in rows around its outer edge. Over it, a large chandelier hung from the high ceiling, the immaculately polished wood of the floor reflecting its brilliance like a sheet of ice. Beyond the circle rose the bandstand, like bleachers in an arena. On it were arranged two full orchestras that would alternate playing every thirty minutes, providing lush dance music all evening without a break. The one on the right featured two complete drum sets, and all the musicians wore the same red elephant logo on their blazers. The main attraction of the left-hand orchestra was a ten-member trombone section, and this troupe wore green elephant masks.

I found a seat and ordered a beer, loosening my tie and lighting a cigarette. The dance-hall girls, who danced for a fee, would approach my table now and then and invite me to dance, but I ignored them. Chin in hand, and taking an occasional sip of beer, I waited for the girl to come.

An hour went by, and still she failed to show. A parade of songs crossed the dance floor – waltzes, fox-trots, a battle of the drummers, high trumpet solos – all wasted. I began to feel that she might have been toying with me, that she had never intended to come here to dance.

Don't worry, whispered the dwarf. *She'll be here. Just relax.*

The hands of the clock had moved past nine before she showed herself in the dance-hall door. She wore a tight, shimmering one-piece dress and black high heels. The entire dance hall seemed ready to vanish in a white blur, she was so sparkling and sexy. First one man, then another and another, spotted her and approached to offer himself as an escort, but a single wave of the hand sent each of them back into the crowd.

I followed her movements as I sipped my beer. She sat at a table directly across the dance floor from me, ordered a red-colored cocktail, and lit a long cigarette. She hardly touched the drink, and when she finished the cigarette she crushed it out without lighting another. Then she stood and proceeded toward the dance floor, slowly, with the readiness of a diver approaching the high platform.

She danced alone. The orchestra played a tango. She moved to the music with mesmerizing grace. Whenever she bent low, her long, black, curly hair swept past the floor like the wind, and her slender fingers stroked the strings of an invisible harp that floated in the air. Utterly unrestrained, she danced by herself, for herself. I couldn't take my eyes off her. It felt like the continuation of my dream. I grew confused. If I was using one dream to create another, where was the real me in all this?

She's a great dancer, said the dwarf. *It's worth doing it with somebody like her. Let's go.*

Hardly conscious of my movements, I stood and left my table for the dance floor. Shoving my way past a number of men, I came up beside her and clicked my heels to signal to the others that I intended to dance. She cast a glance at me as she whirled, and I flashed her a smile to which she did not respond. Instead, she went on dancing alone.

I started dancing, slowly at first, but gradually faster and faster until I was dancing like a whirlwind. My body no longer belonged to me. My arms, my legs, my head, all moved wildly over the dance floor unconnected to my thoughts. I gave myself to the dance, and all the while I could hear distinctly the transit of the stars, the shifting of the tides, the racing of the wind. This was truly what it meant to dance. I stamped my feet, swung my arms, tossed my head, and whirled. A globe of white light burst open inside my head as I spun round and round.

Again she glanced at me, and then she was whirling and stamping with me. The light was exploding inside her, too, I knew. I was happy. I had never been so happy.

This is a lot more fun than working in some elephant factory, isn't it? said the dwarf.

I said nothing in return. My mouth was so dry, I couldn't have spoken if I had tried to.

We went on dancing, hour after hour. I led, she followed. Time seemed to have given way to eternity. Eventually, she stopped dancing, looking utterly drained. She took my arm, and I – or, should I say, the dwarf – stopped dancing, too. Standing in the very center of the dance floor, we gazed into each other's eyes. She bent over to remove her high heels, and with them dangling from her hand, she looked at me again.

We left the dance hall and walked along the river. I had no car, so we just kept walking and walking. Soon the road began its gradual climb into the hills. The air became filled with the perfume of white night-blooming flowers. I turned to see the dark shapes of the factory spread out below. From the dance hall, yellow light spilled out onto its immediate surroundings like so much pollen, and one of the orchestras was playing a jump tune. The wind was soft, and the moonlight seemed to drench her hair.

Neither of us spoke. After such dancing, there was no need to say anything. She clung to my arm like a blind person being led along the road.

Topping the hill, the road led into an open field surrounded by pine woods. The broad expanse looked like a calm lake. Evenly covered in waist-high grass, the field seemed to dance in the night wind. Here and there a shining flower poked its head into the moonlight, calling out to insects.

Putting my arm around her shoulders, I led her to the middle of the grassy field, where, without a word, I lowered her to the ground. 'You're not much of a talker,' she said with a smile. She tossed her shoes away and wrapped her arms around my neck. I kissed her on the lips and drew back from her, looking at her face once again. She was beautiful, as beautiful as a dream. I still could not believe I had her in my arms like this. She closed her eyes, waiting for me to kiss her again.

That was when her face began to change. A fleshy white

thing crept out of one nostril. It was a maggot, an enormous maggot, larger than any I had ever seen before. Then came another and another, emerging from both her nostrils, and suddenly the stench of death was all around us. Maggots were falling from her mouth to her throat, crawling across her eyes and burrowing into her hair. The skin of her nose slipped away, the flesh beneath melting until only two dark holes were left. From these, still more maggots struggled to emerge, their pale white bodies smeared with the rotting flesh that surrounded them.

Pus began to pour from her eyes, the sheer force of it causing her eyeballs to twitch, then fall and dangle to either side of her face. In the gaping cavern behind the sockets, a clot of maggots like a ball of white string swarmed in her rotting brain. Her tongue dangled from her mouth like a huge slug, then festered and fell away. Her gums dissolved, the white teeth dropping out one by one, and soon the mouth itself was gone. Blood spurted from the roots of her hair, and then each hair fell out. From beneath the slimy scalp, more maggots ate their way through to the surface. Arms locked around me, the girl never loosened her grip. I struggled vainly to free myself, to avert my face, to close my eyes. A hardened lump in my stomach rose to my throat, but I could not disgorge it. I felt as if the skin of my body had turned inside out. By my ear resounded the laughter of the dwarf.

The girl's face continued to melt until suddenly the jaw popped open, as if from a sudden twisting of the muscles, and clots of liquefied flesh and pus and maggots sprang in all directions.

I sucked my breath in to let out a scream. I wanted someone – anyone – to drag me away from this unbearable hell. In the end, however, I did not scream. This can't be happening, I said to myself. This can't be real, I knew almost intuitively. The dwarf is doing this. He's trying to trick me. He's trying to make me use my voice. One sound, and my body will be his forever. That is exactly what he wants.

Now I knew what I had to do. I closed my eyes – this time without the least resistance – and I could hear the wind moving across the grassy field. The girl's fingers were digging into my back. Now I wrapped my arms around her and drew her to me with all my strength, planting a kiss upon the suppurating flesh where it seemed to me her mouth had once been. Against my face I could feel the slippery flesh and the maggoty lumps; my nostrils filled with a putrid smell. But this lasted only a moment. When I opened my eyes, I found myself kissing the beautiful girl I had come here with. Her pink cheeks glowed in the soft moonlight. And I knew that I had defeated the dwarf. I had done it all without making a sound.

You win, said the dwarf in a voice drained of energy. *She's yours. I'm leaving your body now.* And he did.

'But you haven't seen the last of me,' he went on. 'You can win as often as you like. But you can only lose once. Then it's the end for you. And you *will* lose. The day is bound to come. I'll be waiting, no matter how long it takes.'

'Why does it have to be me?' I shouted back. 'Why can't it be someone else?'

But the dwarf said nothing. He only laughed. The sound of his laughter floated in the air until the wind swept it away.

In the end, the dwarf was right. Every policeman in the country is out looking for me now. Someone who saw me dancing – maybe the old man – reported to the authorities that the dwarf had danced in my body. The police started watching me, and everyone who knew me was called in for questioning. My partner testified that I had once told him about the dancing dwarf. A warrant went out for my arrest. The police surrounded the factory. The beautiful girl from Stage Eight came secretly to warn me. I ran from the shop and dove into the pool where the finished elephants are stockpiled. Clinging to the back of one, I fled into the forest, crushing several policemen on the way.

For almost a month now, I've been running from forest to forest, mountain to mountain, eating berries and bugs, drinking water from the river to keep myself alive. But there are too many policemen. They're bound to catch me sooner or later. And when they do, they'll strap me to the winch and tear me to pieces. Or so I'm told.

The dwarf comes into my dreams every night and orders me to let him inside me.

'At least that way, you won't be arrested and dismembered by the police,' he says.

'No, but then I'll have to dance in the forest forever.'

'True,' says the dwarf, 'but you're the one who has to make that choice.'

He chuckles when he says this, but I can't make the choice.

I hear the dogs howling now. They're almost here.

ACKNOWLEDGMENTS

A. S BYATT: "The Thing in the Forest" from *Little Black Book of Stories* by A. S. Byatt, copyright © 2003 by A. S. Byatt. Used by permission of Alfred A. Knopf, a division of Random House, Inc. "The Thing in the Forest" from *Little Black Book of Stories* by A. S. Byatt, published by Chatto and Windus. Reprinted by permission of The Random House Group Limited.

ANGELA CARTER: "The Tiger's Bride" taken from *Burning Your Boats* by Angela Carter. Copyright © 1995 The Estate of Angela Carter. Reproduced by permission of the author c/o Rogers, Coleridge & White Ltd., 20 Powis Mews, London W11 1JN

JULIO CORTÁZAR: "The Night Face Up" copyright © 1967 by Random House, Inc., from *End of the Game and Other Stories* by Julio Cortázar, translated by Paul Blackburn. Used by permission of Pantheon Books, a division of Random House, Inc. "La noche boca arriba" (The Night Face Up), by Julio Cortázar, © Heirs of Julio Cortázar, 2010. Reprinted with permission from Carmen Balcells Agencia Literaria S.A.

ISAK DINESEN: "The Sailor-Boy's Tale" copyright 1942 by Random House, Inc. and renewed 1970 by Johan Philip Thomas Ingerslev c/o The Rungstedlund Foundation, from *Winter's Tales* by Isak Dinesen. Used by permission of Random House, Inc. *Winter's Tales* © 1942 by Random House, Inc. Copyright © renewed 1970 by Johan Philip Thomas Ingerslev. Published by agreement with The Gyldendal Group Agency.

NEIL GAIMAN: "Troll Bridge" from *Smoke and Mirrors* by Neil Gaiman. Copyright © 1999 by Neil Gaiman. Reprinted by permission of HarperCollins Publishers. "Troll Bridge" from *Smoke and Mirrors* by Neil Gaiman. Copyright © 1999 by Neil Gaiman. Reprinted by permission of Hachette UK Limited.

URSULA LE GUIN: "The Poacher" from *Unlocking the Air* by Ursula Le Guin. Used with permission of the Virginia Kidd Literary Agency and MBA Literary Agents Limited.

WILLIAM MAXWELL: "The Industrious Tailor" from *All the Days and All the Nights* by William Maxwell, published by Harvill Press. Reprinted by permission of The Random House Group Limited. "The Industrious Tailor" from *All the Days and All the Nights: The Collected Stories of William Maxwell* by William Maxwell, copyright © 1965, 1986, 1992, 1994 by William Maxwell. Used by permission of Alfred A. Knopf, a division of Random House, Inc.

STEVEN MILLHAUSER: "The Visit" from *The Knife Thrower and Other Stories* by Steven Millhauser, copyright © 1998 by Steven Millhauser. Reprinted by permission of Crown Publishers, a division of Random House, Inc. "The Visit" from *The Knife Thrower and Other Stories* by Steven Millhauser. Reprinted by permission of International Creative Management, Inc. Copyright © 1998 by Steven Millhauser.

HARUKI MURAKAMI: "The Dancing Dwarf" from *The Elephant Vanishes* by Haruki Murakami, copyright © 1993 by Haruki Murakami. Used by permission of Alfred A. Knopf, a division of Random House, Inc. "The Dancing Dwarf" from *The Elephant Vanishes* by Haruki Murakami. Reprinted by permission of International Creative Management, Inc. Copyright © 1993 by Haruki Murakami.

VLADIMIR NABOKOV "The Dragon" from *The Stories of Vladimir Nabokov* by Vladimir Nabokov, copyright © 1995 by Dmitri Nabokov. Used by permission of Alfred A. Knopf, a division of Random House, Inc. and Weidenfeld & Nicolson, a division of The Orion Publishing Group Ltd., London.

Everyman's Pocket Classics are
typeset in the classic typeface Garamond and
printed on acid-free, cream-wove paper
with a sewn, full-cloth binding.